AMBER PRINCESS

BY HENRY TREECE

Novels

The Rebels
The Dark Island
The Great Captains
The Golden Strangers
Red Queen, White Queen
The Master of Badger's Hall
Jason

Verse

The Exiles
Collected Poems
The Haunted Garden
The Black Seasons
Invitation and Warning
Thirty-Eight Poems
Towards a Personal Armageddon

Criticism

A Selection of Algernon Charles Swinburne
Herbert Read
Dylan Thomas: Dog Among the Fairies
How I See Apocalypse

Drama

The End of a World
The Tragedy of Tristram
Tristram and the Watchers
The Dark Island

History

The Crusades

AMBER PRINCESS

HENRY TREECE

Random House · New York

FIRST PRINTING

© *Copyright, 1963, by Henry Treece*

Library of Congress Catalog Card Number: 63-9355

PUBLISHED IN LONDON, ENGLAND,UNDER THE TITLE *Electra*

MANUFACTURED IN THE UNITED STATES OF AMERICA

For Barney Blackley,
in all friendship

AMBER PRINCESS

PROLOGUE

BUT, doctor, even you, a Hittite, saw what our Mycenaean shields were like! Oh, don't smile, I may be an old woman, but I know what I am talking about, and if you will be patient, you will understand, too.

Our shields were formed by stretching a hide on to a frame, made with rounded cross-bars at top and bottom, fixed to a central spar of ash or olive-wood. The leather at either side, not having the support of the cross-bars, shrank away and pulled in tightly when it dried out. So the shield took on its own peculiar shape, not round, nor oval, but more like the form of a woman with her wasp-waist lying between broad breasts and wide hips.

You are smiling again, doctor, because you do not understand; you imagine me to be talking of a shield, or a woman's body, but these things are only an example, for I am describing the heart speaking out, the mind as you call it.

You do not see how? Soon you will be saying again that words in our Greek mouths are as slippery as fishes; I know you outlanders. It is because you do not see the wholeness of things, the Virtue, the *aretê*. You observe one fact, the single symptom, like the Hittite doctor you are, but your eyes are blind to the *Ananke*, the whole Order of things which even the gods cannot infringe.

The shield is formed on a frame; and that frame is the will of man. But after the sun and rain have been on it a week, its shape has changed beyond man's guiding; and that is *Ananke*.

It is still not clear, doctor? You Hittites are very stupid: no wonder you accuse us here of cheating. Very well, I will tell you simply: though I began upon a firm frame, the hide of my experience has tautened and twisted until now I am as *Ananke* wills me to be. I am not what I wished, or others wished for me: I am what it was ordained for me to become before ever the seed passed from my father to my mother. I am the cow's hide, tormented to the only

[7]

shape it can be. Now do you see? Do you see that there may be no anger, no regret, no remorse?

We must all grow and die as the gods have decreed, as the pattern has been woven. Man's life is like that of the trees. The wind scatters the leaves to the ground; the vigorous forest puts forth others, and they grow in the spring-season. Soon one generation of men comes and another ceases, just as *Xanthoi*, the brown-haired Achaeans, my own folk, came and flourished where the black Cretans had had their houses. Just as the tow-headed Dorians came and flung our fortress down at last.

That is the endless unrolling, doctor, and I am part of it. I do not weep, for *hybris*, which is defiance of god's will, deserves to be punished by the Furies. All we can do is to try to keep on good terms with the gods. And, in any case, Hope is a snare and a temptation; there is even a sort of joy in the agony, the anguish of the struggle with the god. Beyond that, nothing; a man is only truly happy when he is dead.

Oh, I know you are laughing at me, doctor. We Hellenes are used to that by now. You tidy folk with milk for blood have never understood us. You call us sinful because our word for a fault means 'missing the mark'. While you beat your breast and cry like children to your father-god for pardon, we laugh at our bad marksmanship—and try again, though we know we may fail, may sin once more.

What you have never comprehended is *sôphrosynê*, our whole-mindedness, our persistence in vice or virtue. And this, dear doctor, is the whole secret of my people: we have never given in. Crushed, we have risen again; sons have replaced their fathers and fought under the old helmet-crest as though time had stood still; women have sung in their birth-pains to think that the little child they bear might one day bring the Hellene glory back.

If I could only tell you what it was like in the great days! But you would only rub your long Hittite nose and smile your sly eastern smile. And, in your tent, to your boy, you would say, 'These Greeks! These liars!' I know; yes, I know. All the world says it—and we laugh with them. We do not spit and wail like Phoenicians, or run to the temple for revenge like Egyptians. We laugh—because in our hearts we know that all the world is wrong, and we are right! So we can afford to laugh, doctor. It is a precious thing to be born a Hellene. It is even more precious to have been born, as I was, a princess of the House of Atreus. Yes, that startles you! It will stagger you still more to hear that I am the last of them all, the kin of Atreus. This bent old woman, this wrinkled wine-skin, bone-dry now, the last of them all. Touch my hand. Can you not feel the pulse of Zeus himself in it? God knows what honour I do you in letting you touch the god's own distant flesh!

And still you do not believe. Then I shall convince you. I shall describe what it was like, before your father's father lay upon his woman, tented on the plains at the world's misty edge.

In the beginning, there was Mycenae, and greatest of all since Minos, Atreus himself. I have heard folk praise Tiryns of the High Wall—but it was nothing to Mycenae.

No, I never saw Tiryns, doctor; but why should I go there, when I had Mycenae? And when all the world came to Mycenae to see my father, Agamemnon? Some fools will tell you he had a face like a dog: but I can put you right. His face was that of a lion, all golden and bushy and his eyes and nose showing through his hair and beard. And sometimes, if he was angry, it was like a boar's head, with the white tusks pushing up from the dark bristles and the eyes growing small and red with fury. Now can you see Agamemnon? Can you picture such a man wearing the high horse-plumed war-helm? Do you wonder that the children screamed and the mothers turned away if they were carrying babies? Oh, he was a man. There has never been a man in the world since.

Our city was built on and about a rocky hill that jutted up from the plain of Argolis before the big mountains began. We stood at the world's cross-roads and from Mycenae you could go anywhere. But we stayed there and let all the world come to us, for it was always summer in Mycenae. Not the simple summer of mere sunshine; the high summer of glory, with my father as the High King of that season.

[9]

We knew, as though the god had put it into our inner hearts, that we were the Chosen, born to rule the world of men. Even the dark-eyed Cretans who lived on the lower slopes of our hill felt this, the folk my great-grandfather had first conquered. They had forgotten this conquest, for we treated them well and married into their best families, and now they claimed a share of our glory too.

We were good tyrants, not bad ones, doctor. If there was something to learn, we learned it, though it came from the folk we had conquered, and thought it no disgrace. They showed us how to write, and make pretty dresses, and how to store the wine in great jars, and to drink from pretty little cups with high handles. From them, we learned how to paint pictures on our walls and how to bury our dead with gold masks on their faces to do them honour.

From us, in their turn, they learned to respect land-soldiers—to forget their grandfathers' ships and to give praise to the swift chariot. They were never great soldiers, but at least we helped them half-way towards it.

I don't think the god meant them to be warriors, really. They were an amusing brown-skinned folk with eyes like a deer's, and there was nothing prettier than those tiny bronze-haired babies that came from the mixture of our peoples. Indeed, my own mother had been such a one, coming from the south, from Laconica, where most folk were Cretan.

Yes, we dealt with them well, doctor; there's no gainsaying it. And if, in wine, they bragged about their ancient king Minos, we tried to hold our peace and not boast about our own flaming-haired Pelops, the father of all kings.

It was the same in the shrines. 'Allow us to honour Zeus of the Sky and Poseidon Fish-father, Sea-stirrer, Earth-shaker,' we would say, 'and you shall have as many altars to the Mother as you wish. You can worship her as maiden, wife or crone, and no one will deny you.' This we always did, though some of us hardly approved of their sacrifices. Yet it worked well enough, this give and take. Why, at Delphi itself, we let our Apollo leave his shrine for three months

[10]

in the year, so that their wine-god, Dionysus, could take his place. And down at Amylcae, near my mother's birth-place, we permitted a joint-festival in honour both of their Hyacinthus and our Apollo. There could be nothing fairer than that: though some young barons, my cousins, who had been there, told me that the first day of the festival made them vomit, seeing how the women ate the chosen one. These barons really went down for the second days' wine-drinking, they said, when a man might feel safe and could pay his respects to the man-god who protected him.

Still, live and let live, we said. And there were other things to think about, besides gods and goddesses; though, I confess, they always lay behind our thoughts and deeds. But we shook them off, whenever we could, and got on with our business, until Zeus sent us a warning dream and brought us before his shrine again—or Poseidon made the seas boil and the earth shudder beneath the feet. So, the gods kept us in our places, and we did not hold it against them. It was *Ananke*, Order.

Why, *Ananke* governed Mycenae, from its thatched houses among the olive groves on the plain, to our great family fortress on the hill-top; High Town, they called it. Here, my father, mother, sisters and brother lived, and all our kindred who had no kingdom of their own—with their warrior-companions, servants and slaves. This was as it should be, for the kindred to live on the hill-top: though, naturally, when the distant kings and lords gathered for my father to lead them against the Trojan horse-tamers, there was not room enough at High Town, and our visitors had to lodge down the hill in the pine houses thatched with rushes, and only come up on invitation, to dine in our great hall.

Our hall was in the middle of High Town. Oh, it was magnificent with its tapering pillars and painted walls, and the round fireplace in the centre where the olive-logs blazed noisily. The vestibule was nearly as big, where the lords gathered before coming in. And the white stairway that led down to the small court was the finest in the world, my father said. When I was little I lost count of all the other rooms that led off from the great hall; there was the women's room, the bath-house, the armoury, the dairy. . . . Oh, scores of rooms! There were some I never went in, even; little dark places set within the thick stone walls of our palace.

Then there were the stables and work-rooms beyond that, and the shed for our sacrificial oxen, whose blood must be unmixed with that of lesser breeds.

Mostly, the cattle and sheep grazed beyond our orchards at the back of the palace, round about the ancient bullring that we called the Womb of Hera, and were only brought inside the high walls, into the big outer court, if danger threatened.

There was a grave-circle in the outer court, too. I don't know who lay there, but there were about eleven men and six women, called the kindred because they were perhaps ancestors of ours. My father said that once they had lain outside the wall that clenched its fist round High Town, in the big tombs called tholoi; but that King Atreus had had them brought inside because there were grave-robbers about.

I will tell you about the tholoi some time, doctor. They seemed very strange to me when I was little. My sisters and I used to call them the Beehives, because they had great domes and wild bees made their homes in the dark spaces between the blocks of stone. All through the summer these bees buzzed so loudly, there in the hollow darkness, that you could hear them all over High Town, through the Lion Gate and half-way down the steep ramp that led to the wooden houses and the farms. I can still hear them, doctor; it was a furious noise, as menacing as the bone bull-roarers that the Libyans use before they run naked into battle.

When we were children, my sisters and I used to put our hands over our ears to shut out this droning from the tombs, because we thought the old dead were calling to us, mocking us, threatening us.

While I have been telling you this, I remember now that these bees made every summer hideous for me. It is strange, I had never realised that before. I cannot go on, doctor. You must wait a while.

1

I WAS eleven when my father the king went away in the ships; and my brother Orestes had only just begun to walk a step or two. He was perhaps only a year old. He was always a forward boy, but a very quiet baby.

I can only just remember what Agamemnon looked like then— a huge man, a giant in his bronze armour and with the high horse-tail plume on his helmet. All the lords were afraid of him, though in his presence they did a lot of laughing and even touched his arm. But I could tell.

I do not think that I was afraid. I am not sure now. When he was at home, in High Town, by our hearth-fire, he played with me on his hands and knees, growling like a hill-bear or roaring like a desert lion, and tickling me with his bristly hair and sharp beard. He made all the lords wear their hair long, so that the world should see they were Hellenes who prayed openly and upright to the god with the beard, and not the conquered folk who muttered in the dark at the Mother shrine.

If my mother the queen ever came into the hall while father was playing with me, he would stop and stare at her till she went out again, sniffing and shaking her long bronze-coloured hair. He would stare after her even though she had gone, as though his eyes would follow her down the dark corridors, and push her along to her own chamber. He used to do the same with my two elder sisters, who said they wanted to be priestesses at the Mother shrine when they grew up.

But it was all right when the nurse, smiling Geilissa, brought baby Orestes in. Father would play with him too and call him 'baron'. And though the king was so big, Orestes was never afraid of him, and never used to cry when the stiff beard brushed him. I used to scream out when the king whiskered me, but I was only pretending, as girls do, to see what else would happen.

[13]

But when the king was dressed in his war-gear, with the side-flaps of his helmet down, so that you could only see his bright eyes staring, this did frighten me, because he was no longer my father. He was like Zeus then, with his voice booming out of the closed bronze, and echoing till the words lost all their meaning, like the bees in the tholoi.

Then he would swing me up onto his shoulder and the sharp edges of his corselet used to pinch me. I tried not to say that I was hurt, but I did cry out once, I recall. This made the king very angry with me, and he turned up my tunic and smacked me with the flat of his sword. I can remember what he said while he was doing it. He said, 'You, an Achaean, and howling because you are hurt! What an example to the world!'

The sword hurt me, too, but I didn't mind that kind of hurting. I cannot explain, but in a way it made me love the king all the more for doing it.

And when the king had gone after this beating, I told my corn doll that I would marry him one day. He was the man for me, the biggest man in the world. I was only about nine then, but for the first years he was away over the sea in Troy I longed for the day he would come back, so that I could marry him. It got very bad at times and even turned me against the boys of my own age in Mycenae.

In fact, it was so bad that I used to dream I would take the king away from Clytemnestra, my mother. Such thoughts made me ashamed at first, but Geilissa told me that all dreams were sent by Zeus, so after that I told myself that it was the god speaking in the night, not I.

All the same, in those days, there was nothing wrong about loving your father. Most of the girls I knew, of good family, said they were in love with their fathers and would marry them when they came back from the fighting. Some of them did, I know for a fact, if their mothers had died in the meantime. It was something to do with land-tenure, I think. Only a few, slave girls mostly, liked boys of their own age; but we of the House of Atreus had our own ideas of what was right, and we did not do as the slaves did in those days. Though, the god knows, before we were finished, we lost our pride and were willing to do anything that would put bread into us.

But in those days, it was not so. The only other man I loved was my baby brother Orestes. He was like a little doll to me. I loved washing him and nuzzling his body, which always smelled so warm and sweet. Many times, when the fit was on me, I would put him to my chest and implore Zeus to let milk come out of me. And when it didn't, I wept to hand him back to Geilissa, to be wet-nursed.

Once she said to me, with her crooked smile, 'If you want milk for the prince, then one day there's an easier way of getting it than praying to the Man God, Electra.'

I asked her how, and she told me something that sounded silly and impossible. It concerned her young brother, a cowman in the sheds behind the great hall. She said he was a great hand at it, and her winking and gestures were so confusing that I didn't know whether to run out to him straightaway, or to call the soldier at the door and tell him to beat her.

I ended by putting my hands over my ears, as though I was not listening, but I left a little space between my fingers so that I could hear.

I remember, she laughed and said, 'Oh, 'tis a small thing, lady. Especially for a fine boy like the prince. Someone is doing it all the time—why, even your own mother—and once they are used to it, it gets better and better. You will find out.'

My mother the queen came in while this was being said. She was tall, with bronze hair and a deathly white face. She always painted her mouth very red. I liked her in one way, but feared her in another. This day she smiled at us in her stiff, mask-like way, and said through her sharp teeth, 'If I catch her at it, I will see that she loses all taste for it afterwards. And I'll see that your brother does, too.'

When she went out, Geilissa made a very rude sign behind her back. I did not want the nurse to see that I agreed with her, because we of the kingly folk were not supposed to speak of one another to the slaves, or even to the better class of Cretans. So I went away, too, and ran up to my room above the armoury, where my little loom stood. There I worked at making shawls and ribbons for Orestes, thinking that if I could not suckle him, at least I could help to clothe him.

2

THERE was a loud shouting outside in the lower court before the palace. It was a bright clear morning, with a touch of frost in the air, and the roofs of the barons' houses silvered, the colour a snail leaves behind him in the grass.

I was with my father. This was about a year before he left us. He was sitting on a carved oak stool and I was standing between his knees, tracing the dragons on his breastplate with one hand, and holding my corn doll with the other.

It is strange how clearly I see this—yet I forget what I broke my fast on only yesterday. Clearly, I recall the harsh dry scent of his hair and beard, the chill touch of his bronze armour, the deep tone of his voice that seemed to come from the cavern of his great chest, as water comes from the dark holes in rocks.

It was one of the last few times I was quite alone with my father, so that is why I remember it, perhaps.

I said, 'King, why are you looking so grim? Why do you wear your breastplate every day now?'

He smiled and stroked my hair. 'There are things a little girl would not understand, Electra.'

'Try me and see, father. I can understand embroidery and where calves come from.'

'Those things are easy, daughter. Zeus looks after the one, and a little fish-bone needle the other. But my grim looks and armour are not things themselves, they are the signs of other things, of something that lies back, and back, and back. There, I told you that you would not understand.'

He smoothed my dress and told me that I was getting to be a big girl. I pulled away from him and, dropping my corn doll, took hold of his hair on either side and tugged at it.

'You are a bad father! Other fathers tell their daughters about things. Urana's father tells her how chickens get in eggs, and where the sun goes at night. But you don't tell me anything. And I am a year older than Urana.'

He bent and scratched his leg, where the bronze guard had chafed it. Then he looked up and said, 'Urana's father is only a second-class baron. He can walk round his boundaries in one short morning. A man like that, with only two wives, and about eight cows, has time to bother his head with eggs and where the sun goes. But kings. . . . Ah, kings are different.'

I was always being told this. It was often said with a sort of darkness, as though it was all a secret that children should not hear about. I said, 'Please do not say this again, father. I have seen you in the bath, and I did not notice that you were much different from the boys I swim with in the stream. And if you mean that kings sometimes have to go under the axe, then that is not very different from being a soldier and having a sword hit you—or being a farmer's slave and having a bull gore you.'

Agamemnon held me by the shoulders and said, 'I know, death comes to all of us. But who told you about kings going under the axe, my sweet?'

His hands were so big that they seemed to fold round me entirely. My father the king was the biggest man in Hellas, I thought at that time. He was of the blood of giants, of Titans. I used to think that he could take any man in Hellas and break him apart with one twist. When he held my shoulders so, I wondered whether he meant to do that to me.

Frightened, I said, 'Old Aphaea, the nurse. She tells me the ancient tales when she puts me to bed, father.'

He reached down and sat me on his knee.

'My little Amber Princess, my Electra, half the trouble in this world is that old nurses will tell stories when they put children to bed. Most of our fears come from these old nurses. Especially the Cretan nurses, who will for ever be remembering magic. One day, I must make a rule to stop it. We will have all the old nurses put onto an island out in the sea, then they can tell each other these tales, till the wolves come down the hill and eat them up!'

'You are trying to put me off again, king. I asked you why you always looked so grim recently, and why you wore your armour every day. You are being sly with me, father, and I don't like that. You are a crafty Greek, that's what you are.'

He bent me over and smacked my bottom with his big hand, gently though, and said, 'Very well, princess, if you must know, you must. But listen carefully, and don't interrupt. . . . You see, we are all poor men in Hellas these days.'

I said, 'But, father, we have a great house, and my mother has fine clothes and jewels. Even Urana's father has three swords and a carved chest to keep them in.'

Agamemnon answered, 'If you interrupt again, I shall hang you in the pear tree for the hawks to peck at. That's better, now be silent. I was saying that we are poor men, and by that I do not mean a few swords or a house or two—I mean that we only have what we can grow out of the earth, with our own hands; or only the calves and lambs that our beasts bear. We have nothing to spare, no gold to take to other lands and bargain with. All the gold has gone, my sweet.'

'That is a silly thing to say, father. Gold does not go. It cannot get up on its feet and walk away like a man. How can it go?'

'I wish you had stayed with Aphaea and played with your doll! Your questions make my head spin! Listen now; once we had gold, but much of it has gone back into the ground, into the graves, masks on the faces of the dead ones. Other gold has become arm-bands and neck-rings on ladies who will not give it up, or on warriors who have sailed away and died beyond the world's edge.

Other gold has gone to Hittites and Phoenicians and Libyans. Now do you see?'

'I see only that you are trying to fox me with all this talk, father. Don't you see that I can understand anything, if only you tell me? I am nearly eleven, and in three years I shall be old enough to marry a man, and have a baby of my own. That is *old*.'

Agamemnon gave a little gasp and pulled at the tight neck-ring he always wore. Then he put me down quite roughly, and went to the window. He was so immense, my father, that he blocked out all the light from the window. The room got dark straightaway. I thought he was crying at first, and I didn't know why a great king should cry, especially in our family, the Kin of Atreus. We were not supposed to cry, neither the boys nor the girls. When my mother, Clytemnestra, first told me of this, she said, 'My child, we are as a model for all the world. In us the lessons of the gods are made flesh. What we do, that the gods wish for all men one day. By acting as we do, men may grow to be perfect in the eyes of the gods. Gods never weep. If we weep, then we are betraying the gods. We are showing disobedience and weakness, Electra. So we deserve punishment. Learn always to control your tears, then you will not be beaten.'

I went to my father by the window and said, 'A fine thing, for a king to weep.' But he did not listen to me. Remember, I was only eleven, and so I began to tug at his sword-belt and his kilt, and to stamp my foot on the floor, quite angry. 'Stop this!' I shouted at him. 'If you go on weeping, I shall weep, too. I do not want you to sail away and leave me, but I have not wept about it so far. Do stop!'

Then he half-turned from the window and gazed down at me. His face looked very old and wrinkled and leathery, like a tired god; but his eyes were blinking and his throat was moving, and tears ran down into his rough beard. And that made him seem less than a god, less than a king. It was the first time I had ever seen a man crying, and it was like the end of the world. I began to beat at the king's legs, crying myself by this time. Suddenly, he stooped and picked me up, lightly, like a doll, and said, 'You have seen what no other has seen, my daughter. You have seen a god crying.'

'You are no god! I know now that you are like anyone else, father.'

I said it bitterly, yet even in that bitterness I loved him more than ever.

The king said, 'I do not know. I think I feel different from other men, but there is a little part of me that is like other men, perhaps. The part that is not yet god.'

'You cannot tell me that, now, father. I saw you crying. Why, the tears are still on your cheek.'

I began to wipe them away as he carried me about the room. He said, 'It is when I think of you growing up and taking a man, Electra. That is when I am not a god. Consider; a king, even a great king such as I am, has few pleasures. He must always be at his trade of king, always giving judgement, giving battle, giving men a rule to live by. A king's whole life is giving. So, there are times when he feels as though he wishes to receive, instead of giving. Yet what can he receive from others that his own power could not get for him? It is like giving once again, but to himself this time. Always giving.'

Now I was ruffling his hair and rubbing his stubbly beard the wrong way. I was hardly listening.

He said, 'A king has only the love of his children to receive. That is his only reward for being a king. Only his close dear ones can give him that. So, when you speak of another man, a husband, I weep. Now do you understand?'

I pretended that I did, and said, 'Yes, yes, yes! So tell me why you must sail away with the chiefs and barons and headmen, to leave me. If you love me so much, why leave me? I am ready to play with you in the orchard and on the hills every day, yet you plan to go away. Is that your love?'

He set me down on a table and clasped me round the waist. 'All men, even kings, must often do what they have no taste for. A king is the chosen of his people, and he must do what is best for them. Hellas needs gold, and I must lead the men to get it. Far over the sea, my love, beyond the islands, where the great creatures spout in the waters, there lies a city of gold. The Phrygians who live there sit in gold chairs and eat off gold plates. To them, gold is as bronze to us, no more. Even their children play with gold dolls, and their dogs wear gold collars.'

Then the king walked away from me, beating one hand into the other and saying, 'That gold I must have. I shall destroy the city of the Phrygians, and shall drive them like beasts into the wilderness. Then our ships can sail up along the route old Jason discovered, to get gold from all the distant streams, and no one to stop us.'

I was about to answer him when the curtains opened and my Aunt Helen came in. She was my mother's young sister, but was very different from Clytemnestra, whose face was thin and her hair reddish. Aunt Helen's face was oval and plump, and her hair was so yellow that it looked like spun gold. She wore it down her back, proudly, like an unmarried girl. She had been married to my father's brother, Uncle Menelaus, for ten years, yet she always tried to look like a maiden. Her bodice was so small that her breasts showed, like apples. She used to paint them, to make them even prettier, as unmarried girls did in those days. Her dresses were always very rich and splendid, with gold wire fringes on the skirts, in the Assyrian mode; and lions embroidered all over her cloak. But one never noticed what she was wearing, really. Aunt Helen's body always seemed to be speaking, even through the richest robes.

And there was always a strange scent about her. It was like musk, or some sharp herb. Perhaps like the faint smell of pinewoods, or of aromatic leaves burning in the distance. It was so much a part of her that I would have known if my Aunt Helen was in the room, even with my eyes shut.

She came to me as I sat on the table, with my legs dangling, and kissed me, letting her thick hair fall all about me until it seemed as though I was in a tent of gold. I touched her breasts, and even nibbled one of them, in game. She pretended to smack me and said, 'You are as bad as your father, Electra!'

The king frowned and lifted me off the table. 'Go into the cow-shed,' he said, 'and see that those lazy slaves have milked all the cows.'

Aunt Helen saw my look, and said, 'Then after a while come back and I will have a present for you. But do not hurry, for I have not got the present ready yet.'

I saw her glance at Agamemnon in a secret way I did not like. So I pretended to go to the barn, but turned round and came back, quietly along the passage, and hid myself among the curtains, where I could peep into the room.

3

ALL my life I have remembered what I saw and heard in that room, and the guilt of my listening has often run across my body at night like little mice scuttering, or small birds pecking inside me.

Agamemnon loomed like a dark bronze statue in the corner by the window, while Helen stood before him, simple as a farm girl now, clasping her narrow hands. Her voice, low and rough as a boy's, said, 'What of my family, brother? There are Menelaus and Hermione to think of.'

The king rubbed at his beard. 'Not again, for god's sake. We have been over it all before, woman. In this life there are tasks for us all. Does the young bull-leaper grovel on his knees whenever he smells the dung in the straw? Does the priestess draw back from catching blood in the libation cup?'

Helen lowered her gold head. 'These you mention are trained for their work. I, wife and mother. . . .'

Agamemnon began to laugh and to thump his hard brown fist against his armour.

'Zeus! Zeus! Zeus!' he kept saying. Then, 'You get too nice, sister. I could name a dozen young fellows who have assisted at your training.'

[22]

But Helen would not let him say more. She swore with words that I had only heard among the slaves before, then ran at him and beat her narrow hands on his bronze breastplate, like a frantic woman chased by wolves, trying to get past a village gate.

Agamemnon was laughing down at her. He was so tall, she could not reach up to his face with her fists. Then he suddenly put his arms around her and drew her onto his armour. She was crying now that it hurt her, that he was bruising her, that she would have to explain the marks to Menelaus when she reached home again. But the king only growled at her, and bent over her, rubbing his harsh face against her smooth one. He was like a great bear, nuzzling its cub. Aunt Helen had stopped squealing out and was sighing and shuddering and trying to pull off her robe.

For a moment I almost thought of running into the room, to help her wrestle with my father, thinking that this was a game they played. But something stopped me, something that seemed to whisper at the back of my head, 'Don't go! Don't meddle! This is not for you!' I know now, what it was, but I was only a little girl then. So, I waited and watched, as far as I could, the curtains being in the way of some things. I saw the king wrap his heavy cloak round them both, and I heard Helen crying and laughing. I was very puzzled. I think I went to sleep for a while, in the hot afternoon, with the flies whirring round me in the dim passage-way.

Then all at once the curtains by me swung open waking me, and my father swept out, striding with long steps, his bronze sword-scabbard hitting against the stone walls, his cloak flaring out and taking all light from the place. I was glad that a fold of the curtain fell over me and he did not see that I had been spying on him.

For a while I sat there, then I heard Aunt Helen crying, and I went into the room. She was surprised to see me, but she sat up from the floor and arranged her robe. Then she wiped her eyes with the back of her slender hand and began to smile. I smiled also, because her hand had lain on the dusty floor and now her tears and the dust had left a smear across her painted face, giving her a comical look.

She drew me onto her lap and said, 'Where have you come from, Electra? Have you been listening outside, then?'

I nodded my head. There was nothing I could think to say. Her gilded breast showed over her torn bodice and I touched it, as she often let me do. But this time she drew away from my hand with a little grimace. Then she smiled and patted my head.

'There were things happening that you could not understand?'

I said, 'The king was hurting you, wasn't he?'

Helen shrugged her shoulders. 'They almost always do. Kings, princes, barons, slaves. . . . They are all men. And men become furious and thoughtless. They can't help it, Electra. Zeus made them like that. And perhaps it is just as well. If it were only like slipping into a warm bath, then we wouldn't know it had happened, would we?'

I nodded, but I didn't know what she was talking about. I got up and sat on father's stool. Aunt Helen still sat on the floor, like a cat stretching when it wakes.

I said, 'My father's armour has scratched you, aunt. It is bleeding a little. Shall I get a cloth?'

She wiped her fingers over the scratch, then ran them down the skirt of her robe and smiled. 'It is not the first time, and it will not be the last.'

In a while, she rose and came over to me, standing before me so that I smelled her musky scent. She reminded me of a mother cat, all furry and soft and warm.

She said, 'Do you ever dream of Zeus, my love?'

I nodded that I did. She said, 'What shape does he take in your dream? A bull? A fish? A goat?'

I said, 'No. He is always like my father, the king. Always big, with a beard and red eyes, and that armour he wears. With the smell of horses on him. Like that.'

Aunt Helen sat down beside me and said, 'Yes, that is how it is with me. I will tell you a secret—I think that Agamemnon *is* a god. No, not the highest god, perhaps—but a god, all the same.'

I took hold of her hand and held it to my cheek, as though it were a bird that had fallen from its nest and needed warming.

[24]

'We both love him, do we not, Electra?'

'I would do anything for him, aunt. I would lie down and let a bullock-cart roll over me. I would jump into the sea from the highest cliff. I would let him hack my head off, anything.'

Helen nodded, and hugged me to her. 'So would I. If Agamemnon wanted to eat me in a pie, then I would let the cooks chop me up into steaks. If he wanted to eat me raw, I would hold out my arm and say, "Here it is, lord. Devour me!"'

We both began to laugh then, our arms round one another, as though we were one flesh. Many folk said that we looked as alike as two twin sisters. That made me glad, because Helen was very sweet and pretty.

At last she said, 'Men talk of freedom, but that is only a word. There is no freedom; there is only serving the god. And if the god is the king, then freedom is serving the king. Serving Agamemnon.'

I agreed with her. She said, 'Just as the king must sometimes die for his people, as their Shepherd, so we must die for him if he wishes it.'

Her voice was so hushed and hoarse that I looked at her, fearing she would weep again. But she shook the tears away from her eyes and smiled.

'I shall tell you another secret, Electra. And you mustn't tell your cousin Hermione about it, or she will cry and have nightmares. Do you promise?'

I nodded my head, and she whispered, 'Soon I am to be sacrificed. What do you think of that?'

I almost pulled away from her with shock, but she held me close, laughing. 'Silly goose! Silly goose! I don't mean *like that*— dead flesh, white, with no blood, just smelling cold.'

I hugged her warm body again and laughed in relief. 'I am so glad, aunt. Our cat caught a shrew yesterday and bit its body open. I saw what was inside. It was horrible. I would not like you to be like that.'

She said, 'There'd be much more of me, and different, I can tell you! But no, it's not that.'

I said, 'What then?'

She made me wait a long time. She was thinking how to say it, perhaps.

'You know we have no gold in Hellas?'

'Yes, the king told me about that. The Horse-tamers have it all now.'

Helen said, 'Someone has to get it from them.'

I began to laugh, seeing my aunt wearing hard armour over her soft body and facing bearded Phrygians with a heavy sword in her little hand. She knew what I was thinking and she said, 'There are other ways to fight than with a sword, Electra.' But she was laughing, too. Helen always laughed a lot. Some of the men called her the merry queen. They never called my mother, Clytemnestra, that.

'In a way, though, I am the sword of Hellas. The instrument, the tool. If I go to Troy, then the Hellenes will fight to get me back. They will kill the men of Troy, and then there will be gold in Mycenae once more.'

I scratched my head. 'It seems wasteful. Could not the men of Hellas just go in their ships to Troy, without sending you there first? Why put you to the trouble, Aunt Helen?'

She made her eyes small and looked up at the rafters where the doves perched.

'It is no trouble. There is a prince there I would like to meet; Paris, the son of King Priam. And besides, both the Phrygians and ourselves pray to Zeus—so we must have a good excuse to offer to the god if we are to kill his other people. I am that excuse. In a way, I am almost sacred, you see. Being the chosen one has made me different from all the others.'

I said, 'Does Uncle Menelaus know this?'

She smiled at me then and said, 'I have not spoken to him about it. It lies like a wall of silence between us. But I think he knows. These things one does not talk about.'

I said, 'Then, if he knows, all the other kings will know, and the barons and the soldiers.'

She nodded and said, 'When I walk among them, all talk stops,

They stand with their heads bowed until my shadow has passed by them on the pavements. They are proud if I notice them or smile at them. It is a great honour to be chosen.'

'But what if it goes wrong, aunt? What if you do become like the shrew, with the inside showing, and smelling cold?'

Aunt Helen rose and flung her cloak about her. She kissed me on the forehead and said, 'I try not to think of that, Electra. That is what my dreams are about, every night. But in the sunlight, I do not think of it. I meet everything as it comes. That is the only way to live, my dear. You will discover that, as you get older.'

At the door she turned and said, 'If you do not, then you will go mad.' She went then, along the dark passage-way. I think she was weeping again, but suddenly I found a little beetle trying to carry a mud ball on its back. When I had finished helping him, my aunt had gone, and I ran out into the sunshine.

4

I WAS in my mother's room and the soldiers had stopped drilling. Some of them, the leaders, were on a small dusty mound outside the palace, lying about and laughing, waving their hands and showing their white teeth to the sun. Most of them were boys; yet they were kings and chieftains in other parts of Hellas. They sprawled carelessly, in their short kilts, their legs burnt deep brown by last year's good summer, the summer that had scorched our crops and left us too often hungry.

My father the king stood on the mound above them, enormous in his full growth. He balanced on one leg, leaning on his tall spear, his other leg wrapped about the ash-shaft, like a waiting herdsman.

The young men laughed at his jokes, and made jests back at him. He threw up his head and laughed at times, and the sound of his laughter came into the room to us through the undraped window.

All at once, my mother said, 'Come away from the window, Electra. Those young kings are shameless, lying about there.'

I came away, for no one disobeyed Clytemnestra; but I felt she was unfair. I thought the young men looked well in their breast-plates and short kilts, with their high-plumed helmets lying beside them, and their swords piled in a heap, as though they had forgotten about war.

Clytemnestra was weaving at a little olive-wood loom, passing the shuttle between the strands of the warp nimbly, with long white fingers. She was very different from Aunt Helen, more clever, but stricter. Yet just as pretty in a fiercer, thinner way. One of her eyes was deep blue and the other grey, and this always gave her a search-ing, sneering look, even when one knew about it. Her name meant 'fierce lover', but as she sat at the loom, her dark robe tight about her throat and her thick bronze hair covered with a black hood, there seemed to be little love about her.

I said, 'Are you going to weave a picture of the king in the cloth, mother?'

She was long in answering. 'No, this is a scarf for your sister, Iphigenia. If she is to become a priestess of the Mother, then she should have such a scarf, with all the symbols on it.'

I said, 'But its is Chrysothemis, the eldest, who is the priestess of Hera's shrine, here in the palace. Iphigenia is like me—she only wants to play, and have babies of her own to nurse and dress. She does not want to shut herself up and do those things at sacrifice times.'

My mother's fingers halted a little in their weaving.

'Iphigenia has no choice, Electra. She must do as the gods wish. So must we all. Besides, it is very convenient, and we who rule the land must always think of that.'

'What does convenient mean, mother?'

She smiled now, and looked for a moment as though she might

pick me up and hug me. But that mood passed, and she went on with her work.

'When the men have gone away,' she said later, 'we shall need all the priestesses we can get to keep Hellas in order. The slaves will only obey priestesses—you know that. They worship the Mother, secretly in the straw, whatever the king commands. There must be a hundred clay images scattered here and there among our own stables.'

'But there are other folk besides slaves in Hellas, mother. Hellenes who pray to Zeus, as we do.'

Clytemnestra gave another of her smiles, but a wrinkled one this time, and said, 'When the men are gone to the war, there will be no one left between Mycenae and Olympus worth bothering about. And when the men come back, your two sisters will be too old to make a good marriage.'

I said, 'What do you mean? I asked you what convenient meant, mother.'

'And I am trying to tell you, child. While this war is on, I cannot have Chrysothemis and Iphigenia running off and marrying the first brisk young peasant who touches their legs. So, they shall be kept safe in their shrines. And when your father comes back, if he ever does, there shall be no peasant bastards haggling at him for his throne.'

My mother never explained things to me simply, as Agamemnon did. She lacked the patience to find words I would understand. She was impatient in all things—which is why her name was what it was.

After a time she said, 'Why are you standing sulking, child? Be off and feed the hens, or see if little Orestes is crying.'

I stared at her then began to cry. She left her loom and came over to me, putting her arm round me and drawing me to her.

'There,' she said, 'I see now; it is because I said your father might not come back. . . . Is that it?'

I nodded, and she smiled. 'You think he is a god, don't you, Electra? One who could walk through a raging fire unmarked?'

I nodded again. 'He will come back,' I said. 'He could come out of the jaws of Poseidon unhurt, or kill a bear with his teeth.'

Clytemnestra was not warm, like Aunt Helen. Under her shift, her body was as cool as a stone in a stream. She said, 'It is right that little girls should make their fathers into gods. But you are eleven now, and you must be starting to grow up, Electra. Agamemnon is not a god, whatever you think. He is only a man; a strong man, certainly, but a man. Do you know, he weeps if he hears a sad song?'

I said, 'Of course I know that! Do not the gods weep? Is that not rain?'

Clytemnestra shook her head. 'I can see that you will be hard to convince,' she whispered. 'Then hear this; your father the king has the name, through all Hellas, of being the bravest man, the most resolute warrior. Yet, I can tell you, he never sleeps before a battle. He prowls the room all night, weeping, and being as sick as a dog. What do you think of that?'

I hated her for telling me, and said, 'It is a lie! I have seen him sitting in the saddle as they started out, laughing and throwing his sword up into the air with the others. And I have seen him when they come back, shouting and yelling out for drink to wash the dust from his throat. And the heads of the defeated kings hanging from his horse's neck. Is that not brave, then?'

My mother left me and sat down at her loom again. She said, 'He puts on a good show, as a High King should. But his warriors do not see him in his bedroom at night. They think that they are the only ones who are sick with terror, so they respect him. Yet, one day, perhaps, he will be a head hanging from a horse's neck. Then men will know that he is not a god after all.'

I could stand this no longer. Suddenly, hardly knowing what I was doing, I ran at my mother and struck at her. She was startled, but the smile never left her face. Her annoyance showed only in her strange eyes. She tried to hold my hands, but my fingers caught in her fine shift and tore it open. Then I drew back, afraid, for I had never seen her body before, and it was not what I had thought.

From ribs to knees, she was marked with a tracery of blue and red, the flesh slightly raised where the marks were. I saw that there were snakes and palm trees and even bull's horns on her. At first she was about to cover these things up again; but then she thought a little longer and just sat there, showing herself to me, and smiling.

'I have worn these since I was your age, Electra,' she said. 'It was the fashion in Laconica, before I married your father. All the princesses were pricked with bone needles and dyes rubbed in.'

I said, 'Aunt Helen is not like this. I have seen her, and she is all clean and the colour of honey.'

Clytemnestra shrugged and answered, 'She may be the colour of honey, but she is not clean. I should know that, she is my sister, and I know most of her secrets.'

She quickly wrapped her shift about her and fastened it with a strand of red wool.

Then all at once she said, 'Electra, you know well enough that I love you. Yet you know that I cannot always find the words to tell you so. It is as though there is a coldness in me, a shyness, that ties my tongue down. Your father is different. He can come out with it and make his heart known. Helen is the same. She can sing as freely as a bird, all that is in her. Yet she forgets just as freely. I am not like that. What I feel, I feel for ever. Yet I am dumb to tell what I feel, at times, even when I feel it the most strongly.'

I was still staring at her, thinking of the marks on her body that I had never seen before. I said softly, 'Mother, it comes to me now—you are a witch. Those marks mean you are a witch.'

She did not even hear me, and perhaps it is just as well. Instead, she said, 'I was not always like that, my dear. Once, I was as brisk and warm as Helen. That was years ago, when I was a young girl. You do not know this, but I may as well tell you, for no doubt if I do not, someone else will, before long.'

Her voice flowed on, harsh, like water over sharp stones in the dry season, when the shrivelled reeds crackle in the sun. I was thinking of the marks, not of her words, until she said, 'And in those days I had a husband, a boy as young as I was, Tantalus.'

Now I began to prick up my ears, for this was new to me. I said, 'But Agamemnon, mother . . .?'

She waved me aside and said, 'Tantalus and I lived as though each

[31]

day was a lifetime, and every wood and field a whole world. The sun shone for us alone; the streams flowed only for us; the early aconite came up out of the cold earth only to cheer us. All the folk adored us in those bright spring days, and ran to the doors of their cottages to watch us pass, our arms about each other, singing. And then we had our baby, and Tantalus stood by me while it was born and wiped my forehead. We loved that child, perhaps too much. One day warriors raided us and burned down our house. Their king put his sword into Tantalus, and then struck off the child's head as I held it in my arms, at the breast. I could show you the mark now, where the sharp bronze bit into me, too.'

She began to wipe her eyes on her shift, though I saw no tears. Then she said, 'They were hard times. When all the kings fought together like dogs, each tearing at the bone in the other's jaws.'

I said, 'And did my father, Agamemnon, save you from the raiders, mother? Is that it?'

She began to laugh and to rip at the strands of wool on her loom, spoiling the cloth.

'Your father *was* the raider. He was the man who put the sword into Tantalus and killed my first-born.'

Somehow, I knew that she was going to say this. The scent of it had passed across the room to me even before the words were spoken, just as a farm-dog knows a wolf is about, even before he has seen him. And at the same time, though I had come from her body, I knew that there was something of me my mother hated, some part of Agamemnon.

I ran out of the room, crying, 'A witch! A witch!'

She did not try to follow me, and I was soon ashamed of myself. In the courtyard, near the well, my sister Iphigenia sat, combing her hair and whistling to the doves on the red roof of the great hall. She was two years, perhaps three, older than I was, and her body had begun to show under her shift, making me envious. She stopped whistling and said with a smile, 'Hey, what's the matter? Or have you broken your doll?'

I fell at her feet and said, 'Sister, our mother is a witch, and our father is a murderer. And mother's body is all marked with blue lines and red lines, right down to her knees, like the warp and weft on a loom.'

Iphigenia began to comb my hair then, and patted me so hard on the back that I choked. 'Child, child,' she said, 'surely you have been deaf and blind all your life.'

I looked up and said, 'Did you know, then?'

Iphigenia laughed in the sunlight and said, 'All the women of the Laconian royal house are like that, except Aunt Helen. She wouldn't let the old men do it when she came of marriage age. She fought and bit them when they got the little needles to her, and said they shouldn't spoil her body. Being tattooed doesn't make mother a witch, dear. As for the king being a murderer, it is true that he killed Tantalus. But then, all kings have killed other kings. It is the law, just as it is the law for the king stallion to kill other king stallions and so take over the mares. Bears and wolves and foxes do it, too. It is the law of the god. So there is nothing wrong in it.'

I said, 'Then, one day, another king will kill our father?' I began to cry again at this; I was too young to learn all the truth of the world in one day.

Iphigenia lifted me up and said, 'If Agamemnon is a god, then that puts him out of reach of swords, doesn't it?'

I pushed my damp hair back and said, 'But how do we know he is a god, now? Mother says he is sick before a battle, and surely the gods are not as weak as that? Surely his sickness means that he is mortal, and will fall under the sword of another?'

My sister straightened my dress and wiped the dust off my legs with her hand. Then she said, 'That about being sick is nothing. I'll tell you what it is; father sups milk, as we all do. But on the evening before a battle, he goes into the tents with the other men and also drinks wine. Now, you know what our Mycenaean wine is—sharp and sour as a crab-apple. Put it to yourself, sour wine on top of milk. The milk curdles, you see, and becomes too heavy for the stomach to tolerate. So the stomach throws it up, and the man is sick. Try it some time, when Mother is not about. You will be sick, just as anyone would be. But that will not mean you are afraid.'

I laughed then and kissed her. She had almost made my father into a god again, with a few kind words. I said, 'It is right that you should be a priestess, sister, for you have truth in your heart and can tell it to others.'

Her face became very serious then, and she took me by the arm, pinching me a little. 'Come,' she said, 'let us go out and watch the men throwing javelins.'

5

ANOTHER thing comes back to me again and again, doctor. There are many nights, even now, when its memory pushes through my dreams as a man pushes through a door curtain and comes suddenly into a room, when everyone thought he was miles away.

I was playing on my own at evening, away from High Town, up the grey hillside in one of the shallow quarries where once the masons had dug out the stone that made the tholoi and our palace. I did not mind being alone, among the wild thyme and brown grasses that now covered the dusty basin.

I called this my secret bower and not even Iphigenia knew that I used to go there. In this quarry there were little brown flickering lizards that stuck on the sheer rocks like images, until I coughed. Then they would be away, zig-zagging like the god's lightning, into crevices too small even for my little finger.

And there were wise little old snakes, dusty green snakes, that lay on the tumbled rocks, baking themselves in the sun, not seeming to mind although the stone was often so hot that I could not bear to hold my hand against it.

I used to believe that, with patience, I could find words to talk to them in: I tried Greek and Cretan, and the few bits of Egyptian I had picked up from merchants. And when these failed, I tried various sorts of hissing. But they still went away. Then the notion came to me that such little beasts might only understand the language of the god, since they were always outside and did not live among men in market-places and palaces. So I tried to remember what the god sounded like, in thunder, rain, wind and earthquake, and did my best to make his voice. But a young girl cannot make that awful splitting crash that comes when the floor quivers under the feet and the tall columns sway and then slash downwards, even though she shouts herself raw-throated and puts such a buzzing into her ears that it lasts for days—as I did. My small companions still left me, for their holes and crevices, try as I might.

So I approached them at last in the final way that occurred to me. When I thought it out at last, I was amazed I had been so stupid before. All my life I had watched the priestesses at the altar, supplicating Mother Dia, laying first a row of sea-shells on the marble stone, then a row of pebbles, then one of laurel leaves.

In this way, it came to me: I ran quickly to the secret bower in the quarry with a skirt-full of amber beads, blue clay beads, scallop shells and agate stones. There were even a few old glass seals from Crete among my offerings.

And I went silently and with respect down into the bower, making no sound in the thick grey dust. The lizards and snakes did not move yet, so I sat before a low flat-topped stone and arranged my beads and shells on it, glancing round through my thick hair from time to time, in hope. Yes, they were still there, pretending not to be concerned with me, but watching all the while. I knew they were watching!

Oh, my heart said, if only your clumsy hot fingers can get the pattern right! If only Mother Dia will guide them, as she does those of the priestess, so that the beads and shells and seals will spell out some message of friendship to these shy creatures of the earth!

I could hardly breathe, in my excitement. My heart was beating so hard that I thought it would sound like a great drum to the snakes and lizards, and drive them away before I had finished. In my head I said: Don't go! Please don't go! Give me a chance to show you I mean well, my friends. Please bear with me; I mean well!

I had almost completed the third row and I wanted to weep with joy that my friends were still there, watching me and trusting me. Oh, I was on the edge of the old secret, I knew. Deep down as far as my body went, I knew. My fingers would scarcely obey me now, and I almost dropped the bull-seal I was placing in the centre of the pattern.

It was the hour when the sun fell from the sky, so my side of the quarry was in shadow, though the other half was still golden with light. Heat was coming off the rocks and out of the ground, pleasing the crickets like a baker's oven, setting the clear air shimmering so that straight sticks looked bent, and the bushes of wild thyme seemed to be dancing, though there was no breeze in that hushed evening.

I sat breathless in the purple shadow under the dark lip of the steep quarry-side. Above my head and behind me, the sky was such a deep blue! And before me there was a cloud so richly-red, so bronze, so like my mother's hair, but all edged with pearl, that I wanted to shout out with joy and sadness mixed.

I knew then that this was the magic-time. My hand hovered like a hawk over the altar-stone, for I must get it right, and then the secret would be with me for ever. The bull-seal was slippery with sweat in my fingers. Oh, the agony of choosing!

Then, at the instant when I was within an inch of talking to the snakes and lizards, of becoming one with them, and the earth, the Mother, a sudden sound came down to me that almost made me faint away with shock.

It was a man's deep cough. I heard the lizards scutter dryly away.

I looked up through my hair in fury, but what I saw turned that fury to fear immediately, and I forgot about my shells and agate stones.

Seven men stood dark and terrible against the bronze cloud above me, looking like giants, like awful gods. They did not see me for I

[36]

was under them, in the shadow, and they were staring away up the hill, like blind men.

God, my inside turned over and I almost screamed: they were so enormous, so terrible. Their high horse-hair plumes nodded in the breeze; their long hair and beards flared out from below the bronze cheek-flaps of their helmets; and their bunched cloaks made them look like Titans. On each man's left arm, a great hide shield studded with bronze or dull gold. And the tall spears standing high above them, bristling towards the sky like the ruff of a savage boar when he begins to charge.

Yes, they were savage, savage, savage! Their scent came down into my oven-hot bower and struck at my nostrils like a slap on the face. It was the harsh, savage smell of man. I had never really scented it before, but now, as all my skin prickled and the sweat ran down my face, I knew that it was a fearsome thing. I knew now why all the birds and beasts ran away from man in terror. I knew that I was a woman and weak, as powerless as the wolf and the lion against man.

You are smiling, doctor, but if you had been there you would have wanted to relieve yourself as I did. You think you are a man, but I tell you that these men were of a different, terrible breed. To them, you are no more than an ass is to a screaming war-stallion.

And they stood so long, so still, so huge, together, like one heart with seven bodies, like lovers, like savage lovers, with the dying sun coming off their bronze corselets and the golden hairs on their legs catching the light. They were beautiful and terrible, like gods. One part of me wanted to strike them to stone, to rid myself of the fear that was making me want to vomit; another part of me, that I had never known before, wanted them to eat me, to crush me like wild lavender under their feet, to bruise and ravish me.

My great father stood in their midst and even the tallest of the others were small beside him. He was no less fearsome because he was my father, because the seed from which I had grown was out of his body. No, this made him the more terrible: for this gave him the right to consume me again, to make me nothing again, to destroy me.

God, god, I thought, these monstrous men are the lords of earth, They will eat up Troy as though it had never been.

Then, for an instant, I even pitied the poor Trojan horse-tamers, who could teach a stallion his manage but would run helpless and weeping before these godlike Achaeans.

All at once, a most awful thing happened. My father began to nod his high plume like a mad war-horse, and this nodding spread along the dark line of them. Then all his body began to shudder and nod and twitch, and his lion-coloured legs to quiver and his feet to stamp. The whole company of them moved in harmony with him. Dust began to rise about them in the dying sunlight. Spittle began to spray the air and some of it to fall on me.

They were like black bulls tossing their horns, working themselves into the fury of their death dance.

Sounds came from them, but not words I knew. They were deep rumbling sounds, groans and sighs, mutterings and harsh cries. Suddenly my poor shells and agates and beads seemed so powerless against these sounds.

I had never really been afraid of men before. I had always thought that I was one of them, though a little different in certain small ways. But now I knew that we were not the same creature at all; that it was only by the will of the god we lived together and spoke the same tongue.

This truth came into my heart like a message from Mother Dia, keen like a needle into my heart, and I wondered why I had never known it before—it was so clear and simple. Now I knew why the Mother called for a man-offering in the places where she still governed. She was asking revenge on men, fighting their savageness, holding sway over the wild beast in them.

This knowledge ran through me like a poison draught, burning my inside so fiercely, so pitilessly, that I could stand it no longer.

I think I gave a cry, then, blindly, I got up out of the dust, turned, and began to run away from them, among the rocks and the thyme bushes and the prickly acanthus. I did not know what I was doing. I only wanted to be away from these men—away, away!

[38]

Yet I knew that they would see me, once I had left the purple shadow and had run into the clear amber sunlight at the other side of the quarry. I knew it, but could not help myself. I was like a poor hunted hare that breaks cover when it need not, and runs haphazard into the open, where now the dogs might take it easily.

When I reached the sunlight, sobbing with terror, a high shout went up behind me, as though the hounds had sighted me. My heart almost stopped at that sound, and all the strength flowed out of me. There was a droning in the air behind me, and a great ash-shafted spear clattered on the rock I had just clambered over. Another suddenly stuck upright in the dust before me, casting a long thin shadow across the ground before it tilted and fell into the brush.

Then, as I stumbled on, swaying here and there, they came again and again, whirring and thudding about me. One struck sideways and caught me flat across the back, almost having me down. Another clanged at my heels then shot between my legs, like a vicious snake racing me up the far slope. Even as it went, I recognised that it was my father's javelin, by the gold studs set just below the bronze socket.

Now their voices were like the distant baying of hounds and as the sun dropped below the lip of the quarry a great chill came over all the air and the bright sky darkened.

I fell to the ground breathless and gasping. 'Mother, Mother, you have saved me!' I said, my dry mouth to the dust.

Then, from a little crack in the rock beside me, a hissing voice seemed to say, 'Not yet! Not yet! They will be coming down to gather their spears again. This time, they will have swords in their hands. So, you must rise and go now, if you wish to live.'

And I did wish to live, most savagely I wished to live, if only to find out what man's weakness was, so that I could give payment for the lesson I had just learned.

Though I was sick with fright, and my legs were like water, I went at the far slope and scrabbled at the grey rocks. And all at once it was as though a hard warm hand placed itself in the middle of my back and pushed me upwards, until I reached the smooth grass of the hillside.

I heard their feet shuffling about in the quarry, but I did not dare look back. I ran all the way home to the palace, dry-eyed but weeping in my heart.

My father never spoke of this, nor did I. I do not even think he remembered it. I certainly do not think he ever knew that it was his own flesh he had almost pierced with that ecstatic javelin.

6

OUTSIDE the lowest wall of High Town, there was a grey field of boulders, where the King's Justice was done. Nothing grew there, except a sort of sedge, and sometimes an aconite or two. People said that the earth was poisonous here, because of the blood that had been spilled, and so nothing grew. Indeed, when I was quite small I saw a prince's brains dashed out on one of the rocks. He was of a distant tribe, of course, but what made it worse was that he was only very small, hardly able to walk by himself. But he was still a prince, and the thing had to be done because, as my father pointed out to me while we sat watching under the striped awning, one day this child would grow and be as big as any other man.

Another time, two youths who had been drinking wine and saying that they would face Zeus himself if he came to earth, were punished in this place by being blindfolded and ordered to fight with stone axes. They missed as often as they struck each other, and that was quite laughable; but what stuck in my mind and made me feel unclean for years afterwards was the way they called out pitifully for pardon when their blows did strike. What with those calls and the horrible thudding of their axes, I wonder I ever slept again.

I mention this place of rocks and dead grey earth because it was here that something very strange happened to me, one evening before my father sailed away to fight the Phrygians. I was walking alone in the moonlight by our wall, weeping to myself, and thinking how lonely I would be when Aunt Helen and father had gone from Mycenae, when someone called my name from among the rocks.

'Electra! Electra, come here; I have something to show you!'

It was a rule in our house that the girls should not go down into the lower town at night unless a baron went with them. Only slaves and bad women strolled in the dark in those days. When I heard this voice calling, I knew that I should risk being whipped before all the servants if I went; and I did not like the thought of going into that awful place in any case, where the baby prince had died terrified, and no pretty flowers grew. But the voice was so strange and piercing, not like any other voice I knew, and it kept on crying, 'Electra, I have something to show you.'

I think that I was perhaps curious, in the way young girls are, and wanted to know what the thing was. Perhaps it was a present for me—a cup from Samothrace, a necklace from Crete. . . . And the voice was so thin and sharp and reedy, it went on sounding in my head even when it was not speaking. I even began to wonder if it was some god or other; and I knew that if it was, and I did not go when it called, I should be sorry later.

I did not want to go blind, or lame, or have sores all over me, so I looked round to make sure that no one was about, and then I gathered my skirts up round my waist and ran out of the tall Lion Gate and over the rocky field. It was a stupid thing to do, I kept telling myself as I ran, but the words seemed to draw me, like the voices in the dreams that Zeus sends.

But when I got away from our high stone wall, deep into the bright moonlight, I could see no one there; only the shadows cast by the boulders, or by dry thyme bushes, that had been dead for years. And I was about to turn round and run back into the palace, when a man stood up from behind a rock and nearly frightened the life out of me.

His face was round and white and hairless, and his eyes were as black as marble. He wore a goatskin hood and cape. At first, I thought it was Pan, and I almost fainted where I stood.

But this man laughed and then hobbled over to me and took my hands. I think he was frightened, too, because his fingers were clammy with sweat. The goat smell that came from his clothes made me want to heave, and I drew as far from him as he would let me. He was surprisingly strong, though, once he had got hold of me, I could not free myself at all.

'You have never seen me before,' he said. 'But soon you will see me every day of your life.'

I remember saying, 'I find small comfort in that, whoever you are.'

He answered, 'I am glad to find that you are of a humorous disposition, Electra.' Then he began to laugh in a high bleating manner, and suddenly took hold of my hair, down at the roots, and started to tug at it. Then I was really afraid, and thought this man meant to kill me. It did no good to threaten him with my father's guards, or to say that my mother would have him hunted down. At everything I said, he only pulled the harder, until at last I sank to the ground and wept helplessly. This seemed to affect him more than anything else, because he stopped tugging my hair then and flung the goatskin over me.

'Come, then,' he said, 'now we know who is the master.'

He had his fingers twined in my girdle and was dragging me along at a fast pace. I said, 'Where are you taking me? I shall be beaten for going so far from the palace gates.'

He laughed and said, 'Yes, you may be thrashed, but you must still come with me and see what I have to show you, Electra.'

Beyond the rocky field the wooden houses of the town began. There was one street that led down to the place of tombs, the tholoi. It was a narrow straight street, with hardly any windows in it on either side. The white houses looked blind in the moonlight. It was like going down a gully, or between high cliffs. There was no one to call out to. It resembled the entrance to a great tomb.

I said to the man, 'I beg you, let me go back again. I have never been here at night and I am afraid.'

He chuckled as though I had made a joke, then suddenly drew me into a side-turning, away from the dark street. The change was bewildering. We came out into a little secret place, where vine-leaves straggled and clustered over trellises, and where men and women sat or stood about glowing braziers, whispering to each other and drinking wine from brightly glazed cups.

By the far wall, a young man strummed at a tortoise-shell lyre, and a young woman danced with her body, never moving her feet. The moonlight glowed through the net she had wrapped about her, showing up the tints of her flesh.

White doves strutted about on the ground, or purred from above in the rafters. A great grey she-cat lay in the straw and fed her kittens.

At a brazier, a young Libyan was roasting pieces of goat flesh on a stick of hard olive-wood. The scent that came from it was tempting, and at the same time faintly sickening. It was as though the flesh was alive still, warm and smelling of life, twitching with life, even writhing with life.

I said to the man, pointing, 'Look, it is alive!'

He shook his head. 'No, it is only the fire shrivelling the sinews, drying them up, making them twist.' He smiled at me a while then suddenly put out his damp hand and touched me, drawing his fingers up slowly, letting them rest on me. It was like a spider crawling over me and I pulled away. He shrugged his shoulders and said, 'There is little of the old Mother in you, I see. You are disgusted to see the meat cooking on the fire, and you draw away from my hands. You are altogether too nice, Electra. In the old days it was different. Then the girls were more fierce, more passionate, than the men. When my father's house was great in Hellas, it was because the women drove the men on and on, to do things. But now the men hide behind Zeus and Poseidon. Yes, they clash their spears and

[43]

grow big beards—but that is nothing. They are still only children. They still scurry past the dark corners, in case She is waiting for them.'

I wanted to be away from him, he was getting so excited. Trying to calm him, I said, 'You are making too much of it. People are as they always were, surely. In my family, my father holds to Zeus and my mother is allowed to make offerings to Dia on the special days.'

'Allowed!' he said, and spat into the fire. 'Does one allow the rain and the sea-storms? No, they happen by divine will, which is beyond man's small saying.'

He was pulling at his rags and twisting his face so terribly that I began to wonder how I could best get away, when suddenly from the shadows a dark-faced young man wearing a yellow hat of straw came up to us and touched him on the shoulder, almost like flicking him in derision.

'Well, well, Aegisthus,' he said, showing his white teeth. 'Everything is ready. We thought you weren't coming. She's quite a big girl, isn't she. I thought she'd be smaller than this.'

The man in the skins shook his head, coming out of his dream and said, 'Is the other one here, the boy?'

The young man nodded and grinned. 'He's beside himself with fright, poor thing. The men have been telling him lies about how it's done. I think he's got a terror of knives, or something, He's lost the use of his tongue. Come on, or he'll go mad—then he'll be no use to anyone.'

Aegisthus gritted his yellow teeth and grasped me by the arm, harshly. Then we followed the young man into a dark stable, where there was hay on the floor, and a resinous torch burning in a bronze socket by the wall.

Three men were bending over a boy, laughing at him as he tried to burrow into the hay away from them. One of the men who laughed the most, a red-faced fat fellow, held a knife in his hand. I was furious, all at once, and ran towards him.

'What are you doing, you cowards?' I said. 'Would you dare face Agamemnon like this, laughing?'

[44]

The man turned to me, his smile stiff on his face, and said softly, 'I would face him, the High King, with only a stick in my hand, girl. Or even a stone, picked up from the river bed. And if he let me choose the meeting-place, at a spot where his barons were not lurking behind rocks to have me, I would even face him with these two bare hands. That is what I think of Agamemnon!'

All my life I had thought there could be no one bigger and braver than my father. This man's words angered me beyond bearing. I reached up in my fury and struck out at his face; but he caught my clenched fist easily and held it, bending down to look into my eyes. A heavy smell of garlic came from his mouth as he spoke. He said, 'Princess, oh, princess, I mean you no harm—but do not tempt me. I am a lawless man from over the far hills, and I would as soon taste a bit of suckling-pig as anything else. Do not put me in the way of it.'

I struggled with him, but he was very strong and I could not break his grip. At last I said, 'Let me go and I will not tell the king. Let me go, with this young boy, and I will say no more.'

Then he said slowly, as he loosed my hand, 'Tell the hills, tell the streams, tell the birds! Tell the king, and tell the king's god, Zeus—it is all the same to me. I am of the Mother, and they cannot touch me. Look!'

Suddenly he pulled open the folds of the tunic that hung about him and in the torchlight I saw the snake tattooed across his broad chest, its folds running into the thick black mat. He laughed as I drew away and said, 'So, you see, princess, you are not talking to a straw-haired Hellene now. You are talking to one who can tell you something.'

I put on my best face and said, 'And what can the likes of you tell me?'

He said, almost whispering now, 'I can tell you that the House of Atreus is finished. I can tell you that once the ships have sailed away, that will be that! Then the House of Thyestes will come again, never fear, and Mycenae will know the old ways once more.'

I said, 'You are a fool, man. There is my father and my brother,

Orestes. And there is my uncle, Menelaus . . . all of the House of Atreus. How can it fall? And who of the House of Thyestes still lives?'

The moon-faced man who had brought me to this place pushed in then and took my hand in his damp palm. 'There, there,' he said, 'you ask too much. Perhaps you would not like it if you got the answers! Come, this young boy in the hay is all you should be thinking of, not great Houses and their fall.'

The boy had risen from the floor now and was standing, shivering in every limb, his mouth open as though he wanted to cry out but didn't dare. His black hair hung, uncut, over his shoulders. A lock of it came down the side of his face as low as his jaw. He was very thin, and very dusty. From the leather collar round his neck, he looked to be a slave.

He said to me, in his thick dialect, 'Lady, do not let them hurt me. They said they would, and I am afraid of knives.'

He was perhaps two years older than I was, and quite a big boy. I did not like to see the tears running down his face, making runnels in the dust. It made me want to weep, too, so I slapped him hard on the cheek.

The moon-faced man laughed at this and said, 'Well done, Electra! That is how a wife should treat a cowardly husband!'

I turned on him and he backed away, pretending to be afraid of me. 'He is not my husband,' I said. 'He is only a boy, and I am too young to marry.'

The man with the knife growled and said, 'He is only a boy, but one day he will be a man. You are too young to marry, but before long you will be old enough. And he is not your husband, yet before a man could run to the High Town and back, you will be wed.'

I began to cry out and struggle, but they held me, laughing. The moon-faced man said, 'The choice is yours, Electra. Do as we say and no one will be harmed; or run home to your father if you wish, and tomorrow this boy's heart will be thrown through your window. So choose now, and choose wisely.'

I would still have run away from this frightening place, but the boy began to weep so piteously, on his knees, holding my skirts

[46]

about him, that I gave in and let them do what was in their minds.

In the darkest corner of the byre the men set us face to face, the boy and me, standing so closely together that our breaths mingled and his long coarse hair touched my shoulder and made me shudder. I thought for a while that they would make us do something awful to each other and was glad when this did not happen. The boy was relieved also, I heard his breathing close to my ear, almost a quick gasping which stilled itself when the danger seemed to have passed.

All at once the moon-faced man in the goat-skins came between us and pushed something into my hand, something thin and alive, covered with cloth. 'Take this firmly,' he said, 'and do not lessen your grasp. It is a dangerous thing, so hold it well.'

He seemed to be laughing as he spoke, but underneath the laughter there was a darkness, a threat. I did as he said, feeling the thing twisting in my fingers. Then I heard him whisper something to the boy who stood before me.

All was quiet for a time, except for the twitching of what I held. Then suddenly the red-faced fat man who had spoken slightingly of my father came near us, a long-bladed knife in his hand. 'Are you ready?' he said; then before we could answer, he brought the knife down between us, hissing as he struck. What I held in the cloth gave a violent jerk and I almost dropped it into the hay at my feet. Then it was still and limp in my hand.

A man held the torch over me now and said, 'It is done. Now see what you hold.'

At first I dared not look; the boy in the torchlight seemed pale-faced and agonised. His black eyes were staring, glazed, in the glow. Then I saw that he too held something in his hand, and I found the courage to unfold the linen wrapper.

In it lay the head and half the length of a shiny black snake, the last life still throbbing in it faintly. I saw that the boy held the tail part, staring down at it with his mouth open and his lips shining in the torchlight.

Aegisthus, the moon-face, put his hands on our shoulders and said, 'So! Now each has a half of the Mother's sign. The snake binds you together and you may take no other mates until the Mother gives her permission.'

He took the snake's head from me, and the tail from the boy. 'I will guard the signs,' he said, 'in case either of you needs to be reminded that you belong to each other.'

I drew away and said, 'When my father hears of this, he will come with the barons and punish you.'

The red-faced man laughed again and answered, 'Your father has other things to hold his mind, Electra. He is more concerned with the winds that will take him to Troy than with you. Besides, if he tried to find us, it would be like trying to find where the eagle nests on Olympus. This place is a dream, no more; and who can find a dream?'

I was going to say something angry, but a man came behind me and held his arm across my chest and throat. 'Drink this,' he said, and pushed a clay vessel between my lips, tilting my head back at the same time. I had to drink the bitter draught, or I should have choked. The last thing I heard was the boy's voice, crying out again, pleading. Then I felt myself dropping as though into a deep, dark valley of sleep.

I woke with the moonlight on my face and the bare rocks about me, outside the palace walls. Aegisthus sat beside me, smiling and nodding and fingering a small reed flute. He blew a note or two on it before he spoke to me. Then he said, 'Go straight to your bed and speak to no one about this. Think of it only as a dream, until the time comes for it to be put on flesh and become reality.'

'Where is the boy?' I asked.

Aegisthus shook his head and said, 'He is well. No great harm has come to him, nor will it come to him if you are silent about what has happened. His life is in your hands; do not destroy it. One day you will see him again, if you let him live. That is your destiny now. Go home and do not meddle with what lies beyond your understanding.'

I went back through the gates without seeing anyone. I was

shuddering with a strange fear, but I looked once and saw Aegisthus on a rock, still watching me, and nodding in the moonlight.

7

THE nightmare of the frightened boy, and Aegisthus, and the snake in the wrapping stayed with me for weeks; but I dared tell no one, not even my dear sister, Iphigenia. Perhaps I might have told my father, but as the time went on, and he grew more irritable preparing for war, he seemed less and less near to me, more like a god whose temper rested always at a point just below outright fury. So I kept it all locked inside me, and cried at night in my bed, under the covering so that none should hear me.

My mother must have noticed something, because once as I hung about her door I heard her say to Agamemnon, 'She is growing fast. Would you like to betroth her to one of the princes before you sail? It might keep her from doing something foolish while you are away.'

But Agamemnon shook his great mane and scratched his furry chest and yawned, throwing the covers off him. They had just given him the title of Lion King, the princes, because of his courage and because of the great gates he had had set up, with lions carved on the posts. Seeing him that bright morning, his head and body all hairy, I thought how much like a lion he really was—all but the eyes, which were a bluish-grey and not yellow, like a lion's.

He only said to my mother, 'I have all the world's problems on my back. There are thousands to be fed, princes to be pacified, barons to be paid, footmen to be whipped into obedience. Is that not enough for me?'

My mother rolled over in bed and almost saw me—but I drew back just in time. She said, 'She is your daughter. Is she not worth a father's thought?'

My father was stumbling round the room, rubbing his body with oil and still yawning. He said, 'She is close to my heart, but she is still only a young girl. I am concerned with the fate of the world—and it seems that I have the god himself to contend with now. He must be angry with me, this Poseidon, for he will not give me a wind to drive our ships towards Troy.'

My mother said quietly, 'If you were ruled by me, you would say your prayers to another—not to him. Then the wind might change and let you go.'

Agamemnon sat on the bed to clean his feet. He laughed sleepily and answered, 'I will not change now, woman. The House of Atreus, my own folk, have always offered to Zeus and Poseidon. Ours is the man-god; we could not change and beg favours from the bitch-goddess now. She is well enough for women and slaves, and some of the old outworn families who held this land before my people took it from them—but not for us. We have set our hands to this task in the god's name, and so it shall remain. If we fail, we fail: but there shall be no weeping.'

Clytemnestra was silent a while. At last she said, 'Men are only boys grown bigger. They rush on like stupid boars into the net, all because of their pride. They die for pride, when by a little thought, a little feeling, a little surrender, they might live.'

Agamemnon began to put on his wool shirt and leather tunic. He smoothed his hair and beard, then laughed.

'You women twist words to suit yourself. This surrender you speak of is nothing. What you mean is that a woman lies still while her mate covers her. But that is only to make a consummation possible. It is not true surrender. It is her way of working at the game. For a man, surrender means something else: it means placing your neck beneath another man's foot, it means running at his command, it means sacrifice—and no twisting and turning in a bed can be called that!'

[50]

My mother smiled bitterly then and said, 'I sometimes wonder if men know what sacrifice means. I think men are blinded to the meaning of words by the blind poets themselves. They sing of the gay maidens who gain a joyous freedom by love—but none of these poets has known the joy of being liberated by such frenzied bulls as men are! They sing that a woman in labour feels her time coming like the surges of waves on the seashore, and at last opens like a pretty flower-bud to let a new life into the daylight. But they should suffer it themselves before they sing; they should feel what it is like to be wrenched apart, to be torn, to bleed from the very heart—and all for a life that may well be one too much to feed after all. A life that may well end on the hill the next day. Is it joy to be tortured to provide a meal for the wolf, to wander about half-mad with breasts that howl, with milk no one will suck?'

My father was strapping on his sword. He was whistling and looking out through the window-hole to see what sort of day it was going to be. He said, 'There is one consolation. The pythoness at Delphi has forecast that Troy will fall and that King Priam's House will fall with it. And there is even better news: the Trojan priest, Calchas, who is friendly with our dear Achilles, said only yesterday that if I will give him leave to make an offering the wind will change. He swears it.'

Clytemnestra said, 'You are not listening to me after all. Very well, let Calchas make an offering. Let Priam's House fall. Let the world itself crumble, for all I care. I have been a wife to you, since you took me by force from poor Tantalus. I have borne and suckled your children. And little good have I got from it all my life. Men call you the Lion: but I tell you that once you have led them to where the gold lies, even the mangiest jackal of them all will bare his fangs against you. And at last you will come back home, as old Jason did, your sting drawn, asking only for a quiet place by the hearth and a bowl of gruel in your hand. We shall see the end of the Lion, Agamemnon. We shall hear what roaring he makes then.'

My father's brows puckered. He did not understand why the queen should speak so. Nor did I. He went away, clanking from the room to see to the men. I watched a while longer and saw my mother stagger to the runnel beside the wall and groan above it. She looked so small now, kneeling with her back to me, only like a girl. Even the blue tattooing over her legs and back, which had frightened me before, seemed nothing.

I went to her and placed my hand on her bare shoulder. She started and looked round at me, then smiled and wiped her mouth.

Before I could speak, she said gently, 'All is well, little one. I am not poisoned. It is a new baby in me that causes this. It will pass in time.'

I said, 'Will the king be pleased, mother?'

She looked away and said, 'Does it matter? He is going away, I shall not tell him. It is not his baby, it comes from another. This must be a secret between you and me, to bind us close together, as mother and daughter should be. I tell you this to bind you.'

Then she smoothed my hair out of my eyes and held me to her. I had never known her so gentle and warm and for a moment I forgot my father and even envied the baby within her. I wanted to be as close to her as that.

I whispered, 'Mother, did the god put this baby inside you then, if it is not the king's?'

Clytemnestra nodded. 'You can say that,' she said. 'It is as true as anything else.'

So, though I had always loved and feared my father, this was a secret I kept from him. A month before I would have run after him and told him all I knew: but something was happening to me now that made me want to share secrets with my mother. It had begun that evening in the quarry and it had been finally sealed, this difference, the night when Aegisthus had taken me to that strange dark place of wine and had put me, flesh to flesh, with the poor frightened boy. I was never the same again in my heart. Even my dreams began to change after that, and when I looked at the buds on the trees, or the birds in their nests, I began to wonder where they came from, how they started, what it felt like to have a baby inside one's body, close to the very heart.

[52]

8

BUT I did not think of these things every moment of the day. There were other things in life as well. One morning a man galloped into the city, half-dead with riding, and yelled out that the prince of Troy himself was coming to Mycenae.

All the dark folk ran out and began shouting at once, some saying that High Town would fall, some that we should hack off his head and set it on the Lion Gate, others that the war was now over and we should all feast with wine and bring back Hyacinth.

None of these was true. Prince Paris came up to Mycenae about midday, dressed like any gentleman riding to consult the oracle at Delphi, without armour, and with only a dozen horsemen behind him. He was only half the size of my father, and quite thin. But I liked his yellow hair and the tinkling gold and silver ornaments that hung at his neck and his wrists. He laughed a great deal and spoke our Achaean language with a lisp that interested all the girls. Some of us stood very close to him, so that we could finger the gold fringe on his tunic. He noticed this, and turned his smile upon us, showing his even white teeth. He even leaned towards us so that we could reach the fringe.

His face was shaven smooth, in the old Cretan manner, and his hands were well-kept and their nails trimmed. One of our barons made a comment on this, and on the musky scent that Paris used. But the prince took it all in good part and joined in the laughter of the rough soldiers, so that they had nothing to laugh about then.

Aunt Helen was presented to him and almost fainted when he touched her breast in homage after the Trojan fashion. I saw a shudder run through her. Her eyes went wide open and her lips fell apart as she gasped.

My mother, the queen, whispered to me, 'She'd go to him here, in full view of the people! It's a good thing that your Uncle Menelaus is away in Crete!'

I did not answer, because I had seen my uncle only two days before, dressed in thick country clothes, supping in one of the villages. He was not in Crete, whatever my mother said. He was not more than an hour's ride away.

Hermione, my cousin, the daughter of Helen, muttered to me, 'I would like the barons to kill this Trojan, then all would be happy again.'

I couldn't understand it, either: that my father and all his warriors should have been getting ready to make war on Troy for so long, and now, when the very prince of Troy stood in their midst, no one put a spear into him.

I learned, years later, that Paris had come to Mycenae at the invitation of the Achaean League. He had come as the ambassador of his father, King Priam, who thought that this might be one way of preventing war between the peoples. Yet I understood well enough, later, that he had been fetched to Mycenae so that he would see, and desire, Aunt Helen. His visit would start the very war which Troy had hoped to avoid. That was what all our kings wanted, in their hearts.

But, out there on the tall steps of our palace, in full sight of the folk, it was all laughter and courtesy that day. Agamemnon conducted the prince from one noble family to another, explaining who everyone was. The women all kneeled before him and let him raise them again. I heard him whisper to at least three of the girls, and saw them blush. But when he came to me, he only smiled and ran his fingers lightly through my hair, behind the ears. His touch was like little mice and a strange shiver ran tight down me into the deepest part. He said, 'Amber Princess! Yes, you are rightly called. How I wish you were old enough to come back with me to Troy. You would love the High Town there, and the people would love such a princess. Well, well, so be it. We cannot have everything.'

Then he passed on down the line, and made pleasantries with the girls of other great families. I was trembling as my mother gripped my wrist. She said, 'Behave yourself, Electra. This young man does not mean what he says. It is their custom to make much of little. They are not like our folk, who make little of much.'

She spoke out of a still face, painted almost as white as marble, with her hair all stiffened with horse-hoof glue, so that it looked as though carved from wood. She always made up so on great occasions, the clay-powder on her face often so thick that she could scarcely move her lips to talk. My father, the king, used to laugh at her preparations: he had only to strap on the thin beaten gold mask which had always been in his family since the dawn-times. And whereas my mother was required by custom to mould her hair into the forms of many snakes, setting these locks with glue, his hair was just brushed out, to flare about the edges of the mask like the sun's morning rays.

My father was always careless of custom, though. After the first greeting with Paris, he dragged the mask off and flung it to one of the barons to hold for him. Then he scratched in his thick beard just like any peasant troubled by lice, for everyone to see.

But my mother stood as motionless as a statue, always staring above the heads of the people, as a queen should. I recall, that day, that a little breeze lifted her light linen skirts and showed the tattooing on her thighs, but she affected not to notice this, though all the boys on the lower steps were pointing and laughing. It was said that Clytemnestra could walk naked through the market-place without showing loss of dignity, and I am sure that this was true.

Aunt Helen, on the other hand, could be fully covered with all her silks and worsteds—and yet look as though she was undressed. It was her way of shifting about, opening her bodice, or raising her skirt, with little twitches of the hand, as though she didn't know she was doing it. She seemed always to be on fire under her clothes, and wanting to let air to her body. But my mother was just the opposite. I did not understand this, then; but I do now. It was what destroyed Hellas and let the barbarians in.

After the greetings, Agamemnon took Paris away to a council chamber below the floor of our house, where no women were ever allowed. They were together until sunset, and no one ever knew what they spoke of. I remember that the barons were angry and that many of them got drunk, not watering their wine three-fold as was the rule, and began to boast that they would take the head off the shoulders of Paris before ever he got as far as the coast.

That strange day comes very clearly to my mind, even now, after all those years. There were two great warriors who caused more fuss than anyone else: Diomedes of Argos, who was as handsome as a god, and never made any secret of his love for Aunt Helen; and a strange little hunchbacked king with crow-black hair. This was Idomeneus of Crete. He had a great shield emblazoned with a cock partridge, and a helmet set all about with boars' tusks. Some said he was not a true Cretan, but an Egyptian. Whatever the case, he claimed direct descent from the first King Minos, and had brought a hundred ships to Aulis. Openly he bragged that without his ships, Agamemnon could not make the attack on Troy. And, when he was drunk, which was often, he used to say that he and Agamemnon were the joint generals of the army and would share the glory of destroying Troy.

I had always admired Diomedes for his fine looks, but King Idomeneus disturbed me. I could not forget that on his first evening at our house he had said something to me while my father was out of the feast-hall; and though it had been done with a comforting smile and a caressing hand, I could never see black hair and a brown skin afterwards without recalling this occasion with disgust.

But I am straying from the story. These two, Diomedes and Idomeneus, seemed to make up their minds early on that Paris should die. At the time of his arrival there was a feast in the palace. My mother and Helen were not present, since the first night was for men alone, and the women would be at the tables on later evenings; but all the young girls of noble birth were there, to stand beside the lords and see that their wine-cups were full, this being an occasion too great for mere slaves or serving-men.

Iphigenia and I stood on either side of my father at the board's

[56]

head, so we saw and heard all that happened. So did Helen's daughter, Hermione, who stood at the right hand of Paris in the place of honour.

Diomedes and Idomeneus sat across the table from Paris and seemed determined to make a fool of him. At first they contented themselves with pointing at his gold ornaments and whispering to each other. Then as the wine-cups were filled, and filled again, they grew bolder until, at last, as there came a lull in the talking and laughter, Diomedes said in a loud voice to his companion, 'These Phrygians do not pray to the god as we know him. They have taken up the custom of those cattlemen who live in the little hills behind Jericho. They name him *e-o-i*! Just like children cooing.'

Paris heard this, but went on talking and laughing with my father. However, Diomedes would not let it pass as easily as that. He reached across the table with his long arm and caught Paris by the sleeve.

'Is that not true, prince?' he asked, his lips curled back among his face hair.

Paris looked at him across the rim of his cup and said quietly, 'We have men of many lands in Troy. They each bring their own ways. We do not question them.'

Once more, he would have turned to my father, but King Idomeneus, his dark face reddened with wine, said harshly, 'This god of Jericho, they tell me he requires a strange offering from the cattlemen. Is that also true, prince?'

The face of Paris flushed and he set down his cup clumsily, spilling the red wine on the scrubbed white board. Diomedes thumped the table and laughed aloud. 'There, there!' he called. 'That arrow found its mark, Paris! Come, comrade, onto the table with you and let us see how it leaves a man! Come now, never let it be said a Trojan was delicate!'

I glanced at my father; he was glowering down at his meat, as though anxious not to offend anyone—Paris, or his own lords. I saw my sister, Iphigenia, her eyelids lowered, but her dark eyes turned on Paris as though she hoped he might do as Diomedes said. Many of the older girls were looking the same way, for life in our great houses was very strict in those times, and it was not often that our curiosity was satisfied.

But Paris seemed to recollect himself suddenly and held out his cup for Iphigenia to fill it again. As she did this, her hand shook so much that the neck of the flask chattered against the lip of his cup. Paris turned and looked up at her shortly. 'Do not upset yourself, pretty one,' he said, 'there will be no show.'

Diomedes was beside himself at the calmness of Paris. He turned once more to the Cretan and began to urge him to drink faster and more than his head would stand. Soon, Idomeneus was calling for a harpist and bawling out that he had a song to sing. This was his usual custom and no one gave much heed to it: but tonight there was silence as he wiped his mouth with the back of his hairy hand, and clambered onto the table. Diomedes, already half-speechless, poured wine over the Cretan's head and slapped him on the back, too hard, making him cough and splutter. But at last Idomeneus snatched the harp away from the slave who had come running, and began to sing, in his high, nasal voice:

> A beardless boy
> Who came from Troy
> Met Hermes in the hills.
> 'Come, come, young sir,'
> Cried the messenger,
> 'And judge these pretty girls.'
>
> Three girls he set before the boy,
> One black, one gold, one red:
> 'Come, pick me out,' called Hermes sly,
> 'The one you'd like to bed!'
>
> He took a golden apple
> And put it in his hand.
> 'Take this,' he said, 'and make your choice;
> Be king of all this land.

For that's the prize if you choose aright.'
'But what if I choose all wrong?'
Hermes frowned. 'Then the best you'll get
Is to hear Idomeneus' song!'

As the Cretan's tongue shambled, slurred with wine, over the crowded syllables, Diomedes pointed at Paris and laughed wildly, as though a great joke had been made. Many of the rough up-country barons and squires joined him, nudging one another and beating their cups on the table.

Paris, who had sat with lowered eyes while the song was on, now glanced up, his light eyes as keen as dagger-blades. Then he rose and took the harp from the Cretan and, with one foot on the bench, sang quietly:

What magic lies in wine, sweet wine,
The dark blood of the grape!
It makes fools brave and heroes whine,
Turns gentle love to rape.

Three cups, and dark has changed to light,
Or sea has changed to sky;
Another, and tomorrow's hope
Is last year's memory!

Oh wine, the Maenads' only joy
At the sad sun's decline,
Turns lions of Argos into dogs
And Cretan bulls to swine!

As he sang, the men were silent in the hall, so as to miss none of his words; but as he drew to the finish and flung the harp back to the trembling slave, a hiss sounded everywhere, as though the kings and barons had been drenched with cold water and were catching at their breath.

Diomedes was swaying above the table, his knuckles white on the board, his spittle running into his trimmed beard. King Idomeneus was feeling all round his waist for his dagger, forgetful that he had left it in the vestibule, according to the feast laws in Mycenae.

Only Paris was still smiling. 'Come, gentlemen,' he said, 'a song for a song. Can the Hellenes take a joke no longer?'

Diomedes said thickly, 'Trojan, I will take more than that—I will take your head.'

Then, as the shouting started, my father the High King, the Lion of Mycenae, rose from his carved chair at the head of the table. I had almost forgotten him, and now, as his great head and shoulders thrust up from among all the folk who clustered round him, he seemed like Poseidon the Bull rising up from the dark waves at midnight. He did not speak words, but a deep roaring came out of his belly and his chest. Men fell away from him, from the benches. I trembled so much that my hands let fall the wine flask. I did not hear it shatter on the stone floor, but I felt the cold liquid splash up my legs.

Then Agamemnon was towering above Diomedes and the Cretan king. They were like little children beside him, and their eyes turned up as though their hearts had left them. My father's eyes were so huge and empty that, in the flickering torchlight, I thought for an instant his fury had blinded him, or that Zeus had taken his sight for allowing such words at his table.

Then Agamemnon squealed shrill, like a stuck pig, and brought his clenched fists down on Diomedes, thumping his fine head onto the thick oak board. He struck him again many times, until Diomedes slithered away into the straw and lay still.

And all the while, King Idomeneus stood there, shuddering, but making no attempt to retreat. Even when my father took him by the wrist and twisted it so hard that we heard the sinews strain, the Cretan made no effort to defend himself. The sweat streamed down his dark face and he bit his lips until they bled, rather than cry out.

Soon we were glad when Agamemnon punched him at the side of the neck and tumbled him beside Diomedes in the straw, for that meant the end of his suffering for a while.

And when this was done, we stood away, each moving with

[60]

little steps so as not to be noticed, leaving my father and Paris alone at the table.

It was then that I was most truly afraid of Agamemnon, for he seemed to be seeking another to kill, seeking with his blind, mad eyes, which swung over the huddled company and came to rest at last on the Trojan.

For a while, all wondered what the end would be. The High King mumbled and slavered and then suddenly said, 'Paris the Phrygian! The Trojan trouble-maker! The horse-thief who picks from the mares and leaves the stallions! But for you, this hall would be a happy place. But for you.'

He made half a pace towards the young man, but Paris stood quite still and smiling. Then I saw that in his right hand he held a narrow-bladed dirk that he had pulled from within his feast robe.

He said in his high clear voice, 'Come no closer, Lion. I am not from Argos, nor from Crete, so I shall not stand quiet while you beat my brains out.'

It was as though someone had desecrated a shrine, or left ordure on the Mother's altar. The hall was as silent as death. No one had ever spoken like this to the High King before.

Then all at once Agamemnon laughed, so loud, so hard, that I was almost sick with fear. And suddenly he was holding Paris in his arms, like an old friend who had been lost, and was now found. And Paris was clapping him on the back, as one would clap a worthy horse. His dagger had gone into its sheath again, as quietly as it had come out.

I made my way from that room as soon as I could, and wept alone in my bed, growing more and more aware what it meant to have a god for one's father, what it was to be daughter of the Lion King of Mycenae. It was a wearisome burden.

9

I AM an old woman now, talking to a stranger in the hills. My head is full of half-remembered thoughts that grin like ghosts from behind curtains but vanish when I go to meet them. Days jostle days, and folk push out folk from the memory, like village-dogs fighting for a bone in the famine times. It is hard to make sense of it all. But you must take it as it comes, doctor, for it is the only way I know to tell it.

Paris came and went, without more quarrelling; and one day, before Menelaus returned, we found that Aunt Helen had gone as well. Shortly afterwards, Menelaus came back to Mycenae, riding an unblown horse, and made great show of his grief, knocking his shaggy head against the Lion Gate for all the folk to see, and raising his arms to the sky, calling on Zeus Father to give him satisfaction for his loss.

Hermione, his young daughter, clung to his kilt and wept until all her hair was wet. We other children of the palace wept, too. But afterwards, when the townsfolk had gone away, moved and swearing vengeance on Troy, I saw that the lords and ladies seemed to make little of it. Indeed, it was hardly mentioned: the only talk was of the wind that would not set right to drive our ships towards the dawn, of the harvests that must be seen to, when the army had gone, and things like that; common things.

Even Menelaus stopped pretending grief, and once, sitting at our table, he leaned across to my father and said, 'Did she take the chestnut stallion or the litter, brother?' My father had been drinking wine, too, and was not mindful of other ears. He smiled and said, 'I let her have her own way, Menelaus. She went on foot by night as far as Midea. He was waiting in the hills there with his own horses. His boats lay just north of Epidaurus.'

Uncle Menelaus took another pull at his wine-cup and nodded. Then he said, quite reasonably, 'We must not press too hard, then.

With this wind holding the way it does, he'll find it just as hard as us to make his way through the islands. Let him get to Naxos before we set forth.'

Agamemnon grinned above a partridge leg and said, 'They will light the beacons on Naxos after he has gone from there, then on Paros, then on Siphnos, and so back to the mainland, to Argolis. So we shall know. It is all arranged.'

All the time I was looking into my milk-bowl with my hair hanging down at each side of my face, like a hood. The men did not even notice me. But my mother, the queen, did: she had sharp eyes for everything. And when the king and his brother had gone to drink in the mess-tent with the barons, she said to me gravely, 'We in palaces hear much that is not heard by others; but we do not talk of it. Just as the priest on the hill or the priestess in the shrine hear much and do not mention it.'

I said, 'It is understood, mother.' Then I stroked her cheek and she smiled, and gave me a piece of honey-bread in her fingers. Now she seemed to me dearer and kinder than ever before, since the night when I had seen my father turn into a monster that I did not recognise.

After this, Clytemnestra took more interest in me. She would have me in her bed all night, while the gathering soldiers laughed and sang drunken songs outside, or set fire to the hovels on the outskirts of Mycenae.

Once, as the glow from such a fire lit up the window-holes of the chamber, she hugged me to her and said, 'Have you ever watched fish in the river, sweet one?'

I said that I had.

She asked, 'And what colour are they?'

I said sometimes silver, sometimes blue, sometimes black. They changed as you watched them. It all depended on the light or the shade, whether they lay in deep water or shallow, in the open or under the rushes.

My mother stroked my hair gently. 'That is right,' she said. 'One thing always depends on many others. All life is like that. The man

[63]

who says that there is only one truth tells a lie, and so his truth is a lie and not worth regarding.'

I remember saying, 'But if you take a fish from the water, you see that he was silver all the time. Is that not the truth, mother?'

Clytemnestra whispered in my ear, 'Truly he is silver when he lies on the bank: but then he is dead. That is the dead truth, the sort of thing that is told after a man's death, and you know what manner of thing that is. You know that, when they are dead, tyrants are called good kings, and cowards brave warriors? That is the silver truth about them, not the blue truth, or the black truth.'

I was very sleepy, but I said, 'And all life is like the fishes, mother?'

She answered, 'Yes, my love. You will hear things said about the king, about Helen, about Paris and about me, after we are gone. But it will only be the dead silver truth. So keep your eyes open and watch, as you would watch a fish, while we are alive: then you will know the live truth about us, the changing truth that depends on whether we move in the sunlight or the shadow, in clear and shallow water, or down in the dark deeps.'

I huddled up to her, already half-asleep, and said, 'You and my father will never die, mother. Don't say such things.'

Then I was fast asleep.

10

Now men gathered about Mycenae like flies about carrion. Some of them were so dark-faced that I thought they were from the hot sands of Libya. Others were almost white-haired, with eyes so pale that they looked empty and blind. They often fought because they could not understand one another's languages.

My father took all of us children on one side late one afternoon, when the sun flung long shadows from the cypress trees across the courtyard, and said, 'The time has come for me to tell you this, my children. It is no longer safe for you to go out among the tents to listen to the soldiers' songs, or to watch them wrestling and throwing the javelin. In Mycenae now are men from all over Hellas, and beyond. Some of them have been a year in coming to us from the island of mist at the earth's end. You will know them by their red hair and the blue war-paint they wear on their faces and arms. Do not go near them, for they are not like other men. They pray to stones set in the ground, not to the god, and they offer children in their sacrifice, just as we offer horses to Poseidon. These men are too savage and ignorant to know that you are the children of kings and lords, so do not go near them. Stay safe in the palace. I have put a guard of Achaeans inside the walls. They will not let these out-landers come inside—but you must help by staying where I tell you.'

My sister, Iphigenia, who was older than most of us, said boldly, 'I have heard that these outlanders have gold enough in their own streams; why do they come to share that which we shall gain from Troy?'

The king gave her a hard look. I am not sure that he ever really loved her, she was often too sharp and did not pay him the homage he thought due to a High King. He answered sharply, 'If I say it is frosty, you say it is warm. If I say a creature is a bull, you say it is a cow.'

Iphigenia smiled up at him and said, 'I am not talking about frost or bulls, but about these outlanders who want our gold when they have some of their own.'

Agamemnon pulled hard at his beard and turned away from us. 'Just remember not to go outside the walls,' he said. Then, as he reached the door, 'However much gold a man has, he can still do with more.'

We thought the king was acting strangely: but we were also cross with Iphigenia for angering him so uselessly.

One morning we got a sight of these outlanders, though, without going outside the walls. We stood on the upper steps and saw four of

[65]

them climbing over the walls. Our Achaeans soon caught them when they dropped down onto the ground. How small they were! And one of them was so old, he could hardly jump off the wall.

Iphigenia said, 'They won't make much of a showing against the Trojans, I'll be bound.'

They had only strips of wolfskin about their middles and light deer-hide shoes. They had their red hair done up in buns on top of their heads, and held with bone pins. Their axes and knives were of flint, not like our splendid bronze ones. But the blue war-paint on their faces was certainly fearsome. It made them like strange animals, not men.

The old fellow who was with them wore a ragged grey gown of wool and a crown of oak-leaves round his head. It slipped sideways when he landed and made him look very silly. His hair was quite white and hung down his back. His beard almost reached the belt of clacking shells round his waist. He had a holly stick with a cat's white skull fastened to the top, and with this he tried to beat our Achaeans back.

But they had their orders and closed in with their short swords. I looked away while it was done, but Hermione told me about it afterwards. She said that the younger outlanders were laughing all the time, even when the swords went in, and that the old man in the wool gown almost blinded the Laconian captain with his cat-stick before three of the other guards tumbled him down.

After that I did not want to go outside the walls! I almost prayed for the wind to change, so that these terrible men could be gone from Mycenae, even though it meant that Agamemnon would go, too. I felt it would be a good bargain.

But if our distant allies frightened me, our closer friends seemed more and more noble and trustworthy. They were still allowed inside the palace and I got to know many of them very well.

The most handsome of them was Ajax, who came from Salamis, where they still prayed to the Mother. The rough inland barons used to tease him about this, but, though I was only a young girl, I could tell that they meant nothing by it. Ajax was a foot taller than any other man, save my father, and was so strong that all men wished to be his brother. Actually, he had a brother, or a half-brother rather, called Teucer. This Teucer was just as black as Ajax was golden, and he was no great hand with the heavy bronze sword. His weapon was the bow which, being shaped like the growing moon or the bull's horns, was often the weapon of those who prayed to the Mother. Teucer's bow was a small thing, of layers on layers of horn, bound round with wire and gut, until its strength was such that only an expert could use it. Teucer would draw it to the breastbone, not to the ear as the long Hellene bows were drawn, and let fly arrow after arrow with such rapidity that he could stand easily against five javelin-men. Over a distance of fifty paces, not one would have reached him alive. But Teucer was no use at in-fighting. A girl of twelve could have beaten him at wrestling or dagger-work. It was laughable to watch him, when the armies were practising for the war to come: he would let loose a dozen short stick-arrows at the approaching 'enemy' who, if touched, fell down and pretended to be dead. But if he missed any of them and they still came on with their clubs, Teucer would run for shelter behind Ajax's enormous shield, and would not come out again until the 'enemy' had been beaten off. They always fought together, ate together and slept together. That was the custom among warriors who fought in pairs when I was a young girl. It dated back beyond the time of my great-uncles, Castor and Polydeuces, the Laconians who came from their mother's body together and looked so alike that not even she knew which was which.

I liked Teucer because he was so modest. Once when he shot down an owl from the roof of our palace, with one quick flick of the wrist, I praised him; but he only smiled and shrugged, and said, 'It is nothing, my lady. I have been doing this for more years than you have been breathing air and drinking milk. What would be strange would be if I could not do it, after all that time.'

He promised to teach me how to use the short horn bow; but there was no time before the armies went away, and so I never learned. I was sorry at the time, because we girls liked to boast of what we had learned from the soldiers—sword-play, how to hold a shield up under the axe's blows, chariot-driving, wrestling. We loved the wrestling most of all. In the heat of battle, the men tore off their clothes and grappled with one another all naked, save for a breech-clout. The sweat ran down them, and their big hands slipped in it, as they went at each other with teeth and knees, their hair and beards all over their faces. When the high barons were not about, we girls would strip off our clothes and run in among them, and be thrown here and there in the dust, with the sun over our heads. The younger warriors liked this and got their knees to us just as though we had been other young men. We came away bruised and aching, and some of the older ones with worse troubles, but we loved it. For many of us, it was the first time we had been close to a man, to feel his bone and hair and sweat on us. It was from this beginning that the girls of Achaea gained their name as naked wrestlers. In the generations that followed, such places as Athens grew to be very prim and forbade women even to watch the men wrestling. They called us Mycenaeans shameless hussies for dropping our skirts and plunging into the fray. Not that we cared for what the folk of Athens said: they were born liars, who spoke one word, but meant another. The same elders who frowned and ordered us away from their sports would be just those who tried to take secret liberties with us in the narrow streets or taverns, when the wrestling was over and the wine-feasts began at sun-fall.

I think my father, the king, knew I went out wrestling, but he never commented on it. Clytemnestra did, though. She met me once, as I came up through the vestibule with my cousin, Hermione, and said, 'Fruit that is bruised will soon go rotten and will spoil the other apples that rest beside it. From now on, you must both keep away from the soldiers. Remember who you are, and which House you belong to. All that may be well enough for slave-girls, but not for princesses.'

Hermione, who was always bolder towards my mother than I dared to be, said, 'It is princesses that the men like best. They have told us so.'

[68]

Clytemnestra bent towards her and said, her eyes narrow, 'What more do they do, after the wrestling?'

Hermione just threw back her head and laughed. 'Do you think I am going to tell you that, aunt!' she said, then ran away, her robe trailing behind her in her hand.

My mother turned on me then, and said, 'Hermione is too forward for you. Though you are of the same age, she has picked up too much for her years. Her mother has not kept the watch on her that I have on you. From now on, when you go out with your cousin, you must keep yourself decently covered.'

Later, one of the sewing-women made a small pair of leather breeches for me and I had to wear them under my skirt. They were very thick and hot, and although Hermione tried to ease me of them, she could not, because they were held about my waist with a thong-knot which only my mother knew how to untie. I shall never forget those breeches! They were an agony, especially when the hide got hard with my sweat, and the edges got worn and rough. I thought I would be marked for life—but, as I got older, I came to understand that there were worse torments than a pair of leather breeches, and that being marked for life was a small thing in a warrior-land where hardly any fighting-man went about with all his limbs, or his teeth, or his ears and eyes complete.

But talking of my breeches, which made me look like a boy, reminds me of one of the great lords who looked like a girl. It was Achilles, who was only about fifteen when he set sail for Troy. His beard hadn't come yet and this made him so aware of himself, among the hairy soldiers, that he always put on a fierce face, tightening his mouth so much that he got the nickname of 'the lipless one'. This wasn't the only strange thing about him, though. The rumour was that his mother, having foreknowledge that one day all the princes must sail for Troy, had brought him up as a girl on the island of Scyros. He had been dressed in skirts and had lived among other girls for so long that he was never thought of as anything else, with his long hair and painted eyes, and his clinking jewellery. The story went that Ajax and Odysseus discovered who he really was when they went recruiting soldiers for the war. The tale is variously told, but the version we heard in the palace at Mycenae was that Odysseus got among the court-ladies on Scyros one night and had the ill-fortune to pick Achilles. But I don't know: as far as I saw, Achilles was as brave and nimble as any of the other young ones, even though his high fluting voice made us all laugh. But he had a vile temper, and never really liked my father.

We laughed at Odysesus, too, for that matter, in spite of all his bragging and his great hairy chest. While he was sitting down at table, he looked the grandest man the god had ever made. But once he stood up, everybody roared, because his legs were so short he looked like a dwarf.

He was a very strange fellow, this Odysseus, King of Ithaca. He was always angry, for one reason or another, breaking wine-cups or thumping his fist on the board. After a while, no one took his anger or his boasting seriously. Then he would drink more and more, crunching up the clay cups in his teeth, spoiling our best Minyan glaze-ware, until someone would call out, 'What about your wound, Odysseus? Let's hear about that!'

The men had heard about it a hundred times, but it was always good for another laugh. Odysseus would stagger onto his bench and drag up his kilt to show his body. He didn't care who was present, slaves or women, when he did this. There was a great white and puckered furrow in his brown flesh, that ran down his body into the hair on his thighs, an ugly sight—though he gloried in it. 'Look, all of you,' he would cry, 'this is where the god's thunderbolt entered when I defied him once on Olympus. Which of you could have taken such a blow? Which of you could have walked down the mountain unaided, as I did, and then have lived to carry the scar as long as I have done? Which of you?'

Always the warriors would shout out, 'No one, Odysseus! You are the bravest of all men!'

Then they would laugh behind their hands and get on with the drinking. Even the slaves used to laugh, and I have seen them, when they thought they were alone, exposing their bodies to one another and saying, in their rough dialect, 'Which of you could have lived to carry the scar as long as I have done?' The women and children did it, too; it became quite a catch-word.

Once my father, the king, drew me aside and said, 'You mustn't mind old Odysseus, my love. He is one of my best advisers, but he is a bit of a fool in ordinary matters. That belly-wound of his was got from a boar's tusks, nothing more. But it's the only scar he has to show, so he makes the most of it.'

After that, I got to understand Odysseus better, and men better, in general. I saw how bragging they were, even the grown ones, like little boys. It was from Odysseus and his scar that I learned how rough and hairy old men's bodies were, like gnarled oak-trees. One can learn many things, keeping one's eyes open.

There was one of my father's counsellors, though, who taught me something else. This was Nestor, King of Pylus, the oldest and, men said, wisest king ever to walk the earth. When Nestor came to Mycenae, he was so bent with age that his servants had to carry him to and from the feast table; and his eyes were so like stones that he could not see his hand before his face unless the sun was at its brightest.

But he taught me something. I cannot tell you what it was, doctor, yet awhile. Perhaps I will, one day, when I am in the mood, but not now. It is strange, but even though I am so old, I am often as modest as a young girl from Athens. I think that if my father, the king, had known what Nestor taught me, he would have put the sword into him without delay, even though he was an old man and had come so far to join us with all his javelins and horses. Perhaps it would have been as well. Oh, I don't know. As you get older, things grow more and more confused. Perhaps King Nestor did no harm after all. Perhaps I should have learned about it some other way; from the slave women, perhaps. I don't know, and now I am too old to care.

11

DURING all this time my sister, Iphigenia, was very dear to me. There were moments when she seemed the only unchanging thing in my life; as firm as a rock when my father and mother were full of the whims of a world I had not yet come into. Chrysothemis was always busy with her rituals, her libation cups and sequined skirts, her little sacrifices at the hearth-stone, her prayers to be learned (though she was never very quick at learning and made mistakes with the words which even I could hear), while baby Orestes was still cutting teeth and wetting himself and bawling for the breast. Iphigenia was the only one of my blood-kin I could turn to. Hermione was well enough for a romp in the apple-trees, or a song with the boys, but useless to talk to about the things that bothered me at this time—though she changed a great deal, afterwards, as I will tell you.

But Iphigenia sat, in our secret place among the laurels in the private part of the palace garden, and listened to me patiently. I can see her now, a little on the thin side—though her body was well-formed from the start, and she loved to stroke it when we were alone —her dark eyes big in her narrow face, her lips always shaped into a gentle smile. She could tease, like anyone else, of course, but most often her teasing had a honeyed end to it, of kindness after the sharp word. I told her about Nestor and she waited a while, then said, 'It is always the same with kings, beloved. They are their own law. I think our father may be the same, when he is in other places.'

I said hotly, 'No, no, dear one, our father is not like that. He may be a mad lion but he is too noble a beast for that. Have you not seen him on the palace steps, shouting out the law of the land to the field-folk on the appointed days? Have you not observed his proud beard and his still hands, held out like those of the god? To such a man there is nothing small and nasty, nothing less than godhead, even though that may be terrible, as when he rose against the guests at the feast for Paris. Yet that was not small and nasty; it was grand, though fearsome. Yes, he is grandly mad, but not nasty.'

Iphigenia smiled and shook out her long hair. 'Dear one, dear one,' she said. 'What a baby you still are! Do you think that because a man is a king, and a god, and a great fighter, that there is no smallness to his mind? Can you say honestly that Zeus has never done a nasty, brutish little thing? Or Poseidon, for that matter.'

I came close to tears and answered, 'Our father is always great. Even at his smallest, he is greater than another king's grandest.'

My sister shook her hair over her face, so that it seemed to cascade down to hide her features, like a dark waterfall hiding the rock beneath it. I could not tell whether she smiled or was serious when she spoke, but she said softly, 'How many of the slaves' children are our brothers and sisters, dear one? Can you answer me that?'

I was thunderstruck and said, 'You speak in riddles, beloved.'

Iphigenia parted her thick hair and smiled at me sadly. 'I speak what everyone knows,' she said, 'not riddles which no man can answer. And I tell you that half the black-eyed children who sprawl in the straw with the flies about their heads carry the Blood of the Lion in their veins. They are as well-born as ourselves, if it comes to it, sister. So what is this nobility, this godhead, if any slave may share it?'

I put my hands over my ears and would not listen. Iphigenia took them away gently and hugged me to her. 'Dear one,' she said, 'you want everything to be as you dream it should be. But the world is not a sunlit dream; it is not clean and simple. It is confused and nasty, very often. And the truth of it is hard to find. What do we know, we two sisters? We have lived here in Mycenae all our days—yet Mycenae is but a small village compared with other places of the world. Yes, the folk here bow down when our shadows fall on them in the streets, and the poets call us the children of Zeus, and such like. We lie in bed and think that our dreams are ours alone, and that no lesser one may share them—but all this is nothing. In every farmstead in Laconica, children lie down at night and dream they are the chosen of Zeus, that they are changelings, that one day the god will give them their rights. . . . Each one thinks he is the chosen one, and perhaps that we are tyrants, usurpers, impostors. One day, they dream, all will be right in the world, and the truth will be known to all men. But, I ask you, what is the truth?'

I could not answer her, for I had never heard it put so before. I just sat and rocked myself under the laurels' shade in the sunshine, crying in misery. Iphigenia got up and smoothed her skirt and then began to nibble at a laurel-leaf.

'Dearest,' she said, whispering, 'I will tell you—there is no truth; that is, if by truth we mean the only one and undivided way. There is a truth for each single one of us, and each one will see the truth he wants to see. So each truth is different. There is no more to it than that.' I had said much the same to my mother, but hearing it come from Iphigenia now, somehow made it seem wicked.

There was a little rustling in the bushes and I said, afraid, 'But, beloved, you do not mean this. You are talking as men do, when they have drained the wine-cups too often. Surely, the god shows us his truth? He shows us the only way, gives us our destiny; then, if we do not follow that way, that destiny, he sends the Furies to drag us down and punish us. You know that, as well as I do; you know, besides, that when we do wrong, or when we wish for the god to help us, whether we have done wrong or not, we must make an offering to him, a sacrifice. We must. . . .'

But she would not let me go on. She smiled a thin smile and took two handfuls of my hair and pretended to tug at it.

'Little one,' she said, almost whispering among the rustling leaves, 'in my heart I know none of these things. In my heart. Truly, I *say* such things when I am among the others. But in my heart, no.'

Then she bent right over me and said in my ear, 'Electra, it has come to me in these last days that there is no truth, no destiny, and not even a god!'

I started to jump up, to run away, but she laughed and pushed me down again into the tall grass. Then as I lay, my heart fluttering, she fell beside me and put her arms about me. 'There is no god, and no goddess,' she said, quite wildly, as though a great load had been lifted from her. 'We, the men and the women, have dreamed a god, that is all. There is no god—there are only flowers and rivers and hills, and the white clouds in the sky, and the birds in their nests, and the lions roaring out, far away, up on the mountain. And we are meant for joy, and not for death. The lamb without blemish that is led to the altar at Delphi, so that a mad old woman can dabble in its innocent blood and mumble her stupid dreams, dies for nothing. We are sacrificing to our own fear, not to the god. No god, no god, no god!'

I lay dumb and terrified. I had never heard such words before. The only thing I could think of to say was, 'But our sister, Chrysothemis, is a priestess of the Hearth; and our mother was once a priestess of Dia. How can you tell me that there is nothing to sacrifice to?'

She leaned over and bit my ear hard, as though to bring me to my senses. 'You little stupid,' she said. 'Our sister is a fool, did you not know that? She is pretty, oh so pretty, but she is not right in the head, my love. Tell her that she is a priestess, and she will be one. She will put on the dress and hold the libation cup for the stuff to drip into it. She will go through all the silliness. But ask her the name of a flower, or the distance from Mycenae to Aegira, and she won't know. You might just as well ask her how to fly, or where the night goes to when dawn comes. Poor Chrysothemis would believe she was a fish if mother told her so. She would leap into the deepest lake and try to swim to the bottom for a green morsel of weed. If mother told her she was a bird, our sister would spread her arms and try to soar from the highest tower of the palace. Oh, you are such a baby, you do not know what lies behind her pretty face . . . there is nothing!'

I shuddered and said, 'But surely you would not deny that our mother. . . .'

Iphigenia held her narrow hard hand over my mouth, and said, 'Our mother is our mother. She is the queen in Mycenae. Nothing more. There *is* no more to be—a woman, walking under the sky, eating bread, drinking wine, having her babies, suckling them, and at last dying and falling to dust. Nothing more—all else is dreams.'

I struggled up and pushed her away. 'The god will punish you, sister,' I said. 'I will say prayers for you every night, but he will punish you.'

My sister straightened her skirt and laughed again. She said, 'Pray for me, my bird, as you please. It will do me no good, and no harm. If it eases your mind to pray, then pray. But, one day, you will see the sense of what I have been telling you. One day we will laugh about it all, together. One day, when this heavy dream of blood and altar-smoke lifts from our people.'

All the time she was speaking, somewhere at the back of my head, I sensed that something was about to happen, something ill. Even the sunlit air about us seemed to be thickening. I felt the little runnels of cold sweat going down my back, inside my thin bodice. Over away to the sunrise, in the dry hills, I heard thunder growling like an old lion. The leaves of the trees above us began to quiver, as though the god brushed them with his hand, lightly. It was frightening, and I wanted Iphigenia to unsay all she had told me. I was holding out my hands towards her, to beg her to take back all her words, when a shadow fell across us, hiding the sun. I shut my eyes, and let fall my hands. I waited without breathing for the god to send his lightning into us and burn us up.

Then I heard our father's voice above us. He said, 'There are some things that no heart should think, no tongue should utter, either in the silence of the chamber, or under the wide sky.'

His voice was steady and as chill as the winter breeze. The thunder in the far hills stopped for a moment. The wind that shook the leaves above us was still. All was suddenly so still that I thought I was asleep and dreaming. So still and heavy that I could not have arisen to my feet even if a wolf had run at me then.

I opened my eyes with great effort and saw him standing there among the laurel-leaves, dressed in his armour and holding his sword to his thigh so that its fine scabbard should not be scratched by the twigs. He was not wearing his mask, but that made no difference, for he seemed to have on a face made of dull gold, stiff and carved.

My sister was gazing at him as though she had never seen him before, and her lips were open like those of a drowning girl sucking for air. All her body was shivering, and the silver beads about her white neck were shuddering together like tiny timbrels.

Agamemnon said slowly, 'What has been said, cannot be unsaid. I am as sad as you must be for that. I, on the eve of great enterprise, with half of the world at my call, never thought to hear a daughter of mine defy the god. I, with the god's wind blowing in my face to hold me back, have need of all my persuasion to cause him to stay his hand; yet you, my daughter, taunt him with being nothing, a dream. How can that be good?'

Iphigenia began to cry then, her little hands across her face, and the tears running down below them on to her breasts. She did not dare answer our father the king, nor did I, though I wanted much to beg his forgiveness. We sat, silent and afraid, among the laurels, while he towered over us in the silent world and made all cold.

I do not know how long we sat there. It was the longest time of my life. I have known what it is like to give birth to children, alone in my room, thinking the night would never end—but this, in the garden, was longer than all my childbirths. All sense went from me; no thoughts or words would come to me. I only knew that I was deathly cold and trembling. Every part of me knew that I was wrapped in the Mystery then, powerless in it, nothing, in the presence of the god. I wanted to die now and to feel no more terror, no more pain.

My eyes could see, but only a little way, and only a little circle of light. All else was blotted out—the trees, the sky, the palace walls. And in that small circle of light, I saw my father's great hands come down and take my sister by the shoulders and raise her. Her mouth was set in the shape of screaming, but no sounds came to my ears. I sat as still as a stone and saw her body arch away out of my vision. Then I was alone and she had gone. My father had gone, as well. I was among the laurels; and the harsh grasses, sharp under the sun's drought, were pricking at my legs. I began to see the sky again and the trees. The thunder had stopped in the dry hills and the birds were at their song above me once again. I felt the warmth of the sun on my head once more. I could move my hands now, and turn my head.

'Sister!' I called. But she was not there.

'Father!' I called. But he had gone.

I rose and ran into the palace, but none of the guards had seen either of them. I went down the dark corridors until I came to the place where my other sister, Chrysothemis, tended her sacred fire. I thought my father might have dragged Iphigenia there, to beg the pardon of the goddess. But there was only Chrysothemis, kneeling and fumbling with a little dead bird, and shaking her head like an old crone.

I went to her and took her by the shoulders. 'Where are they, sister?' I said. 'Oh, where are they?'

Chrysothemis shivered and turned round towards me. Her face was pale and still, like a mask carved from alabaster. Her eyes were wide-open and stupid, encircled with their blue paint. She tried to speak for a while, but all she could say was, 'Silver, gold, copper, tin and lead are the sacred metals. Iron that falls from the sky is too holy to use. In Argolis, a slave may be a king.'

Her tongue seemed too big for her mouth, and saliva flowed on to her chin as she spoke. Anyone who had seen her thus, sitting beside the highway, would have said she was stricken by some great sickness. They would not have said she was a princess, a priestess.

Then all at once she began to cackle like an old madwoman, and to drag her nails down her face. I drew away from her, afraid of what I was seeing. Then, when she leaned back and began to fling herself about, frothing at the mouth and plucking at her dress, I ran away, and did not stop until I got to my own room. I did not think to have help sent down to her. All I could think was that Iphigenia had been right; that our sister was a fool.

Either that, or that the god was already beginning to punish our House for the words that had been spoken in the garden, under the sacred laurel boughs.

12

I HID myself under the coverlet, still weeping, while about Mycenae a storm raged. Thunder rattled the doors and roofs; rain came in through the window-holes and swept across the floors, loosening the tiles. Then a great wind rushed through the palace, almost tearing the hangings from their poles, and blowing out the fires.

I was too afraid to leave my bed. I felt so lonely that I knew no one could help me. And though I was as hungry as though I had not eaten for weeks, I fell asleep.

Through that awful night, I suffered an evil dream. It seemed so real that I thought I was living in the middle of it. I felt I could touch everything in it, taste everything, smell everything. It was more real than the bed I lay on, the hangings that flapped about me.

In the dream, I seemed to be in a cave near the sea-shore. The rocky walls were cold and black, and splashed with white bird-droppings. I could hear the waves outside sighing and splashing, and filling the air with a damp and salty chill. I was among others, pushing in a crowd to see what it was the folk were looking at. They were all pressing forward, and making strange sounds—sometimes moaning, sometimes laughing lightly, as though it was but a pretence which they must keep up, nudging one another, elbowing and pinching, then covering their eyes with their hands, yet looking through the fingers all the while.

I was the only one not doing these things, and sometimes those nearest me would turn and whisper that I must obey the law and do as they did. I tried to, but could not see the sense of it. I could not see their faces, either, though in my heart I knew that they were enemies.

At last they let me through, so that I might see what was happening. I leaned forward and peered through the thick, salty air of the cavern. In the middle of the black floor, among all the bird-droppings and the ashes and the brown sea-weed, there was a damp log, rotten at its end, and green with fungus. At first I saw only this log; but then the cavern lightened and I saw that a young girl lay half across it, her head hanging down on the far side, her fingers digging deep into the rotten wood, clenching and unclenching. Her dress was pulled back, covering only her lower body, and I saw that her back was as white as the flesh of the sacred lamb after it has been bled. It was unblemished and smooth, yet shining with oil as though anointed.

I turned to ask one of the crowd the name of the girl who lay across the log, but the dark presence next to me shook its head and said, 'Do not take your eyes from it. Watch! Watch!'

And all at once a great wind blew through the cavern, and from somewhere a high shrill screaming began, then seemed to rise till it filled that dark place to the roof. The green sea began to lap in at the cavern's mouth, then fall away again, leaving behind a scum of sea-froth and weed, and jagged pebbles, and twitching blank-eyed fishes.

It was almost more than I could stand, and I tried to turn and get away from what was happening; but the crowd kept me there, and hands even forced my head back again, so that I must watch.

Then, from the shadows at the far end of the cavern, stepped three figures. The tallest stood in the middle, and all wore damp grey cloths over their heads, reaching half-way down their bodies and hiding their features. They seemed like walking stones, with the sea-fret hanging about them as smoke does round a pine-trunk when the shepherds light their fires to shelter on the hills.

And when these three appeared, the crowd fell silent, as though gods walked the earth once more. All was still in the cave, as the world is still before thunder sounds. I tried to cry out in this dream, but my throat was stiff and dry; no words would come from me. Yet the tallest of the three figures seemed to know what I had intended, for its head beneath the cloth turned towards me and stayed so for a while. I could not see beneath the covering, but it seemed to me that the tall figure could see me, could tell what I was feeling and what I had meant to do. This made me more frightened than I had been before, to see that these figures had entire knowledge, even of that which had not yet happened, or of that which would never happen but which was only intended in the heart. In my dream, I thought how wrong my sister had been to say that there was no god, but only clouds and sky and the careless creatures of earth and air and sea. I heard myself, in that cavern, calling out suddenly, 'Iphigenia lied! She denied the god, and yet he is everywhere!'

As I spoke, the three figures in wrappings turned towards me and said, in tones as deep and inhuman as the sea's voice, 'What then is her penalty, Electra?'

In horror, I heard myself saying, 'Who taunts the god demands death.' As soon as I had said this, I tried to shout out that I had not meant it, that I did not wish to bring the doom on my dear sister. But now no words would come. The tallest figure seemed to bow the head before my judgement, and as it did this, from behind each grey shawl a flickering blue light seemed to grow, like that which shifts over the shallows of the sea in the moonlight, when the shoals of fish come inshore for rock-weed; and in this light I saw the faces of the three figures. The two smaller ones were the Trojan priest, Calchas, and the lard-faced man who had married me to the slave-boy in the tavern of Mycenae. The tall one in the middle was my father the king, Agamemnon himself; but yet not Agamemnon quite, for each of my father's noble lion-like features had some-how suffered a change—his nose was more hooked like an eagle's; his eyes wider like an owl's; his beard more sparse and ragged; his teeth sharper and longer, like those of a wolf, all yellow and gleaming.

Then, as I watched, the blue light died away, and I saw only the grey cloths again.

The one who had been Calchas fumbled under his wrapping and brought out an old, stone-headed axe; it was that same labrys that hung in our palace, above the Mother's holy fire. Bowing, he held it towards the tallest one, who reached out with scaly hands and took it reverently. Then the one who had seemed like Aegisthus bent down and laid hands on the still, white girl who lay across the log. She had not moved all this time, nor did she move now. Only the white, anointed skin of her back seemed to ripple, as though a separate life lay in it. As though knowledge lay in that skin, but not in her heart.

The end of the dream came fast now, like a runner gaining towards the laurel crown.

As though they had done it many times before, the three grey figures turned from us and hunched about the log, hiding all. Then I heard the stone-headed labrys thumping down as though into the rotten wood, again and again, three times. A steady hissing came from the crowd behind me, like breath drawn in with expectation. And at last the thudding axe was silent. In the twilight, I did not know where to look.

Then even that dimness was darkened, for through the cave's mouth came fluttering myriads of bats, shutting out the grey sea-light with their numbers and filling my ears with their frantic fluting. I put my hands over my head to keep the creatures from going into my hair; but it was not me they were concerned with. I saw them flickering darkly towards the cave wall near the log, hanging for a moment against the stone, then falling away to let others come, in a constant stream, like poor folk filing in to empty the lord's tables after a feast, when scraps lay about.

And I heard the tall hooded figure say, 'It is good. The Bull has accepted what we offer. See, they take their libation from the wall where it has spouted. She has gone to the Bull!'

Now my heart was full of terror and warning. I could scarcely breathe, and half-turned to push the crowd at my back away from me; but it was then that I found I was the only watcher, for the others had faded away like the morning mist. And as I saw this, and the great lonely fear came down on me like a mantle, I saw the bats turn like a well-drilled phalanx and sweep out once more through the cavern hole towards the sea. And in their place a bodiless deep voice boomed from the upper air.

'The wind has changed! See, the wind has changed!'

At first I could not tell whether it was a man's voice, or the sea speaking, Poseidon speaking. But the hooded figures heard it too and seemed to turn their heads, listening. I heard one of them laugh as though with relief, and saw that he held a flat wooden dish, such as peasants carve from tree-boles. It was filled with wet clay and wood-ash and, mixed in with this, the grey breast feathers of sea-birds. He was stirring it with his right hand, up to the wrist.

'Come,' he said, 'it is time to stop the hole, or the cask will empty itself. Enough is enough.'

As they all bent, dabbling in the wooden dish and leaning across the log, all fear left me and I ran forward. 'Let me see!' I cried. 'I have a right to see!'

They seemed to know that I would say this, for they opened before me like a palace gate, when well-trained guards draw it back to let a queen enter.

I saw the white body lying where it had been, the fingers still bedded deep in the rotten wood. Then I straddled the log to look down on the face of the girl; but there was no face, no head, only a plastered mess of ash and clay and soiled feathers where the head should have been. I swung round to ask what this meant, but the grey shapes had gone from the cave, and I was alone. Above me the bodiless voice was still booming, 'The wind has changed. The wind has changed.'

And, as I stood bewildered, the white fingers in the log began to twitch and move, as though a new life was stirring in them. It was more than I could bear. I leapt away and began to scream and scream, until my high voice mingled with the deep booming of the one above me, making a terrible chorus in the salty darkness of the cave.

Hands came about me, and suddenly I saw that I was sitting up in my bed in the palace chamber, with Clytemnestra's face near to mine. She was saying, 'There, my dove! There, my little one! All is well now. Do not cry any more. We are here and you are safe.'

I do not think I had ever seen her looking so sad and so concerned. I heard her say to a serving-woman, 'Fetch fresh clothes and bedding. She is wet through. Hurry, woman!'

My father loomed darkly against the window-hole, but I could not see him clearly. I heard him say, 'It is a trouble in the heart, as deep as a wound. This is the heritage of us all, the kin of Atreus. This is the price we must pay for our glory. We must each bear the load alone; no one can help the wounded lion, he must suffer, a lonely beast.'

Then the palace doctor was bending over me, urging me to drink from a scallop-shell which he held to my lips. My mother nodded, smiling, so I drank, for now I trusted her like a baby.

Then my father seemed to lead all the folk from my room, leaving only Clytemnestra beside me. I sank back on my bed, the bitter taste still in my mouth. I tried to reach up to stroke my mother's hair, which hung damply in elf-locks beside her cheeks. She held my hand gently and whispered, 'There, my pigeon. You have taken a fever and we have watched over you for three days. But now you are getting well again. Sleep, my queen, and do not dream.'

I suddenly said to her, 'Where is my sister, lady? Where is Iphigenia?'

My mother the queen smiled down at me and rubbed her cold cheek against my hot one. 'She is well, little one. She went away three days ago, laughing in her litter, to Aulis. That is where the ships lie, my sweet. She went merrily enough, to pray for a wind that would take your father to Troy. If she had known you were so sick, she would not have gone.'

My dream was fading from me every moment, but its edges still trailed behind, as a robe does when its wearer has gone through a door.

'Who sent her there?' I asked, afraid.

My mother the queen began to stroke my brow. 'Your father and Calchas, the priest,' she said. 'And they did rightly, for by her prayers the wind has changed. Now the ships can sail away at last, and we can be happy once more in the palace. Our lives lie in greater hands than our own, so sleep gently, gently, my own.'

I could feel myself falling back into a drugged sleep as she spoke. I tried to fight against it, to ask when my sister would return to us; but no sounds came from my lips. I saw my mother's face above me

[84]

for a while, smiling and nodding, and then even that went misty and far away, and I knew no more.

13

WHETHER I lay in bed two weeks or three, I cannot recall. The palace doctor was with me constantly, giving me potions from the scallop-shell, putting salves on my forehead, and blowing his breath up into my nostrils. I did not see my father, but Clytemnestra came to me many times and sang to me as the women changed my shift. Once she brought Chrysothemis to see me, but had to send her away from the room because she had brought a lame gull with her, and the sight of the feathers made me cry out with fear again.

Then, one morning, I said, 'Mother, I would like a bowl of thick bean-broth, with garlic and lamb meat in it.'

My mother the queen clapped her hands and laughed. 'At last you ask for food,' she said. 'This is the turning-point. You shall have anything your heart desires, I am so glad!'

I said to her, 'Then bring Iphigenia back to me, mother. She is what I most desire, even more than the broth and the lamb meat.'

Clytemnestra shook her head and the smile faded a little on her beautiful face. 'Oh, my dove,' she said, 'that must wait a little longer. Your sister is enjoying her great honour now. Because her prayers have changed the wind, she has gone to the shrine of Upright Apollo, over the sea to Tauris, to help the poor folk there and to bring them good fortune. You would not deny her that honour, would you?'

I clutched the covering and pulled myself up in fright. 'Taurus!' I said. 'Is that the Bull? Has the Bull taken her? Poseidon?'

My mother laughed again and pushed me gently down. 'Oh, you

little mad thing,' she said. 'You never listen! The place is Tauris, not Taurus! One might think your ears were stopped with clay and wood-ash for all you hear!'

I began to cry again when she said this, but at last she rocked me and quietened me. 'If you do not lie quiet,' she said, 'you will not be well enough to go with us on to the wall and watch the soldiers march away. You would like that, wouldn't you?'

I said, 'It is not the soldiers I want; it is my sister.'

My mother put her hand over my mouth, almost harshly, and said, 'Speak no more. Your words might bring them ill-fortune. Never forget, in sickness or health, that we of the House of Atreus are sacred. We sometimes speak with the voice of the greatest ones. I counsel you, little one, speak only of the things about you that your eyes can see—of wood and stone and barley-meal—not of the heart's dreams. We of the Atreus Kin must guard our words as the merchants guard their profits. It is our duty to go up on to the wall, and to wish the soldiers and their ships, and their horses well. So rest now and forget all else. I will come for you when the first company goes out, with your new white woollen robe to keep you warm. Iphigenia's wind blows across the land now, not the sea, so you will take no further chill if we are careful.'

She went from my bedside gently, wriggling her fingers at me and smiling. I thought that she was the kindest mother in the world. But when she reached the doorway, where the servants might see her, she straightened her body and put on a mask-face. Her hands she crossed over her breast, as though she were an image. That is how the queens always walked in Mycenae, in those days; like images. It was how the simple folk thought of them, not as creatures like themselves, of flesh and blood and fear.

14

I REMEMBER little of the men going away. Only that it was a blustery day, with the damp grey clouds scudding almost past our eyes as we stood on a high platform above the wall at Mycenae. But, doctor, I am an old woman, you understand, and I may have imagined those clouds. Perhaps they do not come so low; perhaps it was a sunny day, and the greyness and clouds in my mind, for I was young and sad and very sick. The poets have all sung differently of the leave-taking; I am no lover of poets and I cannot pretend to judge their merits or the truth of their words. I speak as I think I remember—and that may be as true as anything the poets say, for most of them were unborn when the men set out from Mycenae to drag Troy down to rubble.

And I remember the flower-crowned girls running before the armies in two straggling lines, their dusty black skirts flapping at their brown legs in the wind, their unbound hair sweeping in black waves over their excited faces. They clapped their hard narrow hands together as they went, in a strange and fevered cross-beat to the marching men, as though at the one time they both urged them forward and tried to throw them out of step.

It was like a half-disguised game of love, with the girls pulling the men on to them, then pushing them away before fulfilment.

All this hung heavy in the air and came to me, young and sick as I was, as plainly as if it were words said close to my ear. It was as though the black-robed girls, bidding the men farewell, with their white garlands, their thin faces, and their dark painted eyes, pictured both life and death, pain and pleasure, love and hatred. They seemed to be planted like seeds at the beginning of all things, at the deep heart of all things, in the dark belly of time, without knowing it. What they were doing, on the road below the palace, had been done since the first dawn.

[87]

Even their high reed-fluting song, which went round and round like wheels turning or doves purring on the roof-tree in spring, was part of this magic. And their reddened lips, all set in a circle as though they never moved from saying 'Oooo!', were like the ritual ivory masks worn by young women at the Dionysus-festival.

I looked to my mother, to ask about these girls and why my heart should beat so at my ribs; but her own mouth was shaped like theirs, though silent, and her hard narrow hands were close to clapping as theirs did, though frozen, poised in the air, a hawk before it swoops.

I could not bring myself to break her dream, and my question was never asked. Yet in the darkness that was already growing in my body, I suddenly seemed to know the answer, though I had not put the question.

What do I recall? I was in my mother's arms, and weeping. She was telling Geilissa how light I had become, how fragile since my illness. The woman said in return how sunk my eyes were, how much like wax my skin; she said it was her belief that I would not be long in High Town. I heard her say this and wondered where I would be, then, for the palace was the only place I knew to be in. My mother frowned at Geilissa and said something in the secret tongue that the women used in those days, something I did not understand. When I played with Hermione, we used to make up a secret tongue of our own, to be like our mothers, but though it teased the little boys, neither of us could understand it, and we longed for the day when we would be thirteen, grown up, and taken into the women's quarters to learn the proper secret tongue.

When Clytemnestra spoke the secret words, the nurse flushed and made a defiant answer. My mother the queen reached out her hand and struck her across the face. Geilissa fell down and began to kiss my mother's feet, like a fawning dog. I thought at first that she was going to roll right off the tall parapet on to the road below. I wasn't concerned for her, I recall, but just curious to see what she would look like, falling. I imagined her robes spreading out to be a bird's wings, and keeping her afloat on the wind-currents, perhaps sailing her away, across the Isthmus to Pagae or Thebes. . . . I did not know anything about these places, except their names, but they always appealed to me; the shepherds from there sometimes came to our markets and were always bright-haired, gay fellows who sang in a high voice to the oaten pipes.

But the woman didn't fall after all. She kneeled, weeping on my mother's buskins, and I lost interest in her, and looked down with sleepy eyes at the armies below.

Never since the god made earth had so many men gathered together in one place; that much is certain. The fields were black with them, under the grey skies, for as far as eye could reach. Men, men, men . . . and then more men. For years we had had nothing but rumours of this war; all my life men had been coming into Mycenae and drilling outside our town, eating our food, drinking our wine, calling my father their lord. All my life I had heard only that, that my father was High King, Lord of the Earth, the Lion of Mycenae, Master of Laconica, Baron of Peloponnesus, Right Hand of Poseidon, Ring-Giver of Crete, Wolf of the Epirus, Tyrant of Thessaly. . . . His titles and names would have filled a man's memory to bursting, they were so many. There were even Libyans who came to our house who said that in their country he was known as the Elephant of Syrtis; but I never trusted Libyans, because of the way they rolled their eyes and licked their thick lips as they spoke. It seemed to me, even as a child, that they said what men expected them to say, not the truth. I had proof of this later, when I discussed my father's Libyan title with a young Egyptian ambassador who came to do trade with Mycenae. He was thin and pale-faced, and had shaved all the hair from his body. Beside our house barons he looked like a delicate doll-thing; but his dress was so magnificent, and his weapons so beautiful, that none of our men taunted him with his lack of hair. This Egyptian told me, bowing his head and smiling to take away the hurt of his words, that my father was known in Africa, but was simply called 'The Hellene' or, at most, 'Lion of Hellas'. I recall that young man especially because he had three slaves always beside him to scratch his back with ivory spatulas. He was so rich and so grand that he would not scratch his own back—yet I saw him hunting a ferocious boar one day and those frail hands that could not bring themselves to scratch pushed a javelin the whole length of the beast's body, as it charged, in at his tusked mouth and out at his behind, so that the bronze point looked like another tail, under his real one. It takes a brave and strong man to do that, for our boars in those days were at least twice the size and weight of a man.

So I always believed what that Egyptian said; and not what the Libyans told me. Yes, I am sorry, doctor, but I must be permitted these thoughts. I am an old woman, whose days are few now. Let me wander a little, and I will come back to the story in good time. . . . Where was I? Yes, the men who gathered in Mycenae.

Can you picture it? All our lives the world had been centred on us, as though Mycenae was a wheel, and my father the axle. All the valleys seemed to lead down towards Mycenae; and all through every year folk crowded on down towards our city. I could go out into the market and walk all day without hearing a word I understood. And now, after a lifetime, they were going away to sack Troy. . . . And I, a sick child, was being held up on the high wall to watch them go, though I had a fever of the blood that made me rage with heat, despite the chill of the day.

I shall never forget the rumbling of the war-carts and the hourly tramping of feet. The earth shook; our palace walls trembled; the men strode on through cornfields and over garden fences. All fell before them. Where they walked, though it had been green grass at dawn, was parched brown earth by nightfall. Crops were laid low, to become wisps of dry straw when they had passed. Houses fell down and were trampled back to white clay. The cattle ran before them, as though they too were going down to the ships. Thick hordes of birds hovered above their heads, crying in fear, but unable to leave them.

Even your own folk, the Hittites, doctor, were there, marching as though they were proud to be Hellenes, and yelling out, 'Koiranos! Koiranos!' whenever Agamemnon showed himself. They thought it no dishonour then, my friend.

[90]

In truth, my father was master of the world, apart from Egypt, and the owner of every grain of soil for a hundred miles around Mycenae. I have heard it said that, apart from himself and the Egyptian Pharoah, the only other kings he recognised in all the world were Nestor of Pylus, Peleus of Phthia in Thessaly, and Odysseus of Ithaca in the Ionian Isles.

No wonder that every man's eyes were turned up at us, the kin of Agamemnon, as we stood on the walls, watching them go towards the distant sea. In spite of my sickness and the echoes of my ghastly dream, I thrilled at their attention, and shuddered at the glorious hubbub of their thousands of trumpets and drums and bone flutes. My mother was in such a trance that she almost dropped me over the wall a time or two; but my own ecstasy grew so great that I would not have minded. I think the fever and pride in me were so strong that I could have flown through the air like Daedalus of Crete if she had let me fall.

Behind us stood Chrysothemis, with an olive staff in one hand and a tame snake curling about the wrist of the other. She was singing a little song about a milkmaid and paying no attention to the armies, though my mother had dressed her up for the occasion and had gilded her breasts and crimped her oiled black hair. Baby Orestes lay in the arms of his new Libyan nurse, his face buried in her robes, frightened by the noise. Where Iphigenia should have stood, was a space. Someone had stood her distaff there to represent her. I was sorry she was not on the wall to see the men go, and I tried to say this to my mother the queen. She did not even glance down at me as she replied, 'She is better where she is. Few young priestesses have the honour to be called to Tauris these days. Have no regrets. It is well with her.'

All the first day we were there, in spite of the cold wind. Servants brought food up to us, and even put it into our mouths, for the custom forbade us to be seated when the armies went out of the city. By nightfall, we were all exhausted, but still the men moved past, their way lit with resinous torches now, so that the earth seemed on fire. I could see the torches for miles now, on either side of Mycenae. It was as though the procession would never end. Then I fell asleep and did not wake until the dawn.

Midway through the third day, servants brought tall waxen images of us, dressed in our clothes, and set them up on the platform, so that the soldiers below would think we were still there. It would not do to send them away feeling that we had been too weary to look down on them and bless their expedition.

On the fourth day, when the Mycenaean chariots were bringing up the rear, Agamemnon himself came to the queen's chamber to bid us farewell.

He had put aside his parade armour and best clothes now, and it was to accompany him to the ship in three wagon-loads, there was so much of it. He came into the room like a farmer going to market to sell cows, his beard all over the place, his rough hair bunched up with wire to keep it out of the way, his horse-hide breastplate only loosely laced, his kilt hitched up round his thighs to make walking easier. He carried his special sacred iron helmet under one arm. With its flaps down, it looked like another head that he carried, for even the hog's hair plumes were of his own colour. The thought made me smile to myself, that the High King had two heads—in case he mislaid one!

The king saw my smile and bent over me in my bed. 'So, my Amber Princess is more like herself again,' he said, as he kissed me. 'She can smile at her father at last, hey?'

I reached up and held him about the neck, drawing myself up towards him. 'Father,' I said, 'take me with you to Troy. I am tired of being sick and alone. I should grow well again straightaway if you would take me with you.' I do not know what made me say this. It just came to me.

Agamemnon undid my hands from about his neck as gently as he could. Then he smiled and said, 'Why, you goose! We shall not be away for more than one harvest! You can hope to see us again before the snows come down on Cyllene. These Trojans will throw open their gates and run screaming as soon as they see our numbers, my dove. So why disturb yourself with such a long journey for so short a time? Lie still and get better, and when I come again we can play among the apple-trees and forget what swords look like!"

He turned from me, bowed towards my mother, and was gone.

15

I AM too old for any woman to be, doctor. My body is like a wrinkled empty wine-skin, and I do not know what is truth and what dream. I do not know if what I tell you ever happened. Yet I must say it, for it is in me to say.

You smile; I can tell you that once, when I was a young woman, I watched them throw an old king over the rocks, into the sea beside Corcyra. He was white-haired, the pharmacos, the Healer, of his folk, and he went over laughing and calling out to men he knew in the crowd, as though he was thankful to go. I stood and wept to see such an old man falling out of the sky to the fishes. But now I can understand why he laughed. He was glad to be rid of it all. He was glad to know the truth for certain at last. And that is how I am now. I would go gladly, for I am weary of not knowing the truth, weary of hearing my tongue tell lies as though I remembered it all. So let us smile together, doctor. I will tell you more of my dreams, and we shall smile. I will forget that I am a queen, and will smile with you.

Ah, that makes it easier to remember, now. So I will tell you that after the king my father went down to the ships at Aulis, a great calm came over me. I was a sick child, but I was calm. Not calm like a law-giver who thinks on all the world before he makes his utterance, but calm like a cold stone, or a dead partridge; feeling nothing, wanting nothing, content only to be left in my quietness.

My mother would say, 'Why do you stare in front of you, Electra? What do you see?'

If I bothered to reply, I would say, 'I do not know why I stare, mother. I see nothing. What is there to see? Why should I see anything?'

Sometimes she would get angry and answer, 'It is many months since your father went away, and soon you will know what it is to be a woman. Yet you are still thin, though we feed you on the best we have. You sit about in the palace rooms while the other girls go laughing and singing in the sun. If you would only work at the loom it might be better, but your hands do nothing that is useful. They lie for ever in your lap. Are you still dreaming, my own?'

I shook my head. I could not find words to tell her that such a dream as I had had needs to come but once in one's life.

Then one day after her baby had come to nothing and I was twelve, she said, 'We are rebuilding the shrines to the Mother, up and down Hellas, daughter. The men have been away so long that we women fear we are forgotten of Zeus. Now we are bringing back Hera. She may take pity on us and bring good fortune to our houses. If you would like it, I will put you with one of the priestesses so that you may begin to learn the Mysteries. That would be something for your heart to feed on. Shall it be so?'

But I shook my head. 'I have seen enough of my sister, Chrysothemis, mother. She is a priestess, but her heart is still hungry. I have no wish to be like her, the kernel of the nut rotten inside me.'

My mother laughed in scorn and beat her fine hands together as though she wished to hurt something. 'You must not judge by Chrysothemis,' she said, 'Your sister is the god's punishment on this House. She is like the image of a thing—not the thing itself. All is pretty without, but empty within. She is like a sea-shell that seems to hold the voice of Poseidon inside it, howling gently along its whorls; yet it is but an echo of nothing, and if you crush the shell beneath your foot it is only white dust. It is nothing.'

I said, 'She makes great show of her prayers and sacrifices, mother. Is that nothing?'

[94]

Clytemnestra's lips withered from her teeth and she answered, 'Her prayers fly no farther than the roof-tree rafters. Her sacrifices are but the little death of birds and beasts. The glow about her libation cup is only the sunlight gleaming on the glaze. It is not the light from within. But if you learned the Mysteries, it would be different; you have the inner light.'

I said, 'All you have told me of Chrysothemis is what I know about myself. I am as empty as a husk, mother, and I am content to be so. If you find my emptiness a burden on you, then give me the fox-glove to drink and I will go away. I ask no more than that.'

My mother began to weep then and to pull at her hair. Then she dragged me to her and held me so close that I could scarcely breathe. 'Oh, my dove, my dove,' she kept saying. I truly think she loved me at that time; and, in my strange way, I loved her. Yet, when I thought about it, it was a bitter small love that seemed always on the edge of ending, as with a honey-cake that must finish as one bites on at it, however small the bite. There is an end to it, once the edges have been broken into.

Then one afternoon, as I sat dabbling my hand in the water of the fountain that bubbled up in the small court, one of the slave-women stood behind me and touched me on the shoulder.

'Lady,' she said, 'a man has come to the palace at your mother's order. He has brought a playmate for you. It is a boy of your own age, a gentle boy who will not hurt you. His company will be good for you, the queen says. Will you come and receive him, lady?'

I scooped up some gleaming water and splashed it against my face to cool it.

'What is the boy's name?' I asked.

The woman said, 'I think it is Rarus.'

I nodded and said, 'That is a strange name. It means one who was dropped before his time.'

The woman shrugged her shoulders and said, 'They say he was found below the south wall, and was saved from the dogs by a man of Mycenae, a tavern-keeper.'

[95]

I felt the truth in me and said, 'And that man's name is Aegisthus. He is bald-headed and smells like a goat. Is that not so?'

She seemed shocked by my words and pulled her shawl up to her mouth. 'I cannot say, lady,' she answered. 'I was sent to fetch you, not to talk of these things.'

So, to save her more anxiety, I went with her and did not tease her with further questioning. It was as I had thought; Aegisthus stood in the Great Court, before my mother's canopy, rubbing his hands together and licking his lips as though his mouth was dry. The young boy that the men had given me, that night when we held the snake together, stood behind him, dressed in greasy hides, his hands bound by a hempen cord, like a lamb being delivered at a shrine, hobbled so that it cannot make away before the priestess comes out to take it inside and lay it on the stone.

That hempen cord unstoppered the anger in me. I ran forward as best I could in my weakness and shouted out, 'Cut him loose, the poor thing! Is this how a playmate is brought for me?'

The man Aegisthus bowed so low, I thought he would fall over. His hands seemed to go in all directions at once, as though he did not know what to do first. He looked like a man in mortal terror.

Then he stared towards Clytemnestra, as though appealing to her. She was standing on the top step of her throne-place, under the awning, her hair uncombed and wild, her black robe in rags about her—for she had set this fashion among the women recently—and her white face like the mask that Maenads wear when Dionysus must be killed again. Her teeth showed small and sharp between her stretched lips. Between them, she said to Aegisthus, 'Well, man, do as the god's daughter orders you. Cut the cord. Must you be told twice?'

At the time, I took small account of her words and of his quick obedience to them. It did not seem strange to me that a great queen should speak so to one who was little better than a slave, or that such a man should fall into a sweat and slash at the hempen cord, as though death sniffed at his heels. It was much later that I looked back on this sunlit afternoon and recalled the terror of Aegisthus again; then I saw deeper into it, saw that her power over him was great from the start, great in the deepest sense, power that struck down to his darkest vitals, the power of the priestess over common mortal man.

But then I was not concerned about such things. I only wanted the boy, Rarus, to be set free away from this hateful fellow of the tavern who had frightened me at night when I was younger.

I took the lad by the hand and led him away to where the grass stood wild in the garden, among the secret laurel bushes and the luxuriant acanthus with their purple spiked flowers. His hand was damp, as though he was afraid of me, but when I sat beside him and stroked his thin cheek, and told him that I would be his protector for ever, he smiled again.

'Lady,' he said, 'I will love you always.'

I liked to hear him say this, in his rough Cretan dialect, but some contrary thing rose in me, after the way of young girls, and I said sharply to him, 'Do not call me lady. I am more than that; I am a princess. You must remember that, whenever you speak to me and others are about.'

He lowered his head, like a dog that has been struck with a whip. I was sorry at the change my words had made in him, and so did my best to undo the harm.

'When you say you will love me, what does that mean, Rarus?'

He did not look up, but plucked at a piece of braid that hung from my shoulder and said quietly, 'I mean that I will follow you, and fetch things for you, and take messages, and lie at your door by night so that no one may come on you unawares.'

Ill as I still was, his meekness suddenly offended me, and I said, 'No more than that? No more love than that? Is that your love?'

The tears splashed on to his knees and he made no effort to hide them. 'Princess,' he said, 'it is as much as I am able to do. Must I be taunted for what I could not prevent?'

Then I was indeed melted by his humbleness, and saw nothing to offend me in it. I put my arms about his neck and hugged him to me. 'Forgive me, Rarus,' I begged him. 'I am grateful for your love, and you shall have my love too. We will be lovers like two stones lying on the path, two trees standing on a hill, two clouds in the sky. Our love shall spring over the gap between us and be all the sweeter for that.'

So poor Rarus came to be my playmate, my innocent lover, and he was always like a sword that was riveted within the scabbard, or a bull whose horns have been sawn off. He was the gentlest of companions.

16

As for the man, Aegisthus, he never left our house from that day when he brought Rarus to be my playmate. At first he was put to work in the kitchens, among the women, carrying meal-sacks or scraping dirty dishes. But gradually, as the winter came and went, he moved into the palace rooms, and was always standing near my mother. To see them together, both in their rags, one would have thought them brother and sister, not queen and servant.

No one remarked on this, in my hearing at least. I think that two years after the warriors had gone, and the land was in the hands of women and children and old folk, a new spirit had come about. I think it was the folk of Laconica who began it, for they often said it was vanity to wear fine clothes, or to keep a good table. But our people went even further, and neither cut nor combed their hair—which was a thing the true Laconicans were very particular about.

What I am trying to say, doctor, was that in these days it was impossible to tell whether a woman was a lady or a slave by the clothes she wore, or the food she ate. It was hard enough to tell by the speech she used, for now the noble folk copied the common folk in their words and accents. I spoke to my mother about this once, and she laughed and said, 'What does it matter, if we can understand one another? All else is vanity.' I said, 'But once you threatened to whip me for mentioning certain parts of the body. You said that was how slaves talked.'

My mother yawned and scratched her thighs, under her coarse robe, like a fisherwoman, then said, 'That was in the past, Electra. Today, we live in the present. The rules have changed. If we are to please the gods, we must all be equal, and act alike, just as the animals act alike, and the fishes swim alike. One lion roars like any other, don't you think?'

I agreed with her, but said that men weren't lions.

'Yet we were pleased enough to call your father Lion of Mycenae, were we not?' she asked.

There was no answer to that, so I was silent, though I knew that if I had been more clever I might have argued against it.

She said, 'Each age requires different manners from men. In this age, when we all wait for victory over our enemy in Troy, we must use the manners of humbleness, of degradation, so that the gods will think we are poor slaves to be treated kindly. Think on that, Electra, and count every humbleness as a prayer for victory.'

I left her then, convinced by her words, and from that moment I began to speak as roughly as any field-slave. I delighted in going for days unwashed, the dust thick on my legs and body, my hair tangled and even verminous. When Rarus tried to comb it for me, I pushed him aside, laughing and said, 'Don't be such a silly little idiot! Why, I'll wear a cow-pat for a hat if I choose!'

He looked so shocked that I started to say even worse things; until he began to cry. Then I began to cry, too, because I did not like the new self that was growing in me. It is a terrible thing when one first begins to recognise the self in one; all was so simple before, but now it was like learning to live with a stranger in one's body and heart.

I think that Rarus was just starting to see the self too, and was feeling unsure, grieved at the death of his childhood. I know that we lay together in the straw that night, in a byre, and cried one another to sleep. That was how it was in the new Mycenae, and, indeed, in all Hellas. Folk lay together in the straw, taking comfort from each other, in a world that had lost its certainty, and stood shipless and warriorless, surrounded by the darkness of no news. It was as though, with the going-away of the men to Troy, Hellas had gone blind and deaf, and was waiting, waiting, waiting, for life and strength to come back to it one day, no one knew when, after the monster had been finished, after Troy's stranglehold had been broken. It was like waiting, in the deep snows of winter, for the first spring sun to shine once more. It was like waiting for the dead to rise again and stretch their limbs and yawn and walk about the burial chamber.

You must know, doctor, that in those days, after the great empire of Crete had long decayed, and the foraging ships of Minos no more roamed up and down the middle sea, bringing daily news from everywhere, we of Hellas had come to lead a closed life, without knowing it. Each kingdom had been so busy with its own affairs that there seemed to be no time, and no need, for news of anything outside Hellas. Now, with the men gone, and the old urgency gone, all the drilling finished, and the ships fitted out and away, we were like lost creatures, with nothing to do but wait.

Those of us who spoke about these things said that this was the most important moment in the story of the world. This was the moment when the gods would decide whether everything should come to a stop, whether Hellas should go on growing, or whether Troy should now be master, and all our folk sink back to savage slavery. You can see that it was a time of great importance in our hearts; yet you can also see that, with nothing to do but tend the crops and the flocks, and wait, many of us fell into a sort of despair, feeling that our lives were wasting away while all the great things were going on across the sea, at Troy. That is why such unusual things happened in Hellas; we did not know which way to turn, while we were waiting helplessly, our future depending on others whom we could no longer see or talk to. We lost touch with the men, as though they had all died.

Certainly we got news—but nothing that we could trust. Sometimes a carrier-pigeon would drop out of the sky in some village square, with a message tied to its leg that said Troy had fallen, or that

Agamemnon had been killed, or that the loot-ships would be home next spring. . . . Sometimes a pirate smack would put into one of the coastal places and tell strange yarns of what was going on at the world's edge. Sober, the pirates might say that Hellas was triumphant, but when the grateful landlord, who had three sons in the expedition, had given them skin after skin of wine, they would switch their story round, and, out of sheer devilry, say that Ajax and Achilles and Menelaus had been hung in chains to rot from the highest wall of Troy, and that all the Greek ships had foundered.

There was no believing anything after a while. Young boys grew into men and rigged up boats to follow their fathers, always vowing to send back news of what was happening; but the news never came, and the young ones went no one knew where. Not a house in Hellas but had some share in this uncertainty and loss. All able-bodied free men had gone; and after the first five years, even slaves began to put on airs and itch to go, too. And many of them did. Men are like that; they make great show of despising war, and saying that all differences can be settled by talk about the hearth fire. Yet, deep down in them is a love of war; not of the fighting itself, perhaps, but of the freedom war gives them, to see other places and lie with other women. This is a fact, and is as old as man himself. Man is a great liar; he pretends to love his wife and his home, but in his heart he wants to wander away, to fall in love again and again. With women it has always been different, for they need the warmth and the comfort of a settled place, where they can conceive and carry and bear their children. They need shelter, where they can suckle their babies; but men have no part in this. In the world, there are two races—men and women. If the gods would only undo the chains that bind us all, this would be seen clearly enough; one race would stay in one place and bear children, the other would roam and sing about the world. In my life-time only one folk have ever dared to put this thought to the test, the Amazons. Knowing that men are as they are, these women sent them packing and led their own lives. This meant defending them-selves, of course, and so they learned to ride and to fight, as well as they needed to. This is not difficult for a healthy young woman; it is

[101]

only natural, in fact. Most women could ride and fight as well as most men, if the men would allow it. But men are so full of vanity and pride, they bring the women up to think that their place is away from swords and saddles, until, as the generations pass by, women come to take this part in life, being passive and lazy creatures by inclination.

I think that if the Hellene men had been away much longer in Troy, our women would all have become like the Amazons. As it was, they went half-way towards it. They began to pray entirely to the Mother, and neglected Zeus and Poseidon; they began to dress, as men would say, immodestly, and didn't care who saw their secret bodies; they put on rags, like any careless warrior; they washed if they wished, but otherwise went dirty.

Few women I remember in those times but carried the scars of sword-play on their bodies; on thigh or chest or forearm. Many of the younger ones took up the fashion of tattooing their faces again, a custom which only the old savage folk of the hills had used; and it became a mark of womanhood to display a broken nose, or a hand with the forefinger gone, as often happened when one used the long slashing sword, which needed the finger across the guard to manage it. So that small member took the worst of the fight, and often got lost in the heat of the moment, without the loser knowing this till later, when the hand began to howl.

In all, the men were away from Hellas for ten years, a season less or more, and I think the women had got used to being without them. Women can do without men, but not men without women. That is strange, doctor, don't you think? I see, by your shaking of the head, that you don't follow me. Well, look at it this way—man is all the while itching, by day or by night, in winter and in summer. His body never gives him peace, and he will satisfy its hunger one way or the other, at any time. But women move at a different pace, sometimes fast, sometimes slow, in accordance with certain seasons of the blood. They are closer to nature. They are like their goddess, the moon, who begins as a curved bow of silver in the sky, and at last grows full and round, like a coin or a cheese. Then back she goes to a thin bow of silver in the sky; and so on, through most of her days. Only when she is full and round does she need that furious hunger of the blood to be satisfied; and then she takes what comes, until the quiet time when she shrinks back into the sky, closed and modest. It might be a slave, or the caresses of another woman like herself. I see, by your frowns, that I am disturbing you, doctor, but you must not feel like that. I am an old thing, worn out and beyond blushing. Have no thought for me; it is but a matter of words with me now, not feelings. I speak of the world like a goddess, you know; as though I am looking down at it, but am no longer of it. So do not flush and turn away to gaze at things which are not there. Ha, I have caught you, my friend! I can see it! So, you can smile again, and I can go on with my tale.

17

In a way, Hellas had brought itself to the edge of madness by attacking Troy. No land can afford to send all its strong men away and still hope to stay sane, its rule left in the hands of old men, women, children, and slaves. Even though I was hardly more than sixteen years old, I could see that. Riding about the countryside with Rarus, as my mother allowed me to do, to keep me occupied, I saw many things happening in the villages that the lords and barons would never have permitted had they been back at home.

About Tegea, the slaves had taken control and had refused with smiles, to get in the harvest for two years. They had taken what they needed for the moment, and had let the corn re-seed itself as it pleased. There, the olive groves had withered, and the vines had straggled, unpruned and wild, even into the windows of the houses. The noble folk could do nothing about this, for they were all old or crippled, and lived like swine in hovels, while the slaves drank and gorged and fought each other into a condition of ruin.

At Eleusis, the air was heavy with terror, yet for another cause than slave-riot. Here, the women, slave and free, had seen a mass-vision one night, in which Mother Dia had told them to leave the town and settle in the sacred groves. When Rarus and I rode through Eleusis, even only three years after the soldiers had left, the houses were already crumbling; roofs were moss-grown, water-conduits flooded streets and floors, woodwork rotted, rats ruled the dairies and the beasts bellowed in the fields, their udders full of agonising milk.

It was like this wherever we rode. But later in the hills it was worse. There, even as close at hand at Thaumasius, and Thornax where the Tanus rises, the folk had gone back a thousand years, ate grass and offals, painted their bodies with woad-juice, and went clad in deer-skin or horsehide, whatever the season. No traders, not even the Phoenicians, dared visit them with cloth, for fear of being robbed or even flayed alive. And, as you know, the Phoenicians are usually willing to take a chance on almost anything, if there is profit of any sort to be had.

What troubled me more than all this waste and savagery was that the shrines of Zeus and Poseidon had been defiled. Many of them were used as common stables by villagers, who delighted in throwing mud against the images and in filling the libation cups with dirt. Worship became a mockery, and now the women called for the Feast of Dionysus at all seasons, not only at the grape-treading, which was the lawful time. Every female thing thought herself a Maenad, and the men of whatever age went about like hunted deer, starting at every shout or shadow.

You may wonder that my mother allowed us out in the country at such times. I have often thought of this myself; perhaps she had gone beyond caring; or perhaps, having had us tattooed across the forehead with the fish-sign of Poseidon, she thought we would be well enough guarded by the god. I do not know. Certainly, no harm befell us, and though the folk in the backlands did not respect us, they offered us no violence.

There were houses where we were welcome, of course, for the sake of great Agamemnon; houses in Laconica, and Pylus, and Hermione by the sea-shore. Yet, at Nemea, which is only a day's walk from Mycenae, where the servants had always come out with milk or wine and honey-cakes, at the command of the lady there, Megara, we met a rude surprise one day. As we passed through the yard-gates, a javelin clattered across the paving-stones at us, its ash-shaft striking my pony on the chest and making him rear suddenly. I was flung down, and kicked in the side by the gelding that Rarus used to ride. In spite of the pain, I sat up and glowered at the red-bearded man who had thrown the thing, and was now sitting on the bottom step of the doorplace, laughing his ugly head off.

I remember saying, 'Are you tired of life, then, slave? I will have a word with your mistress, Megara, she will know how to treat a stable boy who has so little respect for Agamemnon's daughter!'

He only laughed the louder at this, as though it was all a great joke. 'If I'd wanted to kill you,' he said, 'I should not have cast the way I did, woman!'

This made me so angry that I got to my feet, in spite of my aching ribs, and picked up his javelin. The god was roaring in my blood at the time, and I swear I would have pinned the slave to the post where he sat, if I had been strong enough. But before I could get the clumsy weapon up, another voice called out to me from the top step. I saw that Megara stood there, her robe about her waist, her grey hair hanging unkempt over her chest. 'Leave well alone, girl,' she said, 'and go on your way. There is no wine or honey-cake for you today. All that is over!'

I was shocked to hear her speak so roughly, for she had once been a lady-in-waiting at our palace, and came of good stock. I said, 'Megara, are you out of your mind? You can see who I am, can't you?'

She only smiled, and came down the steps and began to fondle the laughing slave so immodestly that I found it hard to bear. She said, 'Yes, I see who you are—the daughter of a dead king and a palace whore. I see also that you are not better than I am, for we both have a taste for slaves, now that the warriors are away.'

Rarus, who had begun to forget that he too was baseborn, flushed at this, and wanted to turn away and go without delay. But I held his bridle until I should have said the last word, which was my privilege. I said, 'What god do you worship here, may I ask?'

This question, coming from one who claimed descent from Zeus, was meant to upset Megara; but she only laughed in her wild, cracked way, and left the answer to the slave man at her feet. He hitched up his garment and gestured. 'Why, Upright Apollo, lady!' he said. 'What do you think?'

We left then, their stupid laughter filling our ears as we rode blindly through the gates again. Outside, I said viciously to Rarus, 'So, they too have dug their grave. When the queen hears this, she will send to them by night. Their days of laughter will end, that I promise you.'

My anger lasted me until we had stabled the horses and I had strode into the feast-chamber. Then it drained from me like water from a broken cask. My mother was lolling at the board, her tilted cup spilling wine down her breast, her hair as matted as a dog's. She was holding the hand of Aegisthus, who sat in royal robes, in my father's chair, chuckling and fat.

I must have stood in the doorway aghast, for Aegisthus suddenly shouted out in his hoarse voice, 'Come, girl, is this the way to greet your new father? Is this the famous courtesy of Mycenae? I thought we might expect better than this, daughter!'

I said, 'You are not my father. You are not even fit to stand in his shadow. If he were here, Agamemnon would beat you into the yard with the other dogs.'

His face darkened and he struck on the board with the ivory haft of his meat-knife. My mother still smiled with purple-lipped stupor, and said thickly, 'It is a wise child that knows its own father, Electra! Why are you so sure that Aegisthus is not your begetter? How do you even know I am your mother? Surely you are old enough to know, now, that there are many about Low Town who say Helen was your mother. What of that? If Helen, why not Aegisthus? Does a lamb among a great flock know from which ewe it came?'

Aegisthus began to laugh again at these words, and beckoned for a slave-woman to pour more wine for them both. He drank noisily, like a swine. The sight of his thick red lips all shiny and loose at the cup turned my stomach. He seemed of a different race of men from fearful Agamemnon, in whose every limb and gesture the god spoke clearly for all to hear and see.

I fell on my knees before the queen and said, 'Do not torment me, mother. Tell me that I come from you, and that Agamemnon was indeed my father. Tell me, I must know!'

In truth, the words that had just been spoken had raised such a strange doubt in my mind that for a while I felt certain of nothing. It was all a great shock to me.

Clytemnestra gazed down at me, as though trying to see me clearly. She had drunk too much of the strong unwatered Samian wine, I could see that, and her habits were usually frugal in such matters. She began to ruffle my hair with her thin hard hand, and then to stroke my cheek. She spilled wine on to my shoulders and neck, without meaning to. Then she saw this and tried to wipe me dry with her robe. She was very clumsy and careless; I had never seen her so before.

At length she said, 'There, there, my dove. You are weeping when there is no need. It is always painful to pass from the dream of childhood to the dream of the grown world—yet it must be done, at some time or other, and now is as good as any time.'

She stopped then, as I gazed at her waiting, as though she did not know how to go on. But Aegisthus got up clumsily from his stool and came over, limping, to me. He swayed beside me, so close that his sour breath came at me in sickening waves.

'You must force yourself to tell her the truth, Clytemnestra,' he said. 'If she is to live on here in this house, she must know. It is her right—though, the god knows, she has few enough rights, poor little bitch!'

He held out his cup for me to drink from, as though doing me a great favour; but I saw the scum of chewed food at the cup's edge, where his lips had been, and I turned away.

Clytemnestra pulled me to her and said in low tones, 'Yes, it is time for the words to be spoken—but not here. Women need secrecy to speak their minds, Aegisthus. I can tell her more fittingly if we are alone. Stay at the board and drink on at the wine, while I take Electra to her bed and uncover to her the truth of our life.'

I remember little more, until I was lying on my hide-thong couch, with Clytemnestra beside me, soothing my hair and kissing the tears from my burning cheeks. My first despair had worn itself out and I waited, shivering, for what she might tell me.

I think that she was finding it hard to begin, for she plucked at the fringed coverlet, or scratched at her body a while. Then, like a swimmer drawing in his breath before he plunges into the cold spring waters of the river, she said, 'We live in a time of great change, daughter, when it seems that the world is set to destroy itself, when the few of us who are still alive must admit the truth to themselves, or go down into the darkness with the truth unspoken. We are all at the edge of death, and what we do here on earth is of little account, provided we make clear to one another what meaning lies in life. It is time to reveal what the gods intended for us—and how we, small headstrong men, have twisted the gods' intentions for our own pride and pleasure.'

Her hoarse and mumbled words flowed over me, without lodging in my mind, like the swarms of birds which migrate in the latter-year, winging past tree-top after tree-top, unable to find a proper nesting-place.

Impatient, I said at last, 'Mother, why do you treat me like this?'

The queen held me so hard against her that I thought she would hurt herself, or me. She said, 'I love you, Electra, so much—so much more than any other child that has come from me, save little dead Tantalus. I cannot say to you how much I love you. It is like a sword going through me.'

She did not answer my question; but suddenly that did not seem important to me. I clung to her and wet her shift through with my tears.

[108]

18

AT last she said, 'Dry your tears, my own. I swear that you are my daughter. I was only teasing you. I do not know what got into me. Perhaps it was the wine that spoke, not I.'

'And, mother, is Agamemnon my father?'

Her whole body stiffened. 'I lay with him before I got you,' she answered, 'but I always like to think the god was with me, not him. Either that, or that Tantalus had left seed in me that flourished after his death; but not him, not Agamemnon.'

She spoke so violently now that I drew a little away from her, almost in fear. I did not know whether I hated or loved her at that moment. But I had gone in too far to back away now. I said, 'Why do you hate the king so, mother? I know that he killed Tantalus and your baby; but that is long past, and you have us, your other children, to comfort you now. Can you not forget your young pride and glory in the older pride of being Agamemnon's queen?'

Clytemnestra twisted at her lips viciously, as though she would have torn them off in her spite.

'The women of my kin never forgive a wrong,' she said. 'I hated Agamemnon even when he bedded me the most sweetly. My love, you will come to learn that a woman is like those strange Carian flasks, with two divisions in them, so that they can hold both oil and wine. Tip the bottle and oil comes out; twist it a little sideways and then tip it again . . . now it will pour wine, bitter wine!'

I was impatient at her riddles, and said, 'Stop, mother, stop! So, you hate Agamemnon; I will believe that, and will hope that one day, when he returns in glory and the world is sane again, I can get you to love him. But first you must turn this fellow, Aegisthus, from our house. Send him away, anywhere you wish, mother. Give him treasure to go away; but let us be rid of him. He is like a horrible dream, leering at me always from behind hangings.'

My mother rose from the bed and began to arrange her hair, carelessly, passing time until she was ready to answer me. And when she was ready, she said, 'What I shall tell you lies at the heart of the matter, Electra. Listen carefully, my daughter, for this will uncover to you all that was secret before. In the long-dead past, there was a great king of all Hellas, whose name was Pelops. He was so sacred that men say the god himself begot him. This son of Zeus had two sons of his own, Thyestes and Atreus.'

I could have laughed, despite my tears, at my mother's serious face as she spoke these words. I said, 'But, mother, I know all this. Atreus was my own grandfather. The king has told us of him.'

Clytemnestra stopped speaking and stared at me. And when I was silent again, she said, 'What I shall tell you, you have never heard before. It is not likely that Agamemnon would have told you what I shall tell you.'

She ignored my sigh of impatience and went on. 'In the old days, kings went foraging about Hellas to find themselves a kingdom and to raise their own House. Thyestes was such a young rover. He had always more about him than his brother, Atreus. He was a true Hellene of the finest mould, and Artemis looked over him from the start and brought him victory in battle when he played the sword-game for Mycenae. King Thyestes of Mycenae, the Lion of Hellas; that was what he became.'

I started to question her, but she put her hand across my mouth and went on. 'As for your grandfather, Atreus, he was a brooding stay-at-home; one who sat in the corner and bit his nails off to think of his brother's fame. Afraid to risk his precious body among the javelins, Atreus sought his distinction in an easier way. At the time I speak of, more than forty years ago, there was a stern king in Crete, named Catreus, of the old blood of Minos they say. This Catreus, a fierce upholder of the ancient shrines, had a wilful daughter, Aerope, who was trained as the Servant of the Mother, but she lent herself to all comers in the secrecy of the shrine. Her ways became so well known that young bucks from half-Hellas made the journey over the seas to worship at the Cretan shrine. Your grandfather, Atreus, was among them—but, clumsy as ever, he let King Catreus catch him at it. That was the measure of your grandfather's wit, my love.'

Much of this passed by me; but some of it stuck. My father had always talked of Atreus as though he were a god on earth; but Clytemnestra's words belittled him strangely in my mind. I was shocked not by the love-making in the sacred shrine, but that my hero-grandfather should have been surprised by a mere Cretan kinglet.

I said, 'But, mother, you make it sound as though my kin were fools or common rogues, yet, as all the world knows, they were royal folk.'

Clytemnestra smiled bitterly and answered, 'Fools! Common rogues! Royal! All these are words, my own, just words. A man is not a word—he is one, in the image of the god, who acts; and your grandfather acted very stupidly for a well-born man. King Catreus would have been within his right to pin them both to the bed with his javelin; but he was a man of some pride and dignity. In open court, he commanded your grandfather to return home to Hellas in disgrace. As for Aerope, she was sentenced to the death she deserved —she was to be thrown to Poseidon's fishes from the harbour wall at Miletus. But when she heard her fate, she set up such a mewling and beating of the breast that silly Atreus bought her life and married her in the court chamber. He paid for her what, nowadays, a farmer would pay for a second-grade ewe; no more, and at a time when a good wife cost a hundred sheep. That was your grandmother, who bore great Agamemnon and his famous brother Menelaus of Laconica! Now do you see what seed you come from, daughter?'

I grew angry then, and said hotly, 'But, mother, you describe the adventures of a young man, and of a priestess who failed in her duty for love; what is there in that? The Athenian, Theseus, is praised by the poets for running away with the priestess, Ariadne, from the same island. Why should I despise Atreus for doing the like?'

Clytemnestra turned away from me, as though in disgust.

'Because,' she said at last, 'your grandfather's vileness did not stop there. Once she had borne him sons, Aerope was used by your grandfather to trap King Thyestes, his brother. Oh, she was pretty enough, in that brown Cretan way, that full-bodied way; and she knew all the tricks of love. No doubt she enjoyed tempting Thyestes, she was that sort; but your grandfather should never have put a noblewoman to such use. Like a crafty fox, Atreus picked his time to expose Thyestes in bed with Aerope, and so shamed him that the people of Mycenae rose and gave Atreus the crown. Atreus got the throne of Mycenae not in war, but by putting his wife in sin with his brother. Now do you see?'

I nodded and clutched at the sheet which covered me. The threads of the pattern were at last coming into line and drawing a picture before my eyes. 'What happened then, mother?' I asked, in spite of myself.

Clytemnestra said flatly, 'When he had usurped Thyestes, your grandfather had silly Aerope put away by night. So she died violently after all, you see. There is no escaping the god, or the goddess. Then, as though to bring the greatest horror on Thyestes, Atreus called a feast in this very palace where we now are, and let it be known that he was friends once more with the brother who had seduced his wife. They fetched poor half-blind Thyestes up from the dungeon and set a dish before him. Since he had been fed for months on offals, he fell to ravenously and ate the tender flesh that was put before him. When he dared to ask what meat he had been eating, the servants laid a dish on the table, and, uncovering it, showed the heads, hands, and feet of Thyestes' own youngest sons, Orchomenus and Aglaus! No, do not cover your ears, Electra; all this happened, at the very table I have just left, in the feast-hall along the corridor. I will tell you something worse—your own father, Agamemnon, and his brother Menelaus, stood one on either side of Thyestes and forced him to gaze on the mutilated parts of his children. Agamemnon was only a lad himself, at the time, but strong enough to deal with an old man who had been starved in prison for months.'

As her voice went on, I saw my father standing high among the chariots, waving up to us, as he went forward towards the ships. How could such a god act as my mother had told me? I shook my head, trying to drive away the thought, but a blackness was coming over me now, and somehow I knew that Clytemnestra was telling me the truth.

She said, 'You shake your head! Aye, and poor Thyestes shook his, as well. He tried to shake the yelling madness out of it, but that did not work. Thyestes ran from our palace like a crazed bullock whose horns have just been sawn off, slavering and moaning, blind with the agony inside his head. They let him go, laughing at him, thinking that they would go after him when the wine was finished, and put a sword to him. But the god had some mercy and let night cover him. In the morning, Thyestes was not to be found in Mycenae, and the wild beasts of this House gave him up for dead, and went about their own vile affairs.

'There is no sense in life, Electra. This you will learn, more and more, as you get older and see more of the world. The god who had covered Thyestes' escape from the palace now began to play with him as our cats play with wounded mice. Wandering in the outland, Thyestes came one night to a little village where a young woman washed his sore feet and gave him bread to eat. Seeing that he was helpless, she tried to soothe him to sleep, stroking his brow. But Thyestes misunderstood her kindness, and with a madman's strength, compelled her to give him greater soothing, greater comfort than she had intended. You understand what I mean, daughter? He did not mean to force her, I am sure; but her gentle body so close to his was more than the poor wretch could stand. Perhaps he thought she was Aerope come alive again; I do not know. The gods cause men to do strange things in cases like these.

'I can only tell you that in the morning he found that this girl, Pelopia, was no other than his own child, by one of those careless unions that happened to warrior-kings in those days, when they celebrated their victories over outland-folk by bedding the most comely of the women.

'I declare to you, Electra, that Thyestes was not to blame. How could he have known? I do not defend him, but only pity him, you understand. Just as I abhor your grandfather, Atreus, for causing such

[113]

a situation to arise. If the blame must lie anywhere, it lies with Atreus. Your grandfather was the foulest man in Hellas. If you doubt that, I will go further, and will tell you that Atreus had now got word about Thyestes' whereabouts, and followed him to the village. Here he found the weeping Pelopia, and like a dog returning to his vomit, lusted after her, if only because Thyestes had had her. Or perhaps because he wished to misuse something which Thyestes had possessed, since Thyestes himself had fled from the village towards Delphi that time, and was out of his reach.

'You see, daughter, a man like Atreus is insatiable in his vengeances. In due course, Pelopia bore a son—but it was not of Atreus' doing; the seed of that sapling had been planted in an earlier season, on the night mad Thyestes begged for comfort under the thatch. But Atreus thought the boy was his own, and brought him up here, in Mycenae. In his twisted mind, Atreus had already planned to train the baby to track down Thyestes and to kill him.'

The words were swirling round me now, like starlings gathering to go south. I said, 'You have not told me this boy's name, mother.' I do not think I wanted to know, but it was something to say.

Clytemnestra smiled and pointed through the doorway. 'He is sitting at the feast-table now,' she said. 'It was Aegisthus!'

I rose in the bed, my heart thumping and my head reeling. 'You mean that Aegisthus, whom I called a swine, is of my own kin?' I asked. My mother nodded, and let herself down on a stool, as though she was very tired. 'He is as noble as you are, my love,' she said. 'And, indeed, he has greater right to sit on the throne in Mycenae than Agamemnon, for he is son to Thyestes, the rightful king here. Now do you wonder that I treat him with honour? Do you wonder that he and I understand each other?'

I said, 'But why should Aegisthus hate my father?'

Clytemnestra said slowly, 'The tale has gone on too long, already, daughter. It can be ended briefly. I will only tell you that as Aegisthus grew up, Atreus made him swear on oath to kill Thyestes one day. That day happened when Aegisthus was only seven, imagine that! Your father, a wild young man then, tracked Thyestes down at last, and dragged him back to Mycenae. Atreus put a sword in the lad's hand and Agamemnon and Menelaus held the old madman down while his little son carried out the tyrant's order. Now, while Atreus lies in honour, in the great underground treasury, like a god—murdered Thyestes is buried in a pauper's stony grave beside the road that runs to Argos.'

I was biting at the hem of my robe, and the tears were flooding on to my breast. I said, 'So Aegisthus has come back to get vengeance on the Kin of Atreus for his dead father?'

My mother nodded, and suddenly began to stare out of the window as though she had lost all interest in the affair. As I looked at her in amazement, a great thunder clap sounded in my head, as though the god had struck me in the innermost brain. I held out my hands before me, and they seemed dark with blood. My robe suddenly stank as though I had rolled in a gutter. My hair clung damply against my face, like the farmyard straw in which the swine have dabbled for a season. I was unclean, I knew, from innermost to outmost. I was of the filthy Kin of Atreus, a rotting pear, the child of a usurper, the granddaughter of a tyrant-king who had wallowed in the refuse of a butcher's yard.

I suddenly knew myself for the first time, and I ran from that room seeking the clean air outside. I was the child of foul unions, of treachery, of death. And my father, whom men called great, was even more tainted than I.

As I ran through the courtyard, I searched here and there for a sharp stone to put an end to my pain, to solve a problem that was too great for my heart to carry any longer.

Then all at once I found myself in the stable, with wide-eyed Rarus beside me, stroking my face and asking me what it was all about.

At first I wanted to hit at him, to drive him away, to keep my dirt away from him, not to hurt him. Then, as he held me close, trying to comfort me in his simple way, I heard myself laughing as high as the sky, and heard my voice shouting, 'I am as mad as poor Thyestes! Oh, god, take this from me!'

Rarus was crooning above me, holding me down so that I should not harm myself against the rough stone of the stable. And as his hands held me, the black mist came over my eyes again, as though the god was present in the stable. It was all terrible. It was not me; it was some other I did not know.

I felt my body lunging at Rarus savagely, and I heard a voice yelling, 'Come alive! Come alive! On, on, you fool! I need you now!'

But Rarus only clung to me, like a farmer trying to hold a wild steer at the branding-time, his thin body cool and still against all my urgency; and what I got from him came from my own mad urging, from myself. As I shuddered in the high and awful flight, he breathed softly so as not to hinder me, to cause me to fall to earth before my time.

And when I was myself again, he said so gently, 'I can do no more, lady; but that much, poor as it is, is always yours.'

Now I lay ashamed and sobbing, turning my face from his great eyes. I mumbled, 'Forgive me, Rarus; it was the god, not I. He put too much suffering on me. There was no other comfort, it seemed.'

Then we lay together and wept in the dry straw.

19

I WOKE at last to find men with torches standing above me, and my mother and Aegisthus a little apart, with dark cloths over their heads. They were like pale-faced mourners, waiting for the dead to rise again. When she saw my eyes open, Clytemnestra came and bent over me and wiped my face with her own skirt. Her features were composed and gentle, and her lips curved softly in pity.

She whispered to me, 'Electra, you are a woman now, and there must be no more tears. Your childhood has passed, my love, and must not be regretted. That is the way of life; it is the way the god orders it, and there is no denying his command.'

I reached up from the straw and put my arms round her. She kneeled by me and held me close to her breast. 'We are women together now, my dear,' she said, nuzzling my face with her lips. 'Now that you know the worst, you may look forward to the best.'

At this, Aegisthus stepped near me, into the full light. His face had more dignity about it than I had ever seen before. Even his smile seemed to carry some protection in it now. He touched my kneeling mother on the shoulder and said in a low voice, 'She has not yet seen the worst, Clytemnestra. There is that one thing she must see before she may become a thread in our pattern, such as the god decrees. That one thing.'

My mother bowed her head, and a sob shook her body. 'It is not the time, surely, Aegisthus,' she answered. 'Has she not been through enough today?'

But Aegisthus stood firm and said in his softest voice, 'No, Clytemnestra. All things have worked towards this occasion and the moment must not be let pass. If we wait until tomorrow, the thread will be broken, the warp and woof will come apart and the pattern be destroyed. Little as I wish it, for myself, what is to be done must be done tonight, as the smith strikes upon the iron while the fire's magic thrives within it. To leave it an hour, even, would be to lose the occasion. Come, we are all ready. Let us go about the final business.'

My mother raised me to my feet and put a black cloth over my head. Then, with the torches flaring about us, we walked silently from the palace yard and across the barren place of stones that led down towards the ancient tombs of Mycenae. I had never been right into them before, because of the bees and of the ghosts that howled from the hollow passages when the wind blew in a certain quarter. Only kings and priests went there, and when they did, the guard outside drove all the folk away from the tholoi.

At the dark entrance of the greatest tomb, the torch-bearers halted and handed their flares to my mother and Aegisthus. Rarus waited on the outermost edge of the throng, looking down at his feet, still miserable for my sake.

'Come, daughter,' said the queen, 'and hold these beans in your hand as you tread the deep steps. They will keep all harm from you.'

As we descended, damp stale air came up to meet us, and the darkness rustled with small flapping wings. Once my hand touched the cold wall, sliding on the lichen that grew there, and I pulled away with such a start that my mother took me firmly by the shoulder and guided me along.

At last we reached a paved level where the roof arched over us and, on either side, small tunnels gave on to the chief thoroughfare. Our footsteps echoed back to us in long rustling sounds, however quietly we trod. It was as though the tomb was full of waiting serpents.

I began to whisper to Clytemnestra, begging her to let me run away up the stairway; but I had scarcely finished three words before the echo of my whispering came back from the stifling walls with such volume and vehemence that I stopped, afraid to say more.

Behind me, lit by his resinous torch, Aegisthus patted me on the back, as though in sympathy, and nodded to me when I turned towards him.

At last he pushed past us and halted by one of the narrow tunnels, holding his torch out for us to see what he indicated.

'Look,' he said, in a voice that boomed like a roaring bull of dreams. 'Here he is! Here is the founder of your House, Electra!'

In fear, I gazed, and saw, hunched on a gilded stool, the form of a man, wrapped round with brown strips of linen. He was leaning sideways, as though about to fall; then I saw, in the torchlight, that a short stabbing-spear was set against his right side, keeping him from toppling. About his feet lay heaped cups of gold and silver, bronze daggers inlaid with precious metals, piles of amethyst beads from Egypt, and amber beads from the farthest lands to the north. What held my eye most strongly was the mask on the dead king's face; it was of dull gold, hammered and chiselled to show his great broad forehead and his closed eyelids. His sharp nose stood out like an eagle's beak; his beard hung stiffly downwards and seemed to writhe as though life were in it.

'So,' whispered Clytemnestra, 'that is Atreus, your grandfather.'

Then she was silent, as I gazed on the dead metal face of the man who had distantly begot me. It was hard to see, in those calm features and that wide head, signs of this wickedness. Now he slept impassively like a god whose task is done, who is beyond all caring.

In a sudden anger, I drew back my hand to knock him from his stool, but the queen saw what I was about and caught me firmly. 'No, no,' she muttered, 'he is beyond your reach, and must not be disturbed. Our work is against the living, not the dead. Come away, now.'

At the farther end of the passage-way, we came on a tunnel newer than the rest, its stones still bearing the white marks of the mason's chisel, its earth still carrying a little of the odour of the upper world. When Aegisthus held his torch inside this place, I saw no golden cups and amber beads, no gilded stool and dead king lolling there against a spear. Instead, a small figure, wrapped about in rough wool, lying on its side, hunched up, like a child in bed.

Aegisthus said, 'Do you know who this is, Electra?'

I shook my head, though, already, a chill hand was clenching round my heart.

'Feel inside the tomb,' said Aegisthus, 'and see what your fingers find.'

As in a dream, I obeyed him. There was no gold mask where the face should have been, such as Atreus wore so proudly. Instead there was a rough ball of something like clay. Aegisthus put his hand upon my own to keep it there, and pushed his torch forward so that I should see all. This dead one had a mask of clay, rudely fashioned, but clear enough to the eye. I knew that my fingers were stroking the face of Iphigenia, my sister who had gone to Tauris. As I drew back in horror, Aegisthus coughed, and a small cloud of feathers rose in the air from that disturbance of the tomb, the breast-feathers of a sea-bird. One of them settled on my face and I tore madly at my flesh to be rid of it. It was all as I had seen in my dream.

I swung round at my mother and said, 'But she is in Tauris, is she not?'

Clytemnestra stared back at me with wild bright eyes. Her mouth was shaped as for weeping, but the voice that came out of her lips was as deadly cold and calm as would have been that of Atreus, had he spoken now.

She said, numb as a statue, 'They sacrificed her at Aulis, to gain a wind for Troy!'

So, it was spoken at last. And with the speaking, the spell of darkness, of dumbness, was shattered in me. I ran howling back through the black passage-way, and up the steep stairs, falling, bruising my body, hitting my head against the lichened wall, wakening the bees with my noise, making them buzz above my head in their secret caverns behind the stones.

And at last I was up in the living world again, and still running away from the tombs, away from Rarus who started after me in fear for my reason.

I ran and ran, as light as the wind now, howling until my throat was afire and my tongue was silent, although the breath still came from me. I saw walls of houses, then rocks in open fields, and then rough pasture-grass. I was away from Mycenae, away from that doomed place of foulness and decay. And at length I was soaring over the land, leaping streams and boulders with no effort, my hands pressed to my ears to stop them from hearing what my tormented voice tried to shriek.

'Death to Agamemnon! Death to the murderer! Curse on the Lion of Mycenae!'

Then the last I knew, in the moonlight, was that a black dog suddenly came out from a thicket as I stumbled on and dragged me down, slavering over me and growling at my throat.

20

THEY moved my bed into the great hall, so that I should always have company. They brought me the best doctor in Egypt, who put salves and oiled bandages on my head and throat, to heal the bites the wild dog had given me.

Clytemnestra often sat beside me, with her distaff, twisting the newly-shorn fleece into yarn that she would later put on her loom. I used to watch the carved ivory weight spinning round, and back again, as the length of wool grew longer from between her hard narrow hands.

It was like my own life, growing longer and stronger, though soiled in the making, as fleece becomes when it is handled.

I told my mother this one day. She answered, 'It takes much handling to make a strand of wool, and by handling the wool is dirtied. Yet one day, when it is long enough, we trail it in the stream and make it clean again. Then we set up warp and woof on the great loom, and from what was once a piece of grey wool, we make a glorious white robe, or a gay picture to hang on the walls. One would never think it had ever been rough, and broken, and unclean. So it is with life. All things have helped you to grow, but, in helping you, have soiled you. Now, as you lie recovering, the god is teasing you out into a long strand of wool, and you will rise from your bed at last, as the yarn does from the stream—pure white and ready for the pattern you shall help to make, once you are dyed.'

One day, when I was feeling most weary of life, I said that I wished they had left me to the black dog—but she slapped me on the face in play and answered, 'What! Poor Aegisthus got his arms all bitten before he knocked that savage beast on the head. And Rarus, who dragged you away from its jaws, will carry the fang-marks on his cheeks until he dies. Even I had my robe ripped from me. So you see, a price has been paid for you. You must not waste our suffering by making so little of your life.'

Aegisthus would also come and sit beside me, as the moons waxed and waned—for I was long enough in coming back to my true senses and strength. His face was usually set and thoughtful, and, though nothing would ever alter its fat and foolish shape, he had somehow taken on a sort of dignity, a kingliness, that I would never have believed before. He would hold my hand beneath the bed-cover, often so warmly that I smiled bitterly inside myself and wondered what would happen if the queen saw him doing this. Once, when he felt me pulling away a little, he whispered, 'But Electra, cannot a father hold his daughter's hand, then?'

I looked him in the eye and said, 'Yes—but it may be another thing if a stepfather does so.'

Aegisthus rubbed his flat nose and grinned sheepishly, like a boy being caught stealing plums. He said quietly, 'Come, come, my pretty! You are a big girl now, sixteen years or so, surely? A girl chosen by the god as an instrument of his purpose. If you were a peasant girl, by now you would have a hut of your own, and would be preparing meals for a lusty husband, with three or four brats dragging at your skirts all the while, and maybe even one at the breast at the same time. You feel like a child still because you have lived all your life in the palace, where the girls are overmuch protected.'

I clenched my teeth and said to him, 'Aegisthus, if I were asked to take a husband now, I would put a knife into myself. As I have lain here, coming back to the sunlight from the darkness, I have thought every day that I hate men. All my life I thought that men were the god's image, and that my father, Agamemnon, was the greatest of them all. But now I see that men are brute savages, and Agamemnon the most brutish of men. It would please me well to make all men suffer for what the king did to poor Iphigenia.'

Aegisthus leaned down and held his chin in his hand for a while, his brow clouded. At last he turned to me and said. 'This does not surprise me. Most young riders turn away from horses when they are thrown for the first time—but they come back to it again, when the memory has faded. So, when Agamemnon has died, you will come back to men again. Yet, in the meantime, what you say casts a poor light on me, daughter! Do you not think of me as a man, then?'

I answered, 'Aegisthus, there is something about you that is different from the other men I have known. You seem more like a black shadow lurking in the corners of a room, or up above the rafters. I mean you no disrespect, but that is how you seem to me.'

He nodded, for he liked to think that he was different. He said, 'That is because you know my strange story, how I was born, how I became the tool of Atreus, and so on. The pattern of my life has been different from other men's. But what of young Rarus, your companion? You like him, do you not?'

I turned my head away bitterly. 'You know as well as I, that Rarus is not a man,' I said.

Aegisthus said quickly, 'Then what of your brother, Orestes? He is six or seven now; surely you love him?'

I reached out and took a pear from the bowl. 'My stepfather,' I said, 'six or seven is not a man. Orestes is still a child, a little boy. The man-seed has not yet come into him to make him savage. I have hardly seen my little brother since you came to High Town. I would dearly like to have him back, to play with, and go riding with. Why is he away?'

Aegisthus scratched his nose and said, 'Once as he played with a wooden sword, he shouted out, "I am Agamemnon." This did not please me in the mood that clouded my mind then, and I persuaded your mother to put him out to nurse in the hills. He has been with honest peasant-folk, old Cretan stock; so his father's Hellene pride may have gone from him by now. If you would like him back, I will ask the queen to send for him. Now that you have cursed your father, I feel more secure here. You will be able to persuade Orestes to hate Agamemnon for killing his sister, just as you do. So, with the queen beside us, we shall be a united House. Is that agreed?'

I nodded and said, 'When a great storm blows down a village, men come out from the rocks again and begin to build another place

[123]

to live in. I feel that I have suffered such a great tempest, and that now I must start to live again differently. Send for Orestes to be my companion and I will do as you say. He and Rarus shall be my playmates.'

At this time, my cousin Hermione, who had been away, also used to visit me, sitting sucking the ends of her auburn hair and making great eyes at the guards who kept the great doorway safe. I know that she hated Agamemnon, too, and also her father, Menelaus, because they had sold her mother to the Trojan prince. Often, Hermione brought my dull sister, Chrysothemis with her, all decked out in her sequined bodice and tinkling flounced skirt. Chrysothemis, whose eyes were always painted blue, like an Egyptian's, and her long finger-nails stained red like a leopard's claws when he has been at the carcass of a sheep.

They both were with me, thinking as I did, that we women should keep together and wrest justice from the men for the sufferings they caused us.

All the same, I could not resist teasing Chrysothemis, when I got to feel a bit better. Though she looked like a grown woman, she had the heart of a child of nine. Every gesture she made had to be carried out as though she were conducting a ritual at the Mother shrine. When she turned her head to look at anything, her whole body went round with it, stiffly, as though she was an image; and even then, she affected to stare through a thing, rather than look at it. With her decorated clothes and her painted face, and her crimped hair that hung like snakes down her back, Chrysothemis seemed more like a sacred doll than a living girl.

I always used to greet her by bowing, from my bed, and holding my hands, fingers together and straight, palms upwards, like a devotee about to pray. And I would say, 'Greetings, goddess, your light casts away the darkness. What truth of the Mother do you bring today?"

Usually she would stare through me and say in a thin, distant voice, 'All who believe shall walk in light. The Mother sends her blessing and tells you that the truth shall one day be known to you. You must ask for no more this day.'

But one hot morning she almost ran into the megaron, scratching her middle under the flounced skirt, and streaming with summer dampness. She was looking very human this day—not at all like a sacred one—with the blue paint running down her cheeks and her snake-hair all tangled and unoiled.

She flung herself on my bed and said, 'Electra, news has come! Things have not gone well at Troy. Agamemnon and Achilles have quarrelled over some woman, who was Achilles' prize. Without Achilles' army, the king cannot take Troy, himself. The messenger who brought the news has been a year coming, and he says that by this time Agamemnon may already be dead, for he thinks that Achilles will go over to Troy.'

I sucked in my breath and clutched at the covers. 'We may not see him again, then?' I said.

Chrysothemis nodded. She said, 'It is most unlikely, the man says. And Agamemnon has made yet another mistake; he has taken as his concubine a woman already dedicated to the Mother, a woman whose head is turned by the truth. Her name is Cassandra and she is of the royal blood, of King Priam's blood. Agamemnon has got two children on her, and so must answer to the Mother for defiling a priestess.'

I said, 'Has Clytemnestra heard this news?'

I could picture my mother's fury at learning of her husband's behaviour. Chrysothemis nodded and said, 'Yes, and all she said was, "So, by little and little, he digs his own grave." She was no more angry than if she caught the cat stealing a piece of mutton from the table.'

I must confess that when my sister brought this news, I felt a still coldness creep through all my body, like a sign from the god. And as I sat stiffly in bed, I suddenly knew that my father, Agamemnon, was as good as dead. In a way, I hoped that the next messenger would bring word of the High King's funeral pyre; for that would save much trouble. Though I hated him and had cursed him, when I thought of helping to put an end to him, my hands shook and my courage failed me.

I

Under the bedclothes, I whispered, 'Let him die out there, in the outland; do not let him come back. I do not want his blood on my hands, Mother. Let all be clean here from now on. Let my father end away from home, as though in a dream.'

From that morning, Agamemnon seemed dead to me, as though he was nothing but a dream I had had when I was a little girl, five years before.

After that, I got stronger each day; and when they brought Orestes back to the palace, I felt that life had begun again, like a clear spring morning, with the new buds bursting and the white lambs jumping under the blue sky, unmindful of the butcher's knife.

21

I AM old now, doctor, and things which took years to unfold seem to have happened all in a few hours. After Orestes came back, my life at Mycenae was one long afternoon, always sunny, always clear, with the birds singing and the tall acanthus blooming, and the late crocuses under our feet as we ran across the hills, and the wild lavender sending up its scent behind us as we crushed its leaves in our running.

Surely, there must have been snow, and blustery winds. Rain must have come in through the hole in the palace roof which was always to be mended, and never was. . . . But if these things happened, I do not recall them.

What I remember was joy, and myself as the queen of the children, for somehow, since my sickness, they all seemed to take me as their leader in everything.

I formed a Company of my own, the Elect of Electra, we called it, and thought it was a great joke to make.

There were Orestes, Rarus, Hermione, Chrysothemis and myself. We got my mother to give us white ponies, and we persuaded Aegisthus to let the palace armourers make helmets and corselets and short swords for us. I even chopped off my hair, to be like a boy; but Hermione, though she agreed not to paint her face and fingers any more, would not do away with her long oiled tresses. So we told her she would be an Amazon who rode with us. Orestes thought it all the greatest fun, and became a real danger with his sword, because he used to live so much in our play-dream that he took it all for the final truth. For example, though he was only about seven, or perhaps eight, he was a strong boy, and big for his age, and he would fall so deeply into the game we played that he would really try to put his sword into anyone whom we pretended to be our enemy.

Once, as we came down the hill into a village one evening, Rarus said, 'Let's pretend that we are savage Dorians sacking this place.'

We cantered through a farmyard where an old peasant was trying to get a black goat into its pen. He turned and waved at us, but Orestes set his pony at him and badly wounded the old fellow's head with his flailing sword. It was as though Orestes could not tell truth from dream. He never grew out of this, I am afraid.

The old peasant? Oh, we bound his head for him, while Hermione held Orestes. I explained that it was a mistake. The old man said, ''Tis not the sort of mistake that should happen too often, my lady. Yon little lad bears too much of the stamp of the bad king for my liking. I remember Agamemnon as a lad; he and Menelaus used to ride like that, sword-mad. We should not want to see it all again, lady. Now we are rid of it, we should not want it to come back.'

I consoled him and promised it would never happen again.

When I told Clytemnestra about it, she pursed her mouth and said, 'Yes, he is like Agamemnon. It is as well that we know, for now he can be trained differently. We must muzzle him, for we cannot have a little lad upsetting all we are building among the folk. I will see that the smith knocks the edge off his sword, and if that does not do, then he shall have a wooden one.'

Orestes was so upset about his sword that we hadn't the heart to punish him further, and so we let him go on calling himself Agamemnon, in our secret games. We thought it a small price to pay at the time, though, honestly, I think we did him much damage by our leniency, for it is my belief that the boy somehow thought he really was Agamemnon, come again.

I must say now, doctor, that my brother, Orestes, was never quite like other boys. Any more than Chrysothemis was like other girls. It was as though something ancient worked in them, without their knowing, just as wine works in the cask before it is ready to drink. I cannot explain it, but I often used to think that Orestes and Chrysothemis belonged to a distant time that all others had forgotten. They would have been better living when old Cheiron galloped the hills, or when Hera walked the roads of Hellas, like any market-woman. You cannot teach such children to come out of their dream and act like others. Yes, they can seem to be like others, for a time; but suddenly something sets them off, a clap of thunder, the earth shaking under your feet when Poseidon rumbles, a breath of wind from a new quarter, and so on. . . . Then they are off, and no words in the world can bring them back until their dream has played itself out and they have fallen asleep.

But we got on well enough. We could not see the end of the god's pattern at this time, how he would use Orestes and Chrysothemis for his purpose. We were only children and we did not know the end of things. We lived for each day as it came, no more.

One of the things we enjoyed was watching the New Army being got ready. This was Aegisthus' idea, though my mother supported him in it. In my father's time, every man, noble or merchant or peasant, had his own place, and could not shift from it. The lords fought and learned the usage of arms—the chariot, the javelin, the sword, the shield—merchants moved from place to place, on mules or ships, bartering their goods; peasants stayed on the land and tended the crops and the cattle.

But after Agamemnon went away, the merchants plied their trade in the outland, mixing with the Phoenicians, and taking trade away from Hellas. As for the peasants, they became unruly, and often got too drunk and rebellious to sow the corn, or milk the beasts.

Aegisthus put a stop to this. He issued a command which made every man a soldier for half the week, and a merchant or a peasant for the other half. They did not like this new law, but after a while it gave them a pride they had never known before. Aegisthus, who was never much of a soldier himself, and was lame into the bargain, made only one rule about the manner of warfare; he commanded that it should be conducted not in the Mycenaean manner, with chariots and swords, but in the ancient Cretan way, on foot, with the spear and the bow. All farmers could learn to use such weapons, though few of them had the skill to manage swords and shields. And I have never yet met a peasant who could manage a chariot properly. A farm-cart, yes, but not a light-wheeled chariot.

In any case, most of the peasants and the merchants came from the old stock of the first folk, the Cretans, and they preferred, if they must fight, to do so with the weapons their ancient fathers had used. So there was sense in what Aegisthus made them do. If he had tried to put them in chariots and teach them sword-play and so on, they would always have felt he was trying to make them into Hellenes, and he would have been defeated before he had started.

Instead, by the time I was eighteen, the New Army of Mycenae, of part-time soldiers, was thriving. I will not say that the men looked as fine as the warriors I had seen in the old days, when the High King was gathering his host; after all, the peasant army wore no metal, but only horse-hide tunics and helmets. But they were not hampered by the weight, either, and most of them, used to running up hills after sheep, or dragging hard on the ploughing-stick, were hardy and strong, and as active as wild cats, in their thin-muscled way.

I think these soldiers had a soft spot for the Elect of Electra, though we went about the country, dressed Hellene-style. Perhaps it was because they had the traditional respect of peasants for their Achaean overlords. Once, when the New Army was having a great parade outside the palace, with half the countryside gathered to watch them, their farmer-general, who was called Phanus, and was as dark-skinned as a Libyan, asked me if I would lead my Elect at the head of his army, and so show Mycenae that at last freedom had come to the land, that the children of the ruling House were one with the men who worked on the soil.

We rode before them, and later that night, among the tents they had set up about the city, we lounged about the fires and ate and drank with them, pushing our fingers into the mutton-dish as they did, sharing all, then passing the horn wine-cup round the ring, not caring if it was clean, not caring whose mouth it had come from last.

I do not think that Aegisthus liked this, but my mother patted him on the arm and said, 'Let be, sir! They are safe enough—and suppose the girls were tampered with, out among the tents, they are old enough now. They would take no great harm from it.'

I overheard this, and thought: Little do you know, mother! We are as safe from that as Olympus is of falling down in a thunder-storm! I love only Rarus, who can get no children; Hermione only loves Orestes, in whom the man-seed has not risen; Chrysothemis only loves the Mother, who, strong as her magic is, cannot beget offspring!

You are smiling, doctor. Is that because I sound simple? Well, you should know by now that we are all simple. Even you, with your scrolls and medicines and instruments, and so on, are simple.

Man is simple; he is nothing but arms and legs and head and stomach. Oh yes, he thinks he is crafty, like old Theseus, or old Jason, but in the end he is just a simple animal who dreams he is a god.

I tell you, put a knife into a man, and where is the god in him then? Just red on the floor, and the man lying white and still, for all his courage and poetry. We make too much of things, doctor. We call our dreams by all sorts of strange words, and think that this makes them more important. But in the end it is all a word that started it, and the word dies when the man who speaks it dies. That is why I never did like the poets, the singers. They sit on their backsides and breathe out words and words and words—but do nothing. Think of all the lies they told of Jason. They made him out to be a great hero; yet he was only a simple horse-herder who got himself into adventures on a ship he couldn't manage. Any young fellow could have done what Jason did, if the luck was with him.

Sometimes, as I have got older, I think that nothing much really happens in a man's life; it is only the red wine that makes it seem something. And I count poetry as little more than the drunkenness of red wine.

Consider what I have told you so far; it is straight out of my head, and for all you or I know, it may all be lies. I may be like the poets, just saying words and words and words.

That is the great trouble with us Hellenes, my friend. We will talk. In our great distant days, when our forefathers came down from the grasslands in their wagons, there was never all this talk. If there was, then it has been forgotten, for most of us know nothing about our past other than that we are descended from Zeus, or Hera, or Poseidon. And that is almost like saying 'God knows who our fathers were!' Don't frown so much, doctor, if I am being insolent to the god, whoever he is, then it will be I who have to suffer the punishment, not you! It is all my affair, and I am willing for that to be so.

Very well, stamp away if you please; but send your apprentice to me; it is time for my evening draught. I cannot sleep without it.

22

DID I tell you that life was like a constant season of summer? Yes, that was it. All Hellas seemed to flower, all men smiled, as though freedom had come again, as though the Golden Age might be round the corner. And Agamemnon and his hordes had gone from our memory as though they had never been. Hellas was the Land of the Common-folk now, and the stern and angry kings were like the demons of the night, cast away at dawn, like Furies whose wings had been clipped and their teeth drawn.

Men and women sang in the streets. Peasants walked in the fields with their heads held high. The sun shone on everyone. The crops almost leaped from the rich soil, as though crying to be harvested. Cattle bore their calves as though they wished to cover the earth with them. There was so much milk that no one drank water. The olive groves burgeoned with their fruit. The apple-trees almost broke down beneath the weight of their laden boughs. Bees hummed in the blue air loud enough to smother thunder. God, it was rich; it was full; it was fertile!

And the folk looked on Clytemnestra and Aegisthus as the Rain-makers, the Spring Queen and the Corn King. With these two in the palace at Mycenae, who needed gold? Men laughed at the memory of scowling Agamemnon, wasting a thousand lives for a few scraps of yellow metal, when in Hellas we now had all the abundance of the earth to enjoy.

They made a song that they sang about the streets. If I can recall it, it went like this:

> Into the dark belly of the year
> Rain shot his darts;
> Apollo warmed the rain, to raise
> Barley and oats;
> In all the crevices of earth,
> Spring the green
> Shoots of corn, swift growth
> As from King in Queen!

They were a merry, sloe-eyed folk. I do not think I had ever noticed this before, in my father's time; then they were just the field-folk, as we called them, hardly human creatures at all.

But now I had to notice them, for they wouldn't take no for an answer, at their Corn-sowing and Wine-treading festivals. They would come, red-mouthed and tipsy with wine, right into the megaron of the palace, and drag us out, the young women, crying, 'Queens, Queens, out with you to bless the feasting!'

Hermione and I were both taken, a number of times, by these laughing farmers with their long black eyelashes and their waists pulled in by thong-belts till they looked like harvest-dolls themselves. Both my cousin and I had the cup pressed many times at our lips and, lying in hay, let the warm wine run in. Perhaps, at first, I wondered if it was as pleasant as the songs made out; perhaps I wondered if old Nestor's play had not been better. But after a festival or two, I fell into the way of it gladly, and no harm came of it.

Though, I must confess, to see poor Rarus standing at the stable-door, waiting for the thing to be over, troubled me. Especially as he was always so kind afterwards, and wiped my lips with his own garment if the wine had spilled about me too freely.

My mother got to hear of it, and took me aside. 'Daughter,' she said, 'we women all know that this must happen at the feastings, but do not talk of it freely among the men. Aegisthus, for instance, would not like to hear of it.'

I was sleepy with dancing and wine when she said this, and did not pay the heed to my answer that I should. I said, 'It strikes me that Aegisthus tells us too much of what we should do, and what we should not.'

My mother frowned and answered, 'That may be. Whatever the case, all will come right at the end. There is a pattern for Aegisthus, just as there is for all others. All I say is, do not let him know that you have been with the wine-dancers. He thinks you are with Rarus at these times.'

I must have been drunk, for I answered, 'Of course I go with Rarus! He stands and waits for me. And no one could have more patience, for I am not a fast drinker, mother!'

Clytemnestra smiled and nodded, and then bent and slapped me quite hard on the backside. 'You are like me, and like your Aunt Helen,' she said. 'We hold the cup to our lips so long that our cup-bearer grows weary and faint. But if the wine is to be enjoyed, then why gulp it down? When the thirst is quenched it is long enough before one can face the next cup, especially in a three-day festival, when the drinking stretches out before one like eternity.'

Then she became solemn again. 'But remember my words. Aegisthus is such a one as likes to sow the seed himself, and reap the harvest. You will be safe from his wrath as long as he thinks you travel with Rarus, who carries the seed-bag but not the grain. Is that understood?'

I nodded and said, 'Aegisthus is afraid that some other king might rise, is he not, mother? I have seen him look longways at my brother, Orestes, when the lad has called himself by my father's name.'

The queen stroked her silk bodice flat against her, carefully, and said, 'Try to teach Orestes not to use that name. Aegisthus has a temper as unsure as that of a wild dog at some times. That is why I sent your brother away to nurse, when he was small. But if we keep a watch on him, you and I, it should not be impossible to ward the danger off.'

She brooded, dark-faced, for a while, running her long thumb-nail the carved length of a clothes-chest that stood by my bed. Then she half-looked up at me under her lowered lids and whispered, 'And if the worst comes through the door, between us, you and I have power among the peasant-folk now. More so, now that they have known your company. They would follow you as the dog-fox follows the vixen and will not harm her. You are their Wine-princess now, daughter, and that counts for a great deal. So, if ever we needed their aid, there might be a festival when all dangers could be got rid of.'

I smiled and said, 'You make me think of the Feast of Dionysus, mother. You make me think of the Maenads, the flower-decked maidens, with the purple on their mouths, hurrying the Chosen King to his fierce glory. Is that what you mean, mother?'

Clytemnestra smiled back at me and said, 'You spoke the words, not I, daughter. But it may not come to that, if Aegisthus remembers his place in this house. It is one feast I did not want to bring back to

Mycenae, because it can be so uncertain, its choice so painful at times. It goes well enough in the islands, where they have hardly yet heard that Minos is dead—but here, in Hellas, we have put it away because it wastes young men so needlessly.'

She paused by the door and said over her shoulder, 'But if need be, I will not let Hellas stand in the way. I will bring back the ancient world so entirely that a man would think he had slept for ten generations, and had wakened on the day Pasiphäe first doted on the bull.'

So it was that I got to know what lay in my mother's heart. Now I loved her above all others, and thought that I was growth of her seed alone, flesh of her flesh, and closer to her than anyone alive.

23

THE god must have thrown back his head and laughed till the skies shook, at my presumption. For, quite suddenly, Clytemnestra was brought to bed with a child, a baby girl. I do not know why, when I thought I was most near to my mother, I had not noticed her condition. Though it may have been that, in those days, she wore many-folded and heavily-flounced skirts. Also, the baby was a very small one; though, the god knows, it caused her enough trouble to be rid of, for she was past the age for child-bearing.

I saw it all happen. Aegisthus dragged me from my bed to be a witness. 'Come, come,' he grunted, spilling wine from his cup over my face, 'one of the House of Atreus shall be there to vouch for the new dynasty!'

He dragged me along the passage-ways and stood me close to her couch, next to the old nurse, Geilissa, who had brought both

Orestes and myself into the world. But this night, Aegisthus had called in his own doctor to effect the birth, not trusting any servant who had worked at the palace in Agamemnon's time. Geilissa was weeping, not smiling now, and well she might. My mother's agony was dreadful to observe.

Again and again, as the pains came on her, she tore at her tangled hair and howled. Her lips were all bitten and raw, and her great eyes, staring without sight up at the rafters, as though she saw the Erinnyes perched there, rubbing their leather wings.

I almost went out of my mind, seeing the sweat stream down her thin white face, the cords of her neck tautened as though about to break, the savage jerking of her frail body, the poor pathetic markings on her thighs where the tattoo-man's needle had been in her youth.

With every moan and every screech, I thought she would surely die, and I tried to go to her: but Aegisthus, drunk and staggering as he was, held me back, half-smothering me in his evil-smelling embrace.

'Ah, be still, be still, my dove!' he laughed. 'This is as it was decreed. The Mother will look after her own!'

Even as I struggled with him and as the palace guard clustered, curious, about the chamber doors, whispering their wagers whether it would be boy or girl, my mother gave a great gasp and then, immediately, a harsh dry shout that stopped deep in her throat, such as a hard-pressed spearman makes with his final despairing thrust. Then the blue tattoo-marks over her thighs were suddenly covered with another colour, and the incubus had burst from her into the torchlight.

Aegisthus laughed hoarsely and almost broke my teeth, trying to make me drink from his wine-cup; the watching soldiers cheered and beat their swords against their bronze bucklers; old Geilissa fell on her knees, sobbing, by the bedside, while the doctor dragged at the baby as though he was a rough-handed farmer delivering a calf.

My mother's pale face seemed to shrivel to half its size and all about her closed eyes the flesh was hollow and blue. Her head fell to one side and her arms, flung out in a gesture of despair, now dangled loosely on each side of that narrow birth-bed.

I struggled in Aegisthus' grasp, but he would not let me go to her. 'Mother! Are you alive?' I called.

Her pale lips moved and she said, 'If it is a girl and lives, call her name Helen, after my poor sister.'

Then she fainted away while they were washing her twisted body.

And Aegisthus, now almost out of his mind with wine and delight, bundled me from the room with him. 'See, see,' he stammered, 'I have got a child! A child on Agamemnon's woman! The Mother is with me, after all, to let me take so sweet a vengeance on the House of Atreus!'

I was so stunned by what I had seen, I could not even protest—though, at that moment, if I could have made Poseidon the Thunderer hear me, I would have caused the ground to open and smother him, even if I had had to go down into the sulphurous blackness with him to see that vengeance was carried out.

Then I think my wits left me, for the next I remember I lay in my own bed, with Aegisthus leaning hard on me in the darkness, my flesh wet from his, his sour wine-laden breath in my nostrils.

He was gabbling, 'Now, now, Electra, be kind, lie still! Am I not of your kin now? Has a kinsman no rights in your family? Do you deny me my triumph when, by right, the red wreath should be placed about my neck?'

Struggling, I prayed: 'Mother Dia! Mother Dia! You who watch over women, show me your mercy and I will follow you all my life, I swear. I am with you against the men!'

Then the walls of the palace shuddered and the caverns below it rumbled. Dust fell out of the darkness on the bed and on my face. Aegisthus rolled away, groaning and saying, 'Is this my triumph? Am I to be treated thus? There is a pain in my stomach, daughter. Have you stabbed me?'

I lay still in the shivering dark and heard him crawl, across the tiled floor, from the room. I slept no more that night for the chattering of my teeth and the shaking of my limbs.

The new day came up, hot and sunny, with the blue sky smiling and the white birds sailing in from the sea as though the Golden Age had come again. But the Golden Age was not in my heart: there, all was smouldering darkness, as on an altar underneath the stifling thatch.

I went early to my mother's room, but the two men outside her door crossed their javelins and would not let me pass. When I commanded them, they smiled and shook their heads, and said that Aegisthus the king wished no one to enter. They professed not to know whether my mother was well, or even alive.

I went down to the kitchen, where old Geilissa cuddled me to her, calling me her lamb and her kitten and trying to make me break my fast with fresh milk and honey-cakes. But the thought of them made me want to heave and I went away outside, into the clean air.

My cousin, Hermione, was waiting for me with the Elect, sitting on their white ponies, all looking very grave and silent. They were dressed in their play-armour, but that morning I was in no mood for such game, yet there was something in me that called for me to get away from the palace and its dark memories.

I mounted and led the party, still in my shift, with my hair un-combed and no food in me. I felt I had to be off, somewhere, any-where.

We rode over the low hills that fringe the town, and so down into the green valleys where the white cottages lay scattered, here and there. Peasant-folk waved to us and shouted that it was good news, the birth of a child to Mycenae, but I did not answer. It was as though, by what I had seen that night, I had been set apart from those around me. It was almost as though I had been dedicated, by my mother's blood, to something that lay outside the knowledge of common men.

After a while, as we passed by rows of poplars, and cornfields heavy with the golden grain, past hedges, and stone walls and apple orchards, past rich pastures where oxen, goats and sheep grazed carelessly, and women in straw hats, with their skirts bunched up to their waists as they swung their sickles, Hermione pushed her mount beside mine and laid her cool brown hand upon my leg.

'They tell me the girl-child will be called Helen,' she said. 'That is my dear mother's name, Electra, but I count it no honour that a child got by Aegisthus should share it.'

We were now riding through an olive grove, where the luxuriant green leaves seemed to hold all the richness of earth in their rustling darkness. I thought of my mother, as I had last seen her, worn out and wasted, in that brooding great fortress of a palace, where Atreus' grim ghost seemed to overbear everyone and bring them to disaster.

I turned suddenly on Hermione and struck her across the face with my riding-switch. I hardly know why I did this; but perhaps it was because I thought she should have been mourning for my mother, not for her own. By good fortune, the cheek-piece of her helmet took the main force of my blow, and only the tip of the lash curled across her cheek and cut the smooth skin.

She gave a little cry and then suddenly kicked at her pony's ribs and cantered off away from me. Behind me, Orestes started to say something by way of a protest to me, but Rarus, always-gentle Rarus, quieted him and told him to mind his own affairs.

Then, later, Rarus promised my brother a pomegranate when we got back home, and Orestes was contented. He was only ten, and a simple child, it seemed to me, though as handsome as a god—a little god.

As for me, I was ashamed of what I had done to my cousin, and I pressed on after her. The rocky hillside rose again, and among the pines there, I came on a man wearing a goatskin hat and leather leggings, who told me he had seen a soldier-boy galloping and weeping in a farther valley.

We came on Hermione when the sun was above us, sitting behind a boulder, her helmet beside her, her ruddy hair tumbled about her neck, sobbing. A little way from her a shallow stream flowed clear and bubbling over the smooth, round pebbles, but she did not seem to hear its cool voice. Her own tears were water enough for her.

I got down from my white pony and kneeled beside her, smelling the sun's warmth coming off her bronze corselet. All about us the grey-green wild lavender flung up its sweet and bitter scent. The flat and cloudless sky seemed to suck up all flavour from the earth and all who walked on earth. I felt that it was sucking everything from me, like a great mouth taking away the poison from a wound, leaving all clean, leaving all featureless and mindless, careless, nothing.

Under such a healing sun, in the clean and panting heat, with the voice of cool water in my ears, and the smell of herbs in my nostrils, I began to feel reborn, remade, cleansed and changed. All my sadness and my anger had left me, and my heart was as empty of foreboding as was a stone, baking in the sunlight.

I sat beside Hermione and put my arm about her shoulder. The hard bronze burned into it, but I let it lie, as though the burning itself was a pleasure. Then I put my face beside her hot face and rubbed my cheek against the wound I had made on it, so that her blood came on me.

I even kissed this wound and tasted the salt of it.

I said, smiling, 'I have not broken my fast today, dearest.'

My cousin turned and looked at me with great wide eyes. Her tears had made little runnels through the grey dust that lay upon her cheeks, and suddenly I kissed away these marks, holding her to me, pressing at her armoured body.

She let herself lie in my arms, and smiled back up at me. 'Thank you for striking me,' she whispered. 'You taught me my place, princess. All the years my mother and my father have been away, you have cared for me, and yet I am an ungrateful thing, speaking to you as I did.'

I let my hair hang over her face, tickling her and making her eyes screw up. Then we both laughed at each other, like children with a new toy, a doll that will obey all commands, will move its limbs this way and that, a doll whose dress one may strip off, or put on, as one chooses at the moment.

Under the breathless sun, this truth came to us both so suddenly that it was like a slap across the face, but given by a smiling lover.

[140]

Behind us, I knew the two boys came up on their ponies, and as I bent over Hermione, smothering her in my hair, I heard Rarus call out, 'Come, Orestes, these girls are occupied at their game. They do not want us! Follow me along the stream; there is a cave farther down where the ancient folk set clay images. Let us find them.'

Then the thudding hooves faded from us and we only heard the crickets praising the sun in their endless chorus.

I whispered to my cousin, 'Dearest, I am straight from my bed. I must smell of the sheepskin coverlet, of the flock mattress. Lie in the shade and wait for me while I bathe.'

She nodded, sleepily, and I walked, waist-deep, in the stream, where the pebbles shelved and made a little basin. The sun had warmed the surface of the water, and it lapped about my body pleasantly; but below, about my feet and ankles, it was still as cold as though it had just come down from high Olympus when the first snows melt. A silver fish, mottled with blue, came flickering down between my outspread legs. I bent to take it in my hands, letting my tangled hair drag in the water; but the fish flicked its tail like a gay dancer and was away. Laughing, I fell back in the water and pretended to be a fish myself. From the shadow of her rock, among the lavender, Hermione watched me and clapped her hands, pleased as a child at my clowning.

Helpless to wait longer, I climbed out, all wet and shining, and went to her across the hot stones, laughing as they burned my feet, my heart thumping in me like the echo of the ponies' hooves.

As she lay cradled in my arms, Hermione smiled up and said, 'Now you smell like Aphrodite, fresh from the waves.' And I said to her, 'And you are of earth, of lavender and musk, my dear.'

And as we spoke so, there was a fluttering in my ears, as though wings were beating there, deafening me, rendering me helpless. Dazed, I saw that my cousin's face was suddenly blank, too, as though she had heard the same. A voice said, 'Man, the destroyer, the swine grunting in the straw!'

But whether she or I said this, I do not know. I can only remember that, in the purple shadow of the tall rock, we put our arms about each other, and felt the warmth of sun and earth pass through us, as the crickets carolled and the sweet and bitter herbs came at our nostrils.

For me, it was much as when I was with Rarus that night in the stable, but gentler, less of an agony, or, if an agony, a pretty one. And Hermione's smiles told me that she was of the same mind. Somehow I got pleasure from the hard pressing of her bronze corselet; its rounded edges stirred some distant memory of my father, accoutred for war, when, as a little one, he swung me up on to his shoulder. Yet I hated my father, but I loved Hermione; why did I think of him, of his armour?

I thought also of old King Nestor, with his nodding sheep's head and his shaking hands, as he stood me between his knees and told me that one day I would become the Glory of Hellas.

These dreams came and went, as sleep came and went, under the rock, with the kind sun always cleansing us, burning the fear from us, hour by hour. Together, we laughed and we wept, though our weeping was of joy, not sadness now.

Once, as the sun sank in the sky, and we paused, my cousin whispered hoarsely, 'Electra, this day I have seen the god's pattern for the first time.'

I placed my hand over her mouth to silence her, but she bit it sharply and made me draw it away. Then she said, 'We are of the one blood, Amber; our mothers are sisters and our fathers, brothers. So, we are like the leaves on one tree.'

I was feeling this, as well, as she spoke, and I whispered back to her, 'Times may change, and the world may tumble about like a drunken man, but we must always hold together, dearest. You must marry my brother, Orestes, and be his queen and my king; then we shall always be together.'

Hermione nodded and pushed back her hair so that she could see me better. 'Yes,' she said, 'that was in my heart. He is only a boy now, and I am twice his age; but he will grow, yes, he will grow; and while he is growing, I can be like a mother to him, and you and I will have each other. All the leaves on one tree share the sap that rises in the trunk; why should we not share our great love?'

As she stretched up to kiss me again, I turned my face and saw that Orestes and Rarus were standing above us, on the tall rock, gazing down on us gently and smiling, the sun behind them, making them look like young gods come down to earth to bless all men.

'What are they doing now, the silly creatures!' my brother laughed.

Rarus put his arm about Orestes' shoulders and answered, 'They are vowing to love and care for you for ever, my prince.'

Orestes flicked a small pebble down on to Hermione's body and made her wriggle with mock annoyance. He said, 'Am I not capable of looking after myself, without two great girls pestering me all the while?'

The moment was over, and there was no getting it back now. And I was hungry and sleepy after this day in the open. A small chill breeze came over the valley, making me shiver. I put on my tunic again and we went to where the ponies were standing, head to tail, sweeping the gnats away for one another.

I squeezed Hermione's hand and whispered, 'See, in all nature one creature helps the other. It is the law of god, surely.'

She put her lips to my shoulder and kissed me as a baby presses its mouth to its mother, seeking the breast. Orestes did the same to Rarus, but in mockery.

Then, laughing and singing, we mounted our ponies and set their heads back towards Mycenae, as saddle-sore after that lazy day as though we had ridden half-way across the earth.

As we came through the twilight into the last village before the town, we saw torches, and a cluster of peasant-folk bending over something that lay on the ground.

When they saw me, one of them called out, 'Lady, here is a messenger. He has run over the land all this day with his news. He is too spent to reach High Town, but one of the House of Atreus should hear his message.'

The peasant-folk drew back as I leant over the man. He was a thin-ribbed fellow, whose eyes burned darkly in his head. His feet were caked with blood from the rocks, and he wore nothing but an old deerskin clout about his middle. In the rough dialect of Argolis, he groaned up at me, 'Lady, I think I have burst my heart. It was hard going across the hills, and no water has passed my lips this day.'

I nodded curtly, knowing what these shore-folk were like, trying to screw the last ounce of reward when they carried a message inland to the city-folk, whom they thought were soft in the head.

I said to him quietly, 'I understand. Give your news and be done with it, man. We all know what it is like to suffer thirst. Give your news.'

He stared up at me as though I was a ghost. Then he began to laugh, fighting for breath. I shook him to make him speak, and even got my whip ready again, lest he needed more persuasion. But the headman of the village came behind me quite roughly and snatched the whip from my hand. I offered no resistance to this, for I knew that he was one of Aegisthus' farmer captains of the militia.

So I swallowed my pride and said more gently to the man on the ground, 'I beg you, tell your news, and there will be all the reward you deserve.'

The messenger smiled and then laid his cheek against the dusty pathway. I could hardly hear his voice, so hoarse and weary was it.

He mumbled, 'The fires have been burning all night, across the seas, from island to island, each taking up the message from the other.'

'Yes, yes,' I said, my impatience growing again.

'You say you also are thirsty,' he whispered. 'Well, there will soon be blood to drink, my lady. But who will drink it, god knows. Troy has fallen and Priam is dead. Agamemnon is back, the High King is back at last. His ships are already beached at Epidaurus, and he comes as a lamb not a lion.'

I gasped and stared about me. The peasant-folk were clustered together, like sheep when the eagle flies above their flock, shuddering.

Hermione pushed forward and took the man by the hair. 'Tell me, fellow,' she said, 'is my mother with them?'

The man began to laugh in the dust. Then he muttered, 'No,

[144]

woman. Helen is not back; nor your great father, Menelaus. The sea-god has put his jaws about them and munched them up for all the disaster they have brought on Hellas!'

She struck at him again and again with her switch, and no one stopped her now. It seemed that the peasants needed some show of violence to express the dread that lay in their hearts.

The headman spoke aloud and said, 'So, this is the moment Aegisthus trained us for, the crafty devil! Now he will send us against the veterans of Hellas, men who use the chariot and the long sword.'

He turned to the men about him, who stood wavering in the torchlight. 'Brothers,' he said, 'is this just? These hounds that Agamemnon brings back have been fighting, day by day, for ten years. They are the pick of Hellas. How can we, who are scarcely practised to shoot down a wild duck, stand against such men? We are as good as dead, I tell you!'

I could stand no more of this coward's mouthings. I flung a bead-bracelet beside the gasping messenger and we rode away. Whether he lived or died, I do not know. He was a tool to be used, no more, like a sickle or an adze. If the blades stand against their work, well enough; but if they break, then their time has come, and another tool must be got.

24

ALL the next day, the armies came through Mycenae. From the headman's words, I had thought they would be ravening wolves— yet now they seemed to me more like beaten dogs; though, to do them justice, they put on the best face they had, poor as it was. And, in a way, I even felt some sorrow for them.

Aegisthus looked like a wraith, his pale face gleaming and working all the while. He was clad in sackcloth, heavy with sweat. Since I had taken him the news the night before, he had been unable to keep any food down; and now, as we stood at the Lion Gate, he was sucking a piece of hard goat-cheese, to give his mouth something to do.

My mother leaned, gasping, between two of her women, with old Geilissa close behind her, in case she fell from the weakness of her recent child-bearing. It hurt me to see Clytemnestra hobbling down the palace steps to wait for Agamemnon, her hair all wild and tangled, her dress hastily put on and dragging behind at the hem, her feet as bare and horny as any field-woman's. Yet, for all her weakness and rags, her constant coughing and clutching at her side, she looked a queen. Not a rich queen of a prosperous land, but a Queen of Despair—one elected by the Furies to represent them on earth, one of Night's Daughters.

I stood with Hermione and Orestes, behind Geilissa. My brother had put on his armour, in spite of my warning that he should not do so, and was telling anyone who would listen that today the two Agamemnons were to meet for the first time. He had no memory of his father, poor lad.

Time and again, I saw Aegisthus glance over his shoulder angrily as Orestes said these things; but there, in public, Aegisthus could not stop the boy's mouth.

A ragged group of Laconians came through the gate, driving a flock of sheep before them, and leading milch-cows on rope halters. The men's ribs stood from their blackened skin, and most of them still wore brown-crusted bandages about arms or legs. Some of them hobbled as best they could on wooden crutches, their feet bound with rags. Few of them had armour worth calling by that name; but every man carried a sword, however hacked, and every man made a great show of smiling and smoothing his hair as he came into public view.

Despite themselves, the Mycenaeans roared to see them, and the Laconians moved on towards the taverns of the market-place, looking neither to left nor to right, as though they had noticed nothing strange about their welcome. One peasant-farmer near to the royal party called out, 'What of King Menelaus? And his queen?'

The Laconian captain, a grey-haired old fellow with his arm strapped to his side, threw back his head and bawled at the sky, 'He'll be back, if the Egyptians leave him feet to walk on. If not, she'll carry him! They have wed again, the fools!'

They said no more, but went on among the crowd, beating a path for themselves by sweeping out the ash-shafts of javelins to make men give way.

A company of Corinthians came next, sitting on carts and playing flutes and lyres. One of them led a leopard on a chain, fondling the frightened beast as he went, his arms covered with scratches. When one of their treasure sacks fell from the cart, the Mycenaeans saw that it contained nothing but sand and sea-shells. The Corinthian who dropped it just laughed and called out, 'You want a show, and we give it to you! But it's your king who brings back all the booty —Agamemnon is the fellow for loot!'

Aegisthus' face grew calmer and calmer, as though, having seen what the returning army was like, his own fear had shrunk. I saw him lean towards my mother and heard him say behind his hand, 'My New Army is stationed all about the city, and in many houses within the walls. But, my dear, I hardly think we shall need them. If we let this tattered tribe drink their fill, they will be on their way by dawn, only too glad to see their homes again.'

Clytemnestra nodded to him, but did not speak. Her hand was at her side, as though she was in pain. Her breathing among the dust set up by feet and hooves and wagon-wheels was harsh and grating. I longed to be beside her, to hold her hand and comfort her. But there was no time for that. A herald standing a little way along the rocky road that led to the Lion Gate suddenly shouted out, 'He comes! The High King of Achaea comes! Make way for Agamemnon!'

It had been ten years since I last saw my father, and I do not know now what I expected to see that day—a rich prince? A god? Or a man raised from the dead?

[147]

I think it must have been the last, for, as in a dream, I saw this man standing on a broken cart and knew him at once, though he was like no king that the world had ever seen before. The hair had gone from his brown and wrinkled head; his beard, that had once been his lion's pride, was but a few thin hairs that blew about in the wind on our upland rocks; his nose had shrunk until it looked a bird's beak, above which his filmed grey eyes gazed, like those of a time-less mariner who must search for some lost coast-line to eternity, blinding himself.

I saw his shoulder-bones almost poking up through his salt-caked hide; the grizzled mat of grey hairs that shrouded his body from throat to waist; the palsied twitching of his great hands on the reins —and I thought: Is this the man I hate? Is this the man who has brought fear and agony to Hellas, to my family?

As the late sun struck down between two pillars on to him, I saw Agamemnon clearly for the first time in my life. He was nothing but a blind old man, a dreamer who had lost his dream, a warrior no longer strong enough to shake a sword. This was the High King of Achaea.

And I looked at my mother, and she was an old woman; no longer beautiful, noble only in name, a gasping creature leaning on a grey stone wall and trying to remember the fire, the rage of youth.

Put the two of them together, out on the road to Delphi, and any peasant would throw an offering of bread to them; no farmer with two acres to his name would stand aside to let them pass. . . .

Then all at once I heard my mother call, 'There she is, the Trojan's daughter. There is his woman and her children!'

Sitting behind Agamemnon in the cart was a girl about my own age, a soiled grey cloth over her black hair, like a head-dress, and a torn robe of wool bound roughly round her body with hide thongs. At her thin breast she suckled one baby; at her side stood a pale, grey-eyed boy, his slack mouth open and the moisture dribbling from it on to his torn shirt.

Aegisthus had time to sneer and say, 'So, this is Cassandra, who foretells the future—if only she could get anyone to listen to her!

In truth, King Priam must have been a crofter-king, some jumped-up peasant, to father such kin!'

Then King Agamemnon came within hearing distance, and all the folk looked to us to give him the proper greeting. I glanced at my brother in his armour, and saw the tears welling in his eyes that this old scarecrow should be his father. Hermione put her arms about him and tried to console him, but he shook her away rudely.

Then Clytemnestra went forward with difficulty, leaning on her handmaids, and stopped in front of the two oxen that dragged the High King's cart.

Somehow she found strength to call in a high, clear voice, 'Greetings, Lion of Hellas! We of your House come out to meet you. How went the war in Troy, my lord?'

Agamemnon bent his head, as though it was painful for him to move his neck, and stared like a man trying to see through a heavy mist. His blank grey eyes wavered for a while, then seemed to find my mother. He held out his hands widely, in the ritual gesture, and said, 'Some died on either side, my wife. But in the end the god gave us the victory and the honour. We return with tribute and in peace.'

Neither of them made reference to Cassandra or to Aegisthus; but Clytemnestra took the head-band of the ox nearest to her and made the motion of leading the cart up towards the palace. As she went, each step a penance, her handmaids close behind her lest she fell, Orestes and I walked at the tail of the cart in silence. Our father half-turned and saw us, his mouth twitching and his brows moving up and down, like a very old man who is beating his brains to remember, but cannot.

I saw that he had forgotten who we were, and this gave me no pain at all. I only wished that Agamemnon had died in the outland, under the Trojan walls—then we could have hated him as much as we chose, but we should have been forced to remember him with respect. Now, he was nothing, a man more valued in death than in this poor life he dragged about on his bent back.

As we went, a great hush fell on the crowd; then, when we were some distance away, a deep, rumbling laughter rose, as though all the poor folk now saw that they were the great ones, not Agamemnon, that they were free at last, and he a broken prisoner to a dream.

Then, up the hill came the Thebans, with the Ithacan contingent who had lost their king and were singing the most lewd and disrespectful ballads about him. The crowd turned away from us, and I was glad.

When we reached the palace steps, Clytemnestra held out her hand to help Agamemnon down, as was her wifely duty; but he had great trouble in making his legs do what he wished, and in the end he almost tumbled from the cart into the dust. The line of Cretan guards upon the steps began to smile at this, at first behind their hands, then quite openly. But my father did not seem to hear them. He turned towards Cassandra and said, 'There is that to do, inside, my dear. Soon they will bid you to the feast. They will treat you well, have no fear.'

As he spoke, the girl buried her face in her hands and began to moan, the baby at her breast forgotten. The boy beside her in the cart moved forward and took the child gently in his own thin hands.

I was standing beside my mother when this happened. Her face was like an ivory mask of tragedy, so wide were her eyes, so twisted down the corners of her gaping mouth. It was as though she tried to weep, but no tears would come.

She whispered to me, as Agamemnon mounted the long flight of steps, 'Oh god, Electra, I cannot do it now that the time has come. He has paid already, daughter. I cannot do it, I tell you. It rests with you now!'

Then Agamemnon stopped, his hand over his heart, breathing heavily and waving his head about, seeking my mother. 'Where is the Amber Princess?' he asked, in his dry old voice. 'Where is my little girl-thing then? I thought she would be the first to greet me when I came back to my house.'

I wanted to turn and race down the long stairway. I was ashamed of myself, of him, of the very world itself. But I dared not run away, and I dared not go to him now.

Clytemnestra stood beside him and said, 'She is resting, Great One. She will soon come to see you, to show you her new corn doll.'

She spoke to him as though he was a simpleton, and he nodded and smiled towards her. 'I thank you, lady,' he said. 'These little girls must have their rest, and their dolls, if they are to grow up in healthy contentment. A child of eleven needs her rest. Sleep puts roses in the cheeks and starlight in the eyes. One day, my Amber girl shall marry a great. . . .'

He broke off then and sat down on a carved stone lion that stood against the balustrade, sighing and trying to get his breath.

'I had a son. Oh, years ago. He must be dead and in the tomb now. Orestes, they called him. By the god, but time flies! I can only picture him as a baby. . . . A baby, tottering from stool to stool, with the milk round his mouth. It is all most strange. Surely, he was a great warrior?'

He pursed his lips and then began to cough. A small patch of red showed suddenly on his cheekbones and a vein throbbed under the parchment skin of his forehead.

He ran his knotted fingers over the carved mane of the stone lion and said all at once, 'On one of the islands we called at—I forget—Cassandra would tell you—close by Leros, I think, or just south of Delos—one of those places—'

His voice faded away, and he began to look round to find the stone lion's tail. Clytemnestra stood over him and said gently, 'What was this you saw, on the island, High King?'

Agamemnon looked up at her with a blank face, as though he had never seen her in his life before. He answered slowly, 'Why, a tortoise, lady. Bigger than a bull, and older than Zeus, they said on the island. I saw three men sit on his shell and go riding. The sound of his eating at midday was like lightning crackling. No, not lightning. Like a herd of wild cows rushing through brushwood. No, not like that either. Like. . . .'

He got up and said, 'Why do you keep me with such foolish talk, woman? Where is the bath-house in this place? Hey, where is the bath-house? I am weary from my journey. Lead me there, I command you.'

The queen, my mother, nodded to old Geilissa to take Agamemnon where he had said. He went with her quietly, not raising his voice again. And, as they entered into the great hall, my mother turned to me and said, 'Well, Electra, now there is no other way. You heard him ask for the bath-house? That is as the omens have foretold—he has asked his way to his death-place. What can we do now but let his pattern run on to the end?'

She spoke so quietly, almost with tenderness, that there, in the sun on the high steps of the palace, I could see no other way, though I tried my hardest to find one, I swear.

I said, 'But I cannot do it, mother. Now that he asks for it, I cannot do it. Yesterday, last month, any other time, and I would have gloried in it—but now all that has gone.'

She leaned against the stone lion and nodded. 'I am the same, my love,' she whispered. 'Yet it must be done. You see he is the husk of a man, he is as good as dead already. Tomorrow, or the next day, another will put an end to him—or worse, will drag him off as a hostage to some place where we shall never find him. Better to put him out of his misery now; then we shall know his end.'

I said, 'Very well; what am I to do?' There was nothing else to say.

Clytemnestra answered in a still, dead voice, 'Go into the bath-house when he is ready and wrap the towel round him, as though you are a servant-girl sent to dry him. But, I beg you, see that the cloth goes round his arms, not under them. This must be done quickly, with no fuss. I do not think I could carry out the task if he broke away and tried to save himself. Take one of the strong new towels, not the old threadbare ones.'

I shook the tears from my eyes. 'I will do as you say, mother,' I told her. 'But first there is one other thing I must see to.'

She began to hobble on up the stairs, her hand at her breast as though her milk pained her. 'Hurry, Electra,' she called back, 'I feel that we have not much time before us.'

As I ran down the steps to where Agamemnon's cart still waited, I knew what I must do; I must try to get the poor creature, Cassandra, away from our palace. Otherwise, with Agamemnon, her protector, gone, she and her defenceless children would become prey to any soldier roaming wild with a knife.

She was kneeling in the cart, cradling the baby, and singing to it in a wordless crooning chant. The thin-faced boy stood watching beside her, as simple as a young calf, his great eyes wide and thoughtless.

I had to call to her three times before she turned and heard me. 'Go away, woman,' I said. 'Lash your oxen away from here. Go with the Laconians, they will care for you.'

She smiled down on me as though I had gone mad. 'But I must be with my husband, the king,' she said. 'Do you not know, I have come all the way from Troy to be here with him at his triumph.'

I shook her by the arm. 'Go,' I cried again. 'He is not your husband, and there will be no triumph.' Then, shocked by her empty gaze and the trembling of her lips, I said, 'If you will not go, then follow me inside this palace. There is a room I can hide you in, that few know about.'

But now she began to tear her hair and beat at her thin breast, wailing for all to hear. 'No! No! I will not come inside that house of death, that tall tomb! I smell blood within it—blood on the walls, blood on the rafters, blood across the floor! I cannot enter!'

So she fell from the cart, the froth at her lips, her arms and legs flailing, her back arching like that of a woman in a birth-spasm. The boy on the cart took up the crying baby and held it to his bare chest, as though he had food for it.

'Go away,' he said to me, 'you have made my mother weep. That is not a kind greeting! We are of a kingly house and deserve better.'

I almost struck the poor wretch across the face. I began to call him a fool and his mother a mad-woman—until I realised that this was just what they were. Then, helpless and ashamed, I swung away from them and ran back up the stairway to be in time for what I had to do.

25

THE bards have lied, singing of a huge king, lion-wrathful, clenching his great fist at fate, roaring his death-defiance as the bloody water lapped about his legs, shaking the walls with his bellowing, Great Bull, Brother to Poseidon, Zeus' Twin, Earth Rattler, the Mighty, Most Heinous in Battle, the Flamer, the Mountain Master!

They have sung that foxes ran to their burrows at the dread din; that wolves rolled in the dust to stop their ears; that eagles flew from the howling so high that the sun left them only a cloud of charred feathers in the evening sky.

They have sung that the strings of every lyre in Hellas snapped as the blow was struck; that all the mothers' milk lay curdled in the breast and the babes unfed for days; that tombs blew open and bones were scattered half-way to Hyperborea; that the moon pulled a cloth across her face, and let fall tears of silver.

But it was not like that when I was in the bath-house.

Steam made the air heavy, and the serving-women moved through it like ghosts, pouring in water and more water from wooden buckets. When I sent them away, they bowed and did not speak. They saw the thick towel in my hands and knew what I had come for. That towel was of the sacred fleece, the Kin-sign of all the House of Atreus.

It was a while before I saw him, lolling in the deep bath, swishing the water between his thighs like a little boy. He could not see me bending over him for the steam, or for his half-blind eyes, I know not which.

I said softly, 'Rise, High King. I have come to put the cloth about you.'

Agamemnon stared down at the water and said, 'I am not such a fool that I do not know why you have come, Electra.'

Then, as I stood, shocked, he smiled at me and whispered. 'I shall

[154]

give you no trouble, my dear. I know the rite; I rise, I place one foot on dry land, one in water, and so I stand until the axe falls. Is it still the axe in Mycenae, Electra? So many other things seem to have changed.'

I nodded down at him and said, 'It is still the axe, sir.'

He splashed the water with his hands a little while, then he said, 'You have not mentioned Iphigenia, my dear. I thought you would speak of her at this time.'

When he said this, so simply, I knew that I wished him dead again, although I had felt such pity for him on the palace steps in the sunlight.

I said shortly, 'Rise, sir, I am waiting.'

My heart was smacking at my ribs. I was listening for Clytemnestra to come along the passage-way so that all might be done according to the custom. Agamemnon was listening, too. As he rose, with some difficulty, he said, 'She is keeping us waiting, Amber! It was always her way. But she does not look so well, does she, daughter? Is she sick?'

I was angry and afraid, the thick mist of steam in the bath-house half-choked me. My shift was sodden and clung to me, chilling my body, though my face burned as if I stood before a furnace.

I almost shouted, 'Will you come out, or must I fetch you, sir?'

Agamemnon looked at me with wrinkled eyelids, and even smiled. 'It is strange,' he said, as though to himself, 'but I have stood where arrows hailed and spears thudded, where horses reared and swords crashed down, for ten long years—yet I do not recall ever being so afraid as I am now, my daughter. Perhaps it is true what Achilles once said, that I have the face of a hound, but the heart of a deer!'

It was as he was saying this, and clambering out from the deep bath, that dark shapes moved in the steam. I heard Agamemnon give a little intake of the breath, as though he was about to sneeze, then, as I wrapped the woollen cloth about him, I saw it grow suddenly bright with blood. He slipped a little way into my arms, so that I had to support his weight, sitting on the lip of the bath.

[155]

Yet it was small weight enough; he was as light as a child, for all his great frame and the grizzled pelt of his body.

He coughed twice, then turned his head up sideways and fixed me with his flinty grey eye. 'It was not my doing—Iphigenia,' he said. 'It was the priest Calchas, and goatherd Aegisthus. They shed her blood.'

As he spoke, the red kept coming from him, down on to my lap and over my breast, in great spurts. Now there were two dark shapes in the steamy chamber. I could scarcely breathe for the water and the blood. I was glad, at last, when I saw my mother come out of the mist and strike down twice with the stone axe we kept above the Hearth Shrine.

Then we were left together, weeping, and the king limp between us, and the door wide open with the steam gushing out into the sunlit corridor.

I remember saying, 'Let us lay him down and catch the one who has escaped. It is he who is our quarry now.'

We ran, weak as we both were now, like hounds. There was uproar about the palace rooms, but we paid it no heed. Once, as we passed the long window above the high stairs, I glanced down and saw three soldiers haggling with their swords at Cassandra as she lay on the ground helpless. The thin boy was still clutching the baby to him, though a javelin-point stood out from him. Before he had gone from view, I saw him kneel down and lie across his mother, as though protecting her.

But at that moment I saw the edge of Aegisthus' tattered robe disappearing through the small door that led up to the battlements. We howled again, the queen and I, then went on after him like Furies.

He was too spent to reach the higher platform, but sat on the dark narrow steps, holding his head in his hands. The murder knife with the copper blade and the ivory handle lay at his feet.

'See,' he called down to us, 'I have laid down the knife, which proves I mean you no harm, my dears! And I do not try to escape from you, you understand. I sit and wait for you, because I adore you both, my wife and my daughter. See?'

[156]

I think we should have torn him to pieces then, but as we mounted the steps together, my mother suddenly groaned and fell sideways. A trickle came from her mouth's corner, and her breathing was harsh and hard.

She said, 'Go on, Electra, put an end to him. My time is near, any-way! We have each served our purpose, he and I—and Agamemnon.'

But all at once I was as cool and steady as a great oak. I had seen the awful fear that Aegisthus had for me, and I knew that, from this time on, I was his master and he my frightened slave. I bent to lift Clytemnestra and carry her downstairs again to her waiting-women. I said to her, 'All is well, mother. He can wait. I know where to get him now, whenever I want him.'

As we reached the floor below, he was still crying on the dark steps, like a child afraid in the night.

26

MY memory is at its tricks again, doctor. Time eludes me like a sly little water-snake. Now it is here: now it is there! Always slithering through the hand that tries to grasp it.

Sometimes, as I try to recall what happened, a single day will stretch out until it seems to have been a year—and, then again, five years will shrink, like badly-dressed cloth, until they seem like one afternoon. . . .

What I have told you of the bath-house must have been a great shock to my mind—like a blow taken lightly in the full flood of battle, but which leaves a man crippled for the rest of his days. And I say this in spite of all my coolness when I had Aegisthus in my power on the stairway.

Much is still unknown to me of that day, and many others which followed it. But I do recall that I shouted for the old nurse, Geilissa, and was told that she had gone from the palace. I thought little of this at the time for I was occupied in getting my mother to her bed. Two handmaidens helped me in this, and after our palace doctor had given the queen a draught to stop her raving, I went in search of Orestes and the others.

Rarus met me in the feast-hall, his face white, his fingers picking at the neck of his tunic. I had to laugh at him, despite myself.

'What,' I said, 'am I so much a Fury that you fall on your knees and cannot keep your mouth still, like this?'

'Princess,' he answered, 'I am left behind to bear the bad news to you. Old Geilissa feared that once the town had tasted blood again, all the House of Atreus would be slaughtered. She has gone away with your brother, and Hermione, and Chrysothemis.'

I put my hands in his shock of black hair and shook his head savagely: that was the mood I was in, as changeable as the wind.

'Gone away? How could an old woman go away, with three big creatures like them? How could they even get away, with the city, and the countryside about it, swarming with soldiers? Answer me!'

Rarus lowered his eyes and said, 'There was a soldier, I did not learn his name, but he was a captain in Aegisthus' New Army—I saw that much. He bundled them all together, after you went with the queen and the dead king up the stairway, and told them their lives were in danger. He had horses waiting for them behind the great byre, and a handful of soldiers to escort them. They rode off without a word. I stayed behind to tell you this. I could have gone, also, my lady.'

I flung him to the floor in my fury and stormed over him, trying to put my heel in his face.

'What!' I shouted. 'You could have gone, also! You, a creature no better than a dog, to ride with kings! And now lie here to torment me! Where have they gone? Out with it or, I swear, I'll have you hung from an apple-tree and stoned!'

Rarus now lay flat on his back, his face resigned and still, which put me off. I am capable of doing many things, doctor, if my blood is up and men contest me: but if they are passive I do not find it easy to hurt them. This weakness has been with me all my days, you understand. Later, when I became the Goddess in the palace, I often found it more than I could do to draw the knife across the throat of a quiet lamb, or strike a cud-chewing bullock with the axe. But if they kicked and struggled, or swung their horns at me, then it was different, easier.

So now I held back from hurting Rarus any more and said, 'Where have they gone, old friend? Forget what I have just said and tell me, quietly, and without fear.'

He still gazed up at me, never moving, his face a mask I had not seen before. Gravely he answered. 'I have never feared you before, princess, but now I shall be cautious of you for ever. Yet I cannot tell you where they went, whatever you do to me, for I do not know. They rode away, kicking their horses' sides, as though they meant to reach the end of the world before sunset. That is all I know.'

I turned from him then, without another word, and went to seek Aegisthus. It was clear in my heart that he had put his soldiers up to this—to get my kinsfolk away, and then have them murdered in some quiet place, so as to wipe out our House and let Thyestes triumph in the end.

I found him in the small armoury at the far end of the megaron. He was sitting on a sword-chest, surrounded by soldiers of his New Army. A young lieutenant was holding a wine-cup at my step-father's quivering lips.

When I went in with my hair flying and the silver droplets on the flounces of my skirt clashing together, they all turned round and stared at me, holding their breath. The lieutenant let the wine-cup fall, as though his hands had lost their use. They all had javelins or short stabbing-spears, but none of them made any move to attack me.

Aegisthus was slobbering as though he saw a ghost. The red wine was coming back out of his mouth and wetting his chin. He made a great effort and held out both his hands towards me, then, just as suddenly, let them fall on his lap again.

Now I stood less than two paces from them, well in range for a thrusting spear. But, though the skin of my back was prickling and a vein in my neck thrumming like a little harp, I stayed very still and said, 'Well, where are they, my brother and sister? Out with it, goat!'

If Aegisthus could have given the sign for one of his javelin-men to make a cast at that moment, all his troubles with me would have been over, and I would have had no power to prevent it. Instead, they gazed at me like frightened sheep, or like timid beasts of the woods, ready to scatter and run if I but clapped my hands.

As I sensed this, the warmth of power rose again from the deepest part of my body, then mounted until it filled my head with fire. There was a feeling as though the strings of a purse were being drawn tight, to keep the power in, to let it build and build before it should burst forth in fury. I felt my mouth opening stiffly, as though a curse was forming itself on my tongue and making ready to break out. I felt my eyes widening until their lids could hardly contain them, as though in a moment lightning would flash from them to destroy all that lay within their vision. I was almost blind with this power.

Then Aegisthus had slithered down from the chest and was at my feet, stretching to hold my ankles in supplication. I kicked him away, and felt my hard heel strike the flesh of his face.

There was a clattering about me in that small room and, for an instant, I expected a spear to enter me. But it was not that: the soldiers had flung down their weapons, and now all knelt before me, their black heads bowed.

Aegisthus was saying, 'Mother Dia, Mother Dia, oh, deal gently with your servants!'

The soldiers took up this prayer. 'Mother Dia, who are come again on earth, have mercy, we beseech you!'

Now, as the godhead ran through my heart and my bowels, like scalding water that suddenly turned to ice, I felt my face set and stiffen into a bone mask. My hands went up in the ritual to cup my breasts, like the images of the goddess that the old Cretans made at

Cnossus. Even the damp hair about my face and neck seemed to move, as though a cold reptile life had come into it without my knowing.

I stood there so long, in my new dream, that I thought my heart had stopped beating and that I had truly become a statue at last. I only knew that time had passed because, little by little, I heard the men who lay before me start to groan as their joints and muscles stiffened on the cold paved floor.

With a great effort I made myself say at last, 'Where are my kin, Aegisthus?'

He did not look at me when he answered, 'Goddess, I do not know. I swear on your sacred shrines, I do not know. It was no doing of mine. This I swear, or may you lay me on the altar at the next festival.'

Although I now both hated and despised this creature, I felt that he was speaking the truth. I turned from them stiffly and went away. They did not even whisper until I had passed the door.

When I entered my mother's bed-chamber, the women fell before me. Even Clytemnestra looked up at me as though she would rather have shrunk back through the bedding. I placed my chilly hand upon her forehead and said, 'All will be well now, queen of Mycenae. Your children have gone away, but one day they shall be found again. Now sleep, and from this time forward, shut your door to Aegisthus, who is a king here only because I permit it. I do not permit him to be your husband in anything but an empty name.'

Clytemnestra said slowly, 'Lady, you have become—her!'

It was as though she saw me for the first time. I nodded quietly. Then I said, 'You shall be well again. You shall be the queen here and none shall gainsay your commands. But I am the queen behind the queen, the shadow that will keep you where you are. If a man's shadow goes, that is the end of him; there can be no man where there is no shadow.'

The queen smiled up at me and nodded. Then she said, 'Now that you are what you are, lady, I am content at last. The pattern is making itself known and we are secure in the hand of the god. But, tell me, lady, did we do right in putting an end to Agamemnon? It is all that troubles me now.'

I looked away from her and said, 'Our hands are clean of blood-guilt, queen of Mycenae. I put the towel about him to dry him; you laid the axe on his neck after he was dead. The one who must carry the burden for the rest of his days is the man who came in between the folding of the towel and the falling of the axe. The man who put the ivory-handled knife into Agamemnon's heart, with us powerless to stop it, among the steam.'

She reached out, hesitantly, and touched my garnet-studded girdle, as though for a token of good fortune.

Then she said, 'My heart is at rest, now, lady. What is next to do?'

I laughed within myself at this, for now I was truly queen in Mycenae, although my mother bore the title. And I said, 'First, we shall raise a tomb to Agamemnon's glory. Then, all the world will know that we are guiltless. Next, we shall so train Aegisthus to do our bidding that he shall seem little more than one of those dancing bears the Phoenicians lead about with them to attract the crowds in market-places. That will not be hard, for he is a man without an army now; they look to me as their goddess who will bring them fortune or disaster, as I please. And, last, when the time is ripe, we shall bring back Orestes to this kingdom and set him on the throne, with Hermione as his queen, in our good time. So our House will be safe to the end of the days.'

My mother sank back in her bed, smiling, as though she was well satisfied.

But one of the serving-women ran forward and bowed before me. 'One question, goddess,' she said, her head lowered. 'What is to become of the baby, Helen, who is of Aegisthus' getting? Is she to be kept, or put out on the hillside for the beasts to take?'

I glanced at my mother, thinking she might have a feeling about this, one way or the other, for after all this child had come from her own body. But her eyes were closed and she was smiling up at the rafters as she had done before.

I turned and said coldly to the woman, 'Ask no more. That will arrange itself in good time. It is not your affair. Do as you are bidden, the burden is on other shoulders.'

So I went away to the Hearth Shrine, whose new mistress I became. There was silence in the palace wherever I walked; men fell before me; women covered their faces with their skirts.

This it was, then, to be a goddess. All I regretted now was that my dear lover, Hermione, was lost to me at that moment. How we might have celebrated, secret in the Shrine! But one day, I thought, yes, one day—and when that day comes, what gifts I shall have to offer her!

27

AFTER the bright-eyed young heralds had called from every rooftop that the goddess had come again to Mycenae, and all the dark-haired folk had rejoiced, the sewing-women of the palace began making my garments, under my mother's supervision.

They sat about, round her bedside, with the rolls of stuff by their stools, and the gold wire looped over sticks, their bone needles twinkling, their fingers pinching in the cloth, flaring it out, stiffening it with cow's hoof glue, and so on.

I did not understand half of what went on, doctor; I was only required to be present, lounging about unclothed, waiting to have this fitted, that tried on, the other altered.

We of the House of Atreus had never dressed extravagantly, and, to tell the truth, my sisters and I had often run about as ragged as the daughters of any hill-farmer; but now I was being garbed royally for the first time.

The sewing-women gloried in dressing a goddess after all these years, and took their patterns from little images of glazed and painted clay that their forefathers had brought across from Crete. They made me a full skirt, of wool dyed red with sea-creatures, and made heavy with six frills, or flounces, of gold wire, one rising upon the other, just as the roofs of Babylon once did. It was a glorious skirt, though it almost killed me to squeeze into its waist—I could hardly breathe, the women made it so tight! One of them, a big-chested girl from Phaestos, whispered, 'You must eat less, goddess, if you wish to wear this one!' I could have pulled her thick black hair!

Among the flounces, they sewed alternate droplets of silver, of ivory, and of amber; so that, by swinging my hips a little as I walked, I could hear them all clash together as though a small army was on the march, beating cymbals. Since I was permitted to wear nothing on my feet, but only have my heels and toes painted, my coming into a room was unannounced, save for the clashing of my skirt. When I wanted to surprise anyone, I would hold the skirt up to my knees, heavy as it was, and only let it fall when I was almost on them. I frightened half the palace guard to death that way.

But I overrun myself, doctor. I must tell of the rest. The husband of one of the sewing-women, a goldsmith, made me an apron-stomacher. It pinched my middle so fiercely that at first I fainted, getting into it, but this wore off, and I loved this thing more than any other garment I had. It fell down at front and back in great ovals of beaten gold, and was studded round its edges with emeralds. Within the edging, the smith had scored criss-cross lines, on the bias, to give it pattern.

Clytemnestra watched this stomacher being fitted the first time and said slyly, though she was very ill at the time, 'Now, daughter, here's an end to any careless dallying. This girdle will make a young man think twice before he approaches you!'

I smiled within myself, because my heart was set on no young man; Hermione, when I found her again, would know the answer to this golden stomacher. But I said nothing at the time; I only smiled, to humour my sick mother, and made some comment about goddesses having to drink less than mortals.

[164]

Then, above the golden girdle, and intended to push my breasts out to their fullest, the women made me a short corselet of stiffened leather, that came up to a peak in the middle, and was tooled about its surface with sea-shells and acanthus leaves. It was dyed red, like my skirt, and was very pretty; but, oh, the agony of wearing it on hot days! It rubbed me almost raw, until my body hardened to its strong embrace.

They also made me a dark blue jacket, with sleeves that barely reached the elbows. This was a welcome thing to wear, for it lay open at the front, and let the cool airs blow on me above the leather corselet. It was of the finest Egyptian silk and, in a shower, turned the water as easily as a turtle's shell. Its colour was to represent the sky; just as my flounced skirt was red for the wine-dark sea, and also for the blood of Man. My stomacher was the Treasure of Earth, all gold, that garnished the inner darkness.

I think I looked well in these things, especially as the hairdressers had trained my long locks to hang like snakes over my shoulders, my breast and my back, all oiled and crimped into ringlets, and bound here and there with little bronze rings set with pearls, the Tribute of the Sea, of Aphrodite.

On feast days I wore a tower-hat made of starched linen, and covered with silver sequins. It was round, and rose in three tiers over my head, getting smaller all the while, until at the crown it was but a palm's breadth. To match this silver hat, I started the custom of wearing silver bracelets about my arms and ankles, fashioned like snakes, with eyes of amber chips.

Many of the great ladies of Hellas took this up after I had been seen in them at one out-door gathering; though, naturally, however rich they were, they did not dare exceed my own bracelets in size, which was very big.

About my throat, at shoulder level, I wore a hoop of copper, inlaid with silver. No lady tried to copy this, because it was so uncomfortable. But I wore it to create a difference, to make them realise that they and I were of different worlds. My mother used often to say that it would throttle me, but I laughed and said, 'Was

[165]

there ever a goddess who died strangled? Name me one, mother. Go on, name me one.' She could not—so I went on wearing the collar.

When the feast days were gay, and not for sacrifice, I also wore a set of ancient Cretan seals at my throat and wrists—small amethyst ones, of bulls and dancers and palm trees, that kept up a symphony of sound with the droplets on my skirts, as I moved this way and that, in the slow dancing.

I tell you, doctor, I got to be so used to being a goddess that I would often stand on the low altar above the Shrine to Hestia, among the sea-shells, and before the marble cross, for hours at a stretch. I learned how to set my painted feet so as to take my weight, then I bowed my head, shut my eyes, let my long hair dangle, and cupped my breasts in my two hands. And this way I could stand still, hardly breathing, until even the watchers grew tired and moved away to their meals or their field-tasks.

Once Aegisthus came to see me at this, after he had been drinking. He had four companions with him, all heavy with wine and half-hoping to make a jest of the new goddess. Had they been sober, they would not have dared. But, this hot afternoon, their senses were a little over the hills. I could see this, squinting at them under my lids, as they entered the Hearth Shrine.

They stood swaying for a while, giggling and trying to make me break my silence and laugh with them. But I set my mind on Hermione among the hot lavender, and they could not break through the walls of that dream.

Aegisthus came forward at last, showing off to his fellows, and took the lowest flounce of my skirt, though hesitantly I noticed.

'See, mates,' he said, 'no lightning has struck me yet!'

Then he began to raise my skirt, to show my legs. 'Look,' he called again, 'we have got as far as the knee and the goddess has held her hand. Let us go farther, and find out if there is anything to be afraid of!'

I felt his hand and smelled his over-sweet, wine-laden breath. It sickened me to have this man exposing me, to bolster up his cowardice before his friends; but for the moment I could do nothing, having no weapons in my hand and no guards about me. He was doing it all so slowly, so deliberately, although his fat hand shook and made my ornaments chatter against each other like hissing serpents.

There came a moment when I was almost afraid myself, and when I heard the watchers beginning to cry out in mockery. Just then, I think the Mother must have spoken to me, in her strange way, for out in the pastures I heard the deep bellowing of a bull. The sound came to my ears like a message.

I said in as low and steady a voice as I could find, 'The king is brave. We all see that his courage lets him unveil what should be hidden. Only the bravest man may do thus. He has shown that he is the master of the goddess, has he not?'

They all began to cheer then and slap one another on the back. Aegisthus thought very well of himself and was about to go farther, when I said, 'Now he must take the next step, to prove himself. Will he do that?'

'Yes! Yes!' he bawled, thinking something different from what was in my mind.

'Very well,' I said, so that all should hear, 'I call on you men as witnesses. King Aegisthus shall dance with Poseidon's bull this afternoon—then no one can deny him anything, for he will have shown his mastery both over goddess and god!'

The drunken companions roared with delight at this turn of the game, not realising the gravity of it all. But Aegisthus saw well enough how the dice had fallen, and he shrank back, wanting to withdraw, but fearing to lose face with his friends.

He waved them away at last, then came to me humbly and whispered, 'For the god's sake, Electra, release me from this thing. I am too old for that sport; look, I am fat and out of condition. That black devil will hurt me.'

I still stood upon the altar, but now I let myself smile as I said, 'What, the Kin of Thyestes frightened of a little sun-dance! I should be ashamed of you, King of Mycenae, if I did not know you jested.'

He knew what was in my heart and left the shrine-room, beating his hands on his head. When I told my sick mother about this, she looked at me calmly and said, 'So, you have decided which way he shall end at last. Now I see that you have outgrown any advice I can give you. I was never so well able to manage men as you are, at your age, or any other age, for that matter.'

I kissed her thin hands and said, 'That is because men are nothing to me, dearest. They are no more than the little tortoises that wicked boys catch on the shore and switch the heads off with willow wands.'

Clytemnestra held me to her and whispered, 'You love your girl cousin, don't you, daughter?'

I nodded but did not speak. I was crying in my heart for sweet Hermione, and there was no language to describe such a yearning.

At last the queen said, 'One day, soon, you must make the journey to Delphi to ask Apollo where Hermione may be. I cannot have you waste away with longing, if it is within our power to bring your lover back to you.'

I went from her bedside then and walked out to see the bull-ring made ready for the afternoon's games, for this was the Festival of Europa, to mark the day when the god became a black bull and swam across to Crete with the daughter of Egyptian Agenor. Usually, at this festival, a dark-skinned girl danced with the bull, but this day I had Aegisthus garbed like a girl, and had the women put a black wig over his bald head.

He came out trembling with fear and drink, into the hot day, and was straightaway swept off his feet by young men and carried to the dancing-pit. I must describe this pit, doctor, because you will see the meaning of it all the better for my words.

28

OUR dancing-pit or bull-ring was more ancient than the city itself. The first of the first-folk had used it, our poets said, and they called it the Womb of Hera, because of its shape. It lay in a narrow little valley that sloped steeply at the back of the palace, and was hardly more than a basin of rock, whose sides fell almost straight down, and then came together more gradually, to form a flat base. This base, or bull-dancing floor, was no more than five paces across, which gave little room for dancer or bull when the pace got furious.

Once this basin had been all rock, like the hills that rose about it, like the palace itself, which grew from the rock and was part of the rock; but over the many generations dust, and clay, and bull-dirt had fallen into it, covering the limestone with a sort of natural cement, that had become smooth and shiny with the years, and with the treading and slithering of many feet. When the bull-ring was not in use between festivals, the small boys of Mycenae would use it in their play, sliding down it on their bottoms, then scrambling up its steep sides again, like gay little frogs. Only the strong and agile could clamber from base to lip without falling in again; and few men could do it easily, unless they were trained athletes.

This was the Womb of Hera. The tread of many years had made the floor dark brown and gleaming, like Libyan ebony-wood. And so close clustered the hills about it that the crowds could gather there and see all that happened. There was a wooden platform, or ledge, at the lip of the basin, where kings and queens and goddesses took their stand. This was made of oak so old that the poets said it had first come from Dodona, from the same grove where Jason's prow had grown. Some said it was part of the one wagon-load of oak that was used when *Argo* was built. Truly, it was old, and the worm had been at it for hundreds of years; and it was riddled through and through. Yet it was as sound as ever; twelve heavy men could jump up and down upon it and never make it budge or shudder. This was always done before a bull-dancing, so that the safety of the kings and queens would be assured, as they gathered on it, watching.

I stood on this ledge that afternoon, with Rarus close behind me, and a waiting-woman to hold the feather fan over my head, for it was a very hot day. On a little stool beside me, sat Aegisthus' young daughter, Helen. She was about two at the time, I would guess, and beginning to take notice of life. Before the dance started, I turned to her and whispered, 'Your father the king is a great hero, is he not?' Helen grinned up at me in the sunlight and nodded, her thin hair blowing in the faint breezes. I thought at the time what a shame it was that she, who was after all my half-sister, would never grow to be a woman. But such thoughts must not be allowed to nest in the heart like pigeons; they must be driven away before the mating starts. I turned from her and gazed at the crowds who lined the hillside, their arms about each other, their brown faces gleaming in the sun, their hard hands passing the wine-skin from group to group.

Herdsmen drove the bull in first. A black four-year-old, with horns that came out before him, longer than swords, in a great curved sweep. In the sunshine his hide glistened like wet silk.

As he slithered down the slope and gained his footing below, I said to Rarus, 'Look, he has been fed, or drugged; he almost seems to smile. This is no way for a bull to come into the ring.'

Rarus came closer to me and whispered, 'I think the chief citizen, Tyndareus, had the tending of him. He would not want Aegisthus hurt, he makes too much profit from the king for that.'

I never liked Tyndareus; he was too much like Aegisthus—fat and bald, and crafty. His dark bright eyes moved everywhere, and spoke a different language from his lips. He had been in the Shrine when the king lifted my skirt, and had laughed louder than the rest. I had set this down in my mind, against the time when Tyndareus' own reckoning should be paid.

Then I signed for the soldiers to blow the horns, and as the blast echoed over the stone hills, Aegisthus came into view. He was not happy, but I must confess that he put on a good show, especially when he saw that his little daughter was on the platform with me.

He held his right hand up in salute and called out, 'Lady, this we do to celebrate the glory of Hellas!' It was a formal speech which all bull-dancers were required to make, and he made it well enough, in a loud clear voice which carried up to the crowd on the highest part of the hillside. They cheered him and flung wine-skins into the blue air.

Little Helen clapped her hands as Aegisthus slithered slowly down the slope. 'Look! Look!' she said. 'The king goes bravely!'

Poor little fool—she did not see the sweat of terror on his brow, or the great effort it cost him to make his fat face smile, as though he delighted in his task. But I did, and I said to Rarus, 'Well, if we see nothing worse than this, friend, we shall have seen a king afraid.'

Aegisthus stumbled and lost his footing when he reached the bottom, because of his lame leg, but the black bull only gazed at him with great damp eyes, hardly interested in him. This gave the king courage, for he went to the bull and patted his rump, well out of reach of the long horns. The crowd called out in praise at this; so Aegisthus plucked up still more heart, and climbed on the bull's broad back. It took him great effort, but the beast stood very still while he did it. The king had to kick his heels into the creature's flanks a dozen times before it would begin to lumber round the small ring. Once more the crowd cheered, though a little less heartily now; they felt that the show was almost over. Tyndareus, the chief citizen, who stood on a rock about ten paces from me, called out, 'Goddess, we have seen the king's valour now. He has proved himself, lady. Shall we throw the ropes down to bring him up again?'

But I ignored him, and stared downwards as though I intended the game to go on. Aegisthus glared up at me as he jolted round the ring, the sweat coming off his brow and chest. Then, as though he felt angry because I had not listened to Tyndareus, he swung off the bull's back and took him with both hands by the left horn, swinging his whole weight on it, his feet off the ground.

The bull tried to shake him off, but he was a young animal, and

Aegisthus was a heavy man. For a while the bull stood still, as though trying to think what he should do next, stupidly, puzzled. Then suddenly he gave a little lowing cry that bubbled deep down in his chest, and began to swing round, in a tight circle, towards the left. Aegisthus kept his feet clear of the ground and began to laugh, like a boy who feels he has the mastery of a game.

The crowd up the hillside laughed too, and so did Helen. It looked as though this could go on for ever, without anyone getting hurt.

Then all at once the young bull in his twirling lost his footing and fell with a heavy thud on his side. It shook the earth. Aegisthus, by some luck, dropped clear and rolled away, safe and grinning.

Tyndareus shouted out to his servants, 'Come, now, fling the ropes down, the show is over.'

I turned this time and said, 'Since when has a mere citizen ruled this ceremony, Tyndareus?'

The crowd did not like this, nor did he like being mentioned by name among the people, and his brown face flushed. But he answered me as politely as his anger would let him and said, 'Lady, you can see that the bull has hurt himself. One of his legs is bruised; he cannot get up!'

I waited a moment, to show my dignity, then said for all to hear, 'Then the king has no more to fear, citizen. We will raise the bull and let them dance their way out.'

Young men slithered down to get the creature on its hooves again. I beckoned Rarus to me and put a little horn-box in his hand. 'Here, friend,' I whispered, 'get some of this powder in your palm and rub it on the tender part, near the black beast's tail. He will forget his lame leg then.'

Rarus slipped down into the Womb of Hera and mingled with the other youths. Suddenly the bull gave a high bellow and began to throw greenish dirt behind him, over his legs and over the youths. They scattered from his flailing horns and, as the beast got angrily to his knees again, scrambled quickly up the slope.

This was a very different bull, and Aegisthus sensed it. He stared at me for a moment, his eyes wide and white, then he had to set his mind to other things, for the beast came at him, swinging his horns like vicious scythes, blaming the king for the sharp pain he was feeling.

The crowd stopped laughing and was silent. The wine-skin was forgotten. There was no breath to blow the flutes with, even.

Now the ring seemed to shrink in size, and it was as though the bull was always on the king's heels, however tight the circle he ran. The dark mess still issued from the creature, fouling the ground, and colouring the lower walls of the basin. Aegisthus went down on one knee once, losing his footing, and he rose scarcely in time, his legs stained, the horns curving up only a hand's breadth behind him.

Tyndareus shouted out, 'This is enough, lady. His blood be on your head if he dies.'

Then, to my great amazement and anger, many folk among the crowd began to shout the same, as though Aegisthus was their hero, as though they did not wish him to die down there. As though they loved him above me.

Soon the bull had put one horn into the king's tunic, and had ripped it from him with one sweep, letting us see the king's fat waist drooping over his thong-belt. I would have thought all Mycenae would have laughed at such a sight—but no one did, except little Helen, who thought her father was doing all this to amuse her.

A gasp of shock passed up the hillside, like a flock of wild geese on their way to the south. And by this sign I knew that if I let Aegisthus die that day, I was as good as dead myself, and so was my mother, who lay on her sick-bed in the palace. I still could not understand why Aegisthus was so well-loved in Mycenae. But I put the best face on it I could, and I moved to the edge of the platform and called down, 'It is finished, Aegisthus. Take care now and we will have the ropes down to you in an instant. You have done most bravely, my king.'

I do not think he heard me, for he suddenly ran out of the track of the bull and tried to scramble up the steep and slippery wall of the basin, the bull close behind him. It seemed that the king would do it, for, as the bull lost its footing and fell back, Aegisthus' fingers scratched at the wall only a sword's length from my feet. If I had bent I could have dragged him up to safety; but my disgust of the man kept me from doing this, though the crowd expected it. His great eyes, brimful with terror, gazed into mine, imploring, and I smiled back at him without moving. The king shouted out, something wordless and afraid; little Helen clapped her hands again and crowed with glee; Tyndareus yelled, close in my ear, 'Hold fast, Aegisthus, the rope is coming!'

But then the king's finger-hold broke away and he slid back, his heavy body plummeting down the greasy slope, to where the furious bull now stood, tossing his mad horns and slavering, and breathing like a bellows.

I do not think the beast even knew that he hit Aegisthus, for his threshing head was rising and falling without meaning now. But we saw the sharp horn go into the king as he lay helpless and spread eagled on the lower slope, and we saw its red point come out again just above the buttock. Then Aegisthus began to squeal like a stuck pig and the gore to spurt over the bull's nose as he tried to get rid of the unwanted burden on his horn.

Now the whole hillside was on its feet, screaming out. Stones began to fly about me. One of them struck Rarus on the back even as Tyndareus' noose fell round the king's shoulders and they slowly dragged him up off the point, groaning and trying to reach backward to his wound. As the horn withdrew, it made a sound like a hungry mouth.

A group of the loyal palace guard came round me with their oxhide shields over my head, to keep the stones from me. They took no heed of my title or my fine clothes, but bundled me away without ceremony, along the back path that led up to the palace. I heard Rarus gasping, and the stones still clattering about us, even when we had got a good distance from the Womb of Hera.

I glanced back only once, between a space in the shields, and saw the citizens carrying Aegisthus on their shoulders, as though he were a great warrior wounded in battle.

Then the lieutenant of the guard gave me a hard push in the back and grunted, 'Get on with you, lady, or they'll throw you down to that black beast! That's the way they are, at the moment.'

I was so afraid just then, I confess, that I took no exception to the man's hard pushing or to his rough speech.

I went straight to my mother and told her what had happened. She gave orders to the lieutenant that the palace guard should be trebled and that no soldiers should be allowed leave until the city was quiet once more. Then, when we were alone, she gazed at me sternly and said, 'So, now you have tested your power, daughter. And see what it has brought you! The title of goddess and a flounced skirt, do not mean quite as much to the citizens as you thought. A queen must always be prepared for the crowd to change its mind, you see. We of the royal blood live for ever on the edge of a chasm. It only needs a little wind to push us off, into the sea, at any time.'

Remembering what the bull had done, I went on my knees beside the bed and wept on my mother's breast. She stroked my head and said mildly, 'There, there, daughter; so now you know how it feels to hurt a man, even an enemy. It is not all glory, is it? Now, perhaps, you will understand what the great warrior-kings have felt, walking the battlefield in the morning, seeing what wounds their merest words can bring to men. Even the greatest heroes weep as you are doing, to think that they have caused such agony, such mutilation. The god himself must weep, at times, to see his children so ruined, my love. Come, dry your eyes and drink some wine. That is what the great kings do; it is the only way. We cannot blame them for it, the wine-warriors.'

After I had drunk deeply and often at the bowl, I said to her, 'What must I do now, mother? I am like a ship without a steersman, I do not know which way to turn in the storm that has suddenly blown over me. I am like old Jason.'

Clytemnestra stroked my head and smiled, as though she was secretly pleased that I still must ask her advice. She said, 'You must stay in High Town for a while, under guard. If you go out, the common people will hurt you, that much is certain. Wait till their temper has died down, and, if there is still anything to nurse, then

[175]

nurse Aegisthus. Let it be known that you care for him after all; let it be thought that you do penance for this day's mistake. Then, as soon as it is safe, be away to Delphi by night, along the narrow roads, and ask the god what is best for you. I can advise no more than that. Perhaps he will tell you where Orestes and Hermione are, at the same time. Then you can bring them back and we may restore some of the old order in this city. Have no fear about going, I shall not die yet awhile. This much I know; that I shall live to see my son again. It was told me in a dream last night.'

I bowed before her and went to see if the citizens had carried Aegisthus back into the palace.

29

He lay in the dark for weeks, shrinking like a wine-skin that is too porous and lets the liquid flow away gradually. His own skin lay about him white and wrinkled. His bed now smelled of his wound.

The doctors put a paste into the hole, of curdled milk, honey, bull's blood and horn-shavings. They said that what caused it would cure it. Tyndareus always stood there, glowering at me, his hand on his dirk, angry that I should even be allowed into the king's room.

At first I was not permitted to go near him; but after a while they were glad to have someone to change the dirty wrappings, and they let me do it, though it made me retch every time, until at last the hole began to skin over.

He was a long while before he would talk to anyone, much less to me, but one day, when we were alone, he stared at me thoughtfully and said in his hoarse voice, 'Very well, Electra; you have had your way, and you see what has come of it. Now are you content?'

I bowed my head and said, 'You will have me killed, father, is that it?'

Aegisthus seemed to like me calling him father; it was a good touch, I thought secretly, because he almost smiled, then answered, 'No, *daughter*. I shall not have you killed, because what you did, you did in ignorance. Besides, there has been blood enough spilled between our families, and it is time for that to stop. Unless we hold together, we shall all perish. I hear that wild men, savages from the north, are moving down all the while towards Mycenae. They call themselves Dorians, and their one desire is to sweep us all away— Cretans, Mycenaeans, Laconians—as though we had never been. When I am well again, I shall try to bargain with them until I can be sure of the New Army once more. Then, perhaps, we will see whether we can drive these incomers back to the sea, and start the world afresh.'

He began to groan soon after this, and I had to leave him in his doctor's hands, for I did not wish it to be thought that I had poisoned him.

I told the queen what he had said. She smiled her withered smile and said, 'All my lifetime there have been rumours of Dorians coming down to sack Mycenae. When I was a little child, no older than the girl Helen, my dreams were full of Dorians. I used to think they had four eyes, beaks like eagles, and great claws on their hands and feet! But they have not come yet—and I sometimes wonder if they are anything but the dark visions of poets, who try to keep men in order by telling them frightening things.'

Later I told Aegisthus something of what my mother had said. He smiled painfully then answered, 'So the queen says they are a dream· Well, you shall see one of them, then you will know. Of course, h is only an envoy from their king, not a great lord himself, but he w at least prove that Dorians exist.'

He knocked on the gong that stood beside his bed, near the tri· that burned continually, and two soldiers came in with a between them.

'Here is a Dorian,' said Aegisthus, pointing.

[17

The servants drew back a window curtain so that I should see the visitor more clearly. He stood no higher than my shoulder, but he was enormous in his girth, and made more frightening by the bundle of sheepskin that he wore as a tunic. His hair was as white as flax and hung in plaits on either side of his broad head, bound round with wire. His pale blue eyes stared out of his red, scarred face; his fringe of beard was so thick that it looked like the brush the grooms use to polish horses' hides. His hands were so big and red, with their nails black and broken, that I shuddered to think of them touching any part of me.

He was bow-legged from much riding, and he bore a broad sword, wrapped in a calfskin scabbard, that reached almost to his ankles.

Over his shoulders he wore a cloak made up of patchwork, of cloths of all sorts, but so threadbare and torn that no beggar in Mycenae would have been seen out in it.

When he took his hand from his face, I saw that he had a little length of ivory pushed through his nose, and sticking out on each side. It gave him a savage look, wherever he turned.

A heavy musty smell followed him, as though, like the lynx, he had his own especial odour, as though he was different from other men.

I wondered what manner of language such a beast would use—would he bark like a dog, mew like a cat, or bellow like a bull?

Instead, he spoke to me, smiling grimly, in a tongue that I understood almost without effort. It was like our own tongue, save that some of the words were twisted round, as though he spoke with a pebble in his mouth. He said, 'Greetings, goddess. Now I have seen all the treasure of Mycenae! What they say of you, up in the hills of Othys, is no lie; you are the most comely of the Hellene women. That is what they say, and what you are.'

He held out his hand to me and, shrinking, I took it. It was as hard and cold as stone. He pinched my fingers together, as though he meant to crush them, but I do not think he even knew that he was hurting me. He was used to holding things like that, rolling them in

[178]

his great hands, letting his fingers think for him, letting them discover what it was they grasped.

I did not cry out. I decided that I must keep still and smile, whatever he did to me, to show him that I was truly the goddess and no ordinary woman. Even when he put his big hand on my breast I stood still. He did not pinch any more, but bowed his head and took his fierce hand away, like a leopard withdrawing its paw after touching a dead deer.

Then he turned to Aegisthus and said, 'This woman would be right for my master, the king. You swear on oath that she is from the loins of Agamemnon?'

Aegisthus nodded as solemnly as his pain would let him and said, 'She is of the blood of Atreus and is out of the body of Clytemnestra. The court scribes shall write down her pedigree before the day is over, if your king wishes it.'

The Dorian walked round me and touched me here and there, like a farmer at a market. 'Yes,' he said, 'my master would want such a pedigree, in case he needed to sell her again. Our people drive hard bargains, and they must always know what it is they are buying.'

As he spoke, I began to see the manner of revenge Aegisthus was working out for me; but I stood quite still, listening to my inner voice that told me all would be well, if I could wait.

Then Aegisthus said, 'And what is more, no man has had her. She would come fresh to your master, ready for his breaking-in, like an untamed horse.'

The Dorian threw back his shaggy head and laughed harshly. 'Zeus,' he said, 'do you think we set any store by such things? Among my people not a woman goes untrained after she is ten years old. When such folk as we are on the move, we do not delay. We take it as it comes, and no one thinks the worse of a girl who has learned her work. I ask you, King of Mycenae, do you demand that each cup you drink from shall come to your lips unused by any before you? Well, it is the same with wives, and every other thing. See, this sword I wear has been through a hundred hands. It is a good sword; it will strike off a pig's head at one blow. Now, should I not be a fool if I refused this sword because others had used it?'

He bent over Aegisthus and put a great hand on the king's bony chest. 'Look you, man,' he said, laughing, 'if I have the taking of this goddess back to my king, I shall not be slow, nor will all my fellow-riders. It would be waste not to; and my master will expect it to have been done. So speak no more to me of these pretty ways of your people. There is no place for them in the hard life we Dorians lead.'

The man left soon afterwards, to go back to his skin tent outside the city walls. When he had gone, I said to Aegisthus, 'So, that is the sort of peace you will make with the incomers? You will use me as your bargaining coin.'

He lay back on his pillow, with his hands under his head, and said softly, 'It is nothing. You make too much of these slight affairs. Suppose you go to their king, it will not be all loss to you. You will be a queen, and will rise in greatness as your husband rises. I am offering you a new life and a new fame, Electra. Besides, suppose you do not like the Dorian king when you meet him—well, it would be a small thing for you to come to some arrangement. They are a simple folk, and you are a clever girl Let us say that you might give him the sort of drink that would keep him quiet thereafter, and so find yourself another husband, if the worst came to the worst.'

I did not know what to do when he said these things. I think that if I had had a knife, I might have risked all and have used it on Aegisthus as he lay smiling up at me from his bed. But his guards always searched me for weapons when I went to visit him, so I was harmless. All I could do then was to weep, though it shamed me to sink so low.

After a short while he reached out his hand and patted me on the side. 'There,' he said, 'I know what is in your mind. You are thinking that a rough Dorian husband would not be so sweet a lover as Hermione. But you must not let such fancies keep you from your greatness. You will find, among the Dorian women, others of the same taste as yourself, others who know a way of passing the time while their lords are away burning and stealing. After all, my dear, what you have discovered with your cousin is no magic; it is not yours alone. Consider the Amazons, who have known how to live without men since the world began. No, girl, your secret is shared by thousands, and has been since Hera first quarrelled with Zeus!'

I left his room and went back to my mother, for I could stand no more of his wicked talk. From his mouth, even the sweetest love seemed to turn sour and bitter. His words laid dirt on everything, and I could not tolerate it.

I told Clytemnestra what had been said, and she answered thus: 'We have come to the breaking-point again, daughter. We have come to a place in the weaving where we cannot see what the god means by his pattern. Aegisthus is more powerful now, flat on his back with the hole in him, than he ever was running about on two legs. That is often the way of life; it is the unexpected that happens. I thought all would be well once we had buried Agamemnon and set the great stone over him. Then, I thought, we could work together and wear Aegisthus down, as water does a stone. But it is not as easy as I thought. You see, I have lost my own children, and have gained only one of his. And in gaining his child, I have lost my strength and am an old woman. Now, unless we can do something quickly, I shall lose you; and shortly, the fool Aegisthus will lose Mycenae to the Dorians—for, mark my words, those beasts will come here whether you marry their king or not. They are not like us Achaeans—they do not abide by the bargains they make. You cannot bargain with a lion or a snake, and Dorians are like lions or snakes. They are not men, as we know men, my dear.'

I sat down and wept. I said, 'In my lifetime, short as it has been, the world has changed, mother. Our family has fallen apart; Hellas has fallen apart; and soon even this great palace may crumble and be grown over by the weed, so that later men may never find it.'

Clytemnestra answered, 'These things are always happening, my child. See, King Priam of Troy must have thought that his city would last until the world ended in a clap of thunder—yet our own men dragged down its walls. Men who once drilled here, outside our house, with their chariots and their javelins. It is the law of the gods that things must change, just as the seasons change, just as the trees change, as the seas and the skies change.'

When this did not stop my weeping, she said, 'Consider, daughter, that Priam's Troy, great as it seemed, was only one of many Troys. There had been others before it; others which lay under Priam's Troy, and on which his city was built. Perhaps other Troys will one day grow upon the city your father dragged down, who knows? And perhaps there will be another Mycenae when we are gone. Another Hellas, another Electra, another Clytemnestra. . . . Others again and again, who will carry on the story that the god wishes to tell himself, just as the weaving-women work and work away to make a piece of cloth that will tell all that there is to know, for ever and ever. All things are timeless, daughter. It is only we who weep; the god does not weep, because he knows, to the end of time, that life must go on and on, and the same stories be told and told again. To him, Cretans, Hellenes, Minyans, Egyptians, Dorians, Libyans, Hittites, are all small grains of sand in a long shore that reaches out of sight. Now do you see why you should not weep today?'

I rose and dried my eyes and nodded. 'I see, mother. You are wiser even than I thought. Now, tell this small grain of sand what she must do.'

The queen half-rose upon her elbow and, with a great effort, since her talking had tired her, said, 'This very night, take two horses, one for you and one for Rarus; and go, cloaked, to Delphi. There, ask the pythoness what is best for us all. That is the only counsel I can give you, Electra.'

I knelt and kissed her burning hand. 'I will do as you say, mother,' I answered. 'Now that you have spoken to me, I feel stronger in my purpose once again.'

She nodded and settled back to sleep. 'Have no fear, daughter,' she whispered. 'I shall be here, and Mycenae shall still be standing, when you return, though your journey will be a long one.'

[182]

30

DELPHI was not, then, as you know it now, doctor. Not tumble-down shacks and grass-grown streets, but tall white columns along the gullies in the rocks, and doves fluttering above the many shrines. An expensive place to stay in, with rich Egyptian and Assyrian sight-seers putting the prices up everywhere.

Old veterans who had fought at Troy lay about the streets show-ing their stumps of limbs and begging for offerings in their rusted helmets, claiming to have been the first through the great gates in that wooden horse they all boasted of, and which, if the truth were told, was only another of the poets' lies.

Three years and the pythoness wouldn't say a word. A drunken old woman, once a licensed girl at the Mother Shrine down the street from the grotto of Apollo, but now so worn that only the beggar veterans went to her.

'No, lady, I cannot hear anything coming up about your brother.'

Another month. 'No, dear, the god is asleep today. He won't say a word about Aegisthus.'

The next year. 'Oh, but you've asked about Hermione so often, the god is weary of your questions. Look, I can tell you where there is one, a black-skinned girl from Colchis. Now if I say the word, she will . . . oh, you Mycenaeans, always in a hurry. . . .'

All wastes, is used up, the substance withers.

'Rarus, the landlord threatens to kick us out tomorrow if the rent is not paid, and we have pawned everything that would raise the price of our lodging. What shall we do?'

'Lady, who am I to advise you? I will see if I can find out in the tavern room. Yes, I will be careful, I know what these Egyptians are.'

Then that evening; 'Lady, the landlord says it can be done easily. In your goddess-dress, at the Shrine of Dia, where the cypress avenue ends, they need a new one there. All comers, I am afraid. But the money's good. The Shrine takes half and you have the other half to pay him off with.'

'Look, Rarus, it is not that I have any feelings about all comers. This thing means nothing to me in itself; but I will not sell it for the Shrine and for him. What I do is for love, for the sweet song of it all. Hermione would be able to understand what I mean. Oh, god, where is she? That crafty old pythoness will not speak a word. She always wants more and more for her fee, and never tells anything. Our room is littered with the shards she has scribbled on, and not one gives an answer I can understand.'

After a long silence, with the sheep bleating up from the street, white lambs being driven in at night for the pilgrims to buy as offerings at dawn: 'Lady, there is another way, though I hesitate to speak of it.'

'Dear boy, dear, dear boy, tell me. You know that I regard you as my brother; my brother who knows me through and through, and from whom I keep no secrets. Tell me, I beg you.'

'Then, lady, there is a place where the four roads meet, at the entrance to Delphi, where the travellers lay down their loads before they start the last trudge into the town. There is a little old stone, an ancient altar. It struck me yesterday, as I was looking round, that anyone who set up shop there would catch the traffic before it got into the town and spent at the stalls and market-place. The simple folk would jump at it, half-starved from the deserts and mountains they must cross getting here.'

'But, Rarus, my dear, I don't know if I dare. It is one thing at the festivals, when all are blind with wine; but in the broad daylight, in public, among crowds, that would be shameful, surely? I could not bring myself to it, and they would want their money back. Oh, Rarus, to have been here three years, and still to be so silly! Tell me, brother, what must I do?'

'It is that, or we starve, Electra. Look, we will hide the goddess-dress away and keep it safe, and you shall put on an old shift, as though you are a street-beggar, a girl left behind by the Phoenicians.

No one will know you for the princess of Mycenae. With dust on you, and your hair tied in a knob at the back, no one will know.'

'Yes, that much is good, Rarus, but I shall know. I shall see them coming, shall know what manner of man it is. I shall see and know.'

'But, sister, there is a way out. Look, I will tie a black cloth over your eyes and tell them all that you have lost your sight in the white sandy-places of Libya. I will collect the fees for you and will stand over you with a staff and see that no one outstays his time. They will not see your face, nor will you see theirs. It will be a blind bargain for both sides, and I will hold the money-bags and keep the accounts. All you must do is be obedient to the customer—and then forget, in time for the next. Is that a good plan, Electra?'

'Yes, Rarus, I suppose so. It is that—or die. And, at the worst, I shall not be as badly off as Aegisthus, with what the black bull did to him that afternoon.'

I tell you, doctor, it was that or death. And always I hoped that the next visit to the grotto would bring me word. The tipsy old woman there must have known what I was at, her spies, no doubt, had been out to the cross-roads, just as my landlord's had, and between them they fleeced me. That made it hard work, through the hot summer and into the first chill of the autumn. But if he failed me in one way, the god looked over me in another; he let nothing come of it. It was as though he had rolled a stone over the sacred place, to let none defile it.

Then, at the next spring, all changed. Sitting with the black cloth over my eyes, dusty once more, beside the flat altar stone where the trade was carried on. And Rarus suddenly saying, 'Hold up straight, dear, and raise the shift a little more. You are not doing yourself justice, my pigeon.'

I heard the clattering of hooves and said, 'Why, who is it?'

'A troop of young men on white horses, led by two wearing great crested helmets. The sort with masks on the front. They are only youths, but they wear swords. The others carry long javelins! Aiee! It is like a porcupine! It is like the old days when the men got ready to sail to Troy!'

[185]

I did as he said, perhaps more too, and I heard the horses halting. Then a muffled voice calling down from above. 'Hey, Cretan! Has your sister got a permit to work here, at the entrance to the sacred town?'

I was frightened by this and thought the police from Thebes had come inspecting. It was the crafty sort of thing they did. But I put on a good face, and, taking my chance, said, 'Here is my licence, sir. Would you like to inspect it?'

I heard a great deal of laughing and for a moment I was ashamed of myself. Then Rarus pulled at my arm and whispered, 'It is all right, pigeon, the two leaders are dismounting to come to you. Look, I will lead you into the grove as usual, and since they are obviously men of some authority, perhaps, this time, we will not insist on a fee. Perhaps that would be wise, for if they are police, then we can say we were not gaining by it. Do you agree, sister?'

I nodded and stumbled to the grassy place by the little stream, which was our frequent place of work. Rarus and I called it Dreamland, because of how it was there, usually, unless you had a wild Thracian to deal with; and then it was more like a fierce battlefield. But most pilgrims were quiet fellows enough, having come so far and being so weary from the mountains.

I rested, waiting, among the asphodel and the tall rushes, hoping that the police would be swift and away, and that the whole troop would not expect to be entertained too lavishly.

I heard the rushes beside me breaking and felt the warmth of another at my side. Then, as I began to do what was required, I heard a high voice cry out, 'Why, by the little god, this must be Electra! She is the only one I know with the snake on her in red and blue!'

My heart thumped so wildly, I tore away my black bandage and saw that the youth in the rushes was Orestes, Orestes with his great helmet off, and his golden hair flying wild. And already he had the fringe of beard growing thick at his chin, and the great bronze bracelets on his arms, nestling among the little curly golden hairs there.

[186]

I flung my arms about him and said, 'Brother, oh brother! The god has brought you here to save me!'

Orestes smiled broadly and said, 'It's Dia you should thank, not old man Zeus! But for her little snake, we might have been in some sort of trouble, you and I!'

I clung to him, weeping with joy, relishing the feel of the harsh hot armour on me, just as I did when I was a little one and Agamemnon picked me up in his war-dress. 'Take me away, Orestes,' I said. 'I have found you at last, without the help of that old bitch of a pythoness. This is the god's answer after three years!'

Orestes stroked my face to quieten me. I was ten years older than he, but now he seemed quite grown-up and capable. I felt that I could leave all my affairs to him. I think that I had become so dispirited by my stay at Delphi that I would have leaned on any man, however young.

'Look up, sister,' he said at last, 'and greet my blood-brother, Pylades. He and I are forming an army to drive the Dorians away. We mean to bring back the old Hellas once again, and all its glory, too.'

I said, 'Pylades! That means, "The Gates of Hades". Yet I see no fire and smoke about him! How did he get his name?'

I spoke to Orestes because I was too ashamed at that moment to address myself to Pylades himself, being still half-shiftless in the grass. Besides, this Pylades was the most handsome man I had ever seen. He was a few years older than my brother, and very tall. His hair was a reddish-gold, with many lights in it, and he wore it in the Laconian style, chopped off straight at the shoulder-line, and tied with red ribbons just behind his head. His face was long and smiling, with deep lines from nose to mouth, and a pointed chin with a thick stubble of reddish beard on it. He wore no gold at throat or wrist, but band after band of soft bright iron. Even his belt, that pulled his waist in until it looked like a wasp's, was of broad iron, all moulded and carved with stags and bulls and twining snakes. His kilt was of thick linen, with little iron bars set side by side on it, running downwards, and rattling at every move he made. I had never seen so much iron in my life before; it made him seem like a god, wearing the god's own sacred metal so.

Orestes rose and put his arm about Pylades' waist, and they stood above me, together, in the sunlight that shone through the new green leaves in that grove. Together, they looked so comely, I could have eaten them! No, doctor, I did not mean to say that, it slipped out. Forget those words; I meant that I could have loved them to madness. I thought that they were second only to dear Hermione in her light armour and her play-helmet, lying among the crushed lavender in the breathless heat of the evening.

I think Orestes knew what was in my mind, because he said, 'In our kingdom, beyond Mount Oeta, where we have set up our camp-place, Hermione still talks of you, sister. We have heard of nothing but you each day since we first came there from Mycenae.'

I arranged myself and ran to him. 'Tell me,' I begged, 'do you think she still loves me, Orestes!?'

It was Pylades who answered. He said, with a strange twitch of the mouth, 'I can answer that! She loves you so much that she has refused to wed your brother. She says that she will marry no one unless you are there, too. Is that answer enough for you, lady?'

I held his hand then and began to weep for joy. Orestes took me by the shoulders and said gently to me, 'This is the moment we have all waited for, Electra. Do not go back to Mycenae, at least not yet. Come with us, beyond Mount Oeta, and see Hermione again. Then she will marry me, and perhaps the god will speak inside you and persuade you to marry my brother, Pylades. For it is in my heart that this was intended by the god, that we should all be joined together, to bring glory back to Hellas.'

I looked up at Pylades, and saw him smiling with the dappled shadows on his long face. And, for an instant, in the greenness of that place, with the magic water rustling about us and the breeze sighing in the tall reeds, I seemed to see Hermione standing just behind him, holding out her arms to me, her laughing head flung back, her hair wafted in the wind, her play-armour cast aside so that I might see what she looked like with the amber sunlight playing over her, too.

I said, 'I will marry Pylades, if he will have me.'

He fell at my feet and kissed my dusty legs. 'Lady,' he whispered, 'it is all I want from life, to marry the kin of my brother, Orestes.'

To fill the silence then, I asked if my sister, Chrysothemis, was well. Orestes laughed and said, 'She is, for all we know, Electra. She went off with a band of Dorians, and they seemed pleased enough to have her.'

So, there, near the cross-roads at Delphi, I got my answers, and my life took yet another course. I recall little else of that meeting, except that when I went back with the two warriors, the horsemen all bowed their great crested heads, and reined in their mounts until they were as still as images. It was as though a great queen had come among them, even though I was dressed in rags, and my limbs were caked with dust and sweat.

One more thing I recall, but with shame, now. As Pylades was helping me to mount the white horse they brought for me, I turned suddenly and shouted, 'Rarus, you will walk! Among great ones, you must keep your place, fellow.'

I do not know what made me say that. I was ashamed of my words the moment they had been uttered. But Rarus did not seem to notice anything. He only bowed his dark head in obedience, and then went to take my bridle-rein and lead me forward among the other riders, on the road out of Delphi.

31

THE deep gorge where my brother and Pylades lived was not green and pretty, as so many other valleys were, but it was secure. No one travelled into it, for there were few sheep and cattle to buy or steal, and hardly enough water to satisfy a herd of horses.

The small dark folk who lived there called it the Iron Valley; and they called Pylades the Iron King. They were descendants of the old Chalybians who had followed Jason back when he returned from Colchis, twenty generations before, to trade their iron in Hellas, where so little of it was ever seen.

They prayed to a goddess called Ay-mari, after the manner of other folk from the land of the rising sun. Some of them believed that she came from the sea, and that her father was the Great Fish. I used to ask them what his name was, but they always smiled behind their hands and drew away without telling me. They were a shy, courteous folk in all things, and never spoke to me unless they were first addressed. The family of Pylades had been their overlords from the earliest day of their settlement beyond Mount Oeta, and had come to be accepted as their priest-kings.

Hermione, who was regarded by them almost as a goddess, could not wait to take me up on the hillside to watch the fires burning down below in the valley after dark.

It was as though the night was full of winking red eyes. Smoke rose from the valley and covered it with a black pall. Hermione laughed with glee to tell me how the other peoples from kingdoms round about steered clear of this place after night-fall. 'They think magic goes on here,' she said.

Then she saw the look in my eyes and stopped talking about that sort of magic. We had a charm of our own to be at, this first time together after so long.

When we came down the hill again, Pylades was stripped to the waist and gleaming with sweat. His face and arms were black with soot. His teeth shone white against the darkness of his features. His fine hair was done up in a tight ring on top of his head, to be out of the way.

He laughed at us, our arms about each other, a great hammer in one hand, and a giant pair of pincers in the other. 'What, you two love-birds back so soon again!' he called. 'I thought we'd have the new smelting out of the furnaces before you came down the hill!'

Hermione told him to stop his teasing and to let us see how the iron was made; but he shook his head and pretended to drive us away with the great hammer.

Later he said, 'One day, soon, you shall both see it, now that we are all together as the god wished. But before that there is a thing that must be done. It is the custom of my people which they brought from their own land lifetimes past.'

I understand what he meant; it was much the same as what the god at Jericho commanded. But among the Chalybians, it was from all alike. Small enough price to pay, I thought, to become a queen, and to have both Pylades and Hermione beside me again.

On the day before the double wedding, the dark folk of the valley built what they called their Great Fish. It was a dark tunnel of brushwood, shaped roughly like a fish, and a hundred paces long. The four of us had to go in through the mouth and out through the tail-end, and, while in the belly of the fish, make our offering. Since Pylades and Orestes had followed the custom of this folk on reaching warrior-hood, we got through all the faster. And since Pylades was the priest as well as the king, he saw to it that Hermione and I were dealt with as kindly as possible. We had both drunk the heavy resinous wine of Oeta before we went into the belly of the fish, and so we made little enough of it all at the time. Though, I must admit that later, when we were alone, we had an indignant word or two to say about Ay-mari and the Fish God; though we said it all laughing, and with fingers crossed, so that whoever was listening would know that we meant no harm.

The next stage in our wedding came at the sword-thrusting. When I heard of this, I was frightened for a moment; but Hermione had seen it done before, and told me there was nothing to fear. All that happened was that the bride held her thumb and finger like a ring while the groom pushed an ancient iron sword through the hole, into a tree. I asked if anyone ever got cut by the sword, but she said there was more chance of that on the wedding-night, when the weapon had to lie between bride and groom until dawn.

[191]

We were all so careful at our wedding, though, that not a drop of blood was spilled. Unless it was when a rough young man from the lower valley put his arm round Rarus, in game, and got a punch on the nose for his trouble. I had never seen Rarus so upset as he was on my wedding-night. Poor fool, he had been with me so long that he thought he owned me. If I had not driven him away with a whip, he would have spent that night at the foot of my bed, as he had always done before.

In the morning, I had to take him aside and tell him that those days were over now; that Pylades, the king, would not like him there. He sulked a little and said, 'But Orestes and Hermione sleep in the same room with you two. What does one more matter?'

It was hard to explain to him that there was a difference; but he came to understand after a while, and left me alone, only tending me when the others were away, and when I called for his company. This I was forced to do because, as yet, I could understand little of what the Chalybians said, and I needed someone to talk to at times. Being alone and silent drives a woman mad a little.

Once, when we were all at the feast-board in the long house where the iron-men ate together, Orestes opened the talk by saying, 'It will not be so long before we go to Mycenae again, sister. Then our iron swords will do the talking, not us! I will lay a red ribbon on my father's tomb, one that you wove for me long ago—so, he too will know that I have come for vengeance.'

I said, 'Brother, there is one thing you must swear, over the bread and the salt.'

Orestes was swaying with wine and he said, 'Why, what should I swear, sweet heart?' He was slobbering, much like Aegisthus now, which angered me.

I said, 'Whatever you may do with Aegisthus, our mother who bore us must never be harmed. Clytemnestra must not be hurt. Do you swear?'

He made a great show of shaking his head in fury. 'Look,' he said, 'she killed my father, didn't she?'

I answered, 'That has nothing to do with the matter, Orestes. This is something different. I have given my word that I will tend her all her days, and if you do not swear likewise, then what am I to do— put a knife into you? Otherwise, I shall be foresworn, you see.'

Pylades began to laugh then, and slapped Orestes on the shoulder like a big brother. 'Come, Prince,' he said, 'do as my wife wishes, or no iron from this valley shall go to Mycenae, I warn you.'

So Orestes swore, on bread and salt, that, when the time came for Mycenae to fall, he would not hurt our mother. After he had sworn, Pylades got into a merry mood and took Hermione and me out to see the iron being made.

It was when I first saw the row of great furnaces, under the rocky hillside, that I knew why he was named Pylades, and all his fathers before him. 'The Mouth of Hades' was the opening in the long tubular clay furnace, with the hole at its base, through which the glowing charcoal could be seen, glimmering at every punch of the goatskin bellows which were set at the top of the furnace and worked by young boys, in relays, hour after hour.

Pylades let me pour in a bucket of sand that came from a special seam on the hillside, and told me that if the bellows-boys only blew hard enough, this sand, on the hot charcoal, would change into specks of iron, and that when the clay furnaces were cracked open, in a day or two, these pieces of iron would have set hard together.

I did not believe him; but he spoke the truth. When he broke open the hollow column of clay, I saw that there was a long ingot of rough iron, mixed with charcoal and the scum of the sand.

Together we chipped away the red iron and then it was put into a cauldron and heated over charcoal until it was all white-hot. Pylades stirred it with a green twig, which, he said, caused the scum to rise, and the pure iron to set, as water sets to become ice in winter.

Shortly after this, he poured the iron out into moulds of stone, and there it lay, hardening and growing dull, in the shape of rude swords.

Pylades wiped his sooty hand over his sweating brow and said, 'A few more hundreds of these, my love, and we shall be ready to take Mycenae.'

Later, when I watched the smiths beating these rough swords out on the anvils, and putting a keen edge to them, I felt proud to be the hard Iron Queen of Oeta. It was better than being the Amber Princess of Mycenae.

32

BUT such glory does not last. The god cannot bear to see us too contented. I had been the Iron Queen of Oeta for only three years when I lost my first baby. It came away from me in the seventh month, when I was helping the king my husband to tip a heavy basket of iron-sand into the furnace-vent one morning. Pylades was as black as thunder with me, and shouted that I had purposely done this, that I did not want him to have a son. This was so cruel, I could not bear it.

The women carried me away to the reed hut where child-birth happened, and there they tried to quieten me, for I was raving with grief all the time, and thought the world had come to an end.

Pylades would not even see me. He smashed the furnaces and let the iron spoil, he was so angry. I remember telling one of the women to lay our dead child on the furnace-top as an offering to their stinking Fish God. She stared at me so horror-struck that I knew I had said a very bad thing, but I was so distracted that I went on and said even worse, just to show her that I did not care what became of me. I even said that I wanted Pylades dead, beside his son.

But at last I calmed down and sent a young girl to fetch Rarus to me. He came with bowed head, and hands crossed on his chest. He stood by my bed, not speaking.

This angered me again, and I shouted out, 'Dog! So you will

make me speak first, hey?' I tried to throw a clay cup at him, but I was too weak, and fell back weeping in my bed. I thought he would come and bend over me and smooth my wet hair, but he stood quiet, where he was, his head still lowered. At last he said, 'Queen, I have no comfort to give you. There is little left in me to offer, after all these years of watching you and longing for your love. You call me a dog, and that is what I am—a dog who has lost his mistress and now must go away and find a kennel in some other place.'

Rarus had never spoken like this before; his words were like a bucket of cold water splashed across my face. Bitterly I asked, 'Where could one like you go, Rarus? Who would want you? Who would want you? No woman, certainly!'

He said, 'No, no woman, lady. But sometimes, during the time I have been shut out from your room, I have remembered that there is a man who might want me, the man who raised me from the gutters of Mycenae and first put food in my mouth.'

I said in amazement, 'You would go back to Aegisthus!'

Rarus nodded and smiled miserably. 'Who else?' he asked. 'I might still be of use to him. I am nothing here. Your brother has threatened to strangle me if I as much as cross his path. There is a madness growing in your brother, lady, which will burst out one day and destroy him. I have watched it coming for long enough now, and I do not want to be here when it breaks forth.'

I thought long on what he had said. Then I answered him: 'Rarus, I think you are speaking the truth. There is something strange with Orestes. He dreams that he is Agamemnon come again, and strikes anyone who calls him by his true name. Hermione tells me that he rolls about awake each night groaning and sweating, and hitting at her whenever she tries to get him back to bed.'

Rarus answered, 'Yes, it is true; I have heard him. One day in his rage, he might well kill her, too. So, I will make my way back to my old master. He may vent his anger on me by thrashing me, but he will not kill me, I am sure.'

He turned and left the hut. I let him go, then wept on to my pillow, for I saw that my glorious new world had been nothing after all.

That night I dreamed of my mother. Her white, lined face filled my eyes, as though she was very close to me. I even scented the sickness of her body as I stared into her suffering face. She had reddened her lips and put clay dust on her cheeks, which made her look like the dead. 'What are you trying to say to me, mother?' I asked in my dream. She mouthed a long while, silently, and then words came from the deepest part of her throat, flying towards me like black birds. 'Come back to Mycenae, daughter,' her words said. 'I am not long to live, nor is the city long to stand. There is much to be done before the darkness falls. Come back . . . come back . . . come back. . . .'

I woke before the dawn, fevered and pain-racked. The girl who tended me lay asleep by my bed, her red hands palm upwards on her lap, her head lolling stupidly down on her breast. She did not hear me rise and stumble about as I put on my clothes. She was still snoring even when I went through the door.

With painful effort, I reached the hill-top and turned once to look down at the stone valley. The furnaces were smouldering, sending out heavy fumes, fouling the air. All looked black or grey down there. I wondered why I had ever thought it a place of glory. Suddenly I saw that it was a place of evil, not magic. A place of foul dreams and sulphurous stench, a valley of madness.

I was glad to be away from it, even though it meant leaving Hermione; but, in any event, in these last months, while the child had been growing in me, I had seen less and less of her, and had felt the love dying between us, like a flower held too long in the warm hand. There was no doubt of it, sad as it was.

Over the first hill there ran a narrow winding road, beside a deep gully where a stream ran between great round pebbles. In summer there was no water, only pebbles, and spiked leaves, grey in colour, like all else in this wilderness. Dead sheep lay in the gully, with the crows at their eyes. I passed this place of agony with my own eyes averted, and my shawl over my head.

[196]

So, it was only by good fortune that I saw Rarus sitting on a stone, picking at a thorn which had lodged in his foot. I might easily have missed him.

He was not looking at me, but at the thorn, and he made no show of even having heard me approaching.

I went to him and said, 'Now it is your right, Rarus, to make me speak first. Come, I will pull out the thorn, then we will go together back to Mycenae.'

He did not answer, but sat quite still until I had finished, then he took my bundle on his back and walked with me, sure-footed among the rocks and rubble, as though he had known we should return together all the time; as though he had always known that we were bound together, part of the same unbreakable pattern, since that awful dark night of our childhood, when we stood afraid with the snake twitching between us, tying us to one another with the ancient knot that no hand could undo.

33

It had been one thing riding up to Delphi and then on, with Pylades' horsemen, to Oeta; it was another thing to set forth, sick and lonely, with one's life a ruin behind one, on foot, in an unknown country whose bitter mountains seemed to block the way at every turn.

I think we should never have reached Mycenae again, but Rarus talked with an old hill-shepherd who told us to follow the river that lay below us; that one day it would bring us to the sea, if the god was with us.

All my life I had heard men speak of the Saronic Sea, or the Gulf of Corinth, and I asked the old shepherd which of these seas we should reach, but he should his head. 'Nay, woman,' he said, "'tis neither. The river is called Euenus and it leads down to Chalcis. Men take it if they want to go to Ithaca, where old Odysseus used to be the king, the one who never got back from Troy. But I know no more about it than that. I am a land-man not a sea-man; I have never seen this sea men speak of, and do not wish to. Land is everything, with its cattle and its crops; who would leave these for sea? My old grandfather used to say: "Go to sea if you must, but only between sowing and reaping—and even then you will be a fool!" Nay, sea's not for the likes of me.'

We parted from him and were going down the hill when he stood up and waved his stick, shouting, 'Take care! Take care! I have heard that there are Dorians somewhere down towards Chalcis. Walk with your eyes open, my friends!'

Rarus shrugged his shoulders and said to me, 'Do not be afraid, Iron Queen; Dorians are behind us, too, coming down the land. They are like death; they stand at every corner. If we let that frighten us, we shall never move a pace forward, but shall lie down and die here, of fear.'

I held his arm and said, 'Rarus, do not call me Iron Queen any more. I am your sister again; all that is behind me now. As for being afraid, though you are not a warrior like the others, I feel safer with you than with anyone. I have always felt like that.'

He smiled gently and said, 'I am glad, sister. We have been through much together in our life; you great, I nothing. It is as though the god brought us together, as he brings the blind man a stick, and us dogs a master.'

There were few villages, and those only scorched hovels where the watch-dogs drove us away before we had a chance to ask for bread. We drank from the river, and ate the red berries that grew on the hillside bushes. Sometimes there were wild vines which carried a tiny harvest for us; sometimes fleshy roots that grew in what thin soil lay on the rocks. Before the winter was on us, we had learned to fish in the shallow reaches of Euenus, in the little swirling backwaters, where the stream only reached the knee. Once Rarus killed a fox

[198]

with a stone, but it was not good meat to eat, being bitter and gristly. It was an old fox, and already half gone before the stone struck it on the head.

Snow came and found us far from any village. I was so weary now that I begged Rarus to go on and leave me. He sat by me for two days, heaping brushwood about me for a shelter, and stones at my head to keep the wind away; then, one morning, he kissed my hands and feet and said, 'It is like cutting off one of my hands, sister—but it must be done, as I see now. There is still so much life in me that if I lay beside you on the hill here, I should live on and on after you lay cold beside me.'

Then he wrapped his own threadbare cloak about me and went away.

I covered my face in my hands and did not watch him going; I should only have lost courage and have called him back to his own death.

And when he had gone, I thought over all my life, and saw at last what a fool I had been, how I had taunted the god, sometimes without knowing it; and I came to the conclusion that I had deserved all that had befallen me. There was no denying it. I said aloud, 'Take me, Zeus; find some place for me somewhere, I care not where; but take me into your arms. That is all I ask. Here on the mountain I have no one's arms about me and I am lost. Punish me if you will, but take me.'

I could hear the snow swirling round the little shelter that Rarus had made, and somewhere above me up the hill a bitch-fox barking sharply, as though she scented her prey, or perhaps cried out for her father whom we had killed.

Then I heard Rarus say, 'There she is, still living, thank god!'

With him stood a very big man wrapped up in wolf-skins and deer hides. He was a Libyan, it seemed, for his skin was jet-black, and his long hair was dressed in a great horse tail at the back of his head. He wore agate ear-rings that hung to his shoulders, and bands of red copper on his wrists. Looking up at him, lazy with the cold, I saw that his nose was fine and curved, not flat as many Libyan's noses are;

and his lips thin and not pouting-thick. He reached out his long fingers and his pink palms towards me and took me up on his shoulder. 'Come,' he said in a deep voice that came out of his chest, 'we have not far to go. Find courage, lady.'

This black man, coming so close upon my prayer, caused me to wonder if he was the god, or if the god used black servants to do his bidding. Always before I had thought of them as lesser-folk and slaves; but now, for the first time, I saw what strength and dignity they had, these black people.

I said to him, 'Are you god's servant, sir?'

He laughed among the snow on the hillside and said, 'Of course! Why yes, of course!'

At last we came to the place where he lived, a low cave in the hillside, formed where a ledge of rock had fallen sideways to leave a sheltered space beneath it. There was a wattle-door before the entrance, and rushes growing before that. A man might live there all his life and never be discovered.

Inside, all was warm and light; a charcoal brazier glowed by the far wall, and clay lamps stood in every rocky cleft. On the floor, among the thick rushes, sat a woman, fashioning a bowl of clay. She was not black; she was of the Hellene folk, with chestnut hair, and brown breasts as freckled as a bird's feathers. Three fair children rolled in play near the fire; a tiny dark baby lay suckling at her breast, even as she turned the bowl with hands that were thick with the wet clay. Her only dress was a deerskin skirt, but she wore long agate ear-rings, like her husband, and seemed a queen.

He set me before her and told her our story. Soon she had left her work and had set down bowls of boiled meat, and cups of apple-ale for us to drink. She watched over us, smiling and making little clucking sounds, as if we were her children, too. Though she could not have been older than I was myself, a great warmth came from her to me, and there were moments when I thought that she must be the Mother herself, the Mother in her gentle mood.

This was one of the sweetest times of my life. All was contentment in that cave with the merry children crawling about and playing through the day, a big brown dog watching over them and letting them do everything they wished, pulling its tail and ears, nestling against its belly for warmth, even trying to ride on its back.

While we stayed there and let the winter wear itself out, I learned to turn bowls and cups of clay from the woman; and Rarus was shown how to glaze them and bake them in a little oven in the rocky wall. The black man taught him this, with long agile fingers which made those of Rarus look like those of a clumsy child, though in most matters his hands were deft enough.

We never learned their names. When we asked, they laughed and said they had thrown away such useless things and called each other simply 'husband', or 'wife'.

I felt so happy with them that I think I could have stayed in their cave for ever; but one morning the woman came to me with a serious face and said, 'A dream visited me in the night, lady. Someone is crying out to you across land and sea; it is your mother, I think. She begged us to send you home again.'

The black man stood by her and nodded. 'It came to me, too,' he said, 'but the voice was so weak that I could only hear it say, 'All is ending, come!''

So Rarus and I set out that day, turning a little from the river, which now fell in torrents over a rocky ledge. Among the mists, distantly, I thought I saw the silver of water, and even ships sailing on it. But Rarus did not see this.

At the end of the second day, we stumbled round a rocky corner on the hill-path and almost fell over a man who sat with his back to the stones, and a tall spear between his knees. His red hair flared out from under a helmet of dull bronze, and his cheeks were streaked with bars of blue war-paint. There was no running away from him; yet, strangely, he seemed in no hurry to catch us. He scratched his stubbled cheek, then poised his spear as though wondering whether to cast it or not. Afterwards, he grinned and showed his broken yellow teeth, like a dog still not certain whether to bite, or to let the hare run back into the corn.

'Who are you?' he asked, in a slow outland voice.

Rarus answered, 'We are brother and sister, Deione and Ares. We go to seek our fortune in Locris, sir.'

The man put down his spear and laughed. 'I wish you well of it,' he said. 'But I fear there will be little enough fortune left for such as you in Locris. Others have been there before you. Come with me.'

We followed him to a bend in the path which overlooked a rocky plain. There, almost as far as the sight could fly, were fires and tents and wagons, and horses tethered. Great herds of cattle lowed; goats cropped what herbage there was, among the stones; and the earth was black with men.

I had never seen anything like this, not even when the kings gathered for the sailing to Troy. 'What is it?' I asked, breathless.

The man laughed at me, in a good humour, then said, 'It is some of my people, the Dorians, woman. We are coming down and down, always towards the navel of Hellas, always towards the proud places where men have lost their hearts for the sake of gold. This gold will we take, and these men will we kill. Then the world will know sense again, and all shall be equal.'

He directed us to a little path that went steeply down the slope, away from the great plain. 'No one will harm you in that direction,' he said, 'and one day, if you are lucky, you will reach Chalcis. But, I advise you, do not try Locris; it is already picked clean, like a white bone. Try somewhere else.'

Rarus had got his voice back by now, and he asked, joking, 'Where shall we try, master?'

The Dorian scratched his nose with the point of his dagger, humorously, then called out, 'Try Libya! Try Egypt! Sail over the seas to the world's edge and try there; for we shall settle in all other places and take them for our own. Good luck to you!'

He went back to his guard-post, as though we were already forgotten, and we staggered on down the hill, among the dried sagebrush.

Four days later we reached Chalcis.

34

It was not a large place at all, in those days, but it was big enough after all our wanderings in the hills. There were four rows of white flat-fronted houses facing the sea, and a long stone wharf where the small ships tied up. Across the strait, about eight miles away, in Achaea, lay the other port of Patrae, and between the two there was a ferry, when there were enough folk or loads of wool and hide to take over.

I stood on the jetty and looked longingly towards Achaea. 'Oh, Rarus,' I said, 'if we only had the price of our fare!'

A shipman who lounged by the sea's edge, winding twine on a stick, heard me and said, 'You had best get your fare quickly, woman. The boats will be leaving Chalcis soon and never coming back. We shall burn this town and clear out before the next moon. Better a burned town than one taken by the Dorians. As for me, I shall take my boat over and then go round the coast to the Isthmus to see what I can pick up. They say that there's plenty of work to be had in Corinth just now, with all the workmen flying for fear of the incomers.'

My heart jumped at his words. If he could land us at Aegira, say, then it would only be a short journey to Mycenae, not more than seven days, even on foot.

I said to him, 'Shipman, would these bands of iron on my arms and legs buy a place in your boat?' They were the only gifts Pylades had ever given me.

He looked at me as I held out my arms, then screwed up his face. 'Woman,' he said, 'at any other time, yes; but now, no. The price has gone up and up, you see, with everyone wanting to be away.'

I could tell that Rarus was angry with the man, but I knew that beggars could not be choosers, so I said, 'Shipman, take us to

Aegira with you, and I will see to it that your night-watches are never lonely ones.'

Rarus hated to hear these words, but by now such a bargain meant nothing to me; I had gone beyond all that.

The shipman put his twine away and we clapped hands together to seal the bargain. Then he got a smith to knock off the iron bands and we went aboard. He was an old liar about folk rushing to get across the Straits, because we were his only passengers, apart from an elderly woman, with a bundle on her back, who cried continuously about finding her lost husband in Achaea. The shipman winked at Rarus and said, 'She's got a hope! The pirates cut his throat, off Ithaca, a year ago. Why, a mate of mine showed me just where it happened. Still, if it keeps her going, then who am I to tell her any different! It is the god's will.'

He was not kind to us, but he got us to Aegira at last. In his wine, he often let things drop that he denied when sober. He said, for instance, that Hellas was now an unclean stable, and the sooner the Dorians got there and flushed it out, the better. He banged the cabin table and shouted out that of all privies, Mycenae was the worst; that it had been the downfall of Hellas, with its rottenness and its mad kings and queens.

I always held my tongue when the shipman was in drink; indeed, I often led him on, as when I asked, 'What of Atreus, then?'

He leaned back until he almost fell from his rocking stool, then said, 'Atreus was sent to Mycenae as leprosy is sent to a man—to finish him by inches. Atreus was the god's curse on Hellas.'

I pretended not to understand and asked, 'But was he not the father of great Agamemnon? And did not Agamemnon make Hellas proud among the earth's people?'

The shipman glared at me as though I was an idiot; then he said, 'You talk like an outlander who has never seen a town, much less a great city. I will explain to you slowly, so that your dull wits will grasp what I tell you: there are some diseases which make a man feel gay and strong, when they are in their first stages and are getting a grip on him. That is a delusion which the god sends, to make men carry on with their old way of life, so that the disease may get a firm hold like a wrestler. Very well, Atreus and Thyestes, Agamemnon and Aegisthus—they are all the stages of a disease. Yes, on the surface they seem to be great, seem to be doing good things—but you must look at the end of a disease, not its beginning. So look at Mycenae now—it is rotted through, as with leprosy the flesh falls away to reveal the dry bone. Now do you see?'

I shook my head and said simply, 'But did not Agamemnon destroy Troy and bring back gold?'

The sailor drank more wine, swilling it about his mouth until he sickened me, then he answered, 'He was one pig rooting out another pig, no more. Troy was one sty, and Mycenae is another. And if you doubt me, then where is the gold now? Where is the trade he promised? Where are the great princes who sailed with him? I tell you, Hellas exhausted herself when she sailed for Troy. All that is left now is the dying old woman, Clytemnestra, who calls herself queen and is but a witch; and that old fool of a cripple, Aegisthus, who got a bull's horn in his backside and has never walked right again. They are all that's left—apart from the mad young prince and his mad sisters, and no man knows where they are. The wolves have eaten them, like as not.'

Three mornings later, as we pulled into the roads off Aegira, he drew me towards him as he stood on deck and said, 'The god forgive me, but I made a mistake when I was in my wine the other night, talking of kings and princes. I said they were all finished—but I made a mistake.'

I was puzzled and asked him what he meant. In answer, he pointed to where a dozen great ships lay at anchor off-shore. I had never seen such vessels in my life before; they stood up high out of the sea and had at least forty oarsmen, besides great purple sails, with hosts of boys running along the yards to furl them. They had high castles fore and aft, crowded with men, and great curved prows that bent backwards, fan-shaped, as though the ships were fine queens cooling themselves in the heat. Each ship, to my eye, was like a palace, clustered with folk, but graceful and sitting on the water as though they were as light as scallop-shells, as though they ruled the sea.

The shipman said, 'They are from Egypt, woman. Not even a blind man could mistake those ships. And they're up to no good, I can tell you.'

I asked him how he knew, and he answered, 'Why, any ship that doesn't mind being seen comes up past Crete and through the Cyclades, to Troezen or Thoricus. That's the way honest sailors come. But these ships have come round-about, and along the Straits, so that no one should see them arriving.'

He bent towards me and said with a smile, 'And who would come from Egypt to within a long stone's cast of Mycenae, hey, my dear?'

I said that I didn't know; but as I spoke, my heart fluttered in me like a frightened bird. I was not surprised when the sailor said, 'Why, Menelaus, King of Laconica, my love! The brother of Agamemnon, darling! The grimmest wolf of all Atreus' brood, my sweeting! That is who it is, I tell you. After all those years away in Egypt, he has come to take his pickings before the Dorians get across the Straits. Now we may look to see the wine flow in all the gutters, before Menelaus puts out again for Egypt!'

That night, after dusk, he set us ashore beyond Aegira, in a little cove a mile from the city, where he would not be seen and pressed into service, unloading the Egyptian vessels. He sailed away again without even wishing us farewell, and I was well rid of him, for he was the worst sort of sea-rogue, the sort who got us Hellenes into bad odour with other sea-folk.

Rarus wanted to strike away from Aegira in the night, but I was driven by some strange madness and I said, 'You can go if you will, but as for me, I would like to see what my uncle looks like. I cannot remember him after all these years, only as a dim shadow. In the end, perhaps our fortune lies with him; perhaps the god has brought us to Aegira so that we should meet him.'

Rarus sighed deeply and gave in to me. Afterwards I wished that he had bound my hands and feet and carried me away from that place, like a trussed lamb. But no, as always, he gave in to me, in his dear way, even when he should have stuck to his own opinion—which was often the right one, for he was always wiser than I was, although he was a slave.

35

IT all began like a gay dream, but ended a hag-ridden nightmare.

The square market-place of Aegira was set about with white-columned buildings, and a fountain always spurting in the middle. Trees were planted on all sides, and from them the crickets sang in the spring dusk. Bright torches, supported in holders about the square, cast a yellow-red light across the striped awnings and the hanging banners, as though this was a wine-festival. One might have thought that the place was prepared for Dionysus to come down again and sign for the dancing to begin.

But it was not Dionysus who reigned in Aegira that night; it was my uncle. On a a high wooden dais, he sat, enthroned in gold, with a woman at his feet.

I would never have known that this was Agamemnon's brother, my own flesh and blood. Beneath the tall flaring crown of gold, his head was shaven smooth, as was his face and body. Even from the edge of the crowd, I could see that his eyes had been painted with black and blue, to make them look larger and more staring. A false beard of black hair hung at his chin on two silver straps, and wagged in the warm breeze that swept across the square from the sea. His great chest was bare, and stained a deep brown. It gleamed with gold, from necklaces and stomachers studded with coloured stones. He sat with his strong brown legs apart, and his pleated linen kilt falling between them. From his golden sandals, and up his leg to the knee, coiled two snakes of some heavy beaten metal which I did not recognise. In his right hand he held a silver sword, and in his left a silver whip, its four thongs standing out stiffly from the head. They were the symbols of his power.

The woman who sat below him was as bare and brown as he, but her long thick hair was jet-black, and her white pleated skirt covered her legs from waist to ankles. Only the colour of her eyes told me that this was my Aunt Helen, transformed as by magic into an Egyptian queen now.

All about us, as we pushed among the crowd, we heard foreign voices. It seemed that the Greeks stood silent to let these sounds sink into their ears, in wonder. The old men of the Council of Aegira stood, white-robed and heads bowed, before the great dais where Menelaus lorded it.

Everywhere, men in Egyptian armour stood laughing and jesting, drinking wine and flinging the delicate cups down to be trodden into shards.

Rarus whispered to me, 'Many of these are Hellenes, also, but painted like the king. They must be the old veterans who left with him after Troy fell. It seems that some of them have brought their foreign wives, too. That woman over there—her hair was never anything but black, her eyes never smaller than we see them. And, look, there are three score Egyptians over there, behind the platform, leaning on their spears. They are no Hellenes.'

A man in a goatskin jacket turned to him and put his finger to his lips. 'Be quiet,' he said, 'or they will have your tongue. That was the order he sent out at midday, and he means it. My brother will speak no more, and only for shouting that Hellas would outlast the world.'

Then a guard in a great lion's head helmet began to glower towards them, and Rarus and the man were silent.

At last, one of the Egyptians stood forward and blew on a silver trumpet, as curled as a ram's horn. Its note was low and mournful, and it seemed to strike fear into all the men of Aegira, for they clustered together as though for comfort. And before the last note died away, from behind the dais, seven black-haired girls rose in their white skirts and clashed upon golden timbrels. The sudden noise came like a shock of lightning. In it lay all the strange foreign power of Egypt, all the magic of that awful land.

For the count of ten, there was only the distant lapping of the waters on the stone jetty, and the creaking of ship's timbers, and the endless shrilling of cicadas in the tamarisk trees.

Then, hardly moving his lips, and keeping as still as an image, Menelaus said above our heads, 'You are gathered here to listen to the fate of the world. Know, then, that I have come from my master in Egypt to bind Hellas, and all that lies in Hellas, to him. Know that you are the tools in his hand, no more, no less. We all lie in the great hand of the Pharoah, men of Hellas. There is no escaping from that hand, I tell you. From this time forward, if Egypt says "live", then we live; if "die", then we die. These things we shall do without thought, without fear, without gladness. We shall do only them and, in doing them, be contented that a new god has taken us into his keeping at last.'

When he had finished, the horn blew again, and the girls clashed their timbrels. Suddenly, as the noise died away, the chief citizen of Aegira, an old man with a crown of oak-leaves on his white head, spoke up in a wavering voice and said, 'What of the Dorians, King Menelaus? Might they not have a word to say about this?'

Menelaus suddenly closed his eyes, and the effect was terrible, for we seemed to be looking into pits of darkness. This was all the answer he gave, all the signal. Immediately four of the Egyptians behind the dais cast their javelins, and for an instant we saw the old man standing upright, staring down at the shafts that stood out of his body. Then he gave a sad sigh and sank out of our view. No one went to raise him; no one said a word of admonishment to the soldiers. It was as though all the men and women in that crowd were in a deep trance and bound by unseen chains.

Then a dark-haired young herald stood before the dais and called through a trumpet, his lips curled in spite, 'This night Aegira shall be burned to the ground. No one shall have it but Menelaus. All men below the age of thirty shall assemble at the harbour to be given arms; all women below the same age shall go to the tents for the comfort of their saviours. It is said.'

Not even at this did anyone call out in rebellion. But Rarus clutched my wrist and whispered, 'If we stay, this is our end.'

I whispered to him, 'If I could but speak to my uncle. . . .'

But he held his hand over my mouth, and drew me back from the crowd very slowly, until we were in a place the light of the torches did not reach. Then he swung me about and began to run, dragging me along. 'Come,' he said, 'we may get out of Aegira before it begins, if the god wills it.'

We were soon in a narrow lane where the houses leaned towards each other over the stone paving-blocks. All seemed clear, but as we ran on round a bend, Rarus stopped and dragged me close to a plastered wall.

'Do not speak,' he whispered. 'There is a guard at the end of the street. I must go to pass the time of night with him.'

He left then, close as a cat to the wall-side, bunched in the shadow until I could hardly see him. This was a Rarus I had not known before, and I crept after him quietly until I came to the bend in the wall.

I saw the tall cloaked figure of the Egyptian, his spear pointing to the stars, his body leaning lazily on his huge shield.

As I watched, a girl passed near him, carrying a wine-jar on her head, and I heard him call out to her, harshly, as though demanding where she might be going. I saw her go to him, saw him put out a hand towards her. Then the distant darkness blurred with an indefinite movement, and I heard the man cry out, the clattering of his shield, the smashing of the wine-jar and the pattering of the girl's feet. Before I could take it all in, Rarus was beside me again, his eyes wide in the darkness, wiping the short blade of a Mycenaen dirk on the skirt of his tunic.

'Come,' he said, 'if it were all as easy as that, then one need not fear any man.'

[210]

I think he was proud at that moment to have behaved so well against a warrior, and in my watching, too.

He sang a little song beneath his breath as we hurried to the end of the street, where the landward wall of Aegira started. There we found a group of women clustered about an ox-cart, on which sat an old Phoenician, his clothes torn, his pointed cap on one side. They were dragging at him, trying to get him off the cart so that they could be away; but the old man was a shrewder bargainer than that, and struck about him on all sides, trying to keep the women back. Yet in another moment, they would have had him down on the ground, their attack was so frantic.

But we ran among them, pushing and striking here and there, and calling out that the Egyptians were on our heels. As they began to run in fear, Rarus jumped on the cart beside the man, hauled me up alongside him, then whipped the dazed oxen forward with the reins.

The old Phoenician pushed back his cap and mopped his forehead. 'By Dagon and all the little fishes,' he said, 'but you frightened me, too, with your shouting! Oh, those poor, poor women! It hurts me not to give satisfaction to my customers.'

Rarus snatched the whip from him and said, 'It will hurt you far more if we are not outside this town very soon. The soldiers are moving from the square even now, I can hear the clank of their weapons.'

Then he stood up in the cart and brought the lash down again and again, until we were jolting along out of Aegira as fast as a man can run.

The Phoenician regarded Rarus with a certain admiration. 'You seem a brisk young fellow,' he said. 'I have never had much respect for Cretans, I must admit, but you are one in a thousand.'

Rarus did not answer; all his care was needed in avoiding the deep ruts that frost had made earlier in the road, and which might easily have smashed our wheels if we had strayed into them.

The Phoenician turned to me and said, 'This young husband of yours is too occupied to listen to an old fellow like me, I can see. When you get a moment, see if he would care to go into partnership with me. I deal in amber, horse-hides, bronze, and such iron as I can get hold of. A young fellow such as he is could do a lot worse than come into the trade with me. There'd be a place for you, as well, woman, if you can write, or if not that, then dance to fetch the buyers in.'

He was babbling on like that until Rarus suddenly swung round on him and said quite fiercely, 'You will be lucky if you are still alive by morning, old man, so save your breath. Our business lies in Mycenae, where there will be no trade for you, I can tell you.'

The Phoenician fell on his knees in the cart and clasped his hands round Rarus' knees. 'Oh, young prince, for the love of Dagon, do not go there, I implore you! I am known in Mycenae and they will slit my throat for a load of salt pork I left there on the way up-country. I was not to know the stuff had gone off in the heat, now, was I?'

Rarus kicked him over the side of the cart, into the darkness, and drove on. We heard him crying out for a while, then nothing more. Either he had seen sense and had held his tongue, or the Egyptians had overtaken him and stopped his mouth for ever.

It was ten miles before our nearside ox foundered and died with a burst heart. The wheels of the flimsy cart, passing over the beast, were shattered with the impact. But now we were away from Aegira, and far enough along the road to Mycenae to let us hope that we might at least reach that city alive, if we could only keep going.

36

WE came up through Low Town at last, among crowds of other folk who sought refuge from Menelaus and his Egyptians. The line of us stretched far back along the dusty hill-roads, like a black and tattered snake. Our approach to the city was announced by the forlorn bleating of sheep and the lowing of cattle, for most of the fearful country-folk had brought all they could with them, even clay pots and pans. The old folk either rode on the top of wagon-loads of bedding, or on the shoulders of a devoted son or daughter. But many of them were left by the roadside as we came up through Cleone, for the eagles to pick at if they chose. When a whole countryside moves, doctor, there is little room for gentle feeling; and the old must die, in any case.

At the Lion Gate the New Army stood in force, turning some away, if they looked poor and too old, letting others into the Outer Court if they had possessions or seemed strong enough to fight.

Tyndareus was in charge of it all. He stood on the outer wall in his chief citizen's robe and chain and his crown of oak-leaves, and scanned us as we hammered on the gate for refuge.

I saw his pig-like eyes sweep over Rarus and me three times, as though he wondered whether to turn us away like the others, but I took heart and shouted up to him, 'Tyndareus, you know us well enough. Do not pretend we are strangers. Let us in quickly, for I have a message of importance for the king.'

He stared about him for a while and then, as though in his own good time, bent and whispered to a young red-cloaked captain, who passed the word down to the guards at the gates.

When they swung open a little way, scores of refugees tried to push through before us; but the soldiers beat many of them back with spearshafts, and so, ragged and bruised, we got into the city, though, I am sad to say, a handful of frightened peasants lay on the ground because of that gate's opening.

Tyndareus was waiting for us, his robe held about his fat stomach to give him dignity. He stared at me insolently and said, 'You have been away so long, we gave you up for dead. You can tell me your message. I will take it to the king. As you see, these days the people have more say in things than they used. Well then, what is it?'

I did not like his arrogant tone, or the way he carefully avoided using any of my titles when speaking to me. I said, 'Tyndareus, we are both old enough to know what is what, aren't we? So, do you mean to say that a princess of Mycenae is denied access to her own home in the palace? Has the law come to that here? Tell me, are you daring to set yourself above me? No, do not turn away, but just answer me in the presence of these soldiers. I ask again: do you set yourself above me?'

This fat tradesman had become so full of his own importance that he must have seemed like the god himself. I must have been the first to speak like this to him for years. His face reddened and his hands shook so much that he let his heavy skirt fall into the dust. But I still stared into his eyes, and at last, afraid that I might belittle him further before the young soldiers, he said brusquely, 'Very well, come with me. I will lead you to the king.'

Rarus could not help himself. He said gently, 'You carry too much fat, Tyndareus, for this hot weather. If you are in the habit of running up and down the palace steps all day, you should sweat some of it off.'

I wished Rarus had held his tongue, though I agreed with what he had said. The chief citizen did not even turn, but said in a firm voice, 'Graves can be dug with words as easily as with shovels, my friend.'

I signed to Rarus to be silent now, and we went up to the citadel in silence, with two lines of soldiers marching after us, trailing their spears. I thought, as I saw them, that they would stand little chance against Menelaus' big insolent Egyptians.

Clytemnestra and Aegisthus were sitting in their gilded chairs at the top of the great stairway, dressed in what was left of their finery; but poor enough this looked when I recalled Menelaus and Helen in Aegira.

My mother did not speak to me at first, but just nodded and smiled down at me, her white face writhen with pain. Aegisthus looked every bit as old and worn, but at least he found the breath to greet me, in his way.

'This is a fine home-coming, daughter,' he wheezed. 'When you might have returned in peace, at any time during the past five years, you come now with the enemy close on your heels and sores on your feet.'

He turned round, painfully, in his chair, to speak to a young girl who stood behind him, a big-eyed creature whose dark hair flowed on her thin brown shoulders. She was overladen with silks and jewels, and wore the same sort of flounced skirt that I had once been proud of, when I called myself the goddess in Mycenae. Her feet were bare and painted, just as mine had been, but there the resemblance stopped, for she was little more than eight years old and had not the fullness of body that the goddess needs.

Aegisthus said to her, 'This is your sister, Electra, my sweeting. I have often told you of her; now you see her in the flesh.'

Aegisthus' daughter, Helen, whose birth late in years had crippled my mother, looked at me with pursed lips, her great dark eyes taking in my rags and dirt and sores. Then she said, 'But her hair is the colour of dust. You told me it was like amber. This is a beggar-woman of the lanes not a goddess, father.'

The king turned to me and smiled. 'You see,' he said, 'children cannot look beneath the surface of things, Electra. They see only what is before them. Perhaps she is right, though; perhaps you are only a beggar-woman now, the way things have fallen out.'

Behind me on the stairway, Tyndareus chuckled, delighted to hear me put in my place at last.

I said in a loud voice to the king, 'Send your dog away, Aegisthus. I will not be his bone.'

The king put on a mock-frown and answered, 'Tyndareus has been my right hand for a long time, Electra. He feels the pulse of the people, and I rely on him most of all.'

I said, 'Send him away, Aegisthus. He is a fat rogue whose only desire is to line his own pockets. I have seen his sort before.'

My mother smiled indulgently as I spoke, all the wits gone from her. Aegisthus turned to her, appealing for her to silence me, but when he saw her empty face, he shrugged his shoulders and gave in.

'Leave us, my friend,' he called down the steps. 'She is still

[215]

headstrong, as you see, but I need her advice. Go, Tyndareus, and I will speak to you later, the two of us together.'

After the chief citizen had gone, grumbling down the stairs, the king called for slaves to carry the two gilded chairs into the great hall. I walked between them, a hand on each, to show everyone my place in Mycenae. To do this, I had to push little Helen out of the way, but this caused me no ache of heart, although she scowled and almost broke into tears to be separated from her father.

Aegisthus saw this, but said nothing to her. Instead he spoke to me slyly. 'You see, Electra, I have never walked very well since that day your black bull got at me. I shall speak of that again to you, later. It has been in my heart a great deal while you have been away.'

Though I hated the man, I had to admire his calm words and forebearance.

Clytemnestra leaned from her chair, smiling vacantly, and said, 'Yes, daughter, poor Aegisthus has not been well at all since that day. The bards sing wicked songs about him, you know. They say he leaps on old Agamemnon's tomb and challenges the Lion to fight for Mycenae; but, I tell you, the poor king couldn't step over a thimble, much less jump on a tomb.'

Aegisthus flushed a little and made clucking noises with his tongue to quieten her; but she went on, regardless, 'And they say he always has an empty chair placed at the table for Agamemnon to come back and sit in, to give the dead their due. But that is false, also, daughter. Aegisthus has two chairs so that he can move from one to the other, if the feast is too long, to rest his poor leg. That is true, is it not, my dear?'

But the king did not answer her. He turned to me and said quite shortly, 'Come now, we are indoors, tell me what you have seen.'

So I told all that I had seen at Aegira, missing nothing out. I then told about the Dorians who were massing beyond the Straits. But Aegisthus waved this away, saying, 'They are nothing, only an undisciplined rabble. We can stand against them, one day, next year, perhaps, when they find the means of coming over to us. I am not concerned with Dorians; it is Menelaus I am thinking of. Tell me, how do you rate his army?'

I answered, 'His men look like veterans. They are armed in a way that Hellas has not seen for twenty years. Though, in number, they are many fewer than your own New Army, I have no doubt that one of Menelaus' warriors would terrify five of yours. That is my opinion, Aegisthus.'

He sucked in his lips and rubbed his sweating hand up and down the stubble on his face. At last he said, 'Would you, then, advise me to treat with Menelaus, to offer him, say, half this kingdom, rather than to fight with him?'

I stood my ground and said, 'Aegisthus, the time for treaty has gone by. Menelaus comes for revenge, not only for lands and gold. He has seen enough lands and gold by now, and knows he can get them easily enough, wherever he chooses. But he can only get his vengeance here in Mycenae. He can only get you here. You are what he comes for, Aegisthus, and no manner of treating will keep him from that. He has hunted you all his life, king.'

As I spoke, the flesh seemed to fall from the king's face; his whole body seemed to shrink. It was as though I saw a man disappearing before my eyes. His chin began to tremble and beads of salt sweat coursed from his sparse hair down his forehead and into his eyes, so that he had to blink many times before he spoke again.

'In your opinion, daughter,' he said uncertainly, 'would this Menelaus accept another for his vengeance? I mean, suppose I granted him this city and went away, taking only what I can carry in a litter, and left behind, say, Helen. . . . She is young, you know, and does not bother about these things; it would be nothing to her, yet it could be much to me. Would that satisfy Menelaus, think you?'

I glanced at his frightened, coward's face, and then at the thin child who stood behind him, silent and patient, not understanding that her father was planning to pass the death-sentence on her. For a moment, I think I would have advised him to offer this Helen to Menelaus, to be dealt with as my own sister Iphigenia had been dealt with. Then suddenly the child put up her small hand and began to pat the king's shoulder. 'Don't cry, my father,' she said. 'You are crying, and a king should not cry. Now, dry your eyes, and all will be well, I promise you. I am the goddess, am I not? And goddesses always speak the truth to kings.'

This decided me. That a man who set himself up as the High King of Achaea should even think of bartering his own poor hide for the life of a simpleton, his own flesh and blood, angered me. I did not love Helen—but I loved her coward father still less.

I said, 'Do what you will, Aegisthus, but you will not escape what is coming towards you. Menelaus will have both Helen and you, to torment as he wishes. This I speak as one who once saw inside the god's heart a little way.'

Aegisthus stiffened and asked hoarsely, 'When do you think he will be here, Electra? How long have we got?'

I answered, 'Today and perhaps tomorrow, for I do not think he will move down until his men are fully ready. Yet, when they do move, it will be quickly, of that I have no doubt. They will strike like the lightning, and will be amongst your folk before they know it. It is my guess that this will happen at the latest by tomorrow night, Aegisthus.'

I spoke calmly, as one might talk of some ordinary thing about the house—the laying of a fire, or the flavouring of a dish. I spoke as though this did not affect me, or my mother, but only Aegisthus. And suddenly, by my manner of speech, I could see that he felt entirely alone in Mycenae.

He drummed his hands on his bare head and all his fat body shook in his chair. I thought that he was about to have a seizure and cheat Menelaus after all. I was so concerned at this, I called for a servant to bring him spiced wine; but the poor wretch could hardly get it into his mouth. It ran down on to his robes and dripped to the tiled floor.

At last I said to the carriers, 'Take the king into the high tower, and stand by him. He will feel more secure there.'

He looked at me with big eyes then, for I think he knew what lay behind my words; in the high tower, there was no escape for him.

[218]

37

WHEN he had gone, my mother turned to me and shook her head sadly. I asked, 'But you do not love him, do you, Clytemnestra?'

She said, so quietly that I had to strain to hear her words, 'Love him? I have forgotten what it is to love anyone, daughter. I only know that he and I are two old folk, too weak now to rule a kingdom, too full of pain to stand much more of it.'

I knelt by her and said, 'Have courage, mother. We still do not know what the god intends for us. Perhaps his pattern might turn out well, after all.'

Clytemnestra shook her head very, very slowly. 'Oh no, Electra,' she whispered. 'That can never be, now. I know that, and you cannot tell me otherwise. Look, ever since you have been away, not one night of rest have I had. The dark has been filled with menacing. There has been no peace for me, my love. The god has found every way to make me suffer. He has neglected nothing, even the smallest things.'

I placed my arm about her and held her like a small child, although the scent that came from her body and clothes was distressing. I said, 'How do you mean, my mother? How has the god been at you?'

I thought that by getting her to speak of these things her heart might be lightened of its load, doctor. You understand.

She said, 'There have been dreams, but dreams so hard and clear that I have not known whether I was asleep or waking. Dreams that have stayed with me, even when the sun has come into the room at dawn, at midday, in the afternoon. And such dreams, my daughter! The god must have kept a writing of all I have ever thought, to bring it out for my torment now.'

I said, 'Everyone has dreams, mother, and they seem worse when one is sick and weak. They are nothing.'

She half-turned from me and put her shrunken hand over the black hole of her mouth as she spoke.

'These dreams are not nothing. Would you like the dream of excrement? It lies everywhere, in my bed, on the table-top, on my body. Each way I turn, my hand encounters it. It fills my mouth. It slides under my feet. It is always where I least expect it. It lies at the bottom of the cup I drink from, though that cup be washed a hundred times. This the god has thought of for me. Then there is another dream, and this goes back to when I was so small, a lonely little girl wandering in my father's great palace, too noble to play with other children. One day, up in the high rafters, in a secret room I discovered, I lifted a floor-board and under it, in the darkness, I found a nest of birds—such birds as build their houses high in palaces, I forget their name now. But this was no ordinary nest; it was left for me to find so that I should suffer. In it were three birds, quite big birds, but still young, alive and opening their beaks for food to be put in.'

I tried to laugh, and I said, 'But a nest of birds is no bad dream, mother.'

She screwed her mouth up in disgust. 'These birds were a bad dream,' she whispered. 'As eggs, they had been laid in this small enclosed space, with beams of wood and laths all about them. And so they hatched out, and grew, as their mother got in among the wood to feed them. But they did not grow like birds, for their poor bodies had to take on every shape, every twist and turn of the wood-work. Their necks grew crooked, as though they were screwed; their breastbones were shaped like a harp, with no feathers on one side; and their poor legs and feet were so twined and twisted, it was a torment to see them. I went up to them for many days, daughter, and at last, when I could bear it no longer, I dropped a stone down on them to put an end to their misery. Now that dream comes to me every night—the crooked bodies, and their open red beaks when they thought I was bringing food, and I was bringing a stone to crush them.'

Clytemnestra bent down and wept as I had never heard her weep before. I tried to stay her tears, but she pushed my hand away as though she were young again, an Amazon. 'And now, at last,' she said, 'comes the final dream. All day the black snake moves inside me, curling in my bowels, sometimes sliding out again into the open to see the light; only to torture me again when he goes in to enjoy my warmth, my darkness, my corruption! So does the god speak to me of my end. Now do you understand?'

It was an hour before her weeping stopped. I had her carried to her bed, and thought she had worn herself out and was sleeping. But as I tried to leave her room, to find out what Rarus thought of it all, her eyes opened and she beckoned me back to her bedside.

'Electra,' she said, 'we have talked of all these things, but yet we have not said a word about what lies nearest to my heart.'

'What is that, dear mother?' I asked her.

She said, 'Your brother, Orestes. Did you ever find him?'

I nodded my head. 'Yes, mother, I found him. He is well, and far away, beyond Mount Oeta. He is a king there, mother, and has his own folk now. He has wedded Hermione, and one day he will be great in Hellas.'

She lay back and smiled. 'At least the god gives us some rewards,' she whispered. 'It has been in my heart lately that he might try to come here again, to take back his kingdom, to sit in his father's chair in Mycenae. But that would be death for him now. One or another would put an end to my son. Thank you, daughter, for your words. I can rest a little, now that I know he will stay safe, far from this dunghill of death.'

Her eyes closed again, and her head fell sideways.

She was at peace, but I was not. Her words had wakened in me a new fear. Orestes had sworn that he would come to Mycenae, despite what I had told the queen. So, he would come, and would be caught between the two mill-stones—either the New Army would murder him, or Menelaus, his tyrant uncle.

I found Rarus sitting in the sunlight at the bottom of the great stairway, talking with a young soldier about iron-smelting. He saw that I was greatly anguished and rose immediately and came to me, under the shadow of a cypress tree, where no one should hear us.

'What is it, sister?' he said.

I said, 'For god's sake, Rarus, help me! I have only just seen where the pattern is leading. How blind I have been!'

He held me to him and said, 'Come, come, sister. Tell me in plain words. Do not leave me guessing any longer.'

I steeled myself and answered, 'Then here it is, my brother. We are trapped like birds in a snare, here in this mad city, come what may, it does not matter very much. It seems to me that this is our pattern, the way our threads run. But there is Orestes still to think of. If he comes here, then he is a dead man. You remember what he said, in Oeta, that he was almost ready to come? Well, he may be on the road here even as we speak. He and my husband, Pylades, and the other men. They would be walking into the trap.'

Rarus scratched his head and said with a wry smile, 'That is the chance they must take, sister. We have taken our chance, all the way, with only our own wits to help us. Can they not do the same?'

I began to hit at his face and to shout at him. 'Can you not see, we have it in our power to stop him from killing himself? It is not often that we poor earthlings can change the pattern for the god, but here is our chance. I beg you, Rarus, you who have been so good to me all my days, help me to keep Orestes alive now.'

He looked at me gravely and said, 'What would you have me do? Go back up the road to Aegira, searching for him? Would you have me cross the Straits again and dare the mountains? Is this what you are asking, sister?'

I nodded, not daring to look into his eyes.

'Yes, Rarus,' I said. 'I would have you find him, whether he is far away or near, and turn him back from Mycenae. Alone, you could keep clear of the armies. A nimble fellow like you could hide in a fox-hole until Menelaus had passed by. You could walk under the legs of the Dorian horses, and they would never know you had been there. Will you do it?'

He stood a little away from me, holding my two hands in his. Then he suddenly bowed his head, once, in a sign of acceptance.

[222]

'I will do it, if the god will sit on my back and guide me,' he said gently. 'I will do this if it is the last thing I shall ever do for you. Farewell, my sister, and may your warp and weft be unbroken if I ever see you again.'

I turned and held on to the cypress tree as he went. If I had not done this, I should have fallen, for now all the strength had gone out of me and I felt as empty as a corn-husk after the threshing-flail has fallen on it and the harsh wind has whipped the grain away.

38

FOR long after the sun had lost its strength, I lay under the old laurels in the hidden garden where my sister and I had once made our house and told each other secrets. If Iphigenia had been there, she would have told me what to do now, with a mad queen and a terrified king on my hands.

But all I could hear that afternoon was the sound of refugees pleading, down at the Lion Gate, and the clattering of wagons as they made their way up the rocky slope to the citadel. That and the frantic crying of captains and sergeants trying to get the New Army into some shape, to withstand the coming shock.

Once, I thought I heard the voice of Tyndareus calling out, 'Come, lads, just do your best and trust to me. Whenever have I not seen you through? Believe me, I can arrange everything, if you will only give me a chance. There now, that's better. Let's have a cheer for Tyndareus!'

The breeze which carried these words past my ears in the high garden also brought on their tail a few half-hearted shouts. I put my face into the grasses and laughed and cried at it all, coming in the end not to know the difference between the one sound and the other. For all was mad, the world itself was mad, and I was as mad as any other creature in that world—no more, and no less.

As the sun began to sink and the deep blue of the sky took on its tinge of purple, I decided what I would do to pass these awful hours; go to the tomb of Agamemnon and say a prayer for Orestes and for poor Rarus. I would beg the dead king to pardon all, and now to keep his son, and my dear friend from harm. What else was there for me to do, in a city that was crazy with its own inner terror, its men scuttering about like ants, this way and that, building barricades that would fall down at the first onslaught, practising spear-thrusts that they had not the courage to use when all came to all.

I bought a white dove from an old blind woman who sat on the steps of the Hera Shrine, beside the Lion Gate. She smiled when I took it from her, but would not tell me why she did so. I asked her, 'Is it because you think all sacrifice is useless, old one?'

But she only turned her blind eyes away, and smiled again as though she would welcome the Dorians coming, or anyone coming, who would put an end to this city which had outlived its day.

When I reached the great stone tomb of Agamemnon, set in its eternal silence beneath the dark cypresses, it was so much night that I mistook a stray sheep for a man lying in the grass. I jumped with fear, then laughed at my mistake, and went into the columned porch where the blurred white of the tomb just showed through the dusk.

Here I stood, as is proper to the Greeks in praying, and addressed my dead father, begging his aid, admitting my foolishness in the past. The white dove gave up its life easily, without causing me any anguish, and I laid it carefully in the centre of the tomb stone, where the High King's bronze helmet still stood, for this would be the nearest place to his heart in death.

It was only when I was taking my hand away again that I felt the touch of something that was not dove or helmet. My finger-tips rested on it a while, before the nature of the thing revealed itself to me. It was a fabric of some sort, some piece of braiding, of linen, yet small. I wondered if it was a ribbon that the wind had whisked from some girl's hair and sent spinning over the wall on to the flat tomb stone.

Yet as I touched it, a strange tremor seemed to come out of it and into my arm, striking to the inner parts of me. I took it in my hand, as fearfully as if it had been a little black snake, and almost ran with it to where a tripod glowed beyond the tomb.

And there I saw that it was a ribbon indeed; the ribbon I had once woven for my little brother, and which I had last seen about his hair in Oeta, when in wine he had promised to come again to Mycenae.

I almost fell to the ground with the shock of this message. It meant only one thing—that Orestes was already in the city, somewhere, perhaps among the refugees. That Pylades my husband would be with him, and even their Band of Brothers, their trusted soldiers. Now as I stood, my legs quivering with weakness, behind the tomb, perhaps they were at their work, up in High Town.

And I had sent poor Rarus towards the enemy to save them from this! 'Oh, father,' I said aloud, 'so my dove was wasted, just as the blind old woman knew, down at Hera's Shrine.'

Now I did not know what to do. I thought of Rarus running along the dark road, listening for the approaching tramp of feet; or hiding behind the rocks as a troop of Menelaus' cavalry rode under him. I began to wonder if there was any chance of my getting through the Lion Gate, and of finding him, and going away with him for ever, away from Mycenae. This I would most dearly have done.

And it was then that my ears first caught the sound of a low moaning, like the cry of a starved and deserted lamb, dropped in the wicked winter weather by a careless ewe.

It came to me that beyond the columns, in the long grasses, a child might be lying, lost and afraid, the child of some refugee, perhaps, left by terrified parents. There had been little tenderness in my heart towards these people, but now, myself lonely and fearful in the darkness by the tomb, and remembering my own lost baby, I went towards the moaning sound, hoping that the god who looked

[225]

over all might deal with me the more generously for this pity I was showing.

'Where are you, child?' I called, softly, so that no one might hear me lower down the slope. 'Where are you? I am a friend.'

The moaning was now nearer, almost beneath my feet, in the dark and trampled grass. Afraid lest I might tread on the crying child, I kneeled and groped about me, until my hand touched something that was not a child. I drew back then, for what I had felt was hair, long hair, damp with something other than dew. As I knelt, rubbing thumb against fingers and knowing that I had touched blood, the moon rode from behind the high summer night-cloud, down upon the upturned face of Rarus. But a Rarus I had not known before.

This was such a face as might be cut from alabaster, yet so ravaged and stained, as though a troop of horse had trampled over it to ruin what the sculptor had created. In the silver moonlight, his eyes were round hollows of purple darkness; his clotted hair hung matted, beside his cheeks, like the flaps of a helmet. His lips were drawn back from his teeth like the voice-hole of an ivory mask, leaving only a dark shadow where the tongue should be.

As I looked down on him, at this ghastly comedy that had been Rarus, he cried out again, yet so mindlessly, so distantly, that I knew there was no knowledge in his cry. He was asking no pity, accusing no enemy; he was crying because this was all now left for him to do.

I kissed his gaunt face but its blind features gave no sign that he had ever known me. I held him to me, staining my shift with his dark blood; but his body was already stiffening and he got no comfort from my rocking. Then, as he fell away from me and rolled helpless over, I felt something drag at my skirt, and, reaching out my hand, found that a long javelin-head, such as become detached from their shaft once they have reached their mark, was fixed deep into his side below the ribs.

It was more than I could bring myself to do, to drag this frightful weapon out. Not knowing where my strength came from, I raised the heavy body of my friend and staggered with him past the moonlit tomb, and up the gentle slope behind the palace, where apple-orchards were. There, where the white and rose-pink blossom starred the grass, I laid him down, beneath a tree whose branches were a canopy, of red, and white, and moonlit green.

And there I kissed his chilly lips, called him my love, told him I would return; and ran away.

Huge and squat, most monstrous now, the palace rose upon its granite base; the House of Atreus, the den of death. I did not dare go up its stark and splendid stairs; and so, I entered through a little cavern, at the back, a door prohibited to all but members of the House. I raced on blindly up the winding steps, that led in secret to the great hall. And as I went, my cold mouth formed the message I would shout: 'Beware, mother, beware, your son is back! Orestes is in Mycenae!'

39

AND yet these words were never said. As I drew back the heavy curtains and looked into the room, I saw that my message would come too late.

My mother was trying to rise from a straw-pallet laid on the floor for her, with the aid of two sticks. Her back was towards me, so she did not see the terror in my face.

Three paces from her stood two tall men, so cloaked that their faces were hardly visible in the flickering lamp-lit room. But I knew who they were, for, from beneath the hood of the smaller, a torn length of red ribbon had escaped and was hanging on his shoulder. It was ribbon I had woven myself so long ago, to keep Orestes' hair in order, when his mother wanted him tidy.

Between the two men stood a tall bronze urn, and each of them had a hand upon its lip, as though they had carried it up the stairway.

My mother's reedy voice asked, 'What did you say again, young gentlemen?'

They saw me as she asked this, but made no movement across the tiled floor. The taller of them, my husband Pylades, answered her and said, 'Lady, as you see, we are two Aeolians from Daulis. A man who calls himself Strophius, a stranger to us, I must admit, whom we met on the road to Aulis, flying from the Dorians, begged us, if we ever got to Mycenae, to bring this urn to you. He said it held the ashes of your son, Orestes. We know no more than that, great lady. But we felt that a mother would wish to have the ashes of her flesh and blood at the last. And so we came. Have we done right?'

By now my mother had struggled to her knees, always leaning on the sticks, and was shuffling her way towards the urn. They made no move to help her, but still stood there, the great cloaks and hoods about them.

She was saying, again and again, 'Oh, little Orestes, my poor Orestes.' Then, 'Good gentlemen, how did he die?'

I was like a cold stone at the doorway, unable to move for horror and weariness. It did not startle me at all when hooded Orestes shouted out, like a man bewitched, 'He died like this, mother!'

And as he said these words, he and tall Pylades bent swiftly, so that their cloaks fell over my kneeling mother, shrouding her. I saw a white hand rise and fall, but in the dim light of the clay lamps, could not say whose hand it was. I only knew that they drew away and let Clytemnestra fall on the painted tiles, her hands clasped to her stomach and a dark gout of blood spurting up like a fountain from between her fingers.

She was saying, 'My son, my son, remember your duty to your mother.' And they were laughing, as though she had been some clever poet making a jest.

Suddenly, Orestes shouted back to her, 'And you remember your duty to your husband, witch!'

Then I unfroze and ran across the room to her, as she rolled on the

[228]

pavement. Pylades waved his hand at me and said, 'Go back, Electra, this is not your business now.'

But I ignored him and fell down beside the queen. She was smiling, not weeping, and now the fountain had stopped its dreadful flow. It was as though she had always waited for this; and, now that it had come, was content once more. As I stooped to kiss her lips, she looked as young as I ever remember her. Her bright eyes flickered over my face and she whispered, 'Daughter, now we are all together. It is good for the family to gather once again, is it not?'

As Pylades tried to drag me off her, she looked up once more and said, 'The nurse, Geilissa, told me that great Agamemnon would be back from Troy in time for this feast. Is it so, daughter? I thought I saw him a moment ago, standing by the wall and nodding down at me. Oh, the god is good to bring us all together at the last, after these hundred years of waiting.'

Then she patted my arm with her red hand and slipped sideways out of my knowing to the floor.

Pylades took me by the hair and yelled in my ear, 'For the god's sake, go! I love you, Electra; do not stay here to die. Their guards may come at any moment. Go, I beg of you, go!'

I shook him away, and as I did so, the curtains at the far end of the hall were suddenly drawn, and Aegisthus ran in, wet and naked, save for the white woollen towel he held about him. There was a gold mask in his other hand. His face was puffed and angry.

In the dimness of the lamps, he could not see what was happening at our end of the great room, and he was calling out, 'What is all this row? Can't a man bath in peace? Can't a queen lie sleeping? What are you servants doing in the chamber at this time of night? Whose urn is that?'

He was hobbling towards us all the time, leaving wet footmarks on the floor-tiles, like a snail.

Then Orestes flung back his hood and faced him.

'It is your urn, swine from Thyestes' sty!' he yelled.

Aegisthus stopped at this voice and stood like a man struck by lightning. Then he gave a low cry, from deep in the belly, and swung round to run away. But his leg was lame from the black bull and his feet wet from the bath. He slipped and fell headlong on the shiny floor, and the two men were on him like hounds on a fallen stag.

I heard the thudding of their dirk-hilts on his body, and heard his sharp sucking-in of breath each time a blow landed. Then, in a great noble voice, Aegisthus called, 'Let me cover my face! Let me go into the shadows like a king.'

He tried to get the gold mask over his features as he lay. I saw then how it was; he must have had this thing in readiness against the day when he should be placed in the tomb. It was his own face in gold, the cheeks fat, the eyes small slits, the loose mouth smiling in a sneer. The goldsmith had made a craftsman's job of that mask.

But Orestes kicked it out of his hand, sending it slithering over the floor. 'Your face shall be covered, with a vengeance!' he shouted. And he and Pylades took up the bronze urn and pushed it down hard over his head and shoulders, as far as it would go.

The sound of Aegisthus' last cries, from inside that urn, were horrible to hear; it was the sound of a bull bellowing under the butcher's pole-axe.

I turned away, for the towel had fallen from him, and there was something I could not bear to see in his fat body and his legs kicking in the air.

When little Helen ran through the door, squealing, in her flounced skirt and her bracelets jangling, it was nothing to me that the two men handled her as they did. No, it was no more than the dove, whose neck I had just wrung, down at Agamemnon's tomb.

Then the two were beside me, their arms about me, pulling. 'Come, you fool!' Pylades shouted hoarsely in my ear. 'If we do not go now, we are dead men!'

Though I struggled to stay in that flickering death-room, they dragged me through the far door and down the little stairway I had come up, towards the orchards. No guard was there to stop our way. The New Army was saving itself.

Outside, in the cold night air, I was sick, and vomited. Pylades stood beside me, leaning on the lower wall of the palace, doing the

same. Orestes struck out at both of us, with the ivory haft of his copper knife, and grunted like a wild boar in anger at our delay. In the moonlight, his eyes were no more human than pieces of agate, or thin slivers of flint, such as the men of Thessaly used to set in their death-masks. He seemed to have lost his power of speech now. He was like nothing more than a Fury that has done its work and is lost in the dark, not knowing how to get back to its master, back into its dark shelter in the ground.

40

WHEN we were among the first trees, Pylades stopped again and whispered, in fear, among the overhanging boughs, 'Steady now, we must not miss the way. Our company waits for us beyond the tomb, keeping guard on the little gap in the wall. In which direction does it lie, Electra?'

I tried to point, but my hand was so shaking that I was not much use to him. Orestes was still hitting out, and pulling at our cloaks, trying to make us move on. He was now less like a Fury than a boy frightened by a nightmare. His mouth-ends were jigging up and down as though in a spasm of silent laughter. And all his flesh was shuddering when I put my hand upon his shoulder. At first, he jumped with fright when I touched him, and then swung round on me, his dirk upraised.

But, distracted as I was, I had his measure. I was his big sister again, as I had been in childhood. I took the dagger from him gently, and he let it go without a protest, his hands as weak as a child's.

I said to my husband, 'What ought to be done with him, Pylades?' Truly, I do not know what was in my heart when I said this; but I think it was what I had just seen, and the dagger in my hand, that made me speak so.

My husband was gazing at me strangely among the moonlit blossom with the blood over his breast and face. Then he shook his head like a swimmer coming up out of the water, and whispered, 'We must take him with us, wife. His men are waiting by the wall. They will finish us if we do not bring him back to them. They are sworn avengers.'

It was then that I heard the low moaning again, from beneath the apple-tree where I had left poor Rarus. God, I thought, still alive! Not dead yet—how is it possible to crawl so long down the tunnel of death? Is there any mercy in heaven for a man to be left so long in agony?

My heart brimful of pity, I cried to Pylades, 'Let me go a little moment. I shall not be long; but I cannot leave until I have parted from a dear friend.'

He nodded, distantly, and I ran into the crowded boughs.

Some blows are struck in anger, some in remorse, and some in gentle kindliness. These last are like a kiss, like a caress, no more. They carry so much love with them that all the pain is stifled in it, and the blow is welcomed, not begrudged.

So it was with the blow I gave, under the apple-boughs. And as I raised my hand to put an end to agony, the knife-blade caught the branch above my head, and clouds of blossom fell on Rarus and on me. It was like a pretty wedding, when the young girls scatter flowers over the bride and groom, no more than that. And all in the moonlight, Dia's moonlight. Calm came to me, at this blessing of our final union; it seemed as though the Mother smiled on what I did, giving consent.

When I went back to the orchard's edge, Orestes was in my husband's arms, sagging like a great doll, his legs too weak to carry him.

Pylades said, 'So, it has come to this. I always suspected your brother, Electra, when it came to final thrust. He has the heart for it, yes, but not the force to carry it through. So, we must carry him.'

Together we bore Orestes through the orchard, down towards the tomb. Behind us, lights flared in the palace rooms, and high shouts warned us that what we had left on the floor of the hall had now been found.

I said to Pylades, 'We have little time, husband.'

He nodded, but did not speak. His face was that of an old man, in the moonlight. I thought how young and peaceful Rarus had last seemed to me, with the moon-lit blossom on his face and his dark tumbled hair.

'Come, come,' I said, 'this is the quickest way, alongside Agamemnon's tomb, not through the colonnade. We have no time to lose.'

When we rounded the far corner of the tomb, we stumbled and fell with Orestes. I did not need to be told what obstacle had flung us down. My hands told me this, plainly enough. Orestes' company lay heaped about, in the rough grass, one across the other, as though they had died holding the gap in the wall. Helmets and javelins were everywhere.

I was already on my knees, about to ask Pylades what we should do now, when, from behind the wall, rose a line of soldiers, some of them bearing resinous torches. Menelaus stood tallest among them, dressed in his fine Egyptian armour and holding up a sword.

His voice rode lightly on the evening air. 'So, niece,' he called, 'the chariot-wheel turns well, and the fox runs into the trap!'

All the dark-faced men about him laughed in their strange, foreign way, at his words. I flung the ivory-hafted dagger at him, through the moonlight, but he dodged it with an easy movement, and then they laughed again and closed on us where we kneeled.

Orestes' mouth was wide open and he was gasping like a man in a fit; Pylades was striking out wildly, as they came to grasp him, but he only hit the air. Then the soldiers thumped at his chest and body with the butt-ends of their javelins, without any mercy, until he rolled away and stopped shouting.

Menelaus himself put his hands into my hair and dragged me down. I think, for an instant, he meant to put the sword into me; but through the dark air there came the rustle of wings, just above our heads. It was perhaps a flock of birds, disturbed from their nest in Agamemnon's tomb by our scuffling; but to Menelaus it seemed something else. He flung his sword away as though shocked by what he might have done.

To a captain he said, 'Enough, enough! This lies beyond us now. It must be settled by the law of Mycenae. Take them to the prison. They are out of our hands.'

And, as we went, the deep droning of the bees from the Tomb of Atreus sounded in our ears, at every step. It was as though I had become a frightened little girl again, and all this had been for nothing: nothing at all.

41

I NEVER saw my Uncle Menelaus again after that. We lay, the three of us, in damp straw upon the stone floor. The prison was a filthy place, with only one small runnel to carry all away.

In the presence of my husband and my brother, I did not like to use the thing. It is strange how nice one may be, even in such a desperate condition. I spoke to the gaoler about it, ordering him to flush it down with water more regularly. But he smiled and said, 'I hardly see what great difference that will make, lady, since you will be here so short a time; and after you have gone up out of this place, such things as modesty and cleanliness will seem mere toys of the mind.'

He went away, and the runnel was never flushed. Yet I was the only one who seemed to mind. Orestes lay in a corner, his eyes turned up, his hands, palms-upwards, on the floor beside him, out of his senses. And my husband, Pylades, was often up near the high, barred window, striking at the walls and calling for his warriors to come and save him. His knuckles were all bloody, but he did not know this.

I had no pity to spare for either of them. I felt alone, though they were always near to me in that small cell.

When the chief citizen came down the steps to visit us, in his fine robe and with a clay tablet in his hand, I was glad even to see him.

I ran to him and said, 'What news, citizen? Oh, what news?'

He flung me away and put on his mincing voice, his official voice, the one he used when he made announcements to the simple peasant-folk in Mycenae.

He said, 'You have been tried by the Council, with myself and Menelaus to guide the jurors. . . .' Even then I smiled inside me to think of this upstart jack putting himself before great Agamemnon's brother. I hardly bothered to listen to the rest of his words, for I could tell by his tone that they boded no good for us now. He went on, 'And we have decreed, we the Council of Elders, that Orestes and Electra, Prince and Princess of Mycenae, are guilty of matricide, and must die the death on this account. Furthermore, we have decreed that the man called Pylades, of another country than ours, is guilty of regicide, and so must die on this account. I have spoken the law.'

More for something to say than anything else, something to keep him talking in that lonely place, I asked, 'What manner of death, Tyndareus? And when shall it be?'

He did not deign to look at me as he answered, 'It will be the hemlock cup, in view of your nobility. And, if I can arrange it, it will happen tonight. You will not know when, until you see the cupbearers come through the door. You will not mistake them, woman, I can assure you. These men are chosen with care. They wear the face of death.'

Then he flung the clay tablet on the floor, so violently that it smashed to small crumbling pieces, as was the custom, and, turning away from us, went between the guards back up the steps.

I sat and watched him go, seeing the thick oak door shutting on us for the last time. Then, for the want of something better to do, I leaned forward and took up a piece of the broken tablet and put it between my teeth. It crunched easily in the mouth and gave me a dull sort of contentment, as though I was consuming death before death took me in its maw.

So, through the afternoon, I ate the whole of death and was glad to see it gone; though when it was finished, I felt ready to retch and secretly I hoped that the clay of that tablet had been poisoned.

When the door was flung wide again, I sat quite still, having decided that I would stare the death-bringers in the eye to the last, and would let them put the cup to my mouth without any struggle. But I was disappointed; it was not the cup-bearers who came in, but my Aunt Helen.

She was dressed as I had last seen her, at Aegira, in all the finery of an Egyptian queen. But though her jewellery and gold ornaments jangled richly, there was no splendour now about her face. I could see beneath its paint and gilding, even in the dim light of the cell. She was an old woman, decked out to look a young one. At a distance this might have been well enough, but, close to, she was the ravaged whore of half the world. Her jet-black hair was grey at the roots, and when it swung from beside her jaw, I noticed how her face had fallen into dewlaps. Above and below her amethyst collar, her skin was as wrinkled as a chicken's neck, plucked for the pot.

I laughed up at her and said, 'So, it comes even to a queen, then? Time has no respect for greatness or nobility, dear aunt!'

Helen's mask of dignity could not stand against this mockery. I could tell that her heart was as warm and soft as ever, despite her Egyptian splendour. She waved the guard away and told him to close the door. Then she came a pace towards me and said, 'Electra, dear one, have some small pity for me. You are soon to go away in the fullness of your powers and beauty, but I must carry this mummy of a body about with me for ever. I cannot be lightened of my load by death. Have kindness, princess.'

Suddenly, she seemed so weak and helpless that I almost laughed. She, a great queen, who had set the world at war, once upon a time; and I, a filthy, ragged prisoner, waiting for the poison-cup, like a heifer brought into the pen for slaughter, the dirt on my flanks, the chain about my neck.

I said, 'Have it your own way, aunt. I am beyond pity, for you or for myself, now. This prison is a wonderful place for teaching one what is important in the world, and what is not. And at this moment I would willingly exchange my smooth flesh for your wrinkled parts!'

She put her hand to her mouth, as though she wanted to cry out at my words. Then, instead, she went on her knees beside me in the dust, regardless of her white linen skirt, and took my hands in hers.

'I beg you, Electra,' she said, 'to forgive me. I had no hand in all this. There has been enough killing already, and I wish for no more. I tried to argue for you all in the Council, but the men would not listen to me. I am only a woman when it comes to these affairs, they told me, though I may count as a queen in other matters. Believe me, I begged for your life.'

I said, 'Much good does it do me now, to tell me this! Have you any more amusing tales to tell me?'

Helen turned her face from me and lowered her head. 'Try to understand, Electra,' she said in a low voice, 'none of us escapes, however great we are, in this life. The god sees that, one day or another, we get what is laid down for us. My own death seems to have been a century coming—but yours will be short, your time of waiting so brief that I envy you.'

I ran my fingers through her dyed hair, ruffling it so that I could see how much grey there was in it. This hurt her more than anything, though she bore my insolence bravely, and did not pull away or push my hand down.

Then, at last, she said, 'Now comes the hardest thing of all. Orestes is truly wedded to my dear daughter, Hermione, is he not?'

I nodded and laughed. 'They make a pretty, crazy pair,' I said. 'A crazy husband for a crazed wife.'

Helen frowned a little and said, 'And Hermione is safe in Oeta, is she not?'

I said, 'Someone has told you truly, aunt. Was it one of Orestes' warriors, before you killed him by the hole in the wall?'

She nodded. 'It was sad,' she whispered, 'but I could not stop the Egyptians, once they had started. They are a merciless people, Electra.'

I answered, 'We are all merciless, aunt, when it suits us; Hellenes, Cretans, Egyptians, Dorians. . . .'

She shuddered suddenly and said, 'Dorians! Oh, god, they are like a fever in the blood to set all men sweating. I am afraid of them, the Dorians. But Menelaus only laughs at the mention of them. He is god-drunk and thinks he can wipe them from the earth as easily as he did Aegisthus' New Army of untried farm-lads.'

I shuffled away from her and said, 'I am tired, aunt. It is very wearing, waiting for the poison-cup. So leave us now, and go back to your king.'

She rose and, as hesitant as a small girl asking for a gift from a strict mother, said, 'The god has put it in my power to save one of you from all this ruin. Understand, Electra, if I had my way, I would save you all, but I have only been able to bribe the captain to let one of you go up from this place.'

I smiled and said, 'Say no more, Helen. I understand well enough; I am not a child any longer. Take him with you, and much gladness may he bring to your dear daughter, one of these days, if you ever find her again.'

So the Queen of Laconica said no more, but led Orestes away as though she were a blind beggar's woman, guiding her helpless master over the cobblestones of a crowded market-place. Pylades sat and watched them go without speaking. Like me, he was now beyond caring. Indeed, I think he was glad to be rid of the incubus of Orestes' madness at last. For he had borne the weight of it longer than anyone else, and a man has only the strength for so much, and then no more.

42

BUT after Orestes had gone and I saw his empty place, I began to weep, my guilt and loneliness heavy on me.

'Why, oh why, did the prince forsake us? Why did he leave us?'

'Be quiet, Electra, it was his duty to go, so that if the dice fall otherwise another year he may come back and reign in Mycenae again. The god wills it.'

I said, 'We shall not be here to see it. We shall lie cold in the tombs, with masks over our faces—if we are lucky!'

Then I wept again. Pylades taught me how a princess should control herself; I was angry and ashamed, rather than grateful, for this. Such is a woman's way.

He said, 'No one must see that we are afraid of death, Electra. The man who brings our food must not see tear-stains on your face. It is our duty to let him carry away the tale that Electra and Pylades laughed and sang as though they were going to a feast. Unless we do this, the common folk will think that the kindred of kings are like themselves. Then all kings will fall, and the lands will be like farmyards, governed by peasants. This would anger the god.'

When I used to give way to my grief, remembering how we had killed so many, especially my mother and poor gentle Rarus, Pylades would say, 'Sweetheart, sweetheart, remember what we once saw on the beach at Alope. When the boys knocked off the heads of the tortoises, did those little beasts complain? No, they lay still under the blows and agreed to die, humbly and quietly. Let us take our moral from them, wretched as they are, for the god made them even as he made us, a part of him is in them.'

I did not care to call a tortoise my brother, but these words did have some force with me, and whenever I felt like crying aloud or tearing my robe in grief, the memory of the little creatures would come to me and then, though I kneeled with my face to the wall in a dark corner, I tried to make no further show of terror. But it was too much, and the waves of fear came in, ever stronger, to beat against the rock of my courage. I fell to the floor, weeping.

Pylades kneeled beside me and said, 'What's done is done, wife. We cannot change it with tears. The god only laughs the louder to see all this useless water flowing from our eyes. Come, sit up now and swallow these things. I am happy to stay behind and take what torments the people offer, so that you shall go unmarked into the shadows. Have no fear, I will join you there before long.'

While I was still shuddering with anger and fear and self-pity, he took a horn box from his pouch and said, 'There are seven pellets here—little balls of a grey substance. They are easy to swallow, I hear, and one only feels cold after taking them. There is no pain.'

His words made me burst out again with tears, but at last, with his arms about me, I was quiet again. He kissed my tears away and said, 'Come, Electra, I will hold the box for you, since you are shaking so much, and put them into your mouth. There is a cup of water left to wash them down. Then you can lie quietly on the bed until the god carries you away.'

He led me on to a heap of straw and laid me down, then as though it was too much for him, he fell beside me groaning. So, it was my woman's turn to console him.

While this happened, I reached behind him and put one of the grey pellets into my mouth, hoping to end my life on a moment of glory, as a singer often ends his song. But it burned my tongue and dried my throat so fiercely that I almost screamed. Had not Pylades been by me at the time, I should have done. But his weight held me down and, besides, there was a silly laughing part of me still alive that told me he would think me too weak and tender to sustain his embraces if I pulled away now. It was a sort of woman's pride that kept me there, as the poison burned in me. In those days the Laconian girls used to boast of what they could stand, in this matter, and say that Europa and her bull were child's play. 'See,' they would say, 'Pasiphaë, the Cretan Queen, thought nothing of it. So why should we?'

I only know that the sudden onrush of the moment drove the poison pangs from my thoughts, and I soared with Pylades for a while.

Then, in the quiet that followed, he said to me, 'It is a hard choice the god puts to us, my wife. If it were left to me, I would say: let us enjoy our last hours so, and so, and so, until when the time came at length, we walked in a dream to whatever death was waiting for us. But that would be selfish, for always I should think that I kept you here for my own pleasure. Here, Electra, swallow the pills.'

But the one I had already taken in secret told me what lay in store for me. My head swam, my hands and feet were as cold as stones, an awful griping pain twisted my bowels, coming and going in great thrusts so that I could hardly keep myself still. Pylades noticed this, but he thought I was still in the after-moments of the dream we had called up together, and took no account of it.

'Come,' he said, 'swallow them now. I have the water cup in my hand, to wash them down.'

But I was deeply afraid, for my eyes had become so dim I only saw a blurred grey shape before them and the pain had come up from my belly to my head. The blood in my temples beat like quick drums, almost bursting my head.

I pushed him away and gasped, 'Not yet, my husband, not yet. Let us wait till the sun goes down; then I will swallow them.'

'Swallow them now, dear one,' I heard Pylades say. 'If we wait until sunset, it might be too late. The cup-bearers might come and treat us cruelly before they give the draught. So, I will hold you while you swallow them.'

But even as his arms went about me, warm and shaking, I twisted away and retched, as deeply as a dog that has eaten dirt. Then, exhausted, I lay back on the bed, too spent to speak.

Pylades bent over me and whispered, 'The god in you has answered me. You are sick with terror, my poor one. Your stomach would not keep down the pills, I see now. Forgive me for pressing you to do this. You are right, and I am wrong, Electra. So, we will wait, as you say, until sunset, for that is the time the god has decreed to you.'

I smiled, for now, after that sudden wrench of sickness, my head was clear again and I could see. Only the pain, deep in my stomach, still echoed on. Shortly, we quenched it together, for a little while, as the time wore on and the red sun sank below the ledge of the little window-hole, high up in the wall.

Slow-spoken and pale, his features now as delicate as though of alabaster, Pylades touched me quietly and said, 'Now, at last, the time has come. I am so parched that, if you do not use the water to wash down the pellets, I shall hardly be able to keep from drinking it myself.'

He was trying to make light of it, I knew. Yet I also knew how thirsty he must have been, for at that moment I could have lain in a cold mountain stream and have let the torrent flow through me, like a hollow stone, or a fish.

So I took the pills in my hand, all of them, and prayed silently to Mother Dia, whose priestess I had been for a while, to let the darkness come down on me swiftly, like the lightning of Zeus. I should not have chosen such a comparison I knew, even as it crossed my mind, because I heard her deep voice reverberate in my head, saying that it would be long and painful, that I must pay for my mistakes, that there was no escaping the final judgement, the long agony, even with these magic pills from Egypt.

My hand shook so much that they fell to the earthen floor. Pylades, now a little impatient, also slopped some of the water as he set the cup down, and got to his knees to seek the poison again. The little pellets had rolled into dark places and were hard to find. Pylades reached for them everywhere, hampered by the twilight that fell over all like a dark cloth.

'Oh, woman,' he gasped, 'this is a fearful thing. What made you do it?'

I did not help him to search, but sat on the bed still praying, still hoping for the Mother's pardon. I said, 'It was the god who spilled them, not I, husband.'

He muttered, quite angrily, and went on feeling about the floor. At last he put five of the little things into my palm and said, 'Come now, place them in your mouth and keep them there until I find the water cup again.'

I pretended to do as he said, and I heard his hands slithering over the clay floor, trying not to upset the cup when his fingers found it. At last, as my heart thumped and the sweat ran down my breast, he said, 'I have it. Now all is set, Electra. Take it gently, for every drop is precious.'

I held the cup in my hands and, in the dusk, felt its coldness, felt the smooth glaze on its sides. Soon, I thought, I may be as cold and my skin as smooth and waxen.

Pylades whispered through the dusk, 'Farewell, wife, and may the journey be a swift one back into the sunlight.'

43

My trembling fingers were on the point of putting the pellets into my dry mouth, when suddenly my ears were filled with a great rustling, as though the leather wings of Furies were being rubbed together close to me in the twilit cell. This sound came so violently, that I almost dropped the cup.

I thought: So now I know that I have chosen wrong all my days, even when I thought I was choosing right. The deaths of Agamemnon and Clytemnestra, of Aegisthus and poor Rarus, are laid at my door. And the madness of my brother. So the god speaks to me in the darkness and tells me of my crimes. Yet he cannot hold me responsible for Iphigenia: I would never have hurt her in ten lifetimes.

I thought again: I did not sacrifice my sister, I only dreamed of her ending in the cavern by the sea-shore. And it was from this sacrifice that all other deaths inevitably came. So, why should I carry their blame? If the god's lightning strikes a tree, then that tree topples and crushes a house, and that house falls and kills a man, whose children starve because he is no longer there to provide for them—who killed the children? Surely it was the god with his lightning? His was the first step in the journey, one would say. Why, then, if there is a law that governs men from above, should the Furies come for me in this cell? Or can even gods fall into error and punish the wrong one? Or are they jealous, like common men, and anxious to prevent another's happiness and escape? Or are they cowards, willing to shift the blame on to others for the wrongful deeds they have them-selves committed? Do the gods, fearing even greater gods too vast for man's understanding, lay their own faults at the door of human-kind, so hoping to forestall judgement on themselves?

All these thoughts came to me in the dark. Then, on an impulse, I whispered, 'Do you hear the rustle of wings, Pylades?'

As I stood close to him, I felt his limbs trembling, and I heard him say, in a dry voice, 'Yes. They are outside the door.'

Someone else heard his whisper also, for a man's voice spoke then, not a voice I knew: a rough voice, speaking words that were barely intelligible to me. It was as though someone with a mouth full of pebbles tried to speak the Hellene tongue, like an Egyptian talking-bird, trained by a Phoenician to squawk Greek, so as to attract a buyer by its few cadences of tone that resembled language, but were not language.

This voice said, 'Is there anyone inside? Who is there? Speak, or I shall shoot arrows. Who is it?'

Pylades was the first to find his voice. He called out, 'Electra, the princess, and Pylades, her consort, are here.'

We heard the brutish voice outside the door speaking to someone else, repeating our names. Then the rustling came again and this time I recognised it, not for the wings of the Eumenides, but the rubbing of sheepskin jerkins and hide shoes against the stones outside.

Through the door's grating the red light of a resin torch glowed, the wood crashed back, and then we were surrounded by men. I could not see them clearly, but they seemed shaggy and big. Their hands were hard and savage; the rancid stench of uncured sheepskins came to my nostrils. One of them shouted in my ear, 'You must come. Our king waits for you.'

Then another bustled against us and called out, 'Let me take her to him. It is my right. I am the son of his oldest wife and I claim this girl as my own.'

The first voice answered, 'She will go to no one. The king will use her for his own before he takes her head. Leave her to me.'

I was pushed about among these men as though I were not a living creature, but a bundle of merchandise without feelings or thoughts. The cup and the pills were knocked from my hands. Now I wished I had them again: now they seemed like friends to me.

I heard Pylades grunting as he scuffled, and about him there was much stir, as though he had dealt shrewd blows in the darkness. But there was a shout, the sound of a heavy thud, and a groan; then things were quieter in the cell and I was rushed towards the corridor, where torches flared. Once, as I was half-dragged along, like a swimmer in a strong sea, I turned back my head and, gazing between shaggy heads, saw Pylades, white-faced and limp, his arms swinging helplessly, following me on the shoulders of four men who carried rude-thonged flint axes. Their broad faces were streaked with soot and red ochre. Their blue eyes stared out from the paint and the ragged hair like the eyes of madmen. They were as strong as the great apes of Libya: they stank like the rams of Leuctra, massed in their closed pens during a long winter. Their smell oppressed me so deeply that I almost fainted.

And all the while, as they carried me along passages and up stairways, their hands were at me, so savagely that I could have howled; and at last so often that I accepted them dumbly and with no more feeling, as a shepherd, out on the bare hills when the thunder rages and the lightning plays all about him, must come to accept the storm —grateful only that he is not burned or riven like the grass and trees about him.

So we came up at last to the Great Court, where the pillars were and soft music used to sound. But in the light of many torches, I saw that the pillars were now hacked and charred, and, instead of sweet music, there was only the sound of rough laughter, the babble of outlandish voices, and the constant clash of weapons. The Great Court was swarming with men, all of them as ragged and dirty as our captors.

Then suddenly I was flung on the broken pavement in the centre of the Court, in a small cleared space. Pylades fell beside me, shook his head, then got to his knees. I had thought him dead and was glad to see him smile again, though painfully.

'Courage, Electra,' he said from bleeding lips.

A whip cracked and Pylades fell again. I looked up in fury and saw that we lay almost under the hooves of a shaggy mountain horse. On its broad back sat a man, his bowed legs, wrapped in sheepskin leggings, bent round the horse's belly, the toes turned inwards as though he had been a rider all his days and clipped his mount close with as natural a motion as other men use in putting meat into their mouths, or cupping their hand to drink from a stream.

This horseman was a man to look at twice. Though his legs were short and thin, as a born rider's are, and his body thick and hunched from much galloping, his face was fine in an untamed way. It was broad and brown and darkly-bearded, but the ears and nose and lips were delicately formed, and the pale eyes were sharp and quick, missing no movement in the Court, yet seeming to be neglectful in their pride. His brown hands were fine and still, too, on the reins, though I noticed that his right hand lacked the two middle fingers. He was a swordsman as well as being a rider.

From beneath his round leather helmet, plated with bronze strips, his thick dark hair fell to his chin, no more, and was then chopped roughly across in a line, as though his camp-barber had used a meat-knife, or a dagger.

He wore no ornaments, save bronze bands at his throat, and about his wrists. His heavy squat body was protected by a horse-hide corselet, shaped in boiling water to his form, so that almost every muscle was reproduced in the moulded leather. This corselet was studded at its edges, at waist, and neck, and arm-pits, with gold nail-heads, which told that he was no common man. A short kilt of black bearskin hid his thighs from me. A thick blue cloak of Dorian frieze hung heavily behind him, on to his horse's back, held at the shoulders by two copper brooches as big as plates, and set with garnets and jet.

At his left side he wore an iron sword as long as a four year's child and as broad in the blade as my wrist. Its haft was bound with gold wire and its edge was full of hack-marks the whole length.

All these things held my eye. He was like one of the rich outlander kings who had sailed with my father from Aulis many years ago; yet not so for I could not imagine this rider so forgetting his own pride as to follow another king; I could not picture him kneeling before my father, and taking the oath of subservience.

He broke the silence, saying abruptly, 'You are mistress of this place? You are Electra, the old king's only blood-kin?'

I nodded, half-afraid. He pulled in his restless horse and said, 'This is your husband, Pylades?' He flicked his broad thumb towards my husband.

Once more I nodded, and dared to say, 'And who are you, sir?'

He threw back his head, so that his stiff black beard jutted upwards for a moment, and laughed. He said, 'No one you know, lady. I am a cattle-king from north of Thessaly. I am the Scourge of God, yes, a Dorian, lady. I come to make a clean sweep of Hellene rottenness, so that the world may begin afresh. My name is Thoas. Does that satisfy you?'

Pylades had got to his knees again. His face was working and I feared he would leap at the horseman and have the sword put through him. I began to plead, my fingers touching the rider's horny feet.

'King Thoas, pay no heed to my husband. He has suffered much and acts without thought.'

Thoas glanced at Pylades, briefly like a hawk, and said, 'Then he is my sort of man. There is a place for him behind me, if he chooses. As for you, lady, it seems to me that you acted with a great deal of thought, from what I hear, dragging down all your enemies so carefully, until there were none left!'

I hung my head and said that all my life I had only acted as the god prompted. King Thoas laughed again and said, 'Was it the god, or the goddess, Electra? Your family seems to have been divided on this.'

I was puzzled and said, 'What do you mean, sir?'

He beckoned among the thick crowd behind him, and a cloaked woman came forward on a white pony. When she was beside him, she opened her hood and I saw that it was my sister, Chrysothemis— but now so grown-up and altered that I hardly recognised her. Her face was streaked with black and blue war-paint and on the sheepskin saddle before her sat a red-haired little boy of about three, mother-naked and twisting at the pony's mane.

'This is my wife, who is renamed Thoasa,' said the man. 'She has told me of the many gods you prayed to in Mycenae. But now there will be only one god, and his name will be Thoas!'

My sister smiled down on me, but so pityingly that I did not know how to greet her. She saved me the trouble by saying, 'All debts are paid, if one but waits, Electra. So now I sit on a horse above you, and find you on your knees.'

I said, 'Yes, sister, and I find you with your face painted like a barbarian. The gods have strange patterns for us all.'

Chrysothemis did not take up my taunts, but only stroked the little boy's head absently and said, 'You thought to be Queen of Mycenae when they were all dead, but, you see, it will not happen so. King Thoas and I shall sit here and rule Hellas. And when we are gone, this little boy will sit on in our place and be the god-king after us.'

I was angry at her words, because I had never wanted to be queen.

I said, 'Orestes is the only king here, sister, and in your heart you must know that.'

She smiled again and half-turned her head away. At last she said, 'Orestes is dead—or so mad that the bears in the forests will tear his limbs from him. That is no king, sister.'

King Thoas coughed as though he was a dog growling. 'Have done with this,' he said. 'We have come here to fulfil the god's command, not to taunt our prisoners. Go back to your place among the other women.'

My sister bowed her head and swung her quiet pony round. There was no leave-taking between us.

Then King Thoas said thickly, 'You may think we are thieves, yet I would remind you that our coming has saved your lives. The chair of Mycenae is little enough price to pay for that, especially among soft-fleshed creatures such as you are. Is that not so?'

When I did not answer, he said, 'If you still have dreams of power, there is a place for you both, behind me—though I must tell you that from now on you will forfeit any claim to noble blood, and will ride among the least of my followers. You see, I come to bring a new order to this crumbling kingdom. The choice is yours.'

I cursed him in my new anger, but he did not seem to mind. He only nodded and said, 'They call us Dorians uncouth—well, it is but a word, and words break no bones. So, I have your answer, Electra, and it suits me well enough. But never think that you will turn the years back. We are here now, and here we stay. Your day is ended, and for the rest of your years you will proclaim to all who see you that your turn has passed and that you hold your life from Dorians. You must carry their mark, so that all shall see.'

Then he turned and shouted over his shoulder, 'Bring the fire, my friends.' Men shambled forward with a low brazier, supported by staves. On to its glowing charcoal they placed two broad-bladed Dorian daggers. As I watched the iron begin to redden, King Thoas called out once more, 'Where, for your sister, Thoasa?' And I heard the voice of Chrysothemis answer firmly, 'Where it was for me—but deeper, since she must carry it always.'

King Thoas nodded down to me, like an impassive farmer judging the quality and growth of his cattle. 'You see how fond these sisters are of one another!' he said. Then, his face still smiling, he gestured to the men about him. They ran forward and took hold of me, bending me backwards over their knees till I thought I would break, pulling the front of my robe open, and holding my threshing limbs firmly, so that I was as helpless as a calf. They must have done the same to Pylades, for I heard him swearing and roaring, like a trapped boar.

Then one of them laid the broad-bladed iron over my thumping heart, bearing so hard on it that the god let me know sleep. I was not away long, it seemed, for when I found sense again, the iron was still there, but lying upon the other side. I wept and heard myself promising them a fortune to let me go.

And when the grief grew too great for bearing, I let the darkness come down over me again, for these hands and their iron stood outside the limits of pity.

They were throwing water over me when I knew myself again. I lay with my lips against the charred and broken tiled floor. Pylades was near to me, his shoulders shaking as though he was a boy again.

The Court was empty of folk now. There was no one to mock at our tears, no one to scorn us as, at last, we searched ourselves to know what injuries we had suffered.

So, later, like poor old folk, we rose and went with our arms about each other from the Court and the palace, stumbling like cripples full of pain, the pride and the anger all gone from us.

There was loud singing and rough shouting everywhere in the palace gardens, and torches flaring everywhere, making small islands of red in the purple darkness. It was a pretty sight, with the silver stars speckling the dark-blue sky like the feathers on a pheasant's breast: but it brought no cries of joy from us. We walked in a broken world together, towards any place that took us away from this last terror.

At the gates of the courtyard, freed slaves sat in the dust, singing and drinking from goatskin bags. A fat dairy-woman saw me in the torchlight and pushed forward, laughing immodestly, towards me, her own marked body bared for all to see.

'Look! Look!' she said, touching me with callused fingers, 'she is one of us now. At last the fine princess has found her level. See, these great ones bleed like anybody else. The Dorians are right—all men are equal!'

I was too weary to push her away, too spent to cover myself from their eyes. A gaunt-faced peasant limped to us and pushed a greasy wine-skin under our noses. 'Come on, now,' he said, 'since we are all brothers and sisters, join us in a drink!'

Pylades took the skin and we shared this last indignity, while the slaves cackled round us. Then, at last, we made our way from the swarming mad city, and staggered into the quieter hills.

Once, as we rested against a rock before forcing our protesting bodies higher up the slope, we turned and looked back on Mycenae, where Agamemnon had once been the Lion of Glory. The blurred torch-glow had changed into spiked and leaping flames, as though someone had put a light to the resinous pines about the palace.

I leaned against Pylades and said bitterly, 'I hope to the god they burn it all down—the palace, everything! It has no longer a place in the world, any more than we have.'

44

There is a limit to what the god will let us bear. Like a stern master, he sometimes loads our cart so heavily, and goads us along so sharply, that we accuse him of having no love for us. Yet, consider; we most often find, at the hinder-part of the journey, that we did draw that load, and that our bodies were able to withstand the goad-pricks.

Those who cannot, die, and find peace from all burdens, and so come as well out of the world as those who stay in it. In the dream-time of their death, they sit beside the god and, laughing now, wonder why they wept so much, before, at what is, after all, only a great jest.

Ask yourself, doctor; do we not set too great a store on our aches and pains, our dreams and our sickness after strange foods? Does not a boy with a cut finger howl more than a warrior with a javelin in his breast? Is there not more blood after a joyful birth than after a death-stab to the heart? You see, there is no rule, no sense, in life— and so it is, as I say, a great jest. Who tries to find more than that in it will go down to the tomb with a wrinkled brow, unsatisfied. Better to sip the good wine, to smell the autumn crocus, to laugh in the dust and the sun, as the chance permits; wine, flowers, dust and sun will pass. Perhaps they will come again, or perhaps they will not; but one thing is assured, tears will not make them stay a heartbeat longer. Joy and pain both pass; that is the one thing we learn before the god takes us, doctor.

When Pylades and I walked away from Mycenae, we had not quite learned this lesson, and our eyes were full of tears at our fall, and the fall of the royal House, and the fall of Hellas. But as the journey unwound, our scars mended themselves, and there were no more tears left to shed.

Sometimes, in the night, lying below a hill or behind a rock, away from the wind, I thought of Agamemnon and my mother, of my sisters and of poor Rarus. And always, by day or by night, Orestes was in my head; I saw him running with his mouth open and his hands outstretched, mindless as a stone, searching for death— he who had once lain so tender in my arms, who had been as pretty as a bird.

But in the end, even Orestes let me be, to live my own life and laugh again. That is the way; you can hack at the boughs, the bark, the roots of a tree, and yet it may live on for another lifetime and spring fresh leaves, and provide fresh shelter, though it was left for dead by the clumsy woodcutter.

In a narrow green valley, where the river Ladon rises from the rock, my husband and I built our house. It was a rough thing, of pine trunks and mud, with a roof of reeds from the river-bed. As we built, we could see on the one hand, Mount Cyllene; and on the other, Mount Pholoe, and far beyond its ridge, high Erymanthus with the white cap of snow at its crest.

With the few bits of gold we had, on wrist and at throat—small things like ear-drops, bracelets and neck-rings—we stocked our little place; a ram and three young ewes first; then a half-dead milch-cow we found over beyond the valley, worn out with seeking water. She was only a bag of bones, with hardly any udder, when we came across her, with the carrion birds standing by her, waiting for her to stop breathing. But we drove them away with sticks and I sat with her while my husband fetched water to her in a wooden bucket. Poor Pylades, we laughed at the memory of it many times, later; he staggering in the hot night, his shuffling feet crushing the oven-dry wild lavender in this desert spot, sending up a trail of bitter-sweetness behind him as he came to feed the sick cow; while I turned my head in every direction, afraid at the long-beaked birds that would not go away and leave their prey.

Such things bind a man and woman together, simple homely things. It does not have to be flaming love to hold them to each other; simple things like rescuing a cow will do it. We called her Glauce when we got her home, for she had such great mournful eyes, like that princess in the old tale, the stupid daughter of the King of Thebes, the girl who fell in love with that old pirate, Jason.

I say that we sold our bracelets to buy sheep—and there is another tale about that. We went together, like a peasant and his woman, in grey wool tunics, down to the little market of Thelpusa. Neither Pylades nor I had ever done any bargaining in our lives; coming of noble blood, such things were not in our training.

The sheep-market at Thelpusa was a small one, and the word soon spread that two strangers were there. The brown-faced dealers stared at us, as we walked uncertainly among the hurdle-pens looking at the wiry hill-sheep, and called out to us that theirs were the best animals in Achaea. Even I could see that some of them were lame with foot-rot, or blind in one eye, or crippled with a dropped back. When I mentioned these faults to the dealers openly, as we used to speak in Mycenae, they set up such an angry cackling that I felt ashamed, with their blunt dirty fingers pointing at us, and their rough voices telling all the village that we were too big for our boots, that we were jumped-up peasants who had robbed a noble house and now thought we, too, were noble ones. Pylades, unused to being so insulted by common folk, flushed and took such a grip on his staff I thought he would go among the dealers like a warrior and strike them down.

Someone else saw this, too; a crop-haired Dorian, who leaned on his own sheep-pen, wearing a war-shirt and a broad sword. His big face was wrinkled with amusement to see Pylades so worried by the teasing sheep-men. And when, harried on all sides, we stopped and set our faces as though this was the last straw, the Dorian shouted out above the crowd, 'Hey, you two, come to me!'

We went, I do not know why; perhaps we were really frightened by the crowd—though if there had been twice as many warriors, on the battlefield, we should not have turned a hair. But we were caught out of our element, like fishes twitched on to dry land by the line.

The Dorian screwed his eyes and gazed at us, looking us up and down, while his thin lips turned themselves in over his teeth. He said, 'A soldier and his woman buying sheep in this god-forsaken pig-sty of a place! What does this mean?'

We were grateful to him for standing on our side against the peasant sheep-dealers, so, though his question would have angered us at other, more fortunate times, now we took it with tolerance and told him that we were tired of town living, and wished to set up in the peaceful countryside as small farmers.

He strode over to me heavily and, without hurry, pulled open the fold of my robe. I heard Pylades gritting his teeth as the Dorian ran his finger across the king's mark on my flesh, but I signalled him to keep his temper and let things go as best they might.

The Dorian covered me again, with respect, it seemed to me, then said, 'So, my people have put their hand on you. It is distressing at the time, lady, but it is worth suffering. You are one of us, now, and woe to any of these cattle who lay a finger on you, for we will come upon them and burn the thatch of their houses and put the spear through their children.'

He turned from us then and bawled at the top of his voice to the staring dealers, 'These two are of my folk. If they chose, they could take all of your miserable beasts without paying more than a curse; yet they have come, gently among you, to bargain. And you have treated them as though they were of the same poor clay as yourselves, taunting them and daring to point your filthy fingers in their direction. What do you say to that?'

A wizened old dealer, whose dark eyes were crossed, called out, 'I know who they are, sir. They are no more Dorians than I am.'

Our friend made a step towards him, and the old fellow drew back behind the hurdles, his hands shaking. The Dorian spat at him and said, 'If I say they are of my folk, will you deny me, fellow? Will you call me a liar, then?'

The old man bowed his head and mumbled that he had meant no offence. When the Dorian was satisfied that he had cowed the folk, he turned to us and said quietly, 'I know well enough that you are Electra and Pylades. It was my own half-brother who put the sign on you in the Great Court. But what of that! Times are changing and great ones have become small ones; and low ones, high ones. Change is in the nature of things. Leaves change, water changes to ice, good meat becomes carrion. What of it! Now you are two Dorians, not Electra and Pylades. So what is there to argue about?'

He led us to a tavern where the awning kept the sun from our heads, and there, on the bench outside, we drank raw red wine with him. Always he kept his sword across his knees, so as to be ready, but this did not stop him from being merry. He was the sort of man who would be just as dangerous drunk as sober.

He said, 'You see, King Thoas puts one of us in every village he takes, just to keep order. One of us is enough, for we are the only folk allowed to carry a sword now, the conquered folk have only staves. Sometimes they rise and kill the guardian—but their joy lasts only a day or two. The king sends others to burn the place down and chop off the hands of the killers. You will see, soon there will be such order in Hellas as was known only in Agamemnon's greatest days.'

He glanced at me shrewdly as he spoke my father's name. I said, 'So you think Agamemnon was a great ruler, sir?'

He nodded. 'That king might have ruled the whole wide world,' he said, 'if he had not made mistakes.'

I said, 'You speak of the nature of things; well, is it not the nature of things for men to make mistakes? Does not the god lay these traps for men, so as to show them how small they are after all?'

The Dorian took a pull at his wine, spat in the dust at his feet, then said, 'All that is old-fashioned nonsense, lady. You ancient folk are too full of the god; you lay all at his door because that relieves you of responsibility. You let the god make those decisions for you that you should make yourselves; and when your lives go wrong, you shrug it off by saying that the god ordered this or that—whereas, if you had used your common sense, things would have been different. Look at us Dorians, lady; we make up our own minds, then get on with the job. We don't wait for dreams and sacrifices and so on. We go through folk like you as a knife goes through a cut of cheese. We are practical folk, you understand. We do not stand on ceremony. That is why we are masters in Hellas now.'

Pylades smiled and said, 'What will you leave behind you, you Dorians? Are you not destroyers? Our poets say you are.'

The Dorian called into the tavern for another wine-flask, then wiping his mouth on his hand, said, 'When a man dies and goes into the ground, does it profit him to leave behind him great palaces and pretty pictures? Did it profit old King Minos on Crete? To be back alive again, drinking good wine and eating good beef, would he not exchange all his palaces and pictures? All his blind stone images? I tell you, Pylades, this flask of wine is worth all your pictures; better to be breathing and drinking, than dead in glory. As for the poets who call us destroyers, do they not breathe out foul air and call it a song? Only foul air from a blind fellow with a lyre. Air he has already used. Such silly fellows sing of a world that never was, and never will be. They are the destroyers—for they destroy truth. They make a world of dreams. I would like to be among them when they call us the destroyers. After this sword had been at work, there would be no more lying songs, I can tell you.'

Pylades smiled at him, then said, 'You have made it all very clear to us, sir. Now we will do what we came here for, buy a few sheep, and be on our way back to the hills.'

The Dorian said, 'What will you pay with, Pylades?'

And when we had shown him the gold we had, he held out his hand for it and said, 'That is exactly the price of my own beasts—a little more or less, counting in the wine we have drunk, and so on.'

In all truth, for that gold we might have bought a farm-house and a herd of cattle. I felt that the man was cheating us, in spite of his friendly words, and I said, 'Are you sure, sir, that you have judged the amount of gold rightly?'

This Dorian was an intelligent fellow, despite his rough speech and hairy face. He smiled and said, 'You are thinking I ask a high price for a ram and three young ewes, hey? Well, perhaps I do; but remember that dagger-brand. It is an insurance, is it not? It makes you a free Dorian, does it not? And so with the price you pay for your sheep. No one will ever take them from you; no one will ever as much as set foot in your valley, for we shall see that it is a protected spot during your lifetime and the lifetime of your children. Is that not a good bargain, my lady?'

Though he spoke mockingly, I felt that he meant all he said. I nodded and the bargain was sealed.

We went from the market-place of Thelpusa with all the peasant-dealers bowing before us, as though we were the Kin of Thoas himself, which, indeed, by his marriage to my sister, we were. And, as the Dorian soldier had said, from that time on, we were not molested in our little valley. The word must have gone round, for the Dorians kept no written records, and we were left alone.

Many times we saw troops of them, riding hunch-back and weary on their sheepskin saddles, passing over the top at the valley's head, but they never came down on us, though the smoke from our chimney was visible for a mile and more. Only once did a Dorian soldier walk to the door, and then he greeted us with great respect, putting his rude copper sword at my feet. He only wanted to know the way to Tiryns; and when I had told him, he left behind a handful of Egyptian blue clay beads.

[257]

'These are for your daughter, lady,' he said, before he took up his sword and went back to his waiting horse. Though I had no daughter, I accepted his offering, for Dorians, though they had a great name for meanness and crafty dealing, when they gave, gave freely and were insulted if their gifts were turned back.

Three months after this man came to our door, I did have a child, but a boy, not a girl. His name was Medon, and he was as much like my brother, Orestes, as one pine cone is like another. A year after this, there was another boy, Strophius; and he resembled poor Rarus. Though this might only have been a trick of the light, for Rarus could never have a son, as you will understand.

So we lived quietly, the four of us. Our flocks multiplied and our fields grew heavy crops of corn. Even in the bad times, we had enough to see us through. We seldom left the valley, doctor, and when we did, it was only to ride to Thelpusa for such things as we did not make or grow ourselves—good wine, or thick woollen cloth for robes and tunics. I was never much of a hand at the loom —though I did my share in the fields and the dairy, once I had got into the run of these occupations. Indeed, it was working in the fields, holding down the ploughing stick while Pylades drove the oxen, that I had my miscarriage of my third child. It would have been a girl, and I was grieved at the loss. It reminded me of that time in the Iron Valley.

After that, there were no more children for us. At first this was a bitter blow, but we grew used to it, as one becomes used to almost anything. At first, Pylades said, 'Do you think if we started to pray to the god again we might be allowed a daughter?'

I was feeling sick at the time, and laughed in scorn, hurting him but not meaning to, in the manner of women. I said, 'After all we have done, all the blood we have spilled, do you think the god would turn his ear towards us? You know, as well as I do, that we are cast out from the god. We are like creatures who live neither on earth nor in heaven. Is that not clear to you? Why else all our suffering? Why else the fall of our family? If the god is pleased with us, why has he taken our little one? And where is Orestes, my brother?

Where even is stupid Chrysothemis? No, husband, the god is blind and dumb to us.'

As I said this, I seemed to feel a little shivering of the floor-tiles beneath my feet, as though the earth's crust was shifting. My head was swimming with my sickness, and I sank to the floor. Pylades kneeled by me, his eyes wide with alarm at my words. I stroked his cheek and said, 'Do not be a fool, Pylades; the god has not thrown me down. All women have these dizzy spells when they reach certain years. It will pass.'

As I said this, I saw for the first time that Pylades also was no longer a young man. The backs of his hands were wrinkled and his finger-nails horny. His hair was white above the ears, and had fallen out from the front of his head. Warts had started to grow here and there on his face. As I sat on the floor that morning, I understood for the first time that he and I were growing old, that we had been a generation away from the High Town of Mycenae.

I got up slowly and leaned by the wall, suddenly bitter that we were growing old, that we had lost our child, that nothing really made sense after all. No, nothing really came to a decent conclusion —all was haphazard and formless. I said to Pylades, 'Husband, it seems to me that life is one long joke, and a poor joke at that. We, poor fools, try to make a sort of sense out of it, but there is no sense there to make. Sense is a mad dream that men have made for themselves.'

Pylades said he would get me a cup of wine to soothe me, but I shook my head and told him to be quiet while I spoke what was in my head; I had no need of soothing, I told him. That was for children, and I was no longer a child; far from it.

'Look,' I said, 'we creatures are born into a world that rages about us, and we are bewildered by it all. So, as we grow, we try to give all things a reason for being so various. We say that the god made them so. And, because we ourselves grow tired at the day's end and fall asleep, we say that the crops and the trees fall asleep when winter comes; we say that they have life and knowledge just as we have. We say that the god has put that knowledge in them, as in us. And because, by reason of our hands, we may take up the wet clay and squeeze it in our palms and fingers to make a ball, with perfect form, with shape and limits, we say that there must be such form in all other things—that the god has made this form, this shape, this truth.'

I was wearying myself and my husband by this talk. He came to me and led me to the bed, and set me there, to rest. 'Wife,' he said, 'you are saying things you will regret tomorrow. Be silent now, and tempt the god no more.'

I looked into his gentle, wearied face and answered, 'That is it, Pylades; it has come to me in recent days that there is no god to tempt. The god is something we have all created to give some sense to what is senseless. Do you not understand? There is no god!'

As I said this, our room suddenly became as silent as a sea-shell; yet with that faint howling round the walls such as swirls in a shell, so distantly that one wonders if the sound is in the air, or simply in one's own head. Pylades gazed at me, his mouth open, his arm shaking as he leaned on the oaken table; an old man now, no longer able to outface life and death as the young warrior does. He was no more a warrior, but only an old peasant-man, staring in grief at his old peasant-wife.

He was like a samphire-gatherer who has followed his quest unthinking, the wicker-basket at his waist, along the narrow ledges of the cliff—and suddenly comes out from his dream to see that a wide chasm opens before his feet, and that there is no going forward, and perhaps no turning and going back either.

I smiled at him and said, 'It is you who needs soothing, dear husband. In spite of your white hairs, you are still a child in your thoughts, aren't you! You still need a mother to hold your hand and to tell you that all will be well.'

What he would have said to this, I do not know, for I think my words had taken all the force, and faith, and trust from him—though I had not meant them so. But we were saved from the problem of this moment by a man who came to our door.

He was a bent old fellow, with a bag on his back and a basket on each arm, a wandering merchant of small things, who walked the hills and valleys, the rivers and the towns, from year to year, bartering anything he had picked up on his journeying—amber beads, strips of copper or bronze for making into knives, glazed clay lamps from Cythera, little blue beads from Egypt, even tiny gold seals from Salmydessus.

He called himself Phaestus, and said he was of the old Cretan stock which had been on that island since time's birth; but though he was dark-haired and brown-skinned, and wore a bull-seal at his throat, it is my belief that he was a Hyperborean, from the far island of mists where the stone circle was. Once, after a cup or two of our good wine, he told us how he had carved a Mycenaean dagger on one of the uprights of that stone circle when he was a youth; and it struck me even then that a wandering Cretan trader would not take such a liberty with the sacred shrine of another people. Only a Hyperborean would dare carve such a decoration, I suspected.

There was another thing that made me think so; when we asked him to say something in the old language of Crete, to amuse the children, Medon and Strophius, Phaestus spoke the same sort of gibberish that I remembered the Hyperboreans, who had gathered with my father's armies, speaking, before they sailed to Troy, a lifetime ago. It was my belief that this pedlar was one of them, who had been left behind and had turned to trading for his livelihood. But I never taxed him with this, in case I hurt his pride and drove him away from visiting us. Out there in the valley we welcomed visitors who could bring us news. And, again, Phaestus always carried with him a pouch of medicines for curing sunstroke, or water-sickness, or easing the birth of calves, or even of babies. When Medon was cutting his teeth, a red rash spread over all his little body, and we thought he might die of it, if the red spots met about his waist. But old Phaestus gave us a grey powder to be mingled with goat's milk for him, and the red rash went away and left the lad whole again.

Then there was the news he brought, which was always worth buying. I think he dreamed much of it as he trudged about the hills,

[261]

telling us what he thought we would like to hear—for that is always an agreeable thing in a messenger.

On this morning, when I had told Pylades that there was no god, Phaestus was especially welcome, to take the heavy load from our minds.

Pylades said to him, 'What news of the world, old friend?'

Phaestus sipped at his wine and munched the barley bread and the goat-cheese I had put for him, then answered, 'It goes from bad to worse, sir. As I make my rounds with the seasons, I see change everywhere, and all the time. Nothing stands still; everything rolls on towards darkness.'

Pylades began to tease him, saying, 'That is always your tale, Phaestus! Come, tell us what is happening, in plain terms.'

Phaestus drained his cup, and let it hang on his finger so that I should notice it and fill it for him again. When I had taken it to do this, he said, 'These Dorians will bring the world to an end, mark my words, lady. They destroy wherever they go—shrines, palaces, all. If there is a crop in the fields, they eat what they can, and fire the rest before they go on. And they are going on, to all places. They have learned boat-building now, and make the run to Crete three times a year. In my town there is scarcely one stone standing upon another, lady. As for Cnossus, they have made a sad ruin of that! If my grandfather could see the place now, he would die once more, of shame. Why, nothing can stop them, it seems. They are into Egypt itself, like sand-flies settling; they blow up out of the desert and put all to the sword. In the great days, the men of Egypt would have blown them away; now even kings go in fear of their lives from these Dorians. They have no sense of the rightness of things, my lady. They say that all men are equal; their kings are shepherds, and their shepherds kings. They have no great families, no great houses. . . . It makes no sense, you see. Since time began, there have been great families, we all know that; but the Dorians point to the cattle they have stolen and say, "That is my family!" And they point to their tents and say, "That is my palace." Who can make anything of that, lady?'

[262]

I said, 'You have come through Mycenae recently. What of the palace there, where my fathers have always lived, Phaestus?'

The old man clucked and wagged his head. 'Lady,' he answered, 'if you went back there today, you would be lost. You would not find your way from one street to another. All that your fathers had ever done has gone. It is as though your fathers had never lived, my dear.'

He pretended to weep a little, wiping the back of his brown hand over his eyes, and then went on, 'They have robbed all the graves in the tholoi, men say, and have beaten the gold masks into trinkets for their wives. Their pigs have rooted up the pretty floors in the palace, and their herdsmen have lighted fires in the fountains and have cracked them. Fast-growing alder has pulled the pillars down; ivy nourishes itself on the stones; the tumbled roofs are deep in cow-dung. There is no palace now. Only a stinking rubbish heap, lady. Vultures have their nest in High Town, and no man goes there any more.'

I turned to Pylades and laughed, for this news was pleasing to me, not saddening. Old Phaestus glanced across uneasily, as though he thought I suffered from heat-stroke. Then, deciding that I didn't, and that I was perhaps taunting him, he did his best to bring me to my senses.

'Look,' he said, 'I have told you only the little things, lady. There is worse to come. Your sister, Chrysothemis, who calls herself Queen Thoasa now, has forsaken her priestly duties and no longer speaks her own tongue. She leads the Dorian women in praying to the stones and the streams, and has forgotten all the correct usages. She paints herself like a warrior-man, and rides at the head of the women's company into whatever forays there are. It is as though she has lost all her senses.'

He glanced at me as though he had gone too far, but I only laughed at him and filled his cup again. 'She was always a fool,' I said. 'What of my other kinsfolk, Phaestus?'

He brooded over his cup before saying, 'Old Menelaus and his wife, the one they went to fetch back from Troy, are dead. The news is that they went into Caria to find themselves a new kingdom and were murdered by some Egyptians there. It is a sad end for such great ones, lady.'

He expected tears from me, I could tell; but I was not concerned with such ghosts of the past. I said, 'They had lived their lives. How they ended is no matter. If they burned on the altar, then they must have sent up a good flame, for they were dry old sticks, with no sap left in them, Phaestus.'

'Lady! Lady!' he said, throwing up his wrinkled hands.

But I waved him to silence without any trouble. 'Tell me, and this is more to the point, has any news come to you of my brother, Orestes?'

Old Phaestus gazed down at his shoes, and watched his toes wriggle in them. Looking up at last, he said, 'He has gone to the goddess, I think, lady. It is like asking where last year's wine has gone—or this year's, for that matter.' He half-held out his wine-cup, hinting, but this time I did not rise to fill it. I thought that if I gave the old man any more, he would lose the use of his tongue; so I made him wait, and asked, 'When was Orestes last seen, Phaestus?'

He mumbled a while, and pretended to catch a fly that was bothering him, though there was no fly to be seen. Then he put his cup down on the table with a clack, and said. 'He was seen in Crete three seasons ago, trying to persuade the folk there that he was old Minos come again. He was in Troy last summer, telling all who would listen that he was Priam's shadow. And this year, when the buds first sprang, he was in Cyphanta, having come off a boat from the far-islands, dressed as Agamemnon and calling for the folk to march again and take Hellas from the Dorians.'

I said, 'How can a man be in so many places, Phaestus? And, if he can, why do you say that Orestes has gone to the Mother?'

The sly trader nodded in the afternoon sun. He shook his head and gazed at me with dim eyes. 'If an old dog like myself can go foraging through the world, lady, then surely Orestes, who is a younger dog, can do likewise. As for going to the Mother, I used that phrase because no one is sure that this dark wanderer is Orestes. These tales blow up and down among the islands, as though the simple folk like to think that Agamemnon will come again—or any hero come again, who will drive the Dorians out and set Hellas free once more. I do not know whether it is Orestes, so it is easier for me to tell you that he has gone to the Mother.'

Pylades smiled and waved to me not to give the old fellow any more wine. 'Lie down and rest, grandad,' he said. 'You have come far and are weary. We will not press you for more news. Now rest.'

But Phaestus shook his head and said slyly, 'You think your wine is too strong for me, sir. But that is not true; all my days I have drunk the good heavy wine of Crete, and my head has not grown so weak that I cannot stand this hillside brew! Look, to prove I have my senses about me still, I will tell you another bit of news. Hermione, the daughter of Menelaus and Helen, is with Orestes, wherever he is. She followed and found him, and swears he is her destiny. Together, they hope to found another royal line that shall be greater than all who have gone before. Now, what of that news?'

I said bitterly, remembering our old love that had faded, 'Hermione is of my own age, Phaestus. If she has waited till now to start a family, then she has left it a little late. She is beyond child-bearing, friend.'

Old Phaestus wrinkled his brows, as though calculating the years, then said, 'Lady, if the Mother blesses Hermione, then she will still be able to raise a family. Have no doubt of that.'

I did not press him further, because his words were already stupid enough and no more good could be got from them. Instead, I asked him what he had to sell us this time. He answered, 'Nothing, lady. All I carry is rubbish which such as you would not wish to buy from me. I called only to greet you and to see how your fine sons were faring.'

Pylades said, 'They are faring well enough, Phaestus. Indeed, they have gone from home now and have farms of their own, over the valley. They have got themselves wives and are busy breeding their own families. You must call on them and give them our greetings, when you leave this house.'

[265]

Phaestus nodded. 'It seems no time at all since they were little lads, running behind me and taunting me for my age,' he said. 'Now they are married, you say? Did they choose Dorian women?'

I answered him and said, 'They did, old man. Good clean girls, apt for childbirth, and able to churn butter with the best.'

Phaestus shook his head; 'The world is coming to something,' he mumbled, 'when the kin of Agamemnon marries Dorians. . . . Aye, aye, it is a sad fall.'

He rose from the stool and rummaged among his packages. 'I have thought of something,' he said. 'I had forgotten that there was something you might like to buy from me. Here it is.'

In his hands he held a small box of horn, a cylinder stopped at either end with wax, through which the sun shone dimly, showing a twisted dark thing that moved in the light as though it hated sunshine and sought darkness. He put the box into my hands.

'What is it?' I asked, as the thing inside it moved, and the movement brought a prickling to my flesh, like a deed twice-done, done in the forgotten past, and then done again in the waking present and still half-remembered, though long-neglected.

Old Phaestus said, 'You may well ask, for it is my most priceless article of trade. It is one of the last of the brood of ancient black Cretan serpents that the old woman at Delphi nourished on her own milk. It is a creature of the most ancient lineage, from the depths of the grotto itself. This I would not offer to anyone but you. I would not. . . .'

I flung the horn box down and moved away from it. 'I do not want it!' I cried. Suddenly I remembered how, when I was only a little child, Aegisthus had married me to Rarus with such a snake, and had wormed his way into our House itself from this marriage. From such a snake all our doom had unfolded, I thought. 'Take it away!' I cried. 'I do not want it!'

Pylades came forward and put his arm about me. 'There,' he said, 'there, old woman, but you take on too much, and in this heat. It is not good for you—and all because of a little black snake that I could crush with one stamp of my foot! Is it decent that the kin of great Agamemnon should behave so, before a common trader, because of a little black worm that lives under a stone?'

I began to weep then, so overwrought, that Pylades led me to my chamber to rest. And later he came to me and told me that he had bought the little black snake, to put in a hole under the rocks, near our water-trough. 'For,' he said, 'though you may not know it, I have a great fondness for these little worms. They are said to bring luck to a house. Moreover, they give warning of enemies, of fire and flood and drought. You shall see, Electra, this little creature will drink his fill at the trough, and then go into his own home and never trouble us. He will catch worms and flies and beetles, and we shall not need to concern ourselves about his keep. Perhaps, once in a while, on a sacred day, we may leave a shrew for him, or any small thing we care to offer.'

As he turned from me, he said, 'Since you deny us a god to pray to, let us at least have a little black snake! Though he was once the Mother's creature, we can think of him simply as a garden-pet, and delight in him, not fear him. Now our children have gone away and left us, we need a small one to watch and to talk about, when we sit by the hearth at dusk. You will see, come next year, you will be telling me all manner of things about his strange tricks. You will be waiting at the gate at night, when I come in from the fields, to tell me where he has cast his skin.'

All I said was, 'Curse that old Cretan, for bringing the doom on this house, too!'

But Pylades had gone through the door and did not hear me, I think. If he did, he made no mention of it again.

45

THE years pass, and the oak-trees fall in the wind, their roots rotten, their bark scarred. The fires in the mountains are slaked. The proud-antlered stag lies a heap of dust at the bottom of a gully. Ten thousand of his children have wandered to the northern grazing-grounds, and their herds are but a memory, for they died a lifetime ago. All passes, the pain and the pleasure, the agony and the glory.

Medon died of a plague and his three sons with him. Strophius took his brother's widow into his own house, and into his own bed for comfort. Then the drought struck his farmstead and he went north, in a wagon, with all his oxen, to find green grass, like the herds of deer.

And we were left alone in our bitter valley, Pylades and myself. Two folk who should have died when the Dorians came to Mycenae, if there had been any meaning in life.

I find it hard, doctor, to remember this part of my tale. After the drought, there came rainy season after rainy season, as though nature had gone mad. All rotted now, just as it had shrivelled before. The very roof-thatch sprang green again, as though it were a corn-field. Damp-mould stood on the bread, and the floors were never dry. The beds stank of wetness, and Pylades woke up one day to find the use of his hands gone.

From then on, I was his mother rather than his wife; for I had to put the food into his mouth, and to clean him, since he could not help himself.

Then we had a swarm of flies in the valley that drove the cattle crazy, and clustered round the ewes' eyes till the poor beasts went blind. One day I spoke to Pylades as he sat at the door on his bench.

'Look, husband,' I said, 'that cloud on the far hill is quite red in colour. What does that portend?'

He waited a long while, then in a dull voice he said, 'My wife, it is useless to pretend to you; I cannot see the cloud.'

I gazed in amazement and answered, 'But, Pylades, it is as big as a corn-field. It is immense, and all blood-red. Surely you can see it, now that I have described it?'

Pylades said in the same heavy voice, 'Electra, I cannot see the cloud. I cannot see my hand before my face. Now do you understand?'

I ran to him then and looked at his staring eyes. They were blank and grey, like agate, and there was a milky ooze at their corners. I had seen the poor ewes in their trouble, and I knew that the flies had brought this misfortune on us.

I began to wonder what had gone wrong. Why should my husband and my children have suffered so in recent years? I searched my heart for the answer, and suddenly, like a thunder-clap from a bright sky, I knew; I had denied the god. Then I remembered how, when our world was young, poor Iphigenia had denied the god in our secret garden, under the laurel boughs.

That night, at dusk, I went to the rocks above the drinking-trough and put my mouth close to the hole where the little black snake lived. Never before had I dared come so close to his house, so close to his flickering tongue. But this night the fear of death was hard upon me. I kneeled and said, 'Black snake, black snake, we are suffering, my husband and I. We gave you a home, and food, and kindness. Now, if you can hear me, speak to the god for me and tell him that I have wronged him and know my sin. Tell him that I believe in him again. If you are of the ancient world, black snake, do this for me, and beg him to send a sign so that we shall know what the end of it all will be.'

I was ashamed of myself for saying these things; but, though I would willingly have suffered the god's wrath myself, I hated it that poor Pylades should be crippled and blinded on my behalf.

'Can you hear me, black snake?' I called.

For a while there was no sound, but the distant rumbling in the far hill, beyond Cyllene, as always happened in the summer. Then, below the sound of thunder, came the creature's sharp hissing, as swift and quiet as milk into the pail. It came and went, and I knew that it had answered me. I went back into the house and brought Pylades to his bed, away from the draughty doorway.

As the sun was setting, blood-red, behind Erymanthus, Pylades sat up in his bed and said, 'Go to the door, wife, and see who is coming.'

I answered, 'Lie down, my love, no one will be coming here at this time. I should have heard them.'

But he said once more, 'Go to the doorway and look. It seems that my ears are still good, although my eyes have the night in them.'

To pacify him, I went. A man and a woman were coming up the sandy hill towards our house, casting their long shadows on our doorstep, like travellers who have come through a desert and are far gone with thirst and weariness.

I called to Pylades and told him. He lay back smiling and said, 'I knew they were coming. I have heard them for the last hour. Now do not doubt me further. The god may have taken one thing from me, but he has given another in its place.'

But I was not listening to Pylades. I was too concerned with the man and woman who approached our door. Though they were ragged and caked with dust, their clothes had once been of the finest weave; and though they staggered like drunken folk, there was in both of them a nobility of motion that is not born into common people. It was the way they held their heads high, and hardly deigned to answer when I greeted them, that impressed me.

I thought: It must have been just so in the far-off ancient days when gods and goddesses visited simple cottagers.

I said, 'Enter, travellers. Here is a place of rest for you this night. My husband and I are poor old folk, but not so poor that we cannot share what we have; and not so old that we cannot tend a guest in our house.'

The man looked down at me from his great height with eyes that glared so dully out of his brown and haggard face that at first I was

[270]

afraid, and I wondered if I had spoken words which he thought out of place. But the woman with him flung back her hood, and let long masses of grey hair free to stream down her back, then she smiled at me and said, 'We are beholden to you, my man and I.'

There was some quality in her face that told me she always did the talking for him, protecting him, despite his great size, much as I did for poor Pylades. I gazed at her face as she led the tall man through our narrow doorway; it had once been a very beautiful face, oval, and curved softly, with broad cheeks rising like little hillocks below her great wide grey eyes. Once, too, her lips had been full and curved. And her hands had been long and narrow and hard-palmed, after the manner of the Achaeans.

Now, of course, all this was ruining, all falling away, like life. One saw the woman not as she was, worn threadbare, but as she had been in her day of glory.

Yet still she had comeliness and breeding, and stood silently in our rough room, beneath the oaken rafters, her robe about her, until I had announced her to my husband. Then she and the man sat unspeaking at our table, gazing before them, like gods.

Pylades said from his bed, 'You have come far, my lord and lady. I smell the sea in your garments still.'

The woman said in her low voice, 'Not the sea, but the waters of Styx, old man. The grey river, not the wine-dark sea.'

Pylades called to me, 'Bring out the best wine, wife. They have a long thirst to slake, I know.'

But once more the woman spoke and said, 'If you have milk, that would be the better. We have little wit as it is, without diluting it with grape juice. Our stomachs call for food, not wine, woman.'

This she said in a matter-of-fact manner, almost in a monotone, and with no feeling behind it, only simple truth.

Yet when I put soft barley bread and goat cheese before them on a wooden platter, she and the man toyed at it with their fingers but hardly ate enough to feed a small child. Their hearts seemed elsewhere.

I watched their fingers as they crumbled the bread; they wore no

[271]

rings, but every finger bore the mark where once a ring had been. It was the same on their arms, and about their throats; there had been gold there once, but now there was only the mark it had left, from all the years of wearing.

Trying to make conversation, I said, 'The Dorians, have they molested you, my lord? Have they robbed you, my lady?'

The man half-turned towards me, as though he was listening to other words than mine. In a distant voice, he said slowly, 'The Dorians have gone, as though they had never been. We have driven them into the sea, for Poseidon's fishes to feast on.'

As he spoke, the tears ran down his hard face and dropped on his clenched hands. The woman dried them with the edge of her robe and crooned to him softly. Then suddenly she turned on me and said sharply, 'We will have no more of that, no more of that! Do you understand?'

I felt like a slave in the house of some nobleman in my father's time. I, a great princess! But she was so masterful, this grey woman with the fine hands.

Pylades said haltingly from his blind bed, 'We are poor old folk, my lady. You must be gentle with us, we mean no harm.'

The woman looked away from him, as though she despised him, and said to the man, 'My lord, make do with this place for one night. I will find something better for you tomorrow, some palace, or some great house. But for one night, I beg you, tolerate these folk; they are rude, but they mean well.'

The man bent his head as she spoke, as though he found it hard to hear her, to understand the words she uttered. He was like a god who speaks only with thunder and great howling winds, and so finds words thin and difficult to grasp. His finger-nails were bitten down to the flesh; his feet were bound in stained bandages. If he was a god, then it was the god of beggars, I thought.

All at once, he turned to me and said above my head, 'I am no beggar, woman. You understand that?'

I was so shocked that he should have heard my unspoken thought, that I bowed and said, 'Yes, my lord, I understand. Forgive me.'

[272]

The woman placed her hand on his, consoling, and whispered, 'Do not disturb yourself, lord. No one thinks you are a beggar. All that is in your own head. Be still, and remember that you are a great king who walks through his own kingdom, visiting his folk.'

The man nodded his shaggy head, and smiled like a simple boy. In that smile lay some memory which touched me to the quick of my understanding. My limbs began to tremble so much that I could not trust myself to go towards the table and tell the strangers who they were. I think I might have fallen to the floor and never risen again, so fierce was the tempest in my heart.

Somehow I laid down straw and blankets for them both, at our room's far corner, and then, when the clay lamps were blown out, I crawled in beside old Pylades. He said to me softly, 'You are shaking, wife. What troubles you?'

With the breath sobbing in my throat I answered, 'Husband, the man who lies beneath our roof is my brother, Orestes—so altered by the years that I did not know him until he smiled. Then I saw his broken tooth that he got, jumping from an apple-tree, once when we were young.'

Pylades waited long, as though considering his words, and at last he said, 'I felt it all along. As I sat at the doorway in the sun, I felt deep in my belly that he was coming here, over the rocks and the hills, guided to our house for some reason which lies beyond understanding. It came on me like a chill wind that blew inside me, not on my outer skin. The hairs of my neck stood up and for a while I thought the use would come back to my hands, the feeling was so strong. I tried to clench my fingers, but the strength lay only in my head, not in my bones. But I knew that something was destined for us then, because since my sickness has been upon me I have sat like a stone, with no thought of moving. Yes, when I called to you that someone was coming, it was as though I already knew.'

I put my arm about his thin shoulders and whispered in his ear, 'What does it all mean, husband? Why should he seek us out? And that woman with him—can that be Hermione, my cousin, after all?'

Pylades answered, 'God, what poor things we are, we men and

women, when we do not know our own lovers, our own blood-kin! It is as though the god makes game with us, not only blinding our eyes, but blinding our understanding also. What can be the purpose? What, Electra?'

Suddenly the woman called from the far corner of the darkened room. 'You have given us a bed, now let us sleep. To give and then to take back is no true hospitality. We have come from far off; let us sleep.'

Her voice was heavy with weariness and it seemed to cause her great effort to utter those words. It was like a voice speaking with difficulty from behind a thick curtain; like the voice of a priestess, drugged with laurel or mandrake, struggling to announce the message before she sank with the weight of her duty.

Indeed, there was a curtain drawn between us, a curtain no eye could see, but one which kept me back from struggling out of bed and going to them, to say who they were. No use to tell me, doctor, that I should have known my own brother, my own cousin; for age plays tricks with the sight, with the memory. We recall our dear ones as they seemed to us when we knew them last, with all the freshness on them, the bright sunlight, the water glistening on them as they rose from the river, the droplets like precious stones. We do not remember them as gaunt and bearded ghosts, their limbs parched and thin, the dirt crusted on their bodies, their hair white. It was over thirty seasons since I last saw my brother or Hermione; and in thirty seasons, with the world falling about one, and a family to raise and mourn, the eye of memory grows weary and dull.

I fell into an uneasy dream while I considered such things, such a sleep as I had once had, before they sailed to Troy, when the storm wrestled with the stones of the palace at Mycenae. In my sleep the old horror came on me again that I should see my sister in the cavern, with the cloaked figures bending over her and the squeaking bats going at the walls for what dripped there.

And in the midst of this terror I seemed to feel a hand held over my mouth, hard and brutal, pinching my lips together. Whether it was in dream or waking, I do not know, but I seemed to open my eyes and find that our room was bright with a flickering glow, like summer lightning. And above me stood the stranger who had come to our house from over the hill. He was gaunt and immense, his shoulders now as broad as those of a god-image of the Egyptians. The left hand which clenched across my mouth to stop me screaming was a god's hand, that can stay all escape. In the right hand was a knife that gleamed like a dark flame in the fluttering lightning. The stranger's eyes gazed down on me without love or hatred. There was no depth in their glossy greyness, no understanding for good or ill.

In my terror, I tried to say, 'My brother! Orestes!' But the great hand seemed to feel the words rising, and squeezed them back, like fingers crushing the life out of a snake.

Then the man's lips moved and said, 'Do you remember Agamemnon? Do you remember the Lion King of Hellas?'

I nodded in a frenzy, and tried to tell the man above me that I had loved Agamemnon once, but the hand stifled my utterance, and the slow voice said, 'You killed him, killed the father. I am Agamemnon come again for vengeance, Agamemnon who has searched for you across the world for thirty harvests. At last I have found you, Electra. I have found the false woman who brought the Dorians down on Hellas by killing the god-king, brought darkness on the world by her treachery, brought plague on the great House by her wickedness. It is just, that the knife which took great Agamemnon away from men should put an end, at last, to his destroyer. Just, that Agamemnon should rise again to claim his vengeance!'

As the muttering words came into my ears, I suddenly knew that this was not a dream, that the stranger who had come to our house indeed stood above me now, the madness in his head, the knife in his hand—the knife Aegisthus had once held in his hand, as I wrapped the towel about my father and waited for Clytemnestra to come through the bath-house steam.

As I broke from my dream, I slid also from that terrible hand, and began to cry for help. Old Pylades wakened beside me and began to mumble, still half-asleep. Then I saw the woman who must be

Hermione clasping the stranger about the arms, her hair wild from her bed and filled with straws, her shift fallen from her. She was saying, 'Let her be, Orestes! Let her be! We are not sure that she is Electra! Come back to bed, my love!'

My altered god-like brother laughed and shook her away as easily as a grown boar shakes off a young hound. 'There shall be no more sleep,' he cried, 'only the sleep of death!'

Then he soared above me like a dark cloud full of thunder, his body swelling in size, his head enormous and glaring. My scream mingled with his hoarse yelling as he brought the knife down at me.

Almost fainting, I felt the bone-bruising blow of his forearm on my breast, but not the bitter edge of the knife. Pylades, close beside me, suddenly gave a great leap, as though the use had come back to all his limbs, then fell back shuddering.

Once more the woman ran at Orestes and cried out, 'Let be! Let be! You have done enough!' And as she grappled with him, I saw that now his great hand held only the bone haft of the knife, the blade had broken off.

Yet haft was hard enough as it struck my forehead in its second plunge. The summer lightning fell away from my eyes and the horrid shouting deadened in my ears.

And when I knew the world again, the sun was coming from Cyllene, in through the window-hole and lying in a golden stream across our floor. The yellow straw in the far corner was scattered wide, and our oaken table lay overturned, one of its legs broken. There was no one in the cottage but Pylades and myself. I shook my head, then almost howled with the pain of that shaking. I laid my fingers to my brow and they came away all glued and red.

Pushing the nightmare from me, I turned towards my husband, and searching the stiffened body found the copper blade still in his breast, driven past the bone and broken off.

'Pylades, my husband, speak to me!' I said, still stupid with the terror of that night. But his face was an ivory mask, the smile on his pale lips frozen, as though he had welcomed this parting from a blind life that was worthless to him now.

[276]

Somehow I got from the bed, my limbs shaking and my breath hard to come by. I have forgotten now what I intended to do; perhaps my memory had gone and I meant to run for aid from my sons, Medon or Strophius; perhaps I meant to ask the little black snake for help, hoping that he might intercede with the god and bring dead Pylades back to me; or perhaps I only wanted to go away from this dreadful house where the last of my world had ended in the night.

I do not know what drove me out, into the sun-baked yard where our cattle were penned in the winter; but I staggered there. And there I saw how far our fateful visitors had got.

They both lay with their heads in the water-trough, their white knuckles gleaming in the morning sunshine as they clutched the stone lip, as though kneeling to drink. But they were not drinking. Their lips were white and as stiff as those of my husband; and their hair floated in the clear water, like grey weed, swaying here and there with all the movements of the water in the hillside breeze.

The knife's bone haft that had killed great Agamemnon a lifetime ago lay between them on the sandy soil, and curled about it the little black snake that Phaestus had brought to the house from Delphi.

I fell to my knees before the snake and gazed at it. Its bright eyes looked back into my own, unblinking. It was quite still, as though it were carved in ebony by some cunning craftsman of Crete.

For a moment, I wondered whether to hold out my own hand to its mouth, so that it could bite me also, and let me go away with the others of my kin. Then a different feeling came on me, telling me to rise and crush the serpent with my heel, if only to test whether there was a god or not, or whether all this suffering was an accident, like the strong oak being blown down by a chance gale.

And it was while I was wondering which of these things to do, doctor, that you came on your mule, with your black slave walking beside you, through the farmyard gate.

EPILOGUE

LATER, washing his hands in the bowl that his apprentice held for him, the Hittite doctor said, 'We must not believe everything a patient tells us, must we, boy?'

The young Libyan's smile widened and showed his white teeth; 'All Greeks are liars, master. Is that what you are teaching me?'

The doctor dried his long fingers carefully and put back all his golden rings. 'Not exactly, my lad. Some of them, the rough ones, Dorians and Spartans, often try to seek the truth—but not the dispossessed, the once-great, the city folk. They still hold on to their dreams. I tell you, boy, great palaces may fall with fire and storm, but those dreams can last a thousand years unharmed.'

The black boy emptied the water away thoughtfully. 'Master,' he said, 'was this old woman the great Electra, do you think?'

The doctor gazed across the far blue hills. 'There are hundreds of women called by that name, up and down this strange country,' he answered, cleaning his finger-nails with a little scalpel.

'Yes, I know; but was she the great princess, in her time? She seems to know much of what went on in palaces and tombs.'

The Hittite smiled distantly and said, 'These stupid poets make our work harder than it need be. Any child, from Ephesus to Leucas, could tell you what Agamemnon wore, what food he ate, his words as he died. And they will all be different.'

'What I cannot understand is why she says so little about Troy. There were great heroes and great battles, master, yet she does not speak of them.'

The doctor shook his head slowly and his golden ear-rings made a small tinkling sound. 'Perhaps she was too young to be interested, or too old to remember, boy. Perhaps we all remember only what happened to us, not to other folk, half-way across the world.'

The boy stood beside him, his head on one side, his fingers tracing the pattern on the doctor's carved chair. 'Now you seem to be saying that she was Electra, master,' he said, smiling.

The Hittite stroked his black beard. 'In our trade, my son, a man has to consider all manner of approaches, and he can never be quite certain. In this case, there is only one thing I am sure about. From my examinations, I would say with my hand to my heart that she had never borne a child.'

The Libyan boy said, 'But, master! The still-born in the Iron Valley, Medon and Strophius the farmers!'

The doctor waved his hand like a fan. 'When you are an old, old man, with no one to gainsay you, might you not swear that you led a company, under the arrows, against Thebes?'

The boy sat in the dust and began to collect pebbles together and build them into a small pyramid, always trying to lodge a bright red one on the top, but never getting it to stay.

'There are too many things in life that puzzle me, master,' he said. 'Life is like an oracle that one can read five ways.'

The doctor patted him on the head and said, 'It will never get any easier, little one, however old you grow. That is all a man ever learns, to tell the truth, though it comes to him in five ways.'

Suddenly the boy stopped playing with the pebbles, and, gazing up, asked, 'In all truth then, master, what have you learned about this woman?'

The Hittite answered very slowly, 'I have learned only what I have seen here, at this ruined farm. When we came through the gate, there was no little black snake. Nor had the dead ones died recently. They had been so for many a season, for their hides were like tanned leather bags, that held only the worm. And the old woman, who calls herself Electra, had tried many times to hang herself. Her neck was scarred with the deep marks of a rope. But there was another thing that puzzled me, much more than all this. She spoke of the mad visitor who broke off the blade of his knife in her man's side.'

The boy stood up, his eyes white at their rims. 'Yes?' he said.

Putting his hand inside his robe, the Hittite drew out a copper-bladed Mycenaean dirk with an ivory handle. 'See,' he smiled, 'it is

[279]

as entire now as when it first came from the smith's forge. How else could it have cut the throats of the three dead ones here?'

The boy did not speak, his eyes were fixed on the blade as it caught the sun's falling light.

The doctor put the dagger away, slowly and carefully. 'If you mean to become a good physician,' he said, 'you must learn more than herbs and philtres. You must learn to keep your eyes open. They are your most precious instruments—not your scalpels and your pincers and your probes.'

At last the apprentice shook his woolly head. 'Why does the god make it so difficult?' he said. 'And who is this old woman?'

The doctor stood up. 'Let us go in,' he said, 'I am hungry after this hard day.'

And as they walked back to the ruined house he said, 'I do not know anything about gods, my boy. Nor does this strange old woman. This she has been trying to tell us, all through her story. It is the one thing about her which interests me, or else I should have left her a gentle poison and gone on my way, which is often the best with ancient folk who will never get well again.'

And at the door he said, ' "Who is she?" you ask. She may have been a temple dancer in her youth. But I would guess that she is one of the sort who dwell too much in the past, and dream that they were princesses, or priestesses, or maenads. The bloody tales they heard at their nurses' knee will never let them go, and in the end they become the creatures of their own dreams. These valleys and villages are full of them still and they can never let the past die in peace. The old ghosts are always with these strange people.'

The boy held open the door for his master. 'Perhaps it was a good thing that the incomers put an end to Mycenae, after all,' he said.

The Hittite smiled. 'We are doctors, my son, not poets,' he answered. Then he stepped across the threshold.

About the Author

HENRY TREECE has had an impressive career as teacher, historian, actor, editor and author. His published work—more than thirty titles now—includes critical essays, poems, and a fictional cycle of prehistoric Britain: *The Dark Island, The Great Captains, The Golden Strangers* and *Red Queen, White Queen*. His last novel was *Jason*, a fresh evaluation of the classical hero; his most recent book, a history of the Crusades. Mr. Treece and his family live in Barton-on-Humber, a quiet market town in North Lincolnshire.